Findi

By

Anna Genov

Table of Contents

Mom, Dad, and forever Mia.

Acknowledgments

I would like to thank Julia Betancourt for her time and dedication to this book. I would not have been able to do it without her.

About the Author

Anna Genov is a high school sophomore in New York. She enjoys reading, writing, playing volleyball and spending time with her younger sister. Anna is an avid traveler and speaks three languages, German, English, and Spanish. She enjoys visiting museums and listening to music.

Chapter 1

Camping. That's where I was going to spend my summer vacation, the only two months when I wasn't imprisoned in the horrible jail cell known as school. Yeah, that's right, two whole months in the woods. I wasn't going to Hawaii like Amy or Paris like Roni. Envy ate away at my insides, knowing that they would be seeing the Mona Lisa or sitting on the beach drinking out of coconuts. Meanwhile, I would be trying to find out what leaves were safest to supplement as toilet paper.

My mom decided to bomb me with the news about two days in advance--clearly, she took pleasure in my misery. The conversation was brief, to say the least.

I remember sitting on my light blue, worn-out, paint-splattered easel. I was sketching a sparrow that had been grooming itself in a tree across my bedroom window. I ignored the spilled water and dirty paint brushes that littered the white and green polka-dot carpet. My room wasn't one that you would consider organized. The walls were a turquoise *Behr Marquee Aquifer MQ6-08* though you could barely see it under all of my paintings, sketches, and pictures tacked up on the wall. My lime green cotton bed sheets were un-made, and my sequined pillow was thrown across the floor.

The closet door was open, and there seemed to be a waterfall of clothing falling out. I couldn't find my brand-new denim apron, so I just threw on one of my dad's cotton undershirts and pinned my hair back into a messy bun.

I bit my lip in concentration, trying to copy the shape of the animal's tail feather when I heard my door creak open. My mom popped her head in, her stringy red hair pulled back into a neat ponytail. She wore a pair of yoga pants and a casual gray top, and of course, she still managed to look stunning. Her green eyes were darting back and forth in a hyperactive sort of way. Knowing her, she was probably calculating all of the work she still had on her to-do list and how quickly she could get it done. With some difficulty, she pushed the pile of clothes out of her way and walked in--uninvented, I might add.

"Hey, Piper, remember that we're going camping this summer for two whole weeks. Uncle Jimmy's letting us use his property. Start packing," my mom had said, leaning against a sky-blue colored desk that was littered with doodles, overdue homework assignments, permission slips, post-its, and my new acrylic paint set. Her voice filled with mild excitement. She moved her foot back, clearly ready to go back to grading papers or doing laundry or whatever it was moms did in their free time.

"Wait what?!" I yelled, causing the bird to fly away in fright. I jumped off my stool, banging my knee against my easel and knocking it over. "I must have heard you wrong. C-camping for the whole summer?!"

"Yes," she said, oblivious to my sudden terror, looking down at my floor with a mixture of exasperation and disgust, "in two days. I told you about this, remember? You might want to bring those hiking boots I got you."

I grabbed my head and sputtered in protest, "But--me--ask--what--two days--uh noo!"

I felt my cheeks grow red. How? What? Who? Why on earth could she spring this onto me two days in advance? I had my entire summer planned out. I had signed up for a free art youth program at school and was going to start sculpting lessons with my best friend Amy when she came back. I had told Mom I had plans.

"Yes," my mom said slowly as if she thought I was incapable of understanding her. "We are going camping." She walked out of the door, clearly in a rush to start something else on her schedule.

I felt my heart quicken as she shut the dark blue door causing a sunset painting I had drawn in fifth grade to swing back and forth. I sat down, staring at my sketch of the sparrow. I could barely even process the situation. I wanted to wring my hair as I envisioned the coming two months. No beds, no wi-fi, possible bear attacks, poison ivy--the list went on. Whose idea of fun was sitting on the muddy floor, eating food out of a can, and never feeling fully clean? Even summer school would beat living like a pioneer for two months.

I stood frozen on the spot for a second and then flung the door wide open and ran after her. I stumbled down the *Cream Eggshell Hec #SD312AG* stairs and nearly knocked down the pine wood picture frames that covered the boring wall.

"Wait, but why!" I said, "Mom, what's wrong with staying in Seattle? I mean, we have a nice backyard, and Amy's coming back from Hawaii in two weeks. Please don't make me. Oh, God, what exactly about this sounds like a good idea? The poison ivy? The bear attack? The disgusting food?"

My mom gave me an impatient sigh as she grabbed the light gray laundry basket off the kitchen island and pulled open the white door that led down to the damp basement. Her red ponytail swung back and forth as she pulled the chain that turned on the single light bulb. As she began separating the darks from the colors, she responded in the same tone that she used with all of her high school students when they were acting out.

"Piper," my mom said in a calm yet cool voice, "I think that this will be good for our family. A nice change of scenery, some fresh air, the woods. It will be so peaceful."

I looked her in the eyes, wondering if she was out of her mind. How on earth did camping sound peaceful? Did she know what camping even was? "I don't think so," I said, my voice rising. "No, I'm pretty sure it will be torturous and an experience that will leave me scarred forever."

3

My mom rolled her big green eyes that were similar to the acrylic paint color *456 Viridian hue (7085) Series 2B*, "Oh, Piper, don't be so dramatic. Jack and Dad are thrilled to get out of the city."

Jack, my little brother, hardly counted; he was enthusiastic about everything. He was a wild, crazy five-year-old who reminded me of a pumpkin seventy percent of the time. With his wild copper hair and freckled skin, a huge grin spread across his face showing his crooked teeth. As for my dad, he was just as much of an outdoor freak as my mom was. When I was seven, he had the brilliant idea to buy a house a little farther from the city of Seattle than I thought was convenient, just so we could have a garden. Oh, please, that's what parks were invented for!

In fact, my idea of a nice home was a small, cramped apartment in the center of the city, covered in paintings with brushes and papers strewn across the floor. When I get my own place, the furniture would be round, colorful, and inviting, with music blasting from every room. None of these pointy chairs that bruised your shins or cold sterilized white walls that infected my house like a disease. Everything in this neighborhood was cookie-cutter. They all had the same *Antique White 34 hue #925f43* paint job, perfect lawns, square furniture, and simple orchids. It was like living in a museum. The thought of it makes me want to crawl out of my own skin. When did a little color or music hurt anyone? For once, I didn't want to see a perfect soccer mom in yoga pants taking her kid to school in her grey minivan. In my place, there would be more than just small family pictures adorning the wall and nicely trimmed yards with white picket fences and uniformed lawn chairs.

"But that's hardly fair." I repeated, returning to the current conversation after my slight mental rant, "I mean, Jack loves everything, and Dad is exactly like you. That's why you two got married. I need another person in the family who thinks like me!"

"Piper!" My mom said, twisting her thumb around, something I had learned meant that she was about to scold me, "You've been outnumbered. We are going camping whether you like it or not. You haven't even been there yet. How do you know that you're going to hate it? Don't you love to paint nature?

"I can paint from the comfort of my room. Or, at the very least, a cabin." I murmured under my breath.

Luckily my mom had already closed the door to the washing machine and left me in the musty old basement. Clenching my hands together, I sighed and ran up after her. Deciding it would be too hard to get her to waver, I began to search for my dad. Walking up the creaky wooden stairs, I opened the door and blinked a few times, feeling blinded by the bright kitchen lights and the strong smell of lemon cleaning spray. Walking past the marble kitchen island and into the living room, I suppressed another sigh. Why hadn't my mom made a bigger deal out of this? I had no idea what she was talking about when she said she had already told me about camping. Since when has this house changed from democracy to dictatorship?

Lost in thought, I walked through the bare, white hallway and hit my shin on the light gray table with the velvety orchid. Cursing, I rubbed my leg furiously and hobbled to the living room. My dad was reading the newspaper (who still reads newspapers?) on the itchy gray couch, with his legs propped up on the glass coffee table (something he only ever did when my mom was not in the room). The walls were completely bare, except for a few silver letters that wrote, "Home is where the heart is." There was a collection of magazines on the table which, as far as I knew, nobody had ever read, and a small candle that had never been lit. I turned my attention back to my dad. His auburn hair was standing up, and he squinted his gray-green eyes, letting them dash back and forth on the black and white pages.

I cleared my throat and went over to my light blue plush chair, the one thing in the room that had some sort of life to it. "Hey, Dad," I said, inching onto the large chair, causing my legs to stretch out straight in front because they weren't long enough for my knees to go over the edge. "I heard that we're going camping," I said, trying to keep my voice leveled.

"Yes, we are!" He replied, his brows unfurrowed. He looked at me excitedly. "It's going to be so much fun. The nature, the fresh air, the grass, the animal–"

"And–" I interrupted before he continued to talk about camping as if it were the latest iPhone– "Were you ever planning on consulting me before making the decision?" I brought my legs up and crossed them, resting my elbow onto my ankle, trying to look businesslike and official, a difficult feat considering I was 5'1".

My dad frowned, setting his newspaper down on the desk, "Mom just came up and told you. Besides, what could be better than camping? Trust me. You won't want to leave."

I snorted, highly doubting the truthfulness of that statement. "I don't want to go camping," I replied, trying to keep myself from jumping off the chair and screaming in protest.

"You don't ever want to do anything," he said indignantly, rolling his eyes.

I glared at him, feeling stung. "That's not true," I replied, my voice losing the mask of calm, "I love to do stuff, like painting, talking, umm…." I felt myself grow warm, "That's not the point."

My dad leaned back in a way that suggested *I won, but I'm going to let you pretend that you still have a chance*, "Look, Piper, my mind is made up, and so is your mother's; it'll be a great family bonding trip."

"No, it won't be," I murmured, sliding off the chair. I began to sulk out of the room.

My dad gave me a sympathetic gaze, and I glared at him. Moping up the stairs, I slammed my bedroom door. This time I didn't bother to pick up the sunset painting as if it flew off the nail again. I sat on the paint-splattered stool and stared at my easel that still lay on the floor. I tried to think of something, anything that could stall or stop the camping trip. I traced a red blob of melted crayon wax on the lower left corner of my easel. Maybe I could try to convince Jack to join my side. He was up for anything as long as I gave him a few blue Sour Patch Kids.

Smiling with a bit of newborn confidence, I swung open my turquoise door and ran across the boring hallway to Jack's room. Halting in front of another white door, I looked up at the sign of a crinkled paper that read *Jack's roum dont cume in*. Smiling slightly to myself, I pushed open the door to his room. It wasn't as colorful and lively as my room, but at least it was something. The walls were colored a subtle orange shade *Field Poppy PPG 1195-7*, and there were large palm leaves on the wall shade *Pillow Mint #90GY 54/334* that I had painted for him a few years ago. His orange bed was unmade, and a few toy cars littered his crayon-stained desk. It smelled faintly of Sour Patch Kids, and I saw a small yellow wrapper that had been hastily stuck in a trash can. Jack gave me a guilty look hiding his hands behind his back.

"Hey, Jack," I said, ruffling his orange-red hair and sitting down on his bed.

"Hi, Piper," he replied, grinning. I noticed that his tongue was slightly blue. "What's up?"

I smiled, realizing that this might be easier than I thought. "Oh, not much, hey, so, did Mom tell you that we were going camping?"

I had hoped that Jack's face would droop in disappointment at the thought, but instead, it lit up. "Oh, yeah, Mom told me."

I frowned, "But you don't want to go, right?" I tried to put disgust into my voice.

"Yeah, I do," Jack said, confusion dawning on his features, "Why wouldn't I? Mom said that we would catch butterflies and eat marshmallows around a campfire."

"No! I mean, what about sleeping on the floor and mosquitos that suck our blood?" I asked desperately, trying to get him on my side, "And no Wi-Fi?"

Jack's lower lip quivered, "But-but, I wanna catch a butterfly and eat a big gooey marshmallow."

"But there will be spiders," I whispered, hoping I sounded dark and mysterious. "And, even worse, no, Sour Patch Kids!"

Jack furrowed his eyebrows and lowered his voice, "No..no sour patch candy?"

I nodded menacingly. Jack looked up at me, and I realized in horror that his olive eyes had welled up with tears. I gulped, knowing what was going to happen next.

"WAHHHHHHHHHH!" Jack wailed, burying his face into his hands, tears streaming down his cheeks. He let out a sob, laying back on the bed.

"Ohh, no, no, no, no, no." I cried softly, shushing him with a desperate tone to my voice. "Shhhh, no, don't cry."

But it was no use. Jack lay back on the bed and howled. I sighed in defeat, knowing what would happen next.

My mom burst into the room, her face almost as red as her hair. "What in the..." She sighed loudly when she saw me, "Of course. Piper, just..."

I felt stung by her words. *Of course*? What was that supposed to mean? I got up feeling hurt and walked across the hallway. Creaking open my door, I helplessly slumped onto my untidy bed.

Reaching into my pillow case, I pulled out a half-eaten pack of Swedish Fish–Jack wasn't the only one with a sweet tooth. Well, there went my last chance of getting someone on my side. Groaning, I rolled onto my other side. I slid off my bed and got to my feet. Getting up, I tucked a strand of ash blond hair behind my ear. I might as well try to get out of it--a lot could happen in two days.

Chapter 2

Two days later, after a large amount of unsuccessful pestering and complaining from yours truly, I stood in front of our stuffy Rino Grey minivan and wondered what I would do for the next two months. It's not like I don't enjoy nature. I do (in theory). I mean, don't get me wrong, it's beautiful: the trees, the sun, the animals...they would all look great in my sketchbook. In fact, I would give up almost anything to paint a good view of a sunset or a butterfly, or a petunia. That small silver lining was all that stopped me from pretending to have the flu or some sort of alien parasite.

My biggest question was, why should we bother living without normal plumbing, Wi-Fi, and heating if we didn't have to? It seemed like hell. People invented modern technology so we didn't have to live in the woods and sleep on hay. Why were we downgrading?!

"Get in the car!" My dad yelled, throwing three green duffle bags into the trunk as my mom chased my brother around the yard. He cackled loudly, running in between trees and up and down the gravel walkway, clearly reluctant to sit still for more than a few minutes.

I stood at my doorstep, pouting and longingly staring inwards at the lights. "Piper, get in the car right now!" My mom yelled after catching Jack around the waist. He was, to say the least, extremely unwilling to get into his new Graco Gotham booster seat.

Sighing loudly, I pulled the metal handle and cracked open the door. Scrunching my nose at the slight smell, I made a slow effort to pull the polyester seat belt over my stomach. I rolled down the window. *Here we go*, I thought miserably while pulling out my iPad.

***

"Are we there yet?" Jack moaned loudly.

I sighed, ready to answer the question that had been asked six times in the past thirty minutes. "Oh my God, no, we're not. We haven't even left the city yet."

"UGH," He pouted, looking out the window. I rolled my eyes, returning to my sketchbook that I propped up on my knee. Attempting to draw an orchid, I pulled out a cheap pack of colored pencils (I had a habit of losing them between the seats) and began sketching out the oval petals.

I felt the car lurch slightly and cursed loudly as all of my pencils rolled off my lap right onto the floor and under the seat. Groaning at the horrible road quality, I bent over and attempted to pick everything up. Tugging at my seat belt, trying to loosen it, I snagged the tip of my paper, and half of the page ripped out. I knew it was just a piece of paper but ripped drawing had always been one of my biggest pet peeves. I felt a tug of annoyance and tried not to sigh. I cursed again, attempting to pick up any stray scraps that may have fallen out of my sketchbook.

"Don't use that language around Jack!" My mom scolded, rubbing her temple.

"My sketchbook!" I snapped, "it's all ripped, and my pencils all rolled under the seat."

"How many times have I told you not to draw in the car?" My dad asked, gripping the steering wheel. I wanted to growl at him as I closed my beloved book up and placed it into my blue canvas backpack.

"I'm soooo bored." Jack groaned, dramatically flopping his head off the car seat.

"Watch your movie," I replied through gritted teeth.

"It didn't download," he complained, holding up his iPad that showed the download sign.

11

I bit the inside of my cheek, trying to keep back an insult then, how about you take your iPad and shove it right up you

"Let's play a game, everyone," My dad interrupted loudly, his eyes still glued to the road.

"Noooooooo," I groaned, covering my face with my hands.

"I'll put on some music," my mom suggested, in a voice that flat-out said, if you all don't shut up, I'm going to scream at someone.

"Oh, oh, oh," Jack proclaimed excitedly, "Play baby shark, oh, please play baby shark."

"No," I said, lifting my pointer finger up, "No, don't you dare play that song. Oh, I swear to-,"

"BABY SHARK DOO DOO DOO DOO DOO DOO BABY SHARK DOO…" My mom's phone rang, drowning out the rest of my voice. I gripped my head desperately, trying to block out the song. Just one verse and the entire song stayed imprinted in your mind like a bad tattoo for the next four days.

This was going to be a long ride.

***

I stretched out my sore leg and cracked my neck vigorously. Stepping out of the car, I took a deep breath. Turning around to look at my surroundings, a feeling of dread built up in the middle of my stomach. We were standing in the middle of a small, overgrown *Monsoon Green #HDFC 08U* lawn where a few trees seemed to have been chopped away. The area was so small that I wouldn't have noticed it had my dad not stopped in front of it. In fact, I had thought it was a dead end.

The space couldn't have been bigger than my bedroom, that was if my bedroom was carpeted with uneven grass that scratched at your

12

ankles. I glared into the dense forest surrounding us on all sides. The thin dirt road was the only path left back to real civilization. I was convinced that I saw suspicious-looking raccoons by the trees and mosquitoes hovering near, waiting for the perfect chance to come to suck our blood. Altogether, we had about forty square feet to ourselves. Even the trees seemed menacing with their looming trunks and dry bark.

"Well," my dad said, dropping all of the gear onto the floor and taking a deep breath, "Here we are." He looked around the campsite as if it was his first love. Honestly, if he was a cartoon, there would be little heart eyes popping out of his face. "This is perfect," he gushed.

I absently wondered if he was hallucinating. There were a lot of thoughts going through my head, but none of them were remotely close to, "This is perfect."

My dad opened the trunk rummaging through it when his good mood diminished slightly. He cursed under his breath and then, in a strained cheerful voice, said, "Honey did you happen to take the second tent out of the trunk."

"No, I didn't," my mom said in an exhausted voice, sounding as if she was on the brink of yelling. It was probably due to the fact that Jack had already jumped out of the car the first opportunity he got and was currently running in the tall, wild, insect-infested grass, WITHOUT SHOES.

My dad cursed again. This time a bit more violently than the first. He threw three metal water bottles to the ground and, causally, let my colored pencils fall towards the damp, dirt-infested grass.

"Careful!" I yelled while wiping them on my shirt, glaring at my dad, "My Faber-Castell Albrecht Durer colored pencils were expensive."

"Yeah, I know," My mom shot back her eyes, throwing daggers, "On account of the fact that I gave you 150 dollars to go grocery shopping, and you came back with that non-returnable set."

I shuddered, remembering all the dishes I had to wash to make up for it.

"Ladies, please focus on the problem at hand," Dad yelled, "we only have one tent. Do you want to drive back home?"

I felt my mood shift and could hardly contain my glee hearing this statement; maybe I wouldn't have to stay here after all. Maybe I wouldn't have to sleep on the cold, wet ground. I might even be able to use a real toilet. Ahh, the joys of living in the twenty-first century.

I immediately began planning the rest of the summer. Hey, I might be able to take the modern art class with Amy when she gets back next week. Maybe we could even try to get a permit to paint the playground near our houses.

Grinning, I said in a light-hearted voice, "Yes, That's a great idea. Let's go back home!" Not being able to wipe the grin off my face, I began to walk to the car, clutching my Faber-Castell Albrecht Durer colored pencils and Portobello Sketchbook under my arm.

"Yeah, no, that's not happening," my mom said sternly, wagging her finger in my direction and pulling me back into the clearing, "All four of us can just share a tent."

I took a step back, my eyes widening in horror at the thought. I bit the inside of my cheeks.

"Forget it," I shrieked, "I'm not doing that, Dad snores, and Jack will kick me. Besides, it's too small. You can't-you can't make me. Can't I just stay with Uncle Jimmy? Isn't this his property?" I sputtered angrily, sounding like an eight-year-old.

My mom gave me a look that had "No," written all over it.

My six-year-old brother wrapped his freckle-covered arms around me and said, "Yay, it's a slumber party."

I groan while patting his little tuff of red hair. I know that I sound like a horrible monster for not wanting to sleep next to him, but in reality, the kid was wilder than a puppy on steroids. I would not survive the next two weeks.

Chapter 3

After the tent had been set up, my parents decided on the next item of torture, hiking. One of the activities that I was most unenthusiastic about. Honestly, why would anyone want to trudge through the damp and dirty woods where the possibility of being attacked by a wild animal or catching hypothermia escaped me? Groaning, I grabbed my hiking boots and put them on as slowly as possible, trying to stall the procedure of leaving.

I was in the process of hooking up the orange and purple shoelaces (why anyone would dare combine those two colors was beyond me) when my mom yelled, "Come on, Piper. We want to be back before the sun goes down, or else wild animals will come out to eat."

I stood up in fear, her words having done their job; being bear food was not on my career list, and I certainly wasn't planning on adding it. Double-checking to see that my sketchbook was in my backpack, I got up and ran toward them.

Pouting, I dragged my feet in the mud, half trying to cover up the hideous shoe laces, half trying to stall in the hope of reducing the amount of hiking time.

"Aww, Piper, it's not that bad," says my Dad in the vain hope of cheering me up, "Maybe you'll love it, and this'll be the reason you become a wildlife biologist or conservation scientist."

"I highly doubt that, considering that I'm already failing science," I muttered under my breath. As we trudge through the woods, my feet begin to blister in the tiny hiking boots. Oh, why had I gotten the size five? Maybe my mom had been right about getting the six. Not that I would ever admit it, though.

"This is my life now." I moaned, "I have climbed this hill, and now, upon it, I shall die."

"Be quiet. We've only been hiking for like thirty minutes," my mom hissed.

After a few hours of hiking through overgrown bushes, hitting my head on low branches, and finding quarter-sized spiders in my shoe, my dad spotted a lake and, for some unknown reason, decided that it would be a great idea to walk over there.

I groaned, "My feet hurt, and I think mosquitos have eaten all of my flesh by now."

No one responded.

"But whatever," I continued. "If you would prefer me as a pile of bones, so be it."

"Maybe then you'll be quieter," my mom muttered.

"I'll make you a deal Piper," My dad said, rubbing his temple, "If you swear not to moan at all for the rest of the hike, I promise I will go back to the tent after we walk down to the lake."

I considered the proposal resting my finger on my chin. As much as I hated to admit it, complaining wasn't getting me anywhere, so I might as well go along with him. Not much to lose if you're already dead.

As we walked down the thin trail, my mind wandered to what Ronni might be doing right now. I bet she was looking at the Mona Lisa instead of trudging through mud and coated in dirt.

The four of us walked through the humid air ridden with bugs. Keeping my side of the deal, no negative words spilled out of my mouth. To be completely honest, I had no idea that I had that much self-control. After what seemed like an eternity of walking down steep muddy grass, or maybe just fifteen minutes, we arrived at a large disgusting *Pantone Bottle Green 17-5722 TCX*-colored pond. It was filled with green algae and was an unpleasant amount of moss.

Breathing through my mouth, I wondered why on earth we walked so far to see this mold-infested lake.

The four of us walked around, and my parents began snapping pictures as if it were the most beautiful sight they had ever laid eyes on. I rolled my eyes, taking a step back to go to the tent, when I felt myself step on a particularly slippery patch of grass. The ground grew closer to me, and I began to slide down on my behind. My butt smacked against the ground, and I let out a yelp of pain. My backpack fell off, and my heart jumped into my throat. There was a tremendous SPLASH. I landed in the lake.

Water soaked through my shoes, socks, and slowly the rest of my body. It was the physical manifestation of an infectious disease trying to get into every single spot of my body. I cursed and flailed, trying in vain to get out. I thrashed around unsuccessfully, trying to get out of the water. I made my way to dry land, glaring at everything. My tailbone was throbbing, and my cheeks grew hot. Soaked to the bone, I stumbled up and glared at my dad, who seemed to be holding back laughter. I pushed my way up.

"Can I complain now?!" I asked sarcastically, trying to cover up the hurt and embarrassment.

I stumbled back to the tent wet, sore, and itchy. All I desperately wanted was to jump into a bubble bath and to binge-watch *Friends*. Was it really too much to ask for!? Unfortunately, my mom decided that all I needed was a good night's sleep and some repulsive canned food that smelled like rotten bananas and was the same color as *Pantone Cashew 17-1137 TCX* She had offered to make me a shower by poking holes into a plastic bag, but I wisely decided against it. Starving from the day, I grabbed a can and shoved some of the (I don't even think that should be called food) down my throat. My eyes crossed, my molar clenched, and I felt sick. Retching slightly, I tried to swallow, but the food stayed stuck in the back of my throat.

My mom was watching me, her eyes daring me to complain. I gulped audibly, trying to stay quiet.

***

I lay in the cramped tent, mushed up against the cheap fabric, with my blond hair sprawled against the side. I wondered for the thousandth time why my family wanted to go camping. When I wasn't terrified about bear attacks or falling into lakes, I was so bored that I wanted to crawl out of my skull. Even nature's beauty had failed me up to this point. There were no exotic flowers or bright butterflies, only poison ivy and raccoons, neither of which deserved a spot in my sketchbook.

I stared aimlessly at a birthmark I had on the inside of my wrist. I always thought it was shaped like a paintbrush, no matter how much Jack insisted it resembled a lightsaber. I fidgeted with my fingers and almost sat up in shock when I heard snoring. I turned around, amazed to see that all three of them were fast asleep at only eight-thirty. How someone older than eleven could fall asleep before ten was beyond me.

I groaned, rolling on my side. There was no point in sleeping. The floor felt like a slab of granite, and the fear of wild animals hadn't worn off yet. All we had was a small piece of fabric between a mammoth-sized bear and us. I needed a breather. Maybe I could go outside, not too far from the tent, but some space couldn't hurt. So, before I could change my mind, I decided to go outside and get some air that hadn't already gone through someone else's respiratory system.

I stood up (slightly hunched over) and tiptoed toward the zipper. I quietly creeped out of the tent, careful not to wake anyone up. I sighed peacefully as the cool air kissed my face and rustled my hair. I looked at the falling sun, feeling a sense of amazement fill my veins. This was the reason I didn't pretend to have the flu. I found the beauty of nature, it had captured under its spell.

It was amazing, really. No matter where you were, the sun would always rise in the east and set in the west. It was a constant that you could always rely on in your life. No matter where on earth you were or what you were going through, the sun would always rise and shine down on humans. We were all so tiny compared to it. It was amazing how it put everything into perspective, all my problems, all of my worries. They were all tiny compared to the mass of the sun. The hot ball of fire was so big and so far away that it wouldn't even notice if something happened to us, yet, we relied solely upon the sun for energy, food, and light. Funny how the universe worked that way. I took my focus away from the setting sun and let my eyes drift toward the sky. The colors were brushed together with the softest of strokes on the canvas of the sky. The orange and gold stretched as far as the eyes could see, blending in the faint colors of deep red and blush of rose petals. The sunset was the heart of the horizon, the sky portraying its love. It was as if the rays were destined to create a work of art so beautiful that I couldn't conceive life without it. I couldn't bother thinking of a paint color similar to it. No human could create such a color out of oil and paste, no matter how hard they tried.

I sighed, soaking up all of the colors. I grabbed my sketchbook that was still tucked beneath my hoodie and opened up to the next black page. I pulled out my pencils and attempted to duplicate the wonders painted across the sky.

Sighing, I rolled the tension out of my neck and allowed myself to relax. The sky had put me into a trace. My mind was blurred. There was only me, the canvas, and the sky. The sun began to fall faster and faster, and I tried to keep up with it. My pencil flew across the page as I desperately tried to copy the colors. My legs began carrying me farther and farther from the tent, taking advantage of my non-existent attention span. The sun began to dip below the horizon, and I felt a sense of emptiness, as if I had just lost my closest friends. The fading colors of dusk began to disappear, and the velvety black sky emerged, knocking all the color out of the sky. I sat on the moist grass and hugged my knees to my chest as I stared up at it in wonder. The darkness filled the sky but wasn't completely taken over yet.

There were hundreds of stars still shining like sugar spilled over black marble. Like little beacons of hope still shining through the night. It was an endless battle every evening, the stars and the sky, the light and the darkness. There always seemed to be more darkness when I looked up. Still, it was a source of comfort, knowing that hundreds and hundreds of stars were shining, keeping the darkness from taking over completely.

I lay back in the grass, not worrying about bugs or dirt, my mind in a dream-like state. I couldn't tear myself away from it. The sky was like a magical portal; I feared that if I glanced away for one second, everything would disappear. I was looking up at the starlight of brilliant pearls resting on a cushion of pure black velvet. I didn't dare even bother to grab my sketchbook; in a million years, I would never be able to duplicate such a wonder that even the sky itself had taken millions of years to perfect. I laughed. Maybe my family was rubbing off on me.

However, as I continued to look up at the sky, I realized something had changed. The darkness had brought in another weapon to defeat the light of the stars. The gray *Sherwin Williams Dustblue SW 9161* colored clouds that were edging towards me weren't the harmless cotton balls that had ridden the sky only moments ago. These were menacing soldiers carrying spears preparing to rain down misery.

I froze, not sure what to do. The spell of the sky had drifted off and was now replaced by a curse that raised the hair on the back of my neck. The wind began to blow through the trees and caused my hair to flail around my head, defying gravity. The air flew in between branches howling like a banshee, and I felt fear tickle down my spine as if someone had just thrown ice down my shirt. I looked around suddenly, not recognizing my surrounding. I stood quickly and dusted my back off. Trees surrounded me at all sides in a menacing manner.

I backed away slowly as my heart began to pound against my chest. My breath quickened, and my head spun. Where was I?

Diamond water drops fell down my face, glistening in the faint light. I grabbed my head, trying to find out where the campsite was. I had been following the sunset west, so I could try to go east. Trying to settle my breathing, I slowly walked towards the trees, not knowing if they were getting denser or thinning out. Sweat poured down my face as I passed yet another tree that was uniform to the rest. The hairs on the back of my neck prickled as the wind whistled around. I slumped down onto a semi-dry rock and put my head in between my knees as hot thick tears glistened down my cheeks. I let out a sob and hiccuped slightly. I stood up and tried to continue walking. My eyes were blurred, and my vision was limited. I felt my foot get caught on a root and flew to the ground. I lay on the damp earth, not bothering to get up. My face was covered in tears, and a bit of dirt was collected in my eyes. Large, wet raindrops were falling at this point, and I couldn't tell the difference between tears and rain. I cursed thickly and stumbled backward. My wet hair had turned an ugly shade of grey-brown. I could barely see, with the droplets landing on my eyelashes.

My head spun. I felt as if I were about to pass out. Fear gripped my throat, choking me. My pulse pounded like a speed boat, and I could barely breathe. I placed my sketchbook underneath my shirt. Letting out a defining shriek, I hoped--prayed--someone would hear me. I strained my vocal cords until they grew hoarse, and all I could muster was a feeble whisper. I coughed loudly. I felt goosebumps along my arm, realizing that I was completely drenched at this point. I had begun shivering. The rational part of me wanted to go find a cave or tree or something to shield myself from the sky. Still, I couldn't bring myself to sit up and walk. Helplessness weighed me down more than the rain. What had happened? How had the sky changed so quickly? I wanted to hug myself and float away from this horrible nightmare. How easy it would be to lay down on the wet earth and not wake up.

"Snap out of it Piper!" A voice yelled inside of my head, "Get up right now."

Numbly I stood and followed the voice. I'm still not sure where it came from. It might have been my subconscious or maybe something else entirely. My feet had turned to ice crystals, and my fingers seemed as if they were about to fall off. I wasn't sure what I was looking for as I began walking, but I hoped I would know what it was when I saw it. I stumbled through roots and thick trees, barely even flinching, when I saw a large spider crawl over my sneakers. A shiver went up my spine as I heard a rustling in the trees. Trying to see through the falling rain, I squinted, trying to make out a semi-large hill. It was made of a few moss-covered boulders. I felt my confidence grow a bit and increased my pace. I prayed there would be somewhere for me to hide.

Approaching the rocks, I was relieved to find a small cave on the hill. I stood in front of it, fear building inside of me. What if a wild animal lived there? What if the rocks collapsed onto me? Unfortunately, the rain was incredibly encouraging, and before I knew it, I had walked in. I sighed with relief and crumbled down to the floor. I was shivering from head to toe, and my lungs already felt as if they were collapsing in on themselves.

I needed warmth. I wanted the heat to spread through my body. Nothing could be worse than the unforgiving chill that was circulating in my system. Maybe I could make a fire? I sat up, trying to ignore the fact that I couldn't feel my toes. I looked around the dimly lit cave, hoping to find some dry wood. My eyes strained in darkness, but I was able to scourge a few dry pieces of bark. Sighing with relief, I stared at the wood in my hands. What should I do now? In the movies, they would rub sticks together to create a blazing fire. I looked down skeptically. Seriously, how exactly was fire supposed to emerge from these two pathetic sticks? Knowing I had no other choice, I furiously began rubbing them together.

Chapter 4

I set down the sticks, trying to regain feeling in my hands. They were in the in-between stage, where they were sweating and freezing at the same time. I had rubbed the sticks together for an eternity, and so far, the only results were hands that were no longer numb from the cold but numb from exhaustion.

I let out an ear-piercing shriek. I pulled on my hair in frustration and wanted to cry. My body was shaking all over. I didn't know if it was from the cold, fear, or anger, but at this point, I didn't care. I collapsed onto the ground, trembling. I was going to die here. I knew it. I would never see my family again. I would never hear Jack's high-pitched shriek or my mom telling me she was right. I would never get to listen to my dad's corny jokes or gossip with Amy again. I sobbed loudly, the sound echoing across the cave.

"Get up," the voice in my head said again, this time a bit more sternly.

I took a deep shuddering breath and racked my brain, trying to figure out what else to do. I could vaguely remember my Jack's favorite survival show, *The Wild*. Maybe I could remember something from that? I blinked, hoping to revive the memory. It was on the tip of my tongue, but I couldn't recall any of it. Something about stone…? Oh yeah, they rubbed flint and steel together. I sighed. My life was seriously depending on a thirty-second clip I heard my brother play. Great, just great. I glared around the cave, trying to find a few rocks. There were a few stones that seemed to have broken off, I wasn't really sure if they were flint or steel or whatever, but at this point, I would try anything. My hands were so numb that I could barely pick up the rocks themselves. My entire body was shaking, and I let out another ragged cough.

I lifted the rocks and looked around the cave some more. I needed something like kindling, maybe dry wood or grass. I shivered and glanced over at my sketchbook. Oh no, no way.

"It's the only chance you have," the logical voice in my head said. It sounded like my mom. "They're just drawings."

"Yeah, but they're more than drawings," a different voice fought back, "They're memories."

My drawings were part of me. They were my forms of expression. They were pieces of my soul. I would burn them as soon as I would burn my hair off.

"Just try it!" The logical side of my brain said, "You don't even know if the fire will work."

I took a deep shuddering breath and stood up. I opened up the sketchbook and ripped out the last fifty pages or so. I squeaked slightly. It was as if a little bit of my heart chips away as the paper tore. Hours and hours of hard work, all gone. I sent them down on the floor and tried not to watch the dry dirt cling to them. I lifted up the two rocks and half-heartedly hit them together.

"Come on. You have to try harder than that!" I scolded myself, "You need fire, just don't think about how all of your drawings will slowly turn to ashes."

I wasn't doing a very good job of not thinking about it. Taking a deep breath, I placed one rock in each hand and slammed them together from left to right. A small spark appears. I let out a gasp. It had actually worked! A mixture of excitement and regret filled my body. No, don't think about that. I looked down at the rocks, this time filled with more determination than before. Bringing one rock onto the other, I angled the small spark toward the pages. They curled a bit and then went out on their own again. Bam! I hit the rocks again. The sound echoed across the cave.

I stared at my pages in amazement. It worked! It had actually worked! The paper was slowly turning dark. The embers glowed and licked the drawings away. Silently thanking my art teacher for always convincing us to use sketchbooks with thick drawing paper. I rolled onto my back, wondering how long the fire would last. Its warmth was limited to a few inches in diameter, and the kindling (I couldn't bring myself to think about it as drawings) was burning out fast. I held my sketchbook the way a mother held her child. I would freeze to death without it, but all of my drawings, half a year's worth of ideas and work, memories, and personal thoughts were here. And here I was, contemplating burning it all.

Trying to stop hot tears from bubbling over, I sniffed slightly and began to rip out more sketches. The bluejay I saw on the window seal, "hiss" Burnt. The portraits Amy and I drew for each other crumpled as the flames licked them. The painting of a dove that I drew the day after midterms, and the banshee I drew when I was fighting with Ronni, all turned into ashes. The flame had jumped to about a half-foot high. I sighed with content as my fingers began to warm up and my clothes started to dry. I could barely see the flame at this point. My eyes were blurred with exhaustion. I sat next to the source of warmth. Oh, thank God for the building the fire had worked, I thought quickly before I felt a wave of betrayal at myself. I needed the fire, but my drawings were sacrificed. Still, the warmth radiating from the hearth was warming my muscles and giving me a chance to relax, thoughts of burning drawings and hungry bears slipped out of my head, and all of my muscles began to relax. I lay down on the dusty dirt ground and rested my eyelids. Maybe I could just close my eyes for a few min--

**

I turned around and groaned slightly when the light began to bleed through my eyelids. I lay on the ground, having forgotten where I was. The light was probably coming from my window, and my mom was about to rip the covers off of me. I opened my eyes and rubbed them a few times. I looked around and realized that I was still lying

26

on the ground. The events from last night flooded into my head, and I felt misery wrap around me like a wet blanket.

My clothes were still slightly damp, and another shiver went down my spine. The fire was extinguished, and I could barely look at the ashes. It was like a corpse. I blinked again, wondering where the light was coming from. I looked at the mouth of the cave, and there were still buckets of rain falling from the dark sky. I looked to my right, the source of the light. From deep within the cave, there was a light growing brighter and brighter. Excitement and joy rippled through me! There must be someone else in the cave. Maybe they have a flashlight or, better yet, food. I ran towards it, praying that there was someone to come to my rescue.

"Over here!" I yelled, waving my arms. "Help me!"

My spirit skyrocketed as the light grew brighter. My eyes began to hurt, and I squinted into the cave. What kind of flashlight were they holding, and why were they pointing it directly at my eyes? I squinted slightly and took a step back when I saw where the light was coming from. It wasn't a person holding a flashlight at all; instead, it was a single, bright marble. I bent down to have a closer look ignoring how my eyes screamed in protest. The marble was shining brighter than the surface of the sun. It also seemed to be spinning. Was it a special piece of technology meant to find people? Maybe my family had realized I had gone missing and called the FBI. This must be some sort of tracker that glowed brighter the closer it got to its target.

"I'M RIGHT HERE, MOM AND DAD!" I yelled towards the marble. "PLEASE COME SAVE ME!!!! I PROMISE I'LL NEVER COMPLAIN ABOUT CAMPING AGAIN."

I felt tears spring to my eyes, but I wiped them away. I was getting rescued now. Everything was going to be okay. I would go back to the campsite and never ever complain about camping again. I picked the marble up and dropped it again immediately. There was something off about it. Something just didn't really feel right. There seemed to be some sort of pulse that was pounding through it. The marble was warm, and there was something odd radiating off of it. I couldn't really put my finger on it. I carefully set it back down on the floor, hoping that it would get help quickly. My stomach was growling so loudly it felt like it was trying to claw its way out of my body.

All of a sudden high-pitched noises seemed to echo through the cave. I slammed my hands over my ears, as the noise seemed to be tiny knives embedding themselves in my skull.

"What was that?" I whispered mainly to myself.

I squeezed my eyes shut, hoping that they would block out the noise. Then the noise stopped, just like that. I sighed, letting my hands drop, glancing around in confusion.

"What in the world was-AHHHH," I dropped to the floor and scrambled backward away from the marbles.

The light was shining brighter, and I needed to rub my eyes to make sure that what they were seeing was real. My limbs turned to jello as I realized what had actually happened. The marble had started to grow, and a person had just melted out of it.

Chapter 5

My heart leaped into my throat. Fear gripped my mind as sweat poured out of my palms. The guy standing less than three feet away from me had a cocky smile covering his face. He seemed perfectly okay with the fact that he had just melted out of a small tiny sphere the way a Google tab would open after you hit the minimize button.

"What the...wha, I don't...but...you," I said, unable to process the current events.

My eyes were straining to find the logic behind this. Had he been hiding in the cave all this time? Was this some sorta new NASA technology I had never seen before? I became dizzy and held on to the wall of the cave as my legs had lost all ability to hold my weight. Fear hadn't even kicked in yet, as the shock was all that my body could process at the moment.

I tried to focus on something my brain could understand; his appearance. He had shoulder-length dirty blond hair that gave the impression he had just rolled out of bed, Malibu tan skin, and long thick eyelashes adorned his deep sea blue eyes. He was handsome in every conventional sense. His sharp jaw line adorned a smug expression that he was wearing, which gave me the impression he was fully aware of his appearance, however fake it may look. He was wearing blue khakis and only a light green vest with no shirt. Aladdin much?

"Well, hi there," he said in a cocky voice that seemed to flow into my ear like honey, "Dear dear, aren't you a pretty Piper. I'm Arius."

I gulp, wondering if I was dreaming. Absolutely nothing made sense; my entire brain was on red alert, and my heart pounded in my ears. I felt slightly light headed. How on earth did this stranger know my name? Was he a stalker?! Had he been following me in the woods since I left the tent? The image of my death in newspaper headlines flashed before my eyes. Oh God, I was going to die. I would never become a famous artist. I would never see my family again, and I would never go to school again. I felt hot tears form in my eyes and threatened to spill over.

The young man, Arius, walked towards me, and my muscles tensed. "Don't touch me!" I shrieked, skitting upwards and trying to get to the exit.

"Stop!" He commanded and ran in front of me faster than I could blink.

I skidded to a halt as he stood in front of the only exit. I cursed, glancing around and searching for another exit. None of this seemed real. I couldn't believe any of it, my heart pumped a million miles a minute, and my pulse raced so loudly I could barely think straight.

"Don't make this any more difficult than it has to be," Aladdin boy said, his voice dripping in annoyance. He walked towards me and wrapped his long graceful fingers around my arm.

"Let go!" I screamed, my voice rising in panic.

I shrieked loudly, desperately hoping someone would hear me. I whimpered as his grip around my arm tightened. I could barely feel anything below my elbow. I pulled harder, squirming around, trying to make my arm go limp so he would let go. I lifted my other arm up and furiously began clawing the Aladdin boy's face. I dug my nails into his skin, slightly pleased with myself for leaving a mark.

"Ahh," He looked more annoyed than hurt, "Damn it, Piper, stay still."

The guy grabbed my wrists and easily held them together with one hand. I shrieked, trying to wring them loose. I resorted to using my leg and pushed my knee upwards exactly where I knew it would hurt.

This time Aladdin guy let out a groan, he momentarily released my hands, and I scrambled over myself to escape. Pumping my legs as fast as I could, I began running deeper into the cave. My brain was still ridden in fear, but I tried to focus on the floor. There were pieces of crumbling rocks, and I had already stumbled over a few. I glanced over my shoulder, the fear nearly causing my brain to become dysfunction. My heart was pumping so quickly spots were dancing in front of my eyes.

I tried to push it all away and focus on running. I heard a rock hit the ground not far behind me, and my pulse spiked up. Was Aladdin guy close? I turned my head back around and vaguely wondered where I would end up. Unfortunately, I didn't have enough time to figure any of that out because, at that exact moment, a pair of hands curled around my neck, cutting off my airway. Darkness fizzled around my vision before I passed out.

***

I rolled around, trying to figure out where I was. My mouth tasted like ash, and my lungs felt as if they were on the brink of collapsing. My blood rushed under my skin, and I felt suffocatingly warm. I opened my eyes to see myself lying on a small couch, covered head to toe with blankets. I was lying right next to a roaring fire, and I immediately wondered where I was. My brain felt fuzzy, and I couldn't remember anything that had happened. I could vaguely remember what had happened, there had been fire, a marble, and some shirtless dude, but it all felt like it had been a dream. Fear shot through my veins as the night's event unfurled into my brain. I turned my head ever so slightly, hoping not to attract any attention to myself. I let my eyes wander the floor until I saw a pair of shiny gold sneakers-- Aladdin guy's sneakers. My spine straightened as I realized it hadn't been a dream at all. He seemed busy, maybe too busy to notice me. I held my breath, praying that my panting wouldn't attract his attention. If I pretended to be asleep, would he leave me alone? I stayed frozen in my position, becoming uncomfortably warm and slightly claustrophobic under the thick blanket. I felt a cool piece of metal against my leg, vaguely wondering what it was.

Maybe this guy isn't so bad, a small part of my brain realized. *I mean, he's letting us sleep and even gave us a bunch of blankets--*

Nah, he's definitely a crazy kidnapper, a different thought replied. *Did you see how he grabbed me?*

Well, yeah, but he got me out of the cave. He's even letting me get some much-needed sleep, the positive side argued.

Maybe he wants me to be wide awake while I'm being tortured.

I don't think so he-- I didn't have time to finish the thought because Aladdin guy decided to stand up.

"Look who finally decided to wake up," he grinned, casually leaning back.

I bolted up, terrified of what was going to happen. I dramatically threw the blankets off, preparing to run, when the Aladdin guy looked up.

"Stop."

I froze. I looked down with horror to realize that my legs were tied to the sofa.

"YOU TIED ME TO THE SOFA!" I yelled, my blood pounding in my ears. Of all the things that could have angered me, this was what really pushed me over the edge, claustrophobia tightening around my throat.

I whimpered and immediately began trying to pull against the tight metal coils. The skin around my ankles grew red and sore as blisters began to form. I ignored the pain furiously, trying to pull them off. I reached down with my hands and began to tug at the restraints.

Tears welled up in my eyes as layers of skin seemed to rub off my ankle.

As I struggled against the bonds, the Aladdin guy gave a mocking laugh, strutting across the room towards me, "Oh, don't even bother," he said, smirking slightly as if he were the most incredible human on earth, "you won't get anywhere close to untying them. I would recommend that you sit your tiny little behind right back down and listen to what I have to say before I turn you into a pile of dead bones."

I froze, my head spinning slightly. The slightly less rational side of my head was offended that he called my bottom small, but the other side was drop-dead terrified. I knew it. This was it. Aladdin guy was going to kill me. I wondered vaguely how, maybe with a gun, short and painless, or perhaps an electric chair. All the true crime podcasts that I listen to in my spare time came flooding back into my mind, no longer seeming like unrealistic stories from a faraway place.

Tears welled in my eyes, and I began flailing all around the floor. I violently thrashed against the chair, ignoring the way my ankles screamed in protest as the skin was eaten away by the chains. I landed face-first on the floor, and my nose exploded in pain.

"Stop it! You're ruining everything," Arius yelled, pulling my arms off of the floor.

"Let go of me!" I screamed at the top of my lungs. I kicked my legs up and nearly gasped in pain as the sofa gave way and collapsed on top of me. "HELP ME!" I shrieked in pain as fire exploded in my knees caps.

"Stop moving!" Arius growled in frustration. "Stop moving, and I'll lift the couch off of you."

I didn't trust him. I kept squirming around, trying to lift the couch up myself. I vaguely heard Arius mumble, "I guess you've left me with no other choice." I turned to him, feeling slightly confused.

He flexed his muscles (I swear I wasn't looking at them on purpose) and grunted slightly. Before I could imagine what he was doing, I felt the couch lift off of me. I momentarily forgot the fear running through my head. I stared up in amazement. The couch was two feet off the ground. How was that happening? I squinted my eyes and tried to figure out how he was doing that. Were there invisible threads? Some weird pulley system?

"MOVE!" Arius let out a strangled sort of cry, "Damn it, Piper, don't just sit there."

Luckily my legs finally decided to function. I scrambled out from underneath the couch. It came down with a *bang*. I hugged my knees to my chest and let out a long shuddering breath. The chains had miraculously disappeared, and I cursed, wondering if I was going insane. My brain was spinning, and I thought my heart was about to collapse from exertion. Arius was panting slightly, and his face turned the same color as a red velvet cupcake.

"How–" my voice squeaked, and I tried again–"How did you do that?"

"That's what I have been trying to explain," Arius replied, leaning against the couch for support.

I wanted to argue and remind him that most of the conversation had consisted of him handing out death threats like free samples, but I decided now wasn't the best time to bring that up. I crossed my legs and sat down on the floor, looking up intently at him. I had forgotten the fear circling in my head and glanced back down at the fallen couch. There must have been some sort of hidden wire. Aladdin guy was probably just some dramatic dude who liked to give people a show before he killed them. Still, I didn't really want to die without knowing how he did it. There was something about the Aladdin guy that was familiar.

"Okay, Aladdin guy," I said, bringing my fingertips together underneath my chin, like a judge on America's Got Talent, "Enlighten me."

Aladdin guy frowned, "Okay, so let's start off with the fact that my name is Arius, not Aladdin guy. If you continue to mock me with the name of some ridiculous peasant who rubs a magic lamp, I will banish you to the fiery realm of Charlid!"

His face had grown slightly red again, and I scooched backward and gulped slightly. I felt the temperature in the room goes up a few degrees. I furrowed my eyebrows, trying to figure, Alad--I mean Arius, out. One second he was kidnapping me, the next second, he was saving my life, and now we were back to death threats, I think. Charlid didn't sound like a place I wanted to be banished to. Delightful.

"Umm...okay?" I said, my eyes darting around for an escape.

I must have been in a room with a madman. That was the only logical answer. I was locked in a room with a psychopath. Wait, so did that make me a psychopath? Would someone lock a psychopath with another psychopath? I gasped slightly. Well, at least that made sense. That was why I thought I saw the couch fly. Tears filled my eyes at the thought.

"Oh, God, am I a psychopath?" I choked out, not wanting to hear the answer.

Arius actually had the nerve to laugh, "No, but I bet you wish you were when you find out

what you actually are."

I gaped at him, not quite sure if I was supposed to be offended or confused. I settled with gazing at him with my mouth hanging open slightly. "Sorry, what? I'm honestly convinced that this is a shock-induced hallucination but care to explain what on Earth is going on here?"

"Hmmm, where to start," Arius said, rubbing his chin the way they do in cheesy old-time movies, and then replied in a dramatic voice, "how about we start with the fact that you summoned me?"

I cocked my head, confused. Arius deflated a bit, clearly hoping his dramatic words would have had a bigger impact on me. Instead, I tried to figure out what on earth he meant by summoned. I mean, that was a word that I would normally characterize with a servant, and I couldn't really picture Arius rubbing my feet.

"Look, I don't know what you're talking about," I said, my fear audible in my voice. "I don't know what you want with me." I resorted to begging, my last resort, "Please, please just take me back home."

Arius chuckled, but there was no humor in his voice, "You don't understand it do you? You can't go home. Not for a while."

My breath hitched in my throat, and I felt the world swerve underneath my feet, and stars danced in front of my eyes. Oh God, this was real. I wasn't going home. Images of all the things that I thought happened to children when they were kidnapped appeared in front of my eyes, and a scream began bubbling up inside of me.

"Anyway, as I was saying, you summoned me when you burned all of your--,"

I let out a scream. I scrambled up and began tearing everything off of the wall. Like a tornado, I pulled colorful paintings off of the beige walls and used my fingernails to scratch off the wallpaper in the vain hope of finding an exit or window. I never broke my high-pitched scream, still praying that someone would hear my shriek and rescue me.

"STOP!" Arius yelled after what felt like a millennium. His voice was filled with venom that I froze in fear.

I felt my spine go straight, and my scream stopped as I gasped for air. I tried to move my legs, but they seemed stuck on the floor. At first, my rational mind thought that I was frozen in fear, but I stared straight at Arius, who had a wicked look in his eyes. I swallowed dry and tried to speak. Nothing came out. I felt like I wasn't connected to my body. I couldn't even open my mouth. I was mentally in my body, but I had been disconnected.

"Ha, not so loud anymore, are we now?" Arius said with a wicked grin that I wanted to slap right off of his smug, perfect face.

What did you do to me?! I wanted to scream out. I felt trapped. I couldn't go anywhere, and I was a prisoner of my own mind. I grabbed my neck and tried to push my voice out, but I couldn't even move my arms.

"Now, allow me to finally explain why you are here. Oh, and I'm truly sorry that I needed to freeze you in place, but I honestly can't have you ripping off wallpaper and screaming like a banshee." Arius continued, not looking apologetic at all.

I wanted to glare at him, but curiosity took up too much space in my brain. What did he mean by "freeze me"? As in turning me into ice? I suddenly had the vision of Arius singing "Let it Go" and accidentally freezing Anna's heart. Oh no, was my hair going to turn white? I strained my eyes, trying to look at the few strands of hair that fell on my shoulder. Did they look whiter than usual? I almost let out a small gasp. What if he injected some sort of serum into my blood that made me lose control of my limbs? I glanced downwards at my fingernails that had been bleeding earlier. The blood seemed to have stopped flowing out as well. I groaned internally. I really should have spent more time watching *The Colony* with my dad. Who knew my life might depend on it?

"Ah, yes, this is much better. As I was saying, when you burnt your drawing, you created a spark. It broke down some sort of wall and let Charlid into the world. So, I, the most powerful deity in the world, have decided to come to you and–"

"Hold on. You're a god?" I burst out, all of my other theories flying out of the window. "Like you have a God complex? Pop off, I guess."

Fear flickered across his face, but it disappeared so quickly I could have imagined it, "How–" Arius cleared his throat and then said in a much deeper voice– "How did you break the freeze?"

I looked at him, slightly confused, trying to understand the question. I looked down at my fingers and wiggled them around a bit just to make sure I could move them again. Oh, thank God, but not Arius. I felt relief flow through my body as I began shaking my legs just to be sure.

"Umm...I'm honestly not sure," I said, slightly glad that we had gotten off the subject of killing me and slightly alarmed, wondering where the conversation was going. "Maybe it just sorta wore off."

"I AM A GOD!" Arius shouted, causing me to jump in fear, "No one breaks my freeze."

"Umm," I said, taking a few steps back and wiping my sweaty hands on the back of my jeans. "I'm really sorry for your godliness, sir. I-I don't know what I was doing. Please don't kill me," I whimpered, my voice squeaking a bit.

"How many times do I have to tell you that I'm not going to kill you!" Arius yelled, irritation dripping in his voice like venom.

Just once would have been nice, I wanted to bite back, but I kept my mouth shut. Aladdin guy seemed very prone to lashing out, and considering that he could make me lose feeling in my limbs or pick up a couch with his mind, it would probably be in my best interest not to aggravate him. I swallowed a lump in my throat and nodded, too scared to say anything else.

"Eveda will have to deal with this. My pay grade is too low." Arius mumbled. "Honestly, what were you thinking, releasing Charlid."

I was about to ask if Eveda was some sort of torture device and what on earth he meant by releasing Charlid, but I didn't even have time to panic when Arius (yet again) grabbed my left wrist, and the world went blank.

Chapter 6

I felt as if I was being pushed into a very tiny compartment. My entire body was being squeezed, my lungs felt as if they were collapsing in on themselves, my throat walls were touching each other, and my brain was about to pop out of my ears. I was spinning faster than the *Twister Mania* ride at the *Wing Over Washington Amusement Park* ride. I squeezed my eyes shut, praying for this to be over. I heard a scream, and it took me a hot second to realize it was mine.

After what seemed like an eternity, I felt my feet hit solid ground. I wanted to groan with relief. Was that what Eveda was? Some sort of awful simulation? My knees gave out, and I collapsed onto the ground, shuddering. My vision turned black, and nausea clouded my senses as the ground seemed to tip slightly. I crawled onto my hands and knees, retching onto the grass that stood underneath me. My face had turned pale and cold sweat seemed to seep from my face. I bent over, breathing deeply on all fours. It was as if my organs had been turned inside out and put in a blender.

"What...what was..that?" I asked, still panting.

"Oh no, we landed in the wrong place," Arius said, frowning a bit, "We need to shift again."

He made a motion to grab my hand, but I pulled it away and stumbled through the grass. I didn't care where I went. There was no way that I was doing that Eveda thing again. Stars danced in front of my eyes as I tried to push my legs forwards and move away from him. I didn't even bother wondering was shifting was. I needed to get out of there.

"No!" I wanted to yell out, but I was about to get out, and a hoarse whisper, "Forget it, I swear to Go–" I paused. If Arius was a god, could I actually swear like that? And were there more gods out there or only Arius? I desperately hoped that Arius wasn't the only god in existence.

Arius chuckled, "Well, have it your way. Not sure if you can make it to Eveda in that condition, but it'll be fun to watch."

He began walking across the lawn to a large stone castle I hadn't noticed earlier. I closed my eyes, trying to fight nausea and confusion. Where was I? Was the stone castle some sort of prison hall where lost children found in the woods were kept? I kept my eyes shut, praying that when I opened them, everything would disappear, and I would be back at the campsite.

"Get over here!" Arius growled, grabbing my arm and pulling before I could trip over the doorway, "Why are you keeping your eyes closed?!"

"This is all a bad dream." I murmured to myself, squeezing my eyes shut, "This is all a bad dream."

I could practically hear Arius roll his eyes. "What in the realms of the garden would Eveda want with you?"

I felt too sick to ask what the realm of gardens was. At this point, what did it matter? It clearly wasn't Earth. On Earth, people couldn't lift couches with their minds. On Earth, gods couldn't freeze me or shift.

"Eveda!" Arius screamed, causing my already throbbing head to feel as if it was being hammered open. "EVEDA SHE'S HERE!"

My eyes flew open, and fear filled my brain. Oh no, this was it. I was being handed over to Eveda, whoever that was. Terror built up in my stomach, expanding slowly like a balloon. Was she going to hurt me? WAS SHE GOING TO KILL ME?! Tears threatened to spill over thousands of times in the past few hours.

I looked around the room, trying to find this Eveda. My eyes scanned the chestnut-colored desk stew with pieces of paper and colorful folders. Open pens and markers leaked onto pages, and I felt a small grin tug on the side of my mouth despite the situation at hand. Maybe it was just my brain overthinking the current situation, but somehow people feel more approachable if they are messy.

I continued to look around, but all of a sudden, my eyes began to lose focus. At least, that's what I thought happened. The air in front of me seemed to bend, almost as if it was unfolding like a piece of paper. I let out a small gasp when I saw an actual person step out of the air. Everything went back into focus and returned to its original place, except for the fact that there was a young woman standing right in front of the desk. I took a step back, unsure of what had just happened. Did she just…" I turned my attention back to her, scared of what would happen next.

She was easily the most beautiful woman I had ever seen. Her long golden locks were the same color as *Clare Golden Hour VoC #234*. It swept between her shoulder blades, and there were a few thin braids that trained from the top of her head to her ears. My eyes drifted towards her nose, which was slightly crooked as if it had been smashed by a heavy object. Something told me she wasn't someone you wanted to mess with. Her heart-shaped face was adorned with freckles that were sprinkled on top of her cheekbones.

Her eyes were the most amazing creations I had ever seen. The colors were constantly changing every few seconds. They started out sky blue, with flecks of white that seemed to have been splattered onto a cobalt canvas. The blue then seemed to fade into green, as if two paints had mixed. Her eyes then turned into Aquamarine gemstones that reminded me of the roaring ocean. The next colors were warmer tones. Like the reflection of a fireplace, Amber, tangerine, ruby, and blonde all blending together harmoniously, causing sparks to fly. They were constantly flickering back and forth, making it impossible for me to concentrate on anything else. However I did notice heavy bags underneath her eyes. She seemed physically and mentally exhausted.

She wore a paint-splattered apron, and I noticed there was charcoal wedged between her fingernails. There also was something about her that seemed to radiate power. It might have been the way her eyes seemed to bore down on you or her perfect posture, which resembled a battle stance. I wondered if she was a goddess as well. For some reason, the thought didn't frighten me as much as the concept of Arius being a god.

"Thank you, Arius. You are dismissed." The Eveda woman said sternly, her gaze still on my face.

"But--" he whined, and for some reason, his intimidating macho stance seemed to diminish.

A terrifying thought struck me as I watched the exchange. If Eveda could scare Arius, did that mean she was even more powerful than him? I swallowed a lump of fear. Arius stalked off, slamming the door, and Eveda turned her attention to me. I wasn't sure if I was supposed to smile or shake.

She looked at me with her multicolored eyes. "I apologize on his behalf. He's a bit, er...dramatic. Being only three-quarters of a God has made him a bit insecure. Best if you kept that between us, though."

I wasn't quite sure what to say, there were millions of questions floating through my head, but my voice didn't seem to be working. I gave her a slight nod and then proceeded to try to hide myself. I hunched my shoulders, hoping to evaporate on the spot.

"Ple-," my voice squeaked, and I let out a small sob, "Please, please don't hurt me." I whimpered with exhaustion and fear.

Eveda's eyes softened in sympathy, and she extended her arm to reach my shoulder, "I promise I will try my best to keep you safe."

I flinched slightly, but I didn't completely shrug her off, "But." I whispered so that she had to bend over to hear me, "Arius said," I hiccuped slightly and took a deep breath, trying to steady myself.

"Arius said that he was going to kill me," I sobbed, "and oh my God, I don't even know what to believe anymore. I don't even think I can say oh my God anymore. I mean, is he actually a god? Are you a goddess? Why could Arius freeze my body? Did we teleport? How did he pick up the couch with his mind? What is going on? Who is Charlid? Can I just please come home?"

I let out a gasp, realizing that tears were streaming down my cheeks. The questions were coming out like waterfalls, but I didn't care about most of them. All I wanted was for Eveda to send me home and end this whole nightmare.

I had given up on my theory that this was a dream; I wasn't creative enough to imagine this. My head was so jumbled up I didn't even focus on the fact that I had just blurted out a whole bunch of questions to someone who was able to make Arius go away. Arius, the guy who could pick up a couch with his mind and freeze my entire body when he felt like it.

Eveda gave me a slight sigh and placed her finger onto her chin, thinking hard. "I promise that I am going to answer all of those questions, but I just want you to give me a few minutes to explain the situation you have entered."

I opened my mouth to speak, but she began to speak in a hushed voice. "Hundreds of millions of years ago, before there was anything at all, there was this." She paused, taking a breath. "Energy. The energy took form in four deities: Breizet, Aquia, Potia, and Emensaly." As Eveda began to speak, I noticed she lost her calm composer slightly as her voice became rushed.

"That's great and all, but how exactly is this supposed to get me home," I asked desperately. I couldn't care less that Eveda might have all the power in the world. I didn't even care that she just flat-out told me that the creation of the world started with only four beings. Well, to be completely honest, it wouldn't have mattered to me. My only thoughts were focused on leaving.

"Patience, Piper," Eveda said, this time a bit more firmly. I squirmed around under her gaze, wondering vaguely how she knew my name. "As I was saying, these four deities began creation. They split up, and each took up a different specialty to create the worlds as we know it–yes, Piper, worlds, as in plural," she specified after glancing at my astonished gaze. "I'll touch back on that later. Briezet took care of the skies. He created birds, pixies, and clouds. He created oxygen to help all of the creatures breathe. The atmosphere was created on each of the worlds to protect all of the specific species. Potia created warmth, the sun, and fire; he's always been a hothead, but never mind that. Aquia created vast oceans, bodies of water, icy cliffs, and all the animals in between. And Emensaly, she made the plant life, the jungles, the mountains, humans, and all other animals that roamed in that domain. In some scenarios, they worked together to create. For example, Potia and Briezet created dragons, Aquia and Emensaly made alligators."

I fought the urge to laugh as she told me two weird gods created dragons. Oh, please, dragons? I wondered if this was a prank. Had my family set this up? I doubted it. They had a sense of humor that couldn't teaspoon. I vaguely looked around the room for cameras pondering if this would show up on YouTube.

"You seem skeptical," Eveda noticed, raising her eyebrow slightly.

I rolled my eyes, "Well, obviously, I mean, you can't actually expect me to believe anything that you're saying. I mean, seriously, dragons? You've got to be kidding me, and this whole, I'm magical god stuff is getting annoying at this point."

Eveda frowned. The conversation clearly wasn't going the way she hoped, "I honestly promise that I'm not making any of this up, but by all means, if you want me to prove something to you, I'm more than happy."

I scoffed but took a step back and made a ridiculous "go on" gesture. Eveda cleared her throat and rolled up her sleeve. She closed her eyes, and all of a sudden, the air began to shimmer. My jaw dropped as the colors became stronger and, all of a sudden were no longer transparent. A blank canvas fell out of the sky and into Eveda's awaiting palm. She began waving her hand, and colors appeared on the canvas. It was as if her finger had turned into a paintbrush causing long strokes to appear on the white background. I walked closer to get a better view of her hands, trying to see if there were any paint cannons or invisible wires hidden. Smiling, she turned the canvas over, and I saw what she had drawn me. An exact replica of how I had been standing and rolling my eyes. I blinked a few times, rubbing my eyes, trying to make sense of it all. I've never really thought of myself as a logical person, even though I couldn't wrap my head around this. I gaped at Eveda again, my mouth opening and closing like a fish out of water.

I closed my eyes, trying to figure out what was happening, I kept looking around for special effect machines, but something in my gut was telling me I wouldn't find any.

"But-how, you what--no why?" I stood in front of Eveda, my eyes trying to process how on earth she did that.

"I'm the goddess of art," She said, shrugging as if it was no big deal.

"You're what?" I asked though I heard her the first time.

"The goddess of art," Eveda repeated patiently.

I closed my eyes, allowing this information to sink in. Art, how dare she drag art into this. Whatever parallel universe I had just entered was confusing everything I thought that I knew. The creation of the world, the religions, and now art. Fan-freakin-tastic.

"I understand this is a lot for you to take in, and I truly wish I could give you more time to settle, but, unfortunately, the clock is working against us." Eveda sighed, rubbing her temple.

"What do you mean, working against us?" I whined, wrapping my hair around my finger. "What does any of this have to do with me?"

"Please, Piper, give me a few minutes to explain," She replied gently. "As I was saying, each deity created a different part of the world. The sister, Emensaly, was always a bit different than her siblings. She was a big fan of humans. Their realm was the only one that was unaware of the other realms. Instead of wanting to control them, she wanted to live among them. Emensaly spent all of her time gazing down at humans wishing that she were one of them. Their lives seemed so simple and careless, as if they didn't have a worry in the world. What amazed her was their number. She couldn't possibly imagine anyone being lonely."

I scoffed.

Eveda ignored me and continued. "At least that's what Emensaly thought. She had taken a liking to a particular human man named Saghaza. Emensaly would follow the young man around all day, never getting bored of watching him. She had become so sick of having only her brothers to talk to. Every single conversation she had with them was about the same mundane thing. What were the current issues in some particular realm? How could they become more powerful? Worst of all, they forbade her from going to the human world. The brothers had already realized that the humans worshiped them more than any other creature. They couldn't allow Emensaly to fall in love with a human. They thought it would make them look weak. They feared the humans would stop worshiping them and see

47

the deities as their equals, Godsforbid." Eveda rolled her eyes, and I sensed there was a little more of the story that she was revealing,

I leaned forward, becoming slightly more interested in the story. "How does human worship give the deities power?"

Eveda shrugged, "I've never really understood the logistics of that if I'm being completely honest. You can ask them later."

My eyes widened, but Eveda held up a hand to silence me. "Allow me to continue."

I nodded.

"The three brothers were ignorant–a habit they unfortunately possess--though that doesn't come as much of a shock, none of them realized how lonely the poor goddess had become. Most days, she was barely able to grow a single flower. At one point, Emensaly cracked, Saghaza was growing older by the day, and it physically hurt her to stay away. One day while her brothers were off, working on a new development in the *pedoes* realm, she went to an empty flower patch and began to grow a Camellia flower. She put all her pain into the flower. Emensaly, let go of all her grief and anguish towards her brothers and towards the world. All her emotions were directed right toward the flower. The little plant became overburdened and began to cry tears of nectar. Emensaly drank that nectar and--."

I winced in disgust.

Eveda let out an exasperated sigh but didn't respond to it, "--ended up in the human world, somewhere in Sumer, near modern-day Iraq. Emensaly found Saghaza, and the two immediately fell in love."

"Hold on, slow down," I said, pressing my hands to my forehead. "So this goddess just pops up in the human world, and this regular guy just falls in love with her, no questions asked?"

Eveda threw her hands in the air, "Piper, I don't have an answer for you. I'm sure she gave him some sort of explanation. She certainly had the ability. From what I've heard, she descended from the sky on a dove made of rose petals. Of course, that's only a rumor."

"Right, right," I replied, attempting to keep my voice casual, "I'm still trying to get used to the whole 'Gods have crazy unlimited magic' part."

Emensaly rubbed her forehead, clearly ready for the conversation to be over. "I'm sorry if I'm overwhelming you, Piper, but the clock is working against us."

I sighed. I was really starting to hate this dumb clock.

Emensaly lowered her voice to continue, "Now, while Emensaly is ecstatically living her life in the human world, her brothers claimed they began to feel weak. Now I personally think that they made up that part of the story, but never mind that. Aquia, Potia, and Breezet discovered Emensaly in the human world mingling with humans. Raging with fury, they appeared before the two lovers and murdered Saghaza on the spot."

Chapter 7

I stepped back, trying to understand the story. So much information was being thrown at me that I didn't even know what was going on, much less what to believe.

"It's a very sad tale." Eveda contemplated thoughtfully, clearly mistaking my confusion for sadness, "Emensaly was devastated. She vowed that she would never return to the golden god kingdom. Instead, she uses her abilities to create a way to transport herself between the realms. Her pain had multiplied after the death of Saghaza, and she went back to the field with the camellia flower. She created hundreds of more flowers. Each one could transport her to a different realm."

"Uh-huh," I muttered, trying not to squirm in my seat.

Eveda gave me a sad smile, "Trust me, this involves you more than you think. Now as Emensaly grew more distant, the three brothers began to lose power, much more than they lost when Emensaly was with the humans." She scoffed, momentarily losing her train of thought. "They had less and less control over the realms. They needed her for balance, to stay powerful. So eventually, someone tried to challenge them."

I paused, not sure where this was going. My stomach growled, and I hugged it, slightly embarrassed. "Sorry," I murmured, "I haven't eaten since…" I trailed off, thinking of the campgrounds. It felt like a million years away.

Eveda sprung up, "Of course, how could I be so rude? Let me draw you something to eat. What would you like?"

"Anything's fine, really," I responded, suddenly feeling self-conscious.

"No, no, that simply will not do. I need you to tell me exactly what you want." She chided.

My stomach growled again. "Honestly, a slice of pizza sounds amazing right now." My mouth watered as I thought of the pizzeria that was a few blocks down from my block.

Eveda nodded, satisfied. I wondered where she planned on getting it. Did super-powerful art deities know how to use Uber Eats? Instead, she did something even more bizarre. She waved her hands to make the sketchbook appear out of thin air and began to draw a slice of pizza. I watched her, wondering if she had gone a bit mad. Did she know the paper wasn't edible? I was about to open my mouth to protest when Eveda waved her hand. At first, I thought she was trying to silence me, but I quickly realized something was different. The drawing was...growing. It was becoming 3-D. The smell of cheese wafted through the air, and I realized that there was a very real slice of pizza now sitting on her sketchbook.

Eveda ripped the page out of her sketchbook and handed me the slide, but I didn't take it. My eyes were practically bursting out of my skull. "I–what–how–you just...drew pizza." I sputtered.

Eveda smiled, "Yes, it's a skill many people in the art realm possess."

I gawked.

"Here, take it," Eveda said, pushing the paper holding the pizza toward me.

I scooted back. "I don't want any of your weird alien food."

She rolled her eyes, "Just take it, Piper. You'll pass out if you don't eat."

"How do you know it's edible?" I asked suspiciously, eyeing the pizza.

51

Eveda reached down and took a bite with a smile, "It's delicious."

My resolve crumbled, and I reached for the pizza. Gooey, greasy, cheesy food was my weakness. I decided that if Eveda was planning to kill me, she would have done it already. Death by weird pizza didn't really seem like her style. "Mmm." I groaned, feeling better than I had in weeks. "Thhis ish reaally goods," I murmured with a mouth full of cheese.

Emesally grinned, and I saw a hint of pride in my eyes. "Glad you like it. Know if we could please continue."

I made a go-on gesture. Now that there was food in my stomach, I felt like I could handle any crazy tale Eveda threw my way.

Eveda began in a low hush, "Now, as I was saying, the balance of the three brothers was unstable. They needed Emensaly to reach their full power. With her gone, someone tried to overthrow the three brothers."

"Charlid," I whispered. I didn't know where I had heard it, but I knew in my gut that's who Eveda was talking about. That he was who everyone was talking about.

Eveda nodded grimly. She didn't seem all that shocked that I knew his name. "The cruelest, most awful creature in all the realms. He is the leader of the realm of Charlid. Also known as the chaos realm. When he got word of Emensaly leaving, he staged his attack on the golden god kingdom, hoping to take power for himself. Realms took sides. It led to a massive battle with thousands of casualties on either side. The brothers were able to stop him eventually, with the help of many others. However, the losses were greater than ever seen before." Eveda held a hand up to her mouth, stifling some sort of emotion bubbling within. She swallowed and continued in a wobbly voice. "There was a massive wall built around the chaos realm blocking off the exit to the flower realm, and all other modes of transportation were exterminated from the realm. This made it impossible for Charlid or any of his people to get out. They had zero access to the outside world. Unless, of course, someone who has no connection to the realm of Charlid entered through the flower garden."

I tried to scoff. There was no way I actually believed any of this. Eveda was just a good storyteller, that's all. Still, there was a small part of my brain that recognized this story as if I had heard it before. I didn't like the feeling of being connected to all of this.

"But what does this have to do with me?" I asked, rubbing my thumb across my knuckles.

Eveda bit her lip, clearly hesitant to answer. "Well, Piper, I've brought you here because the wall to the chaos realm is falling down."

It took a moment for her words to sink in. I laughed, unsure of what else to do. "And what exactly does that have to do with me?"

Eveda held up her hand, and I silenced. "What exactly did you do in the cave?"

I looked at her aghast, wondering why she was bouncing around from topic to topic. Did she not just tell me I was somehow involved with Charlid?

"Please just answer the question, Piper," Eveda said, her emotions masked.

I sighed, playing along, "Well, I went inside because it was raining and I was lost. Then I tried to make a fire, which was actually kinda cool cuz it actually worked like in that one survivor show my dad watches a lot, I can't remember the name, but I'll tell you if I think of it." I rambled, becoming nervous by the tense look on her face. "And then I lay down, the ground was really gross, but I was tired. After that, the light from the marble thing–."

"Yes, yes, I know that part." She bit her lip pensively, "Did you leave anything out, anything at all? It could be crucial."

My eyes stung at the memory of my drawings which were probably nothing but ashes at the bottom of the cave right now. "No, nothing," I responded, trying to keep my voice light.

"Piper!" Her voice became urgent.

I flinched. "Fine, yes, I also had to burn my sketchbook because I didn't have enough kindling. Happy?"

"Not in the slightest." She snapped, letting out a string of curses.

I sat back, wondering what was going on with her. Eveda got up and began to pace around the room.

"Earlier, when you went into the cave." She began. "it wasn't just a random hole in between two rocks. It's a small place dedicated to Charlid. Each realm has a sort of embassy for each other realm. They are impossible to get rid of, but lucky not many people know where they stand. The cave you went into was a sort of temple for Charlid. By burning your drawings, you were offering him a sacrifice. That, on top of the unbalance Emensaly caused by leaving, gave him enough power to start to break down the wall. "

I gulped, "WHAT! That's insane. There is no way. And even if that were true, how could a few of my drawings give someone that much power? None of this is my fault."

Eveda nodded, her colorful eyes wide with understanding, "Your artwork has much more power than you think. More than many others in this realm, and to make matters worse, the three brothers, they've been looking for someone to blame for the unbalance of their power for years." She cursed and looked around in agitation, "This is bad, this is really bad. It was so unbalanced, and then you come along, the daughter of the goddess of art, and burned–." Eveda slapped a hand over her mouth, her eyes growing wide.

I stood with my face growing red, "What did you say?"

Eveda froze and threw her hand over her mouth. She cursed. "No, no, no, no, no, no, this was not how you were supposed to find out." She cursed again.

"Find out what?." I asked slowly, shaking. "FIND WHAT OUT EVEDA?"

She seemed to deflate, all the fight going out of her. "You need to sleep, Piper. This is all a lot to take in. I can take you to your room and–."

"What did you say earlier?" I whispered, my voice low. I uncrossed my legs to stand up.

Eveda seemed to age ten years in front of me as her eyes raced back and forth.

"What. Did. You. Say."

"Piper, I-I," She stuttered, failing to get the words out, "Piper, I'm your, your mother."

Chapter 8

I stumbled backward, "No, no, no, you're not. I have a mother. A human mother. Her name is Melissa Hart, and she's the greatest mother alive. She's my mom, not you. It-it can't be you."

Eveda pressed her lips together, clearly trying to keep herself together. I was shaking my head frantically.

She nodded tearfully, walking towards me for an embrace, but I shoved her off. I shook with fear, my entire life collapsing in on itself. Messing with art wasn't enough for this hellhole. Oh no, now it was getting really personal. Another thought crept into my mind. It made my stomach churn with nausea. But I shoved it away. I couldn't think about that right now. I couldn't.

Eveda bit her lip, clearly aware of what I was thinking. "The man who raised you like a daughter currently camping in Seattle has never had an affair. He is loyal and has always been loyal."

I noticed how she said, 'the man that raised you,' not your father, but at that point, I didn't care. I slumped down, resting my head in my hands. This woman in front of me was my mother. Melissa Hart wasn't. I didn't have enough space in my brain to begin worrying about who my real father was.

Eveda reached over and rubbed my back, and this time I didn't shrug her off. "Come on, Piper, let's get you to sleep."

She reached out her hand and helped me up. At least, I think she did. I can't remember much that happened after that. My mind was numb, as if it were going into shock. We walked for some time, passing endless paintings, doors, hallways, and curves. Eveda eventually led me to a plain, white door that opened up to a room. I made a beeline for a bed without taking any time to look at the rest of the area, or Eveda, for that matter. She whispered something, but my brain tuned her out, already falling into an uneasy sleep.

56

In my dreams? I was wandering through a massive flower garden I had never seen before with an easel in one hand and a paintbrush in the other. I had just propped it down, about to paint, when the ground shuddered before evaporating beneath my feet, and I began to fall. The wind roared in my face making my hair and eyelids shudder. I plummeted downwards, shrieking. When my ribs began to rumble, a deep voice began talking, and a figure with many different faces fell next to me. The faces switched from the forms of Aquia, Potia, and a person, with dark coiled braids falling down their face. Cackling madly, I let out a scream as my entire essence seemed to dissolve.

I sat up in bed, covered in a cold sweat. Panting, I looked around the room to make sure that I was alone. Black spots danced before my eyes, but I felt wide awake. In fact, I didn't think that I would ever be capable of sleeping again. I let my eyes roam around the room, trying to distract myself. It was rather, but the moonlight streaming through the window made everything appear threatening. I was ninety percent sure that a plain white dresser was about to grow arms and attack me and then be joined by the nightstand and mirror. Together they would cheerfully beat me to death. I suppressed the shutter. I had never felt so jittery. I mean, I was thirteen years old, for crying out loud. Why was I scared of a dresser?

I rubbed my temples, feeling more awake. The events of last night began flooding back into my brain, and I threw my pillow over my head, trying to block them out. The brothers, Emensaly and Charlid, becoming stronger. It was odd. What on earth could Eveda be babbling about? My drawings didn't have the power to make some madman stronger. It was all crazy. It couldn't possibly be true. There must have been something else that knocked down this weird chaos wall, if it even existed.

I sighed, trying to calm my racing mind. Could I even believe anything that came out of Eveda's mouth? I mean, she tried to convince me that I had a whole new? Different? Family tree. Could it be true? Was she my mother? It seemed impossible.

But was it?

I racked my brain, searching for any recollection I had of her. A sharp memory appeared, one that I had always mistaken as a dream. The strong smell of acrylic paint, long golden hair, and a roaring fire. Was I making that up in my exhaustion, or was it true? I sighed, but why had I never met her before? Why did I live in the human world if she lived here? Did she get rid of me? I had so many questions. Nothing made sense.

My thoughts drifted to my real family. I wondered if they realized I was missing yet. I swallowed back tears, trying to fight against the emotions burning in the back of my throat. Would I ever see them again? I choked on a sob, feeling a sense of helplessness. Who was kidding? I was never going back home.

I tried to lighten myself. No, I couldn't think like that. I would escape this crazy art lady's lair and find my way back home. Maybe I could even use that weird flower garden if it even existed.

Rolling off my bed, I almost yelped when I looked down. I was wearing different clothes. My mud-stained jeans and tattered t-shirt had been replaced with my favorite flannel pajama pants and light blue "Camp Miliwaldon" hoodie. I looked down in disgust, wondering if someone had put them on me while I was sleeping. A second thought followed, where did the clothes come from? The last time I checked, they were scrunched up on my bed, waiting for me to get home from our trip. I felt a newfound hope bubbling in my chest. There must have been someone here with access to the human realm. I reached for the door handle, planning to find them.

Chapter 9

The bright hallway blinded me slightly as I blinked, adjusting my eyes to the light. Once the stars stopped dancing in front of my eyes, I marched down the hall, not really sure where I was going.

I left the many dorm rooms behind and chose to go down the left hallway. It was a bit dimmer, there were soft lights dancing around the stone corridors, reflecting off of the multicolored painting that adorned the wall. I allowed myself to pause and take a look. On the left side, there was a watercolor painting of a stone fountain surrounded by flowers. I shivered slightly. Everything in this place reminded me of Eveda. With each step I took, I felt as if her multicolored eyes were watching me from every direction.

I'm your mother.

"Shut up." I thought aloud, glancing over my shoulder.

My eyes wandered over to a strange metal statue shaped like a bird with plane wings and then to a marvelous stained glass window. A slow smile grew on my face, but I immediately stopped it. If I wasn't so preoccupied with getting home, I knew I would spend hours here exploring each piece in fascination. Honestly, a world dedicated to only art seemed like the greatest place to be alive. I allowed myself a few moments to imagine what living here was like.

I shook myself. Quit it, I thought to myself in frustration. Going home was my only focus. I turned on my heel walking down the next corridor.

I peeked my head through two arcs in the hall, trying to decide which to go through. The right seems somewhat less threatening. Maybe there were people there that could help me. After wandering for what felt like an hour, I sighed, realizing I was hopelessly lost. The halls kept changing, sometimes made of mosaics, sometimes covered in strange yellow flowers, and more. It was enough to make my head spin. I popped my head out the window a few times, but there was nothing to see in the pitch darkness except for the woods surrounding us, beautiful bushes of flowers, and a gorgeous fountain that seemed to glitter even at night.

I turned to my left and saw a small door with a sign that read, *Welcome In*. I sighed in exhaustion, making the decision to enter. Either way, the door was far more welcoming than quite a few other people I had the pleasure of meeting.

I reached for the nob, half expecting it to electrocute me at the touch. Surprisingly nothing shocked me into low orbit or cut me into little strips of spaghetti when I opened the door. I laughed slightly, considering that a success. I entered and grinned when I looked in. The room was filled with every sort of art supply I could imagine. There were huge canvases and hundreds of paintbrushes in every shape, style, and color. I saw painting knives, cotton swabs, sponges, colored pencils, charcoal, acrylic paint, watercolor, oil paints, erasers, oil clay, scoring tools, pottery wheels, needles, fabrics, and hundreds of other tools that I had never seen before. A warm feeling overcame me.

I giggled like a little girl and looked around the bright studio. Why was it so empty? This place was big enough to house two dozen art students easily. Deciding that it would be a shame to leave all of these items unused, I grabbed a canvas apron, slung it over my neck, and propped the 12" by 17" canvas onto an easel. Reaching for a 3/4 angle brush, I uncapped the nearing bottle of gouache paint and poured it straight onto the canvas.

I smiled, delighted to be back in my element. A weight seemed to leave my shoulders as the random blobs began to take shape. The colors began to blend into a sea of emotions. Helplessness and exhaustion lingered on the painting as the paint fumes caused tears to spring into my eyes. At least, that's what I convinced myself was happening. My mind seemed to clear slightly, and I wiped my hands on my apron.

Looking up, I sat back to appreciate my work. I had painted a small boat in the center, similar to the ones back at home in Pike's Market Harbor. Except in my painting, it wasn't sitting in the peaceful harbor. It was struggling against enormous waves that threatened to pull it under.

Out of nowhere, a strange rumble caused the room to shake. "What the–." I didn't have time to finish because, at that moment, a large hole appeared in the center of my painting, and water began gushing out.

I sputtered and gasped as the room began to fill itself with salt water. It flowed up to my knees, soaking my sneakers and sweeping me off of my feet. I looked around bewildered, trying to figure out where the water had come from. I grunted in surprise when I saw a small red boat about the size of my forearm floating next to me. It was identical to the one I had drawn seconds before. I looked around in amazement, unsure what had happened Had...had I summoned my drawing the way Eveda always did?

I didn't have time to figure anything out when Eveda burst into the room, jumping into a fight stance.

"I'm so sorry, I wandered into this room–I just wanted to paint – " I waved my hand around helplessly.

There were puddles on the floor, and the buckets that held art supplies had erasers and pencils floating to the top.

I half expected Eveda to scream, but instead, she broke into a grin. "Wow, Piper, you managed to channel." Her gaze slid to the painting, and a look of understanding glistened in her eyes. "Ahh, I understand why it must have been so easy for you to transform this image. You relate to it, don't you?"

I nodded, afraid that if I opened my mouth, I would start crying.

"Here, let's clean up and then start your training; I've got a feeling you aren't going to want to go back to sleep."

I opened my mouth. What did Eveda mean by training? Why did I need training? I was going home.

Eveda sighed, clearly knowing what I was thinking, "Piper, I'm afraid you can't go home. Not for a while."

***

"WHAT! Why not?" I demanded, fuming. "You can't hold me here against my will."

"You are not a prisoner." Eveda said sharply, "But I'm asking you to please listen to what the three brothers and have to say before you make your decision."

"Decision of what?"

"Whether you're staying or leaving." Eveda disclosed.

I bit my lip, wondering if it was worth it to argue. Nothing she or the brothers would say could convince me to stay here. I understood if Eveda wanted me, her supposed daughter, to stay here, but how could I possibly concern the big brothers? I let a big breath out of my nose. I may as well go along with what Eveda wanted. It was probably my best shot at going home.

"Fine."

She smiled warmly and beckoned me out of the dripping wet room.

"Where are we going?" I asked in a hurry to keep up with her.

Eveda grimaced, "We're going to go meet your father."

My face grew warm, "Wait, what?" I faltered.

Eveda regarded me with caution, clearly scared that I was going to have another breakdown, like the time she admitted to being my mother. "Yes, I have a lot more to explain to you, but I didn't think it would be safe to throw everything at you last night."

I tucked a strand of hair behind my ear, "Fair enough."

Eveda rubbed her hands together, *"Piper, your father is Potia, the brother of fire."*

My heart began to race. "Oh."

Fantastic, that's perfect, just perfect. My father is Potia. Sure! Why not?

I giggled, trying to hide the panic racing through me. So my entire lineage was a lie? Mom, Dad, Jack? I wasn't related to them at all. I sighed, I loved them, but it all was so much to take in. I didn't even know if I would see them again. Still, a small part of me was excited to be part of this world, a very, very small part.

"I thought you didn't like the brothers," I protested, my heart already racing at the prospect of meeting these three deities Eveda told me about.

She was silent as we walked through the sunlight-filled corridors, across the roof, and into another hall. I was about to ask how big this castle was when she began to speak again,

"I haven't been a goddess for a very long time, Piper dear." Eveda began and gazed into my eyes, "At the beginning of my life, I lived in the mortal world. I was an artist living in France. Potia had taken a liking to me and visited the human realm. The two of us fell in love."

I raised an eyebrow, this contradicted the entire story that Eveda told me the other night about Emensaly.

She smirked, "I know what you're thinking, and you're right. Aquia, Breezet, and Potia are the original hypocrites. They've had lovers in almost every realm. That's why there are so many gods. They fall in love with someone, turn them into a deity, and then move on."

I swallowed, "Is that what happened to you?"

"There's a little more to it in my case."

I looked up at Eveda, nodding. Not looking where I was going, I walked straight into a Corinthian column in the center of the hall. Cursing and rubbing my forehead, I groaned. Who in their right mind would put a column in the middle of a hall? I looked around and realized we had entered an area designated for creating columns. There were kids, adults, and a whole bunch of strange creatures, leaning over pottery wheels, chiseling, hammering, etc. There was a woman with a snake body reattaching the nose of a statue, sitting next to a life-size banana with arms that appeared to be welding.

I blinked a few times, wondering if I was going crazy. Nope, it was still there. I turned back to Eveda, "Sorry, what were you saying?"

She smiled, leading me out of the welding room into another weird hallway. I still didn't know where we were going. Her eyes were currently gazing out the window. They had turned the colors, *Ultra Marine Grey Blue Nom: W29,* as if they could reflect her emotions.

"I had never been so happy in my life," Eveda admitted, "I couldn't imagine anything better. Then we had you, and everything felt perfect."

I felt a bubble of excitement. Finally, I was getting some answers about my parents.

"When you were born, Potia offered to make me a deity. Foolishly, I agreed. My transformation was painful, and I don't remember the weeks following. All I remember is Potia saying that I couldn't keep you."

My mouth dropped open, "Oh." I uttered, unsure what to say.

"Potia was gone for several months after that, and when he returned, he began to tell me countless stories and excuses. That's when I had enough of him and went off on my own. I founded the art realm, well, the idea of it. Hundreds of other deities helped me put it all together." She smiled fondly, "Don't be nervous about seeing him. This'll be my first time seeing him since…" Eveda trailed off.

My stomach churned with all this information. "But why does he want to see me, anyways."

Eveda sighed, "I'll get to that."

I gulped, wondering if it had something to do with Charlid.

"And Piper," She added gently, "I've been watching you, and I want to say that you've made me the proudest mother alive."

My eyes stung with tears as I managed a smile, not quite sure what to say. "Thank you, Eveda."

With a smile, she nodded toward me and then resumed talking. "Now I'm sure you're burning with curiosity about why you've come here."

"More like taken against my will," I muttered.

"Yes, well, you see, as I said last night, your burnt drawings were considered a sacrifice towards Charlid. When you revealed that you had burnt your drawings, I immediately became…distraught. I'm sure you have learned about people offering burnt sacrifices to deities in the human world. Your drawings are immensely powerful, as demonstrated earlier with your painting."

A blush crept across my face.

"Burning something like that in a place that is holy to Charlid has dire consequences. To make matters worse, you are also the daughter of Potia, the brother of fire. This meant that the fire you created also gave Charlid direct access to one of the brothers for several hours while the fire burned." She trailed off, not meeting my gaze.

The back of my neck felt hot. I didn't like where this was going.

"So not only did you give Charlid power from your worship, but you also allowed him to drain Potia, weakening the entire Golden God Kingdom."

I stumbled, "Wha-what?!"

Before I could even begin processing, more words spilled out of Evedas mouth, "That's why I had Arius bring you here, Piper. The wall around the realm of Charlid is crumbling, the brothers are angry, and it's because of you."

Chapter 10

I stumbled backward, blood rushing to my ears. "No, no, I didn't do that. I mean, I did, but I didn't mean to make some crazy guy powerful. That can't be true. I didn't know anything about this world until, like, yesterday. Please, you have to believe me. I–"

Eveda held her hand up, and I stopped. I looked into her tired eyes, starting to understand where the bags were coming from.

"Piper, I understand. You didn't mean to do anything, but the brothers won't see it like that. They've been looking for someone to blame for their mistake of losing Emesaly. Three is an unlucky number for deities. There's been an imbalance for a long time."

I deflated, "Fantastic, just my luck. I wander into a creepy Charlid temple when I get lost. Perfect."

Eveda shrugged, "You were attracted to the deitel energy, or to put it in simpler terms, the magic. A power in-between as yourself, living in a world with no channeling, would automatically go to the first power source they find."

I didn't understand half the words she used in that sentence, but I had bigger problems.

"So what, they're just going to kill me or something?" I lashed out.

Eveda flinched slightly, and I felt a sense of dread.

"That's not a no."

"Piper–."

"Can you at least send me back to the human world?" I begged, "I want to see my real family." The last part was harsh, but I couldn't bring myself to care.

"Well, you see," Eveda whispered, acting as if I were a twig, prone to snap at any moment, "I brought you here because there is a way for you to stop the chaos and calm down the brothers."

I stayed quiet, and she continued.

"You could go looking for Emensaly. If you could find her, it would restore everything back to normal and strengthen all the deities in existence."

I gulped, bile rising in the back of my throat, "What are my chances of finding her?"

Eveda didn't reply.

I threw my hands up in the air, "Great."

"The chances are slim, but it may be your only option."

I licked my lips, shaking, "Wouldn't it just be easier to let the brothers kill me? How do I even start looking for Emensaly? I don't even know how to navigate this realm, much less a million others."

I looked around, feeling defeated. Only twelve hours ago, my biggest problem was wondering how to get a grass stain out of my Nikes, and now there were three bloodthirsty gods angry at me for letting Charlid into the world. My breathing turned shallow. I was screwed, so completely screwed.

I doubled over and laughed, actually laughed. My mind seemed on the brink of hysteria, "Yeah, right, as if I can find a deity in realms with literal dragons. I can't even make toast without burning it." I doubled over in a fit of laughter, trying to catch my breath, "And you actually think I can travel through parallel universes looking for some goddess who, might I remind you, doesn't want to be found."

Eveda gave me a sad smile, "Don't underestimate yourself, Piper. You have many incredible abilities. You simply haven't been able to harness them yet. You'll train in the art realm, and we'll find a companion to go with you."

I giggled slightly, "Yeah, right, like what? Falling into lakes? Oh, by all means, yes, please show me all of these amazing mystical powers I possess."

She frowned at me, "Piper, dear, please try to take this seriously. Yes, you do have many incredible abilities. A combination of what I can do and what Potia can do."

I deflated. She was actually being serious. Eveda thought that I was going to go look for Emensaly. "Why can't you do it?"

"Deities are no longer supposed to travel between realms. It is already a risk for me to take you to the golden god kingdom and back. Deities power going from one realm to another causes more unbalance, feeding Charlid's powers." She explained in worry.

I glared at her. "So you're telling me I'm supposed to travel from realm to realm looking for Emensaly *on my own*."

"No, no, no, of course not," She put her hands on my shoulders, "I will train you, and, with convincing, I'm sure Potia will do the same. And you won't be on your own. We'll find someone suited for the job to assist you."

"Why can't a different half-god do it?"

"Because the brothers want you, Piper. They believe that the best way for balance to be restored."

"What if I don't do it?" I challenged, desperate.

"Charlid is much more dangerous than you could ever imagine, Piper. I remember when he launched his first attack." She shuddered. "It happened before I became a deity, but even in the human realm, people knew about it. I'm sure you learned about World War II."

"You're joking, right?"

Eveda shook her head sadly, "And that was the impact it had on one realm, one that knew nothing about what was really going on. The tragedies that occurred in the rest of the realms." She pressed her hand to her mouth. "Unspeakable horrors. You could prevent that, Piper. You could save your friends, family, all of us."

I bit my lip, the impossible choice on my shoulders. Could I do it? I imagined Jack staring up at me with a big, innocent smile on his face. I thought of my mom and dad with their camping dreams. Memories of Amy drifted into my mind. I would never see them again if I didn't do this. I may never see them again if I do.

The words left my mouth before I could think, "I'll do it."

I'll do it? What was I thinking? I was seriously considering checking myself into an asylum. Why did I say I go looking for Emensaly? I was gonna get myself killed, for crying out loud. This did not seem like the place you just wandered around looking for a goddess that had been missing for thousands of years. Eveda was still talking about my training as she led me to a door.

"We're here!" She proclaimed, fidgeting with a sapphire ring on her pointer finger.

I looked up from my thoughts and noticed a light *Basalisk Green Nom. 23671* colored door with a worn-out paint job. Parts were peeling off, the doorknob looked as if it would swing right off on the lightest touch, and there was a small golden sign that hung in the middle. It was held up but a thin brown rope and a rusted nail. On the sign, there were a few letters, **F OW R GA D N**. I realized that it might have said **FLOWER GARDEN,** but most of the brass letters seemed to have fallen off.

"Yes, it's a terribly depressing door, isn't it," Eveda said sadly.

I wanted to argue that a door couldn't be depressing, it was an inanimate object, but she was right. The door itself seemed to be giving off some sort of death vibe. If Amy were here, she would have said this place was throwing off her aura. I felt a pang of homesickness. I wondered what Amy was doing right now. Maybe sipping a coconut or sun-tanning on the beach of Hawaii.

"It reflects the state of the garden and the wall." She explained, proceeding to walk forward and put her hand on the doorknob. Eveda pushed it, and the door squeaked open. She pulled me through, and I looked around in surprise. I had suspected something a bit sorrowful after the door, but we entered an area that seemed to be full of life. I looked around, trying to process the rainbow of color being thrown my way. There were thousands, millions of flowers in every direction. When Eveda had told me Emensaly had created a flower garden to transport to different worlds, I didn't think that she meant there were this many. I had envisioned a small cut-off area that had maybe twenty different flowers, not fifty thousand!

My head spun as I looked around, realizing how many realms there were. There were bright yellow daffodils, multicolored irises, simple daisies, pastel pink roses, clawed tiger lilies, and thousands more that I didn't recognize. Each is over four feet tall. The smell was nearly overpowering as the colors. It was a combination of lavender, honey sickle, basil, and a hundred other amazing things that shouldn't smell good together, yet somehow they just did. The sun was shining down brightly, reflecting on the multicolored petals. Everything was perfect.

That was, of course, before I noticed a huge *Gray Saddle Nom. 432*-colored storm cloud that loomed menacingly in the distance. I looked at it alarmingly and tugged on Eveda's sleeve. "Er, Eveda, don't we want to get inside before that hits? I don't want to get caught in another rainstorm."

"Don't worry," she replied, looking plenty worried, "That's the wall to Charlid. It can't enter the flower garden."

71

Even as she said it, she wrinkled her eyes looking unsure.

"Wait, so how does the flower garden work, with the whole, gods can or can not enter thing?" I asked, still incredibly confused.

"Well, Charlid and his minions are blocked out of every realm and aren't even allowed to enter the flower garden. Usually, deities are able to travel anywhere that they want, but not since the border around Charlid has weakened. We are encouraged to stay away from using the flower garden except in emergencies. That's why I had Arius get you with the marble. As a 3⁄4 deity, his presence wouldn't disturb the flower garden as much, but I would rather not risk it. There are, of course, times when we are banned from a certain realm. For example, after what Potia did to me, I wasn't able to visit the human world for quite some time. Oh, and, of course, going into the realm of Charlid is forbidden. If you enter, you risk breaking down the wall and exposing the world to Charlid and his followers."

I gulped, "Okay then, no going into the realm of Charlid."

"As I was saying, to transport in the flower realm is simple. All you must do is place and *onre* into the center of a flower and drink."

"A what?" I asked.

"I'll show you,"

She took out a piece of paper and drew an odd straw-like contraption. With a wave of her finger, it fell off of the paper into her awaiting palm. I gaped. I felt jittery, wondering if I would ever be able to do something like that.

"You stick the *Onre* into the flower and drink the nectar. It will then transport you to any realm you want. Unfortunately, not all of the flowers are labeled. We have *Balnxies* whose job is to label all of the flowers, but it's an incredibly dangerous job. They never know where they are going to end up. They could be lucky and end up with the Ledos, or misfortunate and end up with Delargends." Eveda shuddered slightly, "Dear me, I remember when the Chaos realm flower, 'was discovered, we lost eight Balaxies. I was rather close to James, bless his little heart."

"Are *Balaxies* human?" I asked curiously, not quite sure what to expect as an answer.

"Most of them are in-betweens, but there are quite a few deities who enjoy the adventure as well." She replied wearily.

"Are there a lot of in-betweens?"

"Of course. You don't think I am the only person the brothers fell in love with." She said bitterly, "They have been around for ages." They fell in love with all sorts of creatures, humans, demons, pixies, ledos, margen, etc. Once they fell in love, the brothers often turned them into deities. Soon, they grew bored and left them. Then those new deities would fall in love with other creatures and other deities, diversifying and expanding the realms in ways never seen before."

I nodded as another wave of thoughts and emotions crashed onto me. I couldn't imagine someone having that many spouses or that many children. My mom always told me that Jack and I were equivalent to thirteen kids, not two. How could the brothers keep track of them all? They probably ditch them all in the mortal world, just like Potia did to me. I shook my head, trying to ignore those thoughts. I was about to go meet Potia. My…father. The words sounded wrong in my head, like the thought of mixing green and purple. The word father brought back memories of inside jokes, allnighters behind Mom's back, the strong smell of purell and aftershave, microwavable mac'n cheese, and lukewarm Sprite. I locked them in the back of my mind, scared they would be tainted.

Eveda continued, "As I was saying, the Balaxies navigate through the flower realms and label them for us. Give me a minute to look for the Golden God Kingdom flower. I haven't been there in a long time, so it may take me a minute."

"Uh-huh," I said, my mouth hanging open slightly.

I looked around in fascination as she scouted the petal. The garden was like nothing I had ever seen before. I couldn't believe that Emensaly, the goddess of X, created this all on her own. A wave of nervousness overcame me. If this was how powerful Emensaly was so long ago, how powerful were the three brothers that wanted to meet with me?

"Piper, come over here," Eveda called from somewhere to my right.

I jogged toward her voice and approached a majestic lily. There were four petals: one petal was blue, the other was white, the third red, and the last was a sickly green color. Each petal was at least two feet long. I motioned to the dead-looking petal and felt slightly concerned, "Why does this one look so...?"

"Dreadful?" Eveda offered.

"Well yeah."

She looked up sadly and responded, "Each petal represented a sibling, blue for water, red for fire, white for wind, and green for land. That petal has been dying since Emensaly left. It was predicted that the petal would die in fifteen years, but ever since your sacrifice, the deadline has been moved to 15 days, give or take.

Another stab of helplessness, "I swear I had no idea–."

"I know you didn't," She interrupted, looking aghast. "Here."

Eveda hands me the *onre*.

I looked at her with an eyebrow raised.

"You stick it into the center of the flower and drink it." She explained patiently.

I sighed. Not wanting to argue, I stuck it into the center of the massive flower and took a small sip. My tongue immediately tingled. It tasted spicy, with a hint of dark chocolate. The color *Red Earth Nom. 64* sprung to mind.

Warmth spread through my body, almost as if the nectar was extended through my body. It changed to a tingling feeling that grew stronger by the second. Soon my entire body was on pins and needles. Once I could barely take the pain anymore, I began to spin. The wind whipped my face, and my hair stood straight up. It kept going and going until I landed flat on my back, having the wind knocked right out of me. Black spots danced in front of my eyes, and I gasped, trying to breathe normally again.

After me came Eveda, who gracefully appeared, standing next to me. Once I had reinflated my lungs, I glared at her, "A bit of a warning would have been nice."

"Sorry," Eveda replied distractedly, looking around over her shoulder nervously, "I promise you'll get used to it after a while."

"I doubt that."

I struggled to my hands and knees, looking around the place, my eyes widening to the size of saucers. It was magical, there was no other way of putting it. I was filled with awe as I spun around, trying to take every sight in at once. We had landed in a sort of circular plaza. It was made entirely of marble and gold. The sun reflected off of everything so strongly that I had to squint to admire the architecture. The marble glowed in a way that looked like the moon in a clear night sky. I turned to face the center of the plaza, and my eyes rested on a magnificent statue in the center. It was a golden woman. The statue stood on a massive marble cut-out that rose at least ten feet off the ground. She had twelve arms and held all of them in the air while her head was tilted towards the sky."

"That's Genev," Eveda explained as she noticed my gaze. "She's the symbol of the messenger."

"Ah," I replied, still starstruck by the sheer size and smoothness of the statue.

The plaza was surrounded by a building that was designed to circle around the plaza. Its Venetian-style columns adorned the front, and intricate carvings decorated the facade around each glorious casement window. There were four gaps in the building, leading away from the plaza, each equal distance away from the other. "North, East, South, and West," I muttered, unsure how I knew that.

Eveda walked towards one of the openings, and I quickened my steps to catch up. I reached up and made an effort to comb through my hair and wipe the grime off my face. I felt like a piece of coal in a diamond mine in my day-old jeans and grass-stained hoodie.

As we left the plaza, I stopped abruptly, my jaw dropping. This couldn't be real. I was standing in front of a massive city that looked like something you would see in a utopian movie. Every single building was made of glowing white marble and adorned with gold trimmings. The pearl path was bordered by luxurious golden trees on either side. My mind spun as a light breeze flew past, rustling the glittering leaves and creating a small tinkling sound. In the distance, I could tell there was a massive monument at the end of the road. I could make out four spires and beautiful teardrop-shaped windows. Eveda grabbed my hand, pulling me along faster as I spun my head, trying to soak everything in.

"This is amazing." I breathed.

"It's certainly something," Eveda responded with her tone undecipherable.

So this was where Potia lived. I refused to call him my father in silent rebellion. I had a real dad at home. Still, I couldn't help but wonder what Potia would think of me, how he would act. Would he

76

apologize? Would he ignore me? I was struck with the strange vision of us running towards each other in slow motion with music playing in the background. I quickly shook the thought out of my head. I watched too many movies.

As I continued to walk down the magnificent road, I realized something: the golden god kingdom was dead silent. I hadn't encountered a single living thing. Being here suddenly felt very wrong. I had the feeling that I was invading a sacred space, tainting it with my dirty nikes and loud thoughts.

"Eveda, are you sure we're supposed to be here?" I asked apprehensively.

She didn't respond. I met where her gaze was directed. We had made it to the massive monument at the end of the road. I realized quickly that it wasn't a monument, it was a castle, one that looked like it had been conjured out of a children's storybook. The pearly stone glowed in the sun and the large gold stage. I craned my neck, looking up at the stunning spires and golden trimmings. There were three statues in the front of the castle, two on the left and one on the right. I looked left to get a better look. The statues were of two men. The first one I looked at, both of them held his hand in the air, and a real flame was burning within it. His gaze was mischievous. It had a sense of playfulness that I felt as though I had seen before. The second statue was of a man in long billowing robes and an icy glare. The first thing I noticed was that it was floating. Literally floating. I rubbed my eyes a few times, wondering how someone managed to make a ten-foot-tall statue float.

To my right, there was a man with a stern gaze that looked far into the distance. The stature was a lump of marble, yet somehow it managed to radiate power. It was standing atop a wave, elevating the man a few inches above the over. Potia, Breezet, and Aquias, I realized.

As I turned towards Eveda, ready to walk in, I noticed there was a fourth pedestal, there was no statue, and it was unevenly cracked in several places. I noticed in astonishment that it was the first imperfection I had seen in the entire city. A gnawing feeling appeared in my stomach at the thought of what used to stand there.

I entered the castle through an arch with endless elaborate carvings. However, I couldn't focus on the interior beauty. Instead, my eyes went straight to the three figures in front of me. The most powerful beings in existence: the brothers.

Chapter 11

Aquia, Breezet, and Potia, the deities that created everything, were sitting right in front of me. I willed myself not to shake. I forced myself to look up at them. Each deity was sitting on a luxurious-looking cushion. The only thing was that these cushions were floating ten feet up in the air. I tried not to stare as the three brothers acted as if this were a completely normal act. I had half a mind to ask how they got up there, but I decided that may not be the greatest first impression.

I looked at the brother sitting in the middle. His cushion was slightly elevated and farther forward than the other two. I immediately characterized him as the leader of the pack. His seat pillow was made of liquid water. This must be Aquia, I thought. Everything about him radiated power. I swallowed as his *Electric Cyan paint model #LA1217ACYAN* eyes bore into mine. His nutmeg-colored skin and mahogany hair brought attention to the aquamarine tones in his irises.

To his right, I assumed, was the deity Breezet. His cushion was made of what appeared to be a tiny tornado. I couldn't imagine being *that* comfortable to sit on. He sat rigid as a statue, looking into the distance. His expression was dull, and he seemed completely uninterested in the fact that Eveda and I had just entered the room. His chalk-white hair, which stood up in a way that would have made my mother faint, was so similar to his paper-white skin that I couldn't tell where his hairline started. Breezet turned his head down ever so slightly that I caught a glimpse of his clouded, soot-colored eyes. A shiver went down my spine, and the memory of the wind slapping my face after I traveled in the flower garden flooded back into my mind. I had a feeling that was only a small representation of the face when I traveled through the flower garden.

Finally, I turned my head to the left. There was no more putting this off. I stared straight at my father. Potia sat on a cushion that was *literally* on fire. Flames flickered upward, licking at his legs, some going as high as his waist. A mixed wave of emotions tore through me, anger, confusion, frustration, hurt, and dependence. I dug my nails into my palm, trying to turn them all off. So this was my father, huh? I squirted, struggling to try to find our likeness. His hair resembled fresh earth that had been scattered with ashes, long strands of *Pratt and Lambert 29-23 Timeless Gray* and *Cedar #4A3728* intertwined into shaggy hair that fell just above his shoulders. The ashy tones were the only similarity I could identify. His champagne-beige skin was a few shades darker than mine, and his harsh jawline had a striking contrast to my round cheeks. I bit my lip, trying to stop the waterfall of words, questions, and accusations from falling out at him. I wanted to throw something at him, and I wanted him to look at me. I wanted to say something, anything. Instead, my mouth stayed frozen shut, and I stared down at the floor, wishing it would swallow me up.

I was about to look at Eveda and figure out what the heck was going on when a loud booming voice filled the hall. I snapped my neck up towards Aquia, whose bright eyes were directed straight at me.

"Do you know why you are here?"

I nearly jumped, realizing he was talking to me. "Uh-huh." I stuttered.

Aquia raised an eyebrow, unimpressed. I felt my pride bruise, standing up to my full high, granted, being only 5'1, it wasn't very impressive. "Yes I do," I repeated. "Sir."

"You are here because you have opened the door of chaos. You should have known better, you, human." He spit out, glaring at me. His eyes seemed to morph into ice pellets. It took all of my willpower not to whimper.

"Aquia, please," a warm voice that reminded me of warm honey interrupted. "Show some mercy--."

"SILENCE, POTIA!" Aquia bellowed.

I nearly passed out, but I mustered the energy to turn and glare at Potia. I didn't need his help. He abandoned me and hurt Eveda, who, compared to the other deities, didn't seem so bad at the moment. Now was not Potia's moment to play happy-go-lucky Dad. Forgetting my fear, I was about to open my mouth and recommend a nice place where Potia could shove his fire pillow.

Eveda interjected quickly. "Please, Master Aquia," She spoke calmly, stepping forwards to acknowledge the god, "I have fully explained everything to Piper, and I have brought her here for her to acknowledge her wrongdoings and receive your wise counseling."

I was mildly impressed by Eveda's cool composer, but I felt indignant. Since when had we discussed any sort of apology to these entitled jerk bags?

"Do you have something to say to me?" Aquia inquired menacingly.

I gulped, taking a step back, wondering if he could read minds. I heard Potia snicker slightly in the background, and I grinned involuntarily. Aquia growled, and I froze, realizing where I was.

"Yes, yep, that's exactly why I'm here. I would like to apologize from the bottom of my heart for unleashing Charlid into the realms and breaking down the wall surrounding the chaos wall." I amended. "Even though I had no clue that any of this stuff existed and just wanted to stay warm after getting lost on a camping trip, that mind you, I didn't want to go on in the first place." I wisely added the last part in my head.

Aquia sat back and laced his finger together, "Eveda should have informed you of the other realms, but her lack of doing so simply emphasizes the fact that she is thoughtless and incapable."

I gritted my teeth, a flood of curses filling my head. Normally I would keep a reply to myself, but since I suspected that the brothers could read my mind, I decided I might as well respond. "Well, Eveda wasn't allowed to visit me under your brother's order, so I don't see how that's thoughtlessness on her part at all."

Eveda shot me a warning look, and I resisted the urge to sigh, "Nevertheless, I'm sure you will figure out a solution to our *horrifying mistake,* being the incredibly intelligent beings that you are."

Aquia clenched his hands together, and for a moment, I thought that I had gone too far. I could practically see the headlines, *Obnoxious Teenager Blasted into Smithereens by Aquia.* Remarkably he simply pressed his lips together and sighed through his nose. "Well, Piper, as I hope Eveda has informed you, Charlid plans to escape in approximately 15 days. As this is all your fault, it's up to you to solve this. The three of us have come to a conclusion that, as much as we hate to admit it, we need Emensaly to subdue Charlid."

"Ok…" I began slowly, not liking where this was going.

"You will go find Emensaly and bring her back safely before the fifteen days are up."

And if I don't? I thought, wiping my hands on my jeans.

"And if you don't." Aquia answered the question I hadn't voiced aloud, "You and the entire world will regret it."

I bit my lip, attempting to keep my mind blank.

Aquia continued, looking up at the mosaic on the ceiling as if I wasn't important enough for his attention, "You must fix your mistakes. Chaos has already started to destroy the flower garden and is breaking the binding spell. We have already received information that he is wedging his way into other worlds to recruit followers. In fifteen days, it will take over all of the realms and, most drastically of all, the human realm."

I gasped quickly and then tried to compose myself. I knew I probably shouldn't say anything, but my mouth was quicker than my mind. "Since when do you all care about humans?"

To my surprise, it was Breezet who answered me. His voice seemed to cut through the room like ice, and I whipped my head around to look at him. "As deities, our lives are tied to beings worshiping us. While many different beings in different realms have some sort of higher power, they show reverence too. Humans are the most ignorant. They worship blindly, while most other realms are much more informed of their surroundings. Human wills are so easily bent, their minds so easily molded to our advantage. Those weak little beings, well, they have no idea what's going on, and this blind, stubborn belief each of them possesses, that there is something more powerful than them controlling their small, insignificant lives, than us deities, remain omnipotent."

My eyebrows raised in disbelief, "That's horrible; humans aren't some sort of puppets you can just feed off of. They get nothing out of this."

Breezet looked me in the eyes, and I felt a slight shiver run down my spine. I was frozen in his gaze.

"Oh, but dear Piper, they do. Have you ever met a human that wanted to take responsibility for their errors? They find it so much simpler to blame and curse divine forces, hoping that karma will do them justice. Imagine how hopeless your human world would be without their belief."

I gulped, nodding slightly, praying that he would let me out of his gaze. He kept me locked in his gaze for a moment before going back to staring absentmindedly into space.

"You are granted permission to your mission. Find Emensaly, or some other method to stop Charlid. If you manage, I will reconsider your punishment. If you don't, well," He let out a laugh, but there was no humor to it, "You will have bigger problems than my wrath. Goodbye."

I stood transfixed on the spot, about to burst with anger, when Eveda pulled me out of the room. I let her tug me along and keep my eyes on the ground. I had the feeling that Potia was staring at me, but I wouldn't give him the satisfaction of catching my gaze. There was enough on my mind without throwing him into the mix.

"How on earth did you fall in love with one of them!?" I yelled the moment we were out of earshot, "They're barely living, for God's sake. It was like talking to three rocks."

"They are stressed," she answered, but I could tell she was having a rough time keeping her anger under control as well.

"They are stressed? Pssst, oh please, did you hear Breezet? *You have fifteen days to complete an impossible task, or after that, you will have worse problems than me killing you.*" I imitated in an unflattering voice. "What is wrong with them!"

"Shh, Piper, please lower your voice," Eveda begged, "The three can probably hear you, and we don't want Aquia to reconsider and kill you now."

I let out a humorless laugh, "Oh god, yes, it would be just awful for him to kill me now. He was so *generous* to extend my life for another fifteen days. I'm practically bursting with gratitude."

Eveda rubbed her temples and sighed but didn't reply to me. I've noticed I have that effect on adults.

"Is there a possibility that I just don't do anything?" I ask, trying to take my mind off the subject of dying

"I suppose you could," Eveda said, though her tone indicated the opposite, "But imagine the world being run by Charlid. Wars would be waged left and right, and lives would be lost, and people would suffer."

I nodded, trying to stand up straight and hold my head high. I wanted nothing more than to crawl into a ball and lay on the ground. My mind seemed to be overflowing with terrible images of me getting fried to crisps by a dragon, Aqua blasting me into a million pieces, the dark storm cloud looming closer in the distance... I pressed my hand to my ears, trying to get my brain to quiet down. All I wanted was a quick moment to myself, but I could barely see straight, much less figure out how to save the world. I shut my eyes tightly, praying that when I opened them, everything would go away.

"Piper dear, don't stress, okay? I swear we'll figure it out. I'll give you a few days to train at the art academy and get your powers under control, and then you'll be ready to find Emensaly. I'm sure it won't be as hard as you expect."

I tried for a smile, but I'm afraid all I managed to do was a grimace. I gave her a polite nod, not wanting to be rude but not wanting to give into her delusional mindset. The two of us began walking through the city, but I couldn't pay attention to the fantastic architecture.

Lost in thought, I didn't notice that Eveda had stopped until I smacked my forehead right into her back. "Oops, sorry." I said, looking around, "Why did we stop?"

Eveda motioned to a man-made waterfall surrounded by meticulously carved marble. There were small designs of different gods, saving humans, having parties, falling in love, and the usual. I was about to ask Eveda about a rather disturbing engraving near the right side of the waterfall, but I realized that she had disappeared.

"Eveda?!" I called, spinning in circles, trying to spot her colorful overalls or shiny blond hair. "Eveda! Where did you go?"

I felt my heart rate begin to rise in panic when I heard her voice reply, "Oh, sorry dear, I forgot this is your first time visiting."

I wanted to roll my eyes at her. Funny. For some reason, it seemed impossible for me to forget that. "Where are you!"

"Well, I'm in the flower garden. All you have to do is walk through the waterfall. Come on."

The shock on my face must have been visible because she laughed and said, "Oh, don't worry, you won't get wet. It's just like the door we have in the art realm. Each realm had its own sort of portal to get to the flower garden."

I stared at the water skeptically. It seemed pretty real to me. How exactly was I going to stay dry walking through it? I sighed. Honestly, it wouldn't be anything weirder than deities sitting on floating pillows and drinking flower nectar. Taking a deep breath, I plugged my nose, closed my eyes, and plunged into the very real-looking water.

Immediately I felt the ground change into the grass. I opened my eyes, and my jaw dropped. I had landed in the flower garden. I looked down, and my legs, huh, not a single drop of water.

"Wha-? How..?" I stared at even, confusion causing my brain to go blank. I know that I probably should be used to strange things happening by now, but that was definitely my first time walking through water and staying dry.

I turned around to look at the waterfall, but there wasn't anything there. I could still vaguely hear the chatter in the streets of the golden god kingdom, but besides that, not a trace was left. I turned to Eveda, "Do all realms have a door or waterfall leading back to the flower garden?"

She shook her head, "Only the densely populated ones. A lot of people come and go from the art realm and the Golden God Kingdom, so much so that it was getting too confusing for people to find their way back. In most realms, there is just a specific spot that you have to stand on, and it whips you back to the flower garden. It's rather inconvenient, though."

I nodded, trying to wrap my head around everything.

"Ready to go back to the art realm?" Eveda asked.

Chapter 12

I landed in the middle of the art realm's garden right in front of the castle, not quite recognizing my surroundings at first. Everything was pitch black, and my eyes strained after the brightness of the flower garden. I blinked a few times, hoping to adjust my eyes to the darkness. Squinting slightly, I realized that I was standing right in front of the large castle of the art realm. My eyes could make out the faint outline of the gargoyle that stood on the roof with paintbrushes in its mouth.

There was a small fountain in the middle of the neatly cut yard made of *Ballet Shoe Pink Nom. 376* marble. Behind me was a massive rainforest filled with all different types of colorful plants, trees and animals. I took a step back just in time for Eveda to fall out of a small hole in the sky and land right where I was standing seconds ago. She stumbled a few times and then dusted her apron off.

"Dear me, it's quite a bit harder to transport in the dark, isn't it."

"Yeah--" I began yawning widely. I rubbed my eyes and straightened my spine, trying to stay awake.

"Ah, I keep forgetting that in-betweens need sleep." Eveda noticed and motioned for me to follow her to the castle. I walked after her, remembering still a little weirded out that I was being called an in-between.

She led me to my room, and I fell into a restless sleep, my mind plagued with images of Emensaly taunting me and Aquia threatening me.

Chapter 13

The next morning Eveda showed up at my door at sunrise. "Rise and shine Piper. It's time to get you a *pindres*."

"My what?" I asked groggily as she tugged me out of bed.

"Your *pindres*." She repeated, not bothering to elaborate.

"Ok." I was too exhausted to ask for an explanation. I let Eveda lead me to a small cupboard labeled supplied.

I rubbed my eyes and yawned vaguely, wondering why I was dragged out of my room for this.

She opened the door, and I glanced in, not expecting much. I cocked my head to the side, my eyes scanning the room. It was much larger than I expected. The shelves in the front were filled with what would be found in a normal school supply cupboard. However, as we walked in deeper, I began to notice stuff that seemed out of place. There were battle axes lined up on the walls, next to the unopened canvas and aquamarine saxophone.

"You know, normal people don't have supply rooms filled with weapons?" I said as we continued to walk through.

"I'll have you know that each of those weapons has saved someone's life at least once," Eveda responded.

"What about that gun over there?" I asked, pointing to the one hanging on the ceiling.

"Oh, that one's decorations."

"Of course it is," I muttered under my breath.

As we walked in even further, the room expanded into multiple hallways, and I was starting to get the feeling that this wasn't your average storage closet. Eveda led me down a hall that had hundreds of displays of jewelry. I managed to sneak a glance at the other hallways and saw hundreds of different types of armor, ranging from the type you would see in a history book to the type I'd find in the news. A second hallway was filled to the brim with floppy hats, and a third continued with nothing but origami birds made out of folded bits of metal. From then on, I decided to look straight ahead and follow Eveda before I lost my sanity trying to figure out how the change from fedoras to ninja birds was made.

I continued straight, my eyes roaming around the multi-colored jewelry that was displayed on the shelves.

"Wow," I proclaimed, gasping slightly, "You've got your own Tiffany & Co. back here!"

I saw diamond earrings, skeleton rings, sapphire charm bracelets, shark tooth chokers, and hundreds more lined up on the wall.

Eveda let out a small laugh, "Well, no, not exactly, these are *pindres*. They're sort of like...a wizard's wand, if you will. Except these are specialized for children of the art realm."

I looked at her in slight confusion, "So we just--" I mimed, waving a wand around.

"No, of course not, that would be ridiculous," I'll explain that later, "For now, I suggest that you begin to browse around and choose something that really speaks to you."

I wanted to protest that waving magic *pindres* was crazy, but at the same time, people drank nectar out of magical flowers with depression to transport from realm to realm, so this was nothing in comparison. Besides, I had bigger things on my mind. "Umm...the gems on here aren't really right because I'm pretty sure I can't afford them then," I replied, my eyes wandering to the sparkling diamonds.

"Oh, Piper, come now, don't be silly. Children of the art realm don't need to pay for their *pindres*. And yes, of course, these gems are genuine. How else would it work?" Eveda replied as if that was an absurd thing that I could say.

"But then how do you make mon--," I stopped, scolding myself for being a big-mouthed idiot, "Never mind."

Not wanting to stand around feeling awkward, I began to walk around the endless hallway, glancing into display cases. I saw necklaces with rubies the size of my fist and a charm bracelet with small metal dragons that seemed to be flying around. My eyes landed on an elaborate mood ring that had fifteen different stones, and each seemed to be pulsing with energy and color. I took one look at the instruction guide. Sitting next to it, and thought, "Nope."

I continued to walk straight, getting the feeling that I was being dragged forwards by some sort of invisible force. I began to ignore the rest of the jewelry as it became stronger. I found myself running forwards, desperate to know what was dragging me over there. I ran past yet another display rack when all of a sudden, my feet stopped as if they had been glued to the ground. Naturally, I felt flat forwards scratching up my palms. Muttering a curse that would normally get me grounded for a week, I dusted myself off and sat up. Massaging my wrist, I groaned, typical. Hmm, maybe this was my secret power, "Accident Prone Piper–get within ten feet of her, and she will manage to crash or bump into you. Quick, everyone, run for your life."

My cheeks burnt as I stumbled to my feet, nearly crashing into another price jewelry display. I turned around quickly, hoping that Eveda hadn't seen my epic wipeout. Unfortunately, I wasn't that lucky. (Let's be real, am I ever that lucky?)

"You okay?" She called, she was a few hundred feet away, so she probably could see my face turn red.

"Yeah fine!" I called back, turning my back to her, feigning interest in a black choker made of willow branch leaves.

I let my gaze slip past it and finally noticed the necklace that had pulled me toward this shelf. I took a closer look at it. The entire pendant was pulsed with power. It consisted of a small silver chain and a lily with four petals. I realized with a start that it was the flower that I had used to transport myself to the golden god kingdom, except this time, all of the petals were thriving. In the center, there was a tiny old-fashioned paintbrush that extended from the red petal to the green one. In the center, a diamond glinted, reflecting off of the wall. I reached down to grab it, surprised at how light it was. The necklace was rather small. In fact, the charm was roughly the size of the nail on my thumb. I ran my hands over the pale white petal, making my way over to the ocean blue. A spark ignited my finger as it pressed gently against the red petal, but I was intent on ignoring that, disregarding any contention I had with Potia. I turned my focus on the green petal, a wave of sadness crashing onto me.

"I found one," I say breathlessly, turning back to Eveda.

She walked over and inspected it. "Beautiful choice, Piper."

"But, but what do I do with it?" I whispered, my eyes still trained on the pendant's beauty.

"You'll find out in just a minute." She answered with a knowing smile.

***

Eveda led me through a few other multi-colored hallways toward a third room. This one is filled with straw dummies, paintings, sculptures, kazoos, colorful beanbags, and...MY SKETCHBOOK!!!

I ran over, picking it up in relief. "Oh my God, how did you get it!?" I squealed, leafing through all of the pages, my heart pounding, thrilled. Every single drawing was still intact, even the ones I had burnt.

Eveda laughed, "Well, I keep copies of all my children's artwork in a file. Luckily, I was able to find everything and reprint it."

I let out an uncharacteristic squeal and ran over to give Eveda a hug. "Wow, thank you, thank you!"

I grinned at her. My entire day had just been made a thousand times better.

"No problem, Piper." Eveda smiled, giving me another quick squeeze. "Now, have a seat. We're already short on time."

I squatted down on an *Ocean Foam Blue #92* beanbag and propped my head on my hands, grinning.

"So your *pindres* essentially helps you summon any sort of art that you create, similarly to your painting of the boat. However, a *pindres* regulates the channeling. It's also used as a place to store your supplies. For example, your paints or sketchbook."

I nodded, only understanding half of what she had just said.

"Think about it like this." Eveda continued. "Imagine something materializing out of your *pindres*. For example, your sketchbook."

A bit confused, I closed my eyes and willed the flower to change its molecules. Trying my best not to laugh, I sat there for a good long minute. Opening my eyes, I saw in disappointment that nothing had changed.

Eveda smiles sympathetically, "Don't worry," she says, "It takes time, dear."

I bit my lip, wanting to point out that I didn't exactly have time as a luxury. I continued to imagine my necklace turning into a sketchbook, but at that point, all I could think about was how badly I needed to use the bathroom. I shook my hands, trying to calm my nerves. I shut my eyes and imagined the colorful notebook materializing in front of me, growing out of the flower. All of a sudden, my necklace became warm and uncomfortable warm. I felt excitement rush through me as I opened my eyes. There right in front of me, was my sketchbook.

I pumped my fist into the air, grinning madly. It had worked. It had actually worked! I stared in shock at the floor in front of me, my mouth was hanging open, and I let out a gasp. I couldn't believe it. It was the first time I had done something of the paranormal on purpose that didn't end in complete failure.

"Bravo. Piper." Eveda praised. "Could you do it again? This time try and store your sketchbook inside your *pindres.*"

I nodded. I had a newfound confidence blossoming inside of me. I squinted my eyes, hoping that I would be able to do it again. I pictured my sketchbook shrinking and being sucked back into my necklace. I opened one eye, disappointed. Nothing happened.

Eveda noticed my expression, "Don't stress, dear. It takes most people a few weeks to master. You've done great so far."

I gritted my teeth. Well, I didn't really have a few weeks now, did I? I tried again, digging my nails into the palms of my hands, trying to concentrate on what I had done with my sketchbook. Hoping I was able to summon that feeling again, I tightened my hands into a fist and directed all of my concentration and energy straight toward my collarbone, where the pendant was resting. After a beat, it grew warm. Encouraged, I opened my eyes, and the sketchbook was on. I blinked a few times, feeling lightheaded, but it passed quickly, leaving me feeling nothing but excitement.

"This is insane."

After another half an hour of practicing, I was able to summon a pack of colored pencils, my sketchbook, and a few paintbrushes.

94

Collapsing on the beanbag from exhaustion, I groaned, gripping my temple as stars danced in front of my eyes, "I'm-I'm tired," I yawned.

Eveda gives me a sympathetic look, "It's like exercising, Piper. You'll get stronger the more you practice. I would love nothing more than to let you take a nap, but as I've said countless times, we are short on–."

"–time." I finished, trying not to sigh.

She gave me a small, exhausted-looking smile. "Let's turn to something else for now."

"Thanks."

Eveda continued, "So, how about I explain your *pindre* a bit more? The object itself can cause many different objects to appear. The easiest is the arts supplied. To make something more specific appear, such as rope, or food, or anything that isn't directly related to the art realm, is very difficult and requires many years of practice."

I cocked my head sideways. I was barely able to remain conscious at this point, much less understand the laws of *pindres*.

Eveda sighed, "So, in your case, you will only use your *pindre* to summon your sketchbook because you would probably pass out from the effort and concentration of creating anything else. Then, once you have your sketchbook, you can draw something and make that appear. Turning a drawing into an actual object requires far less strength because you aren't creating something out of thin air; you have a base to work off of. Drawing something may be more time-consuming, but in a specific case, it isn't worth trying to summon it."

I nodded, getting an idea; I conjured my sketchpad and some colored pencil (nearly passing out from the effort) and sluggishly began to draw. Setting the brown colored pencil down, I concentrated on the image in front of me and imagined it in my hand. Looking down, I was astonished to see it appear. Laughing out loud, I set the warm coffee down off the ground, exhilarated. I took a sip of the steamingly hot drink, it scorched my tongue, and I grinned. It tasted just like the one I always bought from Starbucks on the way to school. I never had enough patience to wait for the drink to actually cool off, so my taste buds would be screaming in pain by the time I arrived at class. A wave of sadness hit me that life seemed so far away, as if it were a dream.

"Mmmmm," I say happily, my tongue already swelling, "Juust tha way I lake aut."

Eveda rolled her eyes. "Well, I'm glad you're enjoying yourself, but there are a few rules you have to keep in mind when conjuring."

I sighed. Of course, rules.

"While drawing, you can create anything that doesn't require channeling magic," Eveda explained, sitting up straight. "You can't draw up another *pindre* or a magic staff with it, only something that exists in many forms and isn't very valuable. If you are trying to create something that has a mind and power of its own, it can become very dangerous. Do not attempt to create a counterfeit of something with power, understand?"

"Yeh."

"Alright, good job, dear," Eveda praised, clapping her hands together, "Care to practice some more?"

I didn't respond; if I was being completely honest, the only thing I wanted to do right now was take a nap.

Eveda smiled, "I'll let you rest a bit for now; no need to summon something. I'll come back and grab you for your next class."

Eveda came back after an hour with a stiff expression.

"What am I doing next?" I asked, struggling to get up from the beanbag.

"He--," Eveda stopped herself, giving me a strained smile, "You'll see Piper."

I fidgeted with my pinky finger, feeling slightly nervous. What did Eveda mean?

I followed Eveda out, and she began leading me toward my next lesson, whatever that would be. I gulped in an attempt to keep my nerves under control. Treading through the maze of hallways, I couldn't stop myself from gaping at everything we passed. I saw hundreds of different painted sculptures, instruments, and abstracts that reached deserved at least an hour to digest. Not to mention the hundreds of different people that I saw. Well, maybe "people" isn't the right word to use. Eveda pointed out in-betweens, deities, animals, and something that looked like a frozen banana on stilts named Dericc (with two "C"s).

Near a fork in a hallway, a living bat made out of clay was nursing an ear that seemed to have fallen off. Eveda halted and gazed down in exasperation, "How many times have I had to remind those boys to score their clay."

I looked down, still processing the situation.

She kneed down and summoned a bowl of water along with a sharp ceramic tool. I looked down in bewilderment as she clicked her tongue in disapproval. Eveda had just dipped the metal tools into the bowl and reattached the living sculpture's ear when a young boy around the age of eight skirted around the corner, panting slightly. He had skin the color of nutmeg and bright white eyes that were wide in alarm. His corkscrew curls were bouncing up and down as he pushed his glasses up the bridge of his nose. There was pizza on the side of his mouth, and he smelled slightly of french fries.

Eveda sighed, "Oh, Thomas, you forgot to score your clay before the transformation process."

"I'm sorry," He said breathlessly, his cheeks turning red, "But Daniel set his cockroach drawing on me again, and I got distracted."

Eveda smiled in spite of herself, "I'll speak with your brother again. I might need to take his *pindre* away. Here, hand me the bat. I'll attach its ear back on. She expertly grabbed the ceramic tool, dipped it in the water, and made a few small Xs on the whimpering clay animal. Waving her hand, the bat's ear reconnected.

I stare at the conversation in amazement. These children seemed to have grown up around magic and completely normalized it. I shook off a small pang of jealousy. It wasn't Eveda's fault that I lived with humans, I had an amazing childhood, and I was fully honest in saying that I wouldn't trade it for the world. I gazed at Thomas, smiling. In an odd way, he reminded me of my little brother Jack. Thinking of him sent a pulse of sadness into my heart. I held back a surge of guilt, the last time I was with him, I complained about him squeezing me, but at this moment, I would trade everything I had for one of his hugs. I stare at the birthmark on my wrist, remembering when he used to say it looked like a lightsaber from his favorite movie. Honestly, I would give up almost anything to have another argument with him over the design right now.

"Who were they," I ask, my eyebrows furring together, trying to turn my thoughts away.

"More in-betweens," Eveda answers, "In the art realm, everyone raises the children as their own."

I nodded and sped up to match her quick strides when Eveda suddenly stopped in front of a door. She made no move to open the door, instead whispering something that sounded like a prayer. Do gods pray? Does the prayer go to a different god? Eveda turned around, as I noticed with alarm that the look on her face resembled panic. I edged away from the door, wondering what was causing her fear. Eveda shook her hands a few times and then slowly lifted one up to bang on the redwood.

I looked at her strangely. Why was she so scared to knock on the door? Did this, in particular, one knockback? Before I had time to answer, the door swung open. My heart lept into my throat. I gulped, taking a step back. Standing in the doorway with a lazy expression was none other than Potia, my father."

Chapter 14

I stumbled over the door frame, trying to take a step back. My heart pounded quickly, and I looked at Eveda for support, but she seemed to be in the same mindset as me. Once we had left the golden god kingdom, I had envisioned, but now I was too intimate to so much as glare.

Potia wore a black tunic fitted with a red clock. Now that I was closer, I could make out the flakes of silver in his gray eyes, leaving no assumptions as to where I got mine.

"So," I asked through gritted teeth and a strained smile identical to the one Eveda wore earlier, "What--," I cleared my throat, hoping that my voice would stop squeaking.

Potia looked down at me as if he had just realized that I existed. As soon as his eyes met mine, he jumped. A jolt flew through me, and the urge to bolt out of the room became even stronger.

"Our daughter."

Before Eveda could say anything, I began to tirade, "Ok, listen, I honestly don't care if your my father or some all-powerful being that could turn probably turn me into confetti with a glance, but rest assured, you've lost the privilege of calling me your daughter a long time ago. Lying and manipulating Eveda into giving me up took away any hold you will ever have on me."

I grinned, filling up on adrenalin. Now don't get me wrong, the logical and intelligent part of my brain (yes, my brain did have a smart side) was drop-dead terrified. It was screaming bloody murder and trying to convince my legs to run away as fast as possible. However, the slightly less rational side of my brain (The one I do tend to use more often) was giving me a mental high five for not bursting into tears while arguing, something that I considered a major accomplishment.

I took a deep breath and forced myself to look back into Potia's eyes, his power seemed to be radiating off of him, and the hairs on the back of my neck felt like they were already on fire. Right when I was convinced I was dead and done, Potia began to laugh, a full belly chuckle. Wiping tears from his eyes, he said, "Glad to know the human world hasn't taken away your spunk, kid. Guess that's another thing we got in common. As for lying and manipulating Eveda…" He ran his hand through his hair, looking at a loss for words. "You're right. I did take you away from her. I shouldn't have, but at the time, I couldn't think of any safer option. I made the mistake of transforming Eveda too soon."

"What do you mean, 'transforming me too soon.'"

"You were a newborn deity. It was too dangerous for Piper to be around you. That's why I sent her to the human world."

"No, no, no," Eveda retaliated, "That's not true, no, of course, it's not, it can't be. You never wanted the responsibility of raising Piper. You had been thrilled to send her to the human world."

Potia narrowed his eyebrows, voice rising in defense, "I most certainly did not. Have you really convinced yourself that I wanted to send our daughter to the mortal world, never knowing what would happen to her, never sure if I would get to see her again? I wanted to spend every second of every day with her, and I would have had it not been for the disaster in the *Pizar* realm Charlid had caused days after Piper's birth. It wasn't safe to leave her with you, and she needed someone to raise her."

"So this is my fault?" Eveda asked incredulously.

"Of course, it wasn't your fault, love," Poita exclaimed, running a hand through his hair. "Eveda was a newborn deity at the time," Potia explained, "She couldn't control herself. No newborn deity can. Once you have been granted so much power, it can take a few years to get it under control. There had been instances where I would leave you two alone and come back with the entire place in ruins. I was able to restrain you for some time, Eveda, but then…Piper started to get hurt."

"No." Eveda sobbed.

"That's a lie!" I yelled, feeling my face turn red,

"That can't be true," Eveda muttered, looking distraught.

Potia took a slight step back, "You were a newborn goddess. The first few months were filled with trying to control your own headspace. You were in no position to raise a child. As for Piper's injury, it was nothing life-threatening. The only record of it, if my memory serves true, is a small scar on the inside of her wrist."

Simultaneously we all looked down at my right wrist. The one with a small mark that resembled a paintbrush.

"What are you talking about? That's a birthmark." I replied, glaring at Potia, "I've had it forever."

I expected Eveda to back me up, but she was strangely quiet. I turned to her in concern. Her hand was up to her mouth, and tears welled up in her eyes.

Eveda gasped, and tears welled up in her eyes. She took a step back and leaned against the door frame, unable to support her own weight.

"I-I- I thought it had been a dream–"

"Can we just start this lesson?"

I attempted to keep my tone as casual as possible, but I could feel myself blinking back tears. So now my birthmarks were hiding secrets from me too? Was everything a lie? What else would be revealed? Was I not a natural blonde? Am I part dwarf?

"So all of this, it wasn't because you didn't want us." "I would spend forever with you in a heartbeat." My head spun, I had envisioned countless scenarios of how this situation could go, but none of them remotely matched up with this. I was about to turn to Eveda and ask her what was going on when she ran past me right to Potia, straight into his arms.

What. The. Heck.

My jaw dropped as I watched the exchange. Everything was changing so fast. I couldn't process it. How was it happening? Why were they hugging? I thought they were enemies. Now all of a sudden, there was yet another new story surrounding my birth. It didn't make any sense. The earth seemed to swerve beneath my feet, and everything was unbalanced. It was as if someone had just laid a solid foundation underneath me and then ripped it all away. My mind was being pushed and prodded as if someone were trying to squeeze it in a small box. Spots danced in front of my eyes, and the ground swerved under my feet.

***

I open my eyes to a bright light. A pair of strong hands were holding me up by my biceps. Stars danced in front of my eyes, and I could make out the silhouette of two people. Once my eyes started working again, I saw two faces above me which belonged to Eveda and Potia. "What the…. I cursed, looking around, slightly dazed. "Why am I on the floor."

They shot me a guilty look, "We're sorry, Piper." Eveda began slowly, "We understand that this is all very overwhelming."

I looked at them in confusion and then burst out laughing. Trying not to become hysterical, I say, "Don't--" I gasped slightly, "Don't worry about it."

They looked at me as if I had lost my mind, which, come to think of it, was the only logical solution at this point. I barked out another laugh and then took a deep breath,

"I'm okay. I'm okay."

I held in a small giggle.

Potia gave me a concerned smile, "Well then, I supposed we should begin your lesson."

"What exactly are you teaching me," I ask, stumbling to my feet and brushing off my jeans.

"How to control your fire." He answers.

"Good luck with that," I snorted, "Adults have been trying to control my fire for ages."

Eveda laughed, her arm still wrapped around Potia's waist, "He means actually fire, not your attitude."

I coughed, eyeing her hand.

Potia smiled, "If you are going to find Emensaly, you need all possible weapons in your arsenal. Fire is one that will come in handy."

I shivered at the thought of my quest.

"Ok, Piper, this is the plan," Potia began jumping straight into the lesson. "You need to imagine energy flowing out of me, almost like a channel. Now grab the energy and pretend it is like a rope. Pull the rope towards you and then release it."

I giggled but complied. Closing my eyes, I attempted to visualize what he had described. I picture warmth spreading through our bodies, linking us. Opening one eye, I wrung my hands together nervously, "Anything?" I ask doubtfully.

"No." He said, not bothered by this at all, "I didn't expect you to get this on the first try."

I nodded, closing my eyes and trying to remember the way I summoned something out of my *pindre*. Maybe I could use that in this situation. I opened one eye after my attempt, slightly disappointed that the entire room hadn't burst into flames at my every command.

"Care to try again?"

I nodded, closing my eyes and imagining a string connecting me with him. My hands grew hot, and I felt as if a current of heat was igniting throughout my body. I opened my eyes and realized in horror that flames were dancing on my palm and licking all the way up to my shoulder. All thoughts of the lesson flew out of my head as I started to panic. Breathing heavily, I remembered what they told us in second grade: stop, drop, and roll. My legs gave away, and I fell to the floor, rolling around madly. The fire grew stronger and stronger, finally engulfing me in flames altogether. I went haywire, flailing around in the vain hope of not burning. My mind went blank, and all I could see was red. Someone grabbed my arms, and Potia's warm brown eyes appeared in front of me.

"Calm down."

I piped down immediately. My eyes unfogged, and my breathing returned to normal. I looked down to realize that my body was completely unscathed. I look up at Potia, confused.

He looked at me apologetically, "I'm sorry. I didn't warn you that would happen. Luckily you're immune to fire, except of the dark kind, of course. I can't even touch that without the proper protection. Since you are so inexperienced, I thought that you would only produce a feeble flame instead of an entire hearth. On the bright side, you're making great progress. This time maybe try to make the flame leave a small part of your body, maybe your forehead or your hands."

"Ok," I said breathlessly, stumbling to my feet.

Taking a deep breath, I attempted to recreate what had happened seconds before. I linked my soul with Potia and attempted to channel fire out of it. Willing the fire to flow freely in my hand. I aimed for a straw dummy that was on the other side of the room. Unfortunately, I lost my hold and a jet of flames, and it ended up bursting out of my elbows right toward Potia's face.

He sputtered slightly, putting it out with his hand. Eveda giggled. "Well, that was sort of an improvement." He said feebly.

I looked at him in horror, "Oh my God, I'm so sorry. Are you okay?"

Potia grinned, "Your lack of faith in me is somewhat amusing."

I shook my head but didn't respond. My mind felt scrambled as if I was in twelve different places at once. I attempted it a few more times only to find myself at a standstill. "It's not working," I groaned.

"Fire is fickle," Potia said, resting his chin on his palm, "It's not something you can put on a leash and control. You have to flow with it."

I cocked my head to the side, trying not to let doubt creep into my expression.

Potia sighed, "Allow me to rephrase. You have much in common with fire. Neither of you likes to be controlled. The more someone tries, the more you fight back. Stop fighting the fire. Join it."

I nodded slowly, even though nothing he said to me made any sense. "Alright."

I closed my eyes and tried to reach for the fire. I imagined myself flowing down a lazy river of lava. In my mind, I connected the lazy river to the palm of my hand and let go. An explosion rocked through my palms, and when the smoke cleared, the straw dummy seemed to have been reduced to a pile of ash.

I grinned, my eyes growing wide at the sight. I looked down at my palms in amazement "wow." was all I managed to say.

I shook my hair a few times, trying to stop the whirlwind of emotions fighting to break loose in my head. Half an hour ago, I would have told you to stop drinking whatever you were drinking if you had told me that I would form some sort of truce with Potia. Now he was training me how to blast fire out of my hands like Wonder Woman. It was all going too quickly for my mind to process. Still, I grinned, remembering the straw dummy that had been reduced into a pile of ash. I felt so powerful. Maybe there was hope for me to survive this after all.

Chapter 15

Walking into the cafe, I was overcome with a sense of wonder. The quaint little tables were covered in deep red tablecloths with abstract silver sculptures in the center. I could see students and other members of the art realm milling around, chatting and tables or hunched over unfinished art pieces. My stomach grumbled, and I looked around for some food. It was strange; I couldn't seem to find anything. I was about to build up the nerve to ask a random student where the cafeteria was when I spotted Eveda. I hurried towards her table. There were a few other people sitting by her, clearly waiting for her attention, but I ignored them.

"Hey, Eveda." I began breathlessly.

"Hello, Piper, dear." She responded, making a motion with her hands to indicate that I sat next to her.

My mind spun slightly as I sat on the velvet cushion. Not wanting to seem rude, I sat patiently, wondering if we were going to be served lunch.

"Well, get along now," Eveda instructed, currently leaning over her sky-blue sketchbook. I noticed that she was drawing a bowl of pesto pasta. I turned my head to the boy with dreadlocks on my left, molding a banana out of a slab of clay. I was hit with a moment of realization. I had to make my own food.

Summoning my sketchbook and a pack of sharpies, I began to outline a cream cheese bagel and tater tots. Waving my hand, I imagined the drawing coming to life right in my hand. After a beat, the food materialized right onto my paper. I grinned in accomplishment. Oh, I was going to have so much fun with this. I took a bite and almost moaned, glad to finally have food in my stomach. "Mmm."

Licking my fingers, I finished the meal. Feeling a craving for hot chocolate, I began to sketch that as well. Once it appeared in my hand, I took a sip. Bleh, lukewarm. A thought occurred to me: could I warm it up with the channeling Potia had just taught me? A small part of me wanted to show off my new ability to Eveda. Attempting to visualize what Potia had instructed me, I pictured a string attaching us together. Summoning the warmth, I envisioned a jet of fire streaming through the string right toward my hands. Heat built up inside me, and I felt myself getting warm. The fire tugged against my restraint and squeezed my eyes shut, attempting to control it.

Then everything went to hell.

Fire burst from my elbows, kneecaps, and forehead. The guy next to me yelped in pain as his yellow sweater vest caught on fire, and even Eveda, threw herself backward to avoid being hit. Everyone shrieked, running towards the door as half a dozen of the beautiful mahogany tables were burnt to crisps. The drapes by the windows were slowly burning, and the fire began to spread toward the wall.

I cursed.

The cafe erupted in chaos. People ran through the thick smoke attempting to find the exit. Water began to fall from the ceiling, and I could hear Eveda yelling for everyone to stay calm.

I stood rooted on the spot, swerving my head back and forth, frazzled. I heard something that resembled the sound of a clap of thunder and all of a sudden. Everything was still. Eveda stood in front of me with her hands together. The smoke settled, and her expression was calm. Everyone in the room stood still, gazing up at her.

"Everyone out." She commanded, her voice strong. "Now."

There was silence, and then, "SHE'S THE JINX!" A small girl with a hot pink tail screamed.

The commotion started up again, the yelling worse than before, as half the people ran towards the exit while the other half began running towards...me.

I gulped.

I turned to Eveda, praying her glare would kill me on the spot.

"Go behind me. There is another exit. Take it and go to your room." She said sternly.

Fear gripped my throat, but I obliged her command, pushing my chair back. I ran to the back entrance as Eveda began shouting commands.

I frantically tried to remember where my room was, but the hallways consisted of endless twists and turns, and I became lost immediately. The shouting seemed to be getting closer, and tears had already started falling down my face blurring my vision.

I pulled on a random doorknob and threw myself into what appeared to be a dark supply cabinet. I slid down the wall and hugged my knees to my chest, breathing heavily. Trying to quiet myself, I tried to figure out what on earth had happened. I hadn't meant for the fire to get out of control. All I wanted was to show Eveda my new skill. I cursed myself for being so set on winning her pride. Why was I already searching for some sort of motherly approval? She was keeping me here against my will, for god's sake.

I sighed, wishing I had a home. I wanted my old problems like what to wear on the first day of school or how to pass English class. As I shuttered slightly, I heard a slight creak, and light leaked into the room. I stood up, frantically wiping the tears off, and looked around the room for something to defend myself. I grabbed a tube of gray paint and held it up to the door.

A guy around my age entered and looked at me in concern.

"Don't come any closer," I said, holding up the paint. I had hoped my voice sounded brave, but I was shaking.

He grinned, "Ahhh, a paint tube. I'm terrified. You could really mess me up with that." He helped his hands up in mock surrender.

I frowned at him, still holding up the paint. He had messy dark brown hair that looked as if it had never seen the downside of a comb. His facial features remained me of those of a Mediterranean cat, sharp nose and cheekbones, all like arrows pointing towards his yellow-green *Citrus spice Nom. 47* eyes. His ears were pushed out slightly, and I noticed a small scar right about his left eyebrow.

He took a step toward me, and panic erased all sense in my head. I tightened my grip around the tube of paint and squirted it directly at his nose. He let out a yelp and cursed. "What the--!" He ran his hand across his face, trying to wipe some of it off.

"Oh my God, I'm so sorry I-I don't-." I stumbled over my words, hoping he wouldn't attack me.

"Don't worry about it," He grumbled, grabbing a bit of fabric from the top shelf. "But you're lucky I'm the one who found you. Most people don't take it as kindly being squirted in the face with gray acrylic."

My throat tightened at the reminder of the other students, and my eyes burned slightly. No, no, I thought, I won't cry, I won't cry.

He stopped wiping off his arms and looked at me, his expression changing from confusion to horror.

"No, no, sorry, I didn't mean it like that." He continued quickly, "I..er….I mean, uh, are you okay."

I shook my head, not trusting myself to speak. I dropped the arm holding the tube of paint and slid back down to the floor. He stood there awkwardly, clearly unsure of what to do. I waited for him to leave me alone or yell at me, but neither happened. Instead, he sat down next to me and awkwardly patted my back. I hid my face in my hands, half wondering what was going on, half glad not to be alone.

"I'm sorry about the whole lunchroom thing," He said after a pause, "I'm Ethan, by the way, Ethan Marsh."

"It's alright." I sighed, "It's just all be a bit much. I didn't mean to set the place on fire. I understand why everyone wanted to attack me, but I just have no idea what's going on, like all the time."

"Oh, right, you're the new girl. You came from the human world, right?" Ethan asked.

I nodded, ignoring the feeling of a hot spike in my throat at the mention of my real home.

"Wow, that's crazy," He continued, clearly not minding that this was a one-sided conversation. "That must suck, being away from everyone you know and thrown into this wack world."

I massaged my temple.

Ethan "Oo wait, sorry, shouldn't have brought that up."

I laughed thickly, cutting him off, "Don't worry about it. I promise I'm not normally this much of a mess."

Ethan grinned, "You sure?"

I rolled my eyes. "Yes I'm sure."

He laughed.

I bit my lip, unsure how to ask this next question, "Ethan…"

"Yeah?"

"What were those people talking about when they called me the jinx."

He winced, "This is going to sound really bad."

I pinched the bridge of my nose with my fingers, "No surprise there."

"This is going to sound really bizarre, but there was a sort of prophecy. See, the art realm has these owls. They're sort of fortune tellers, if you will"

I snorted.

Ethan paused, "Yeah, it sounds stupid, and most of the stuff they predict is a total fraud, but sometimes people will do anything to pretend they have a solid grip on their future. Eveda won't get rid of them because they give the people hope, and sometimes, just sometimes, they end up being right about stuff."

"But what does that have to do with me?" I asked impatiently.

Ethan hesitated for a second, "I haven't got the whole prophecy memorized, but from what I've gathered, the owls predicted that someone would betray the art realm and unleash Charlid. There are also quite a few lines that mention a storm of fire, jinxing all chances of success."

I cursed, "It keeps getting better and better."

"Yeah, but the word 'he' is mentioned quite a few times, and uh, well, you don't, um, I mean, I don't wanna assume–." He blushed, trailing off.

I tried to brush it off with a laugh, "No, don't worry. Well then, hopefully, the prophecy has nothing to do with me."

He grinned.

"One more thing, you said an owl predicted this?"

"Well, yeah," Ethan responded as if it were obvious.

"Right, ok, well, glad that's cleared up." I propped my hands up against my knees. "Though, at this point, summoning Charlid is probably easier than finding Emensaly."

Ethan's eyes widened, "So you're actually going to look for her? I mean, there were rumors, but I thought she was gone forever. Why are you going?"

I sighed, wondering how much I was allowed to reveal. Eveda never specified that my job was a secret. Feeling a bit rebellious, I told him everything. My words became a waterfall as I began to explain how I got lost in the forest.

"Wow." He stuttered, "So the owls are right, Charlid may rise."

"Yep."

"But why are they making you go? No offense, but you seem like you have no idea what's going on or how to control any of your channeling abilities."

I wanted to hug him, finally, someone who realized my incapability. "Hell if I knew. The brothers have some obscure view of justice. They think that I'm the one that caused it, so I'm the one that has to fix it. Never mind that there are hundreds of people out there who actually know how this world works."

"Well, then, I guess I'm just going to have to come with you." Ethan proclaimed.

I gawked at him, half of me praying he was sincere, the other half wondering if he was for real.

"I'm serious." He affirmed, turning his head to look me in the eyes. "You don't know me very well, but I want to help. I want to save the art realm, the way…" Ethan paused, lost in thought.

"Okay then," I responded when he wouldn't continue. "We're going to find Emensaly."

Ethan grinned, "You bet your gray paint we are."

I was about to reply when I heard a familiar voice yell through the hallways, "PIIIIPERRR!"

I cursed, standing up so quickly that stars danced in front of my eyes, "And that'll be Eveda. I better go, but I'll see you around."

I wanted to say more, but what exactly do you tell a person that was willing to go on an insane suicide mission after finding you in tears in a supply closet?

Chapter 16

"Where were you?" Eveda asked suspiciously, "I told you to go to your room."

"I couldn't find it," I answered crisply.

She raised an eyebrow.

"Eveda, why didn't you tell me about that weird owl prophecy? Is there someone actually trying to release Charlid, or is it actually about me? I promise that I will never betray the art realm."

The words were out of my mouth before I had time to think, and only then did I realize that they were true. This place was magical, and even if I felt overwhelmed and out of place, it wasn't something I wanted to see in shambles.

Eveda smiled. " Piper, dear, I didn't tell you because I thought that you had enough on your plate." Eveda pointed out to her *I only wanted the best for your* voice which was getting a bit old at this rate.

I crossed my arms.

"Besides, those batty old owls predict the end of the world at least three times a week. It's how they keep business up."

"Wait, are these actual owls, as in the bird?"

"What else would they be?" Eveda retorted, "Ever since they've discovered Keratin Feather treatment, those vagabonds will do anything for a bit of cash."

"Okaaaaay."

"Are we on the same page?" Eveda urged.

"We're not even in the same library."

"As for Bella." Eveda continued as if she hadn't heard me. "It's a bit blurry from what we've gathered. She was attacked in the flower garden. Someone stole her *pindres,* leaving her completely defenseless. She was found unconscious a few hours later with a lethal shoulder injury."

"What does that have to do with Charlid?" I whispered fearfully.

"The medics have been examining the wound, and they found something rather disturbing. A colorful paste made of Charlid's hair was apparently injected into her shoulder. This clogged her blood and spread to the rest of her body. She's in stable condition at the moment. However, the question remains, how could someone have possibly had access to the hair of Charlid."

"But why are there people from the Chaos realm just milling around!?" My voice was on the brink of hysterics. "How are the brothers allowing this?"

"Do you remember how I told you that in-betweens have a much easier time going from one realm to another than stronger beings, such as deities? After the war between the three brothers and Charlid was over, everyone that had any sort of hereditary relationship to the realm of Charlid was locked inside. However, it was still possible for any in-between to slip inside. The brothers do not approve of this theory. However, many people have been saying that there have been a few people helping Charlid make his own in-betweens that can come and go as they wish. It was never so much of a problem for us because you had to have the right lineage of an in-between to slip between the wall."

My mouth became dry as I predicted what she would say next.

"However, in light of current events, the wall has weakened, and more chaos in-betweens have been escaping."

I clapped a hand over my mouth, fear growing in the pit of my stomach. I was having a harder and harder time trying to convince myself this wasn't my fault.

Eveda stopped in front of a large red door with a printed-out piece of paper tacked to the front. One word was written on it, "Defense."

There were a lot of students in the classroom, more than I expected. They ranged from the ages of eight to seventeen. After bidding me goodbye, she left, leaving me feeling tiny and terrified. The room was massive and looked nothing like a typical classroom. There wasn't a single chair or whiteboard in sight. Instead, there were test dummies lined up against the wall, shields, spears, javelins, swords, crossbows, machine guns, and other lethal weapons hanging from the ceiling, which I prayed would stay as decorations.

I averted my eyes, pretending I didn't notice all of the glares that were being thrown in my direction. Clearly, not everyone was as open-minded as Ethan. I looked around, wondering if he was in this class.

I made my way to the back of the room, keeping my eyes on my shoes. I made the mistake of colliding into someone wearing a black cloak. I took a few frantic steps back, still jumpy from this morning.

"Sorry, sorry, so sorry." I babbled, looking up. My eyes met with a man at least a head taller than me. His white hair was cut short, and I noticed a tattoo line going down his cheekbone, pronouncing the wrinkles in his forehead and dimples. His dark eyebrows were contorted into a glare that was directed straight at my face.

Boy was glad looks couldn't kill.

"Sorry ma'am, I mean sir, I mean mister, sorry, I just, hemehm, sorry." I turned beet red and took another step back, wishing that the shadows would swallow me whole.

The man flared his nostrils but said nothing. A few of the kids smirked.

"Hehem," He said in a harsh, no-nonsense type of voice that could cut through steel, "My name is Master Reverac. Welcome to defense. I will quickly review the rules for all of our newcomers who have *graced* us with their presence." He threw the word "grace" into the air with so much menace that one would think it was an insult, "There is no channeling of any deities' power during this class. Only weaponry is permitted. If I see any channeling at all, you will be forced to leave the class." Master Reverac proclaimed the corners of his mouth arched downward.

I willed my face to turn back to its normal color.

"Now, let us split the class up. If you are able to summon a sword, bow, and arrow, or any other sort of arms out of your *pindres* come to my left. If you have not mastered the ability to do so, come to my right." He sneered.

Over three-fourths of the class went to his left while everyone under the age of 8 and a strange two-dimensional being that looked like a stick figure went to his left. Just my luck. Master Revac glared at me a moment longer before turning to the older group and instructing them to summon their weapons.

Now I know I said that I'd seen it all, but it took a moment for my heart to calm back down after seeing twenty children manifest real weapons into thin air. My eyes drifted towards a child who looked no older than nine, casually holding a machete and staring up at Professor Revac, waiting for further instruction. I scooched backward, trying to put as much distance as possible between us. I accidentally stepped on someone's toe in the process. "Watch it, jinx." the kid hissed and then disappeared into the group.

I shuddered. Something told me that I didn't wanna be on the wrong side of that child's weapon.

Once Professor Revac finished instructing the other group in perfecting their battle stance, and they began to walk towards us.

He raised his hands and began speaking. "Summoning weapons is very different from summoning any sort of other supplies from a *pindre*. To do so, you must imagine a victorious battle against an enemy. Imagine standing on their corpse and holding your weapons high. I will place an image before your eyes, and it will help you summon it."

I whipped my head around to look at the other students. What was going on? Had we already started, what did Professor Revac mean when–.

A loud clap interrupted my thoughts, and then, the room disappeared. I had been transported to a battlefield. Dead and wounded soldiers littered the ground, and looking down in horror, I realized that I was standing on top of a corpse. I tried to remind myself it was just an image Professor Revac had somehow managed to put in my head, but still, my stomach churned at the images. I closed my eyes and tried to imagine a weapon materializing out of my *pindres*, anything that I could use to defend myself in the current situation.

I gritted my teeth when nothing happened. I tried to remember the feeling of channeling my sketchbook out of my *pindres*. Maybe that would help me out.

"I will not let you out of the stimulation until you have produced a weapon." I heard Professor Revac say, though his voice sounded far away, as if I were listening to him underwater.

I cursed. With my luck, I would be in this thing forever. I tried to stay calm. I thought of Potia and how he said to lick our souls. Maybe he could help me summon a weapon.

Something in my illusion changed. There was a figure running towards me. Potia, I realize. I wasn't sure if he was part of Professor Revac's stimulation or not, but I waited for him to arrive.

120

"Potia, what are you doing here?" I questioned, momentarily distracted from the panic of the atmosphere.

Potia said nothing. Instead, he handed me something. I noticed in amazement that it was a spear.

"You want me to take that?" I asked, my voice filled with doubt. I had a feeling I would end up dropping it on my foot or something. Potia said nothing. He simply kept his hands outstretched.

"Okaaay then." I declared, wrapping my hand around the base of the spear.

All at once, a rush of warmth sparked through me. Holding the spear felt…right. The minute my hands touched it, I sensed a pulse in the warm metal, as if the weapon itself were alive. Flames licked the top of the plated spear, causing the air to buzz.

And with that, the illusion went away. I was standing back in Professor Revac's classroom. Only something had changed. The room was silent, and I noticed in apprehension that every single person was staring at me.

I had just enough time to think, "Oh god, what now?" when Professor Revac walked towards me.

"That's the lost spear of Potia." A girl with short black hair and pink skin yelled.

I looked down in confusion.

Master Revac approached me, his expression full of hate. I took a cowardly step back, shaking vigorously. He reached out and took hold of the butt of my spear.

I yelped, "What's going on? You *wanted* me to summon a weapon."

Someone let out a low whistle, and I turned around, ready to slap them, when I was pushed to the ground. I scrambled up furiously, only to see Master Revac standing right above me. He pulled me up by my T-shirt and held me so close to his face that I could smell his breath. "Summon. Another. weapons." He seethed, releasing me.

"But-."

"NOW!"

Swallowing my anger, I stood up, trying to control the fire inside of me. After a few tries, I managed to absorb the spear back into my *pindre*. Unfortunately, summoning another weapon was deemed to be impossible. Every time I envisioned the battlefield, Potia was there, handing me a spear. I groaned, massaging the tension out of my neck. Master Revac's face seemed to turn a deeper shade of purple whenever the spear reappeared.

After the seventh time, he let out a yell, "ENOUGH!"

I jumped, nearly letting go of my spear.

Master Revac went through a small door in the back of the room, and at first, I thought that he was planning to do some deep breathing exercises in there, but when he emerged, he was carrying a five-inch long dagger. I tensed my legs, wondering if he was planning on gutting me, but instead, he tossed it at me. I let out a shriek and jumped to the side. It grazed my hand, but I couldn't feel any pain. I was shocked, had someone actually just tried to kill?

"WHAT IS GOING ON?" I screamed, panic settling in.

My palms grew warm, and I felt a small flame begin dancing across my fingertips. I noticed a flicker of fear penetrate his mask. Attempting to hide my uneasiness, I smirked.

"I was presenting you another weapon to train with."

The flame in my hand grew larger, and I could feel the eyes of every single person in the class.

"Get out of my class." Professor Revac fumed. "Now."

You don't have to tell me twice, I thought. Turning on my heel, I marched out the door.

Chapter 17

Once outside. I extinguished my hand and stumbled around the corner, leaning my hands on my knees. Note to self, don't set your hands on fire to make a point. I took a deep breath attempting to stop the spinning in my head. My hand bled freely, and I attempted to wipe it on my skirt. I leaned against the wall, wondering if I could get a bandaid somewhere. I retraced my steps back to the lunch room, vaguely remembering that there was a room labeled nurses office right next to it.

Thankfully I managed not to get hopelessly lost, and after a few twists and turns, I found myself standing in front of a pair of stainless steel double doors. I opened it up and was greeted with bright, sterile lights. There were crisp, white hospital beds lined up next to each other, and the walls were lined with hundreds of shelves, each filled with medicine, bandages, herbs, and pointy doctor tools.

However, it was strangely empty. A few beds to the left, there was a boy with dreadlocks who looked around the age of seventeen. He held an ice pack to his right eye and his head back and forth as if he were listening to music.

Ahead of him sat a creature with the legs of a dog and the upper body of a woman. I wasn't sure if she had been cursed to look like that or if it was her nature, but judging by the glare she threw at me, I thought it might be in my best judgment not to ask. A few beds across slept a girl with dirty blonde hair that was sprawled over her exposed collarbone. Her shoulder was wrapped in thick gauze, and her elbow was bent at a crooked angle. I took a step closer to her and was surprised at how closely I resembled her. Granted, her lips were fuller than mine, but she had the same pale eyelashes and splash of freckles painted across her nose.

I felt a bit of unease, vaguely wondering if this was one of Eveda's *other* children. I moved my eyes over to the side of her bed and noticed a pile of cards. I leaned over to pick up the card and read the small handwriting, and dread began to form in the pit of my stomach. "Get well soon, Bella," I murmured, reading aloud.

I sighed and bowed my head, "I'm sorry, Bella. I'll fix this."

I heard the sound of a door opening and turned around to face a short, plump woman with rosy cheeks, tan skin, and long white hair tied into a bun at the nap of her next. She wore white scrubs and plastic gloves. I dropped Bella's card as if it had caught fire and looked up at the woman guiltily.

"I'm sorry, I just came in looking for a band-aid." I faltered, holding up my hand.

Her face lit up with a grin, a reaction most people wouldn't have when presented with a bloody palm. "Oh, you poor darling, come here, lay down."

"Oh no, that's fine. I really just need a--."

She put her hands on my back and pushed me towards the bed, "Don't be ridiculous darling, you look so pale a ghost would be jealous. Have you been exposed to any sort of action that could have caused fear or stress?"

"Not that all."

She raised an eyebrow.

"I'm Julie. So glad you came in today. Really I couldn't be happier, just lay down here, and I'll get you all sorted out."

She sauntered off to grab something off the shelf. I suppressed my bewilderment at her good mood and lay backward. Julie smiled and began pulling different bottles and syringes off of shelves. When the clanking had stopped, she rolled a tray table over to me that was loaded with pills and other medications.

125

I faltered, "That's not all for me, is it?"

"Well, who else would it be for?" She beamed, "You know, it's a miracle you've survived this long with that tumor in your kidney and the brain disease that's been developing."

"WHAT?" I blurted.

Julie was about to continue what I'm sure were many other medical ailments I was suffering when the door flew open, and Eveda sauntered through it. "Piper, there you are. I heard about--Julie, what are you doing!?"

Her eyes turned to the nurse who was cleaning a sharp needle and eyeing my right forehand. "I'm drawing blood, obviously, I want to test this dearie for tuberculosis."

I scootched down the hospital bed away from the syringe.

"Oh, nurse Julie, what did we say about this? How about you go get some lunch?" Eveda asked, her eyes darting between me and the heavily loaded medicine tray.

"No, that's fine." Nurse Julie protested, "Just let me finish up with–."

"Actually, I would prefer to speak with Piper alone right now," Eveda replied firmly.

Nurse Julie deflated visibility and turned around, pushing the cart along with her. Once she was out of sight, Eveda approached me and sighed. I'm sorry about her. We don't normally have a lot of patients in the nurse's office, so whenever one wanders in, Julie gets a bit excited."

I sighed with relief, "Good to know."

Eveda laughed but then turned serious, "Piper, we need to talk about what happened with Professor Revac."

126

"He threw a knife at me." I stammered, my hands shaking slightly. "I don't even know why, but he got so angry when he saw the spear that I summoned and–."

Eveda held up a hand, "Piper, calm down, please. Now, believe me. I never thought I'd be one to defend Professor Revac's character, but there's a first for everything."

I raised an eyebrow.

Eveda sighed, "Twenty years ago, Master Revac was accused of stealing Potia's prized spear. Potia used it during the battle against Charlid, and it was one of the many reasons we prevailed. Now, Revac and Potia had always had a bit of a tense relationship, and a few days before the spear went missing, Potia and Revac had a massive fight. Revac's *pindres* was found in the display case of the spear, but it quickly became obvious that he had been framed as the *pindre* turned out to be fake. Nevertheless, the damage had been done. He was an outcast in his realm for a few years before the rumors died down, and he came to work for the art realm. He probably assumed that Potia gave you a spear to gloat, still bitter about their fight. The two of them have despised each other for ages. Revac must have thought Potia was playing a joke on him, causing the spear to appear for the first time in his classroom."

"Wait, so this spear hasn't been seen for the past twenty years, and it just so happens to appear out of my *pindres*?" I questioned, feeling skeptical.

Eveda shrugged, "Channeling works in mysterious ways. As far as Potia and I are both concerned, the spear belongs to you."

"Uhhh," I replied, unsure what the proper protocol was for accepting a spear with a lot of baggage. "Sweet, thanks."

Eveda smiles, "Come on, I'm sure you're exhausted. Let's get you to bed. You have a long day tomorrow.

***

The next morning I discovered that the news of my little spectacle with Master Revac spread like wildfire, and whispers followed me wherever I went. Eveda had handed me a map of the castle and pointed me in the direction of my next class before running off, claiming to have "plans" with Potia, whatever that meant. I was just turning the second corner when I bumped into Ethan.

"Hey Piper." He grinned, rubbing his forehead, "The school is buzzing with the news of your little fight with Master Revac. It's crazy! I don't think anyone has ever dared channel in his class."

I grinned despite myself, "Well, trust me, I don't plan on ever seeing him again. Do you have classes right now?" I was still unsure about how the whole school/everyone living here thing worked yet.

"Survival 101." He replied, "You?"

"Thank God. I have the same." I sighed with relief. "Where is it?"

"Right here," Ethan announced, pushing open a light pink door covered in floors and vines.

I walked in after him, pushing some of the lower vines out of my face, wondering why on earth someone would want that hanging on their door. "So," I asked as we made our way through an empty white room, "Anything I should know about this teacher? I don't really want to relive Master Revac."

Ethan let out another lopsided grin, "Nah, Ms. Leaf's pretty chill."

"Ms. Leaf?" I giggled, "You've got to be kidding me."

He laughed, "Nope, I'm dead serious. Oh, and be careful around her *Pusity*."

128

"Her what?" I asked, suddenly feeling awkward.

He turned beet red and laughed, "It's a spirit tree."

I blushed, "Oops."

"What did you think I meant?" Ethan cackled.

"Shut up."

Ethan grinned but changed the subject, "Anyway--."

I didn't hear what he said next because I had just walked through an arch into the largest classroom I had ever seen. It went on for aces. There was about thirty square yards of freshly cut grass around us, but if you looked further, you could see some sort of terrain. It kept switching between jungle, arctic, beach, desert, city, and forest.

"Woah," I said softly, my eyes trying to keep up.

I glanced around, wondering if Professor Leaf was here and if I could see this *illegid pusity*. My eyes met with a beautiful tree. It was extraordinary from all angles. The wood was a bedazzling shade of gold going from the tips of the roots to the top of the long slender branches. From the branches sprouted delicate roses, each a gentle shade of pink. What caught my eye wasn't the tree itself, though. It was the woman who had seated herself inside of it. She had long legs and skin the color of caramel. She wore a white knee-length sundress that seemed to sparkle in the sun. Her eyes were pastel pink, and strawberry blond locks hung loosely around her shoulders.

"*She's* teaching us survival?" I wondered if I had missed something.

"Yup." Ethan answered, chuckling slightly, "I know she doesn't look it, but I assure you Ms. Leaf could be scarier than Master Reverac."

I raised my eyebrow but didn't reply.

129

"She's *lurer*." He continued as if that cleared everything up.

"And that is…." I asked.

"A *lurer*, she had the ability to lure you into a false sense of comfort and peace, but the moment you come into contact with her, whether it is a hug or a handshake, Ms. Leaf's nails turn into needles. With one quick prick, she has the ability to control your body and mind."

I shuddered, "And Eveda actually trusts her to teach students."

Ethan grinned, "It's the best way to discipline kids. Besides, the two go way back."

"I'm pretty sure that goes against literally everything the Child Protection Act stands for but okay."

Ethan shrugged and took a few more steps toward Ms. Leaf before sitting down on the freshly mowed grass.

"So what's the deal with the shiny tree, or *pusity* whatever?" I asked, sitting down next to him and warily glancing at Ms. Leaf.

"I think it's a present from her sister." Ethan answered, pulling a bag of Cool Ranch Doritos out of his right pocket and chewed pensively, "See all of the fancy roses? They each give you different abilities. The light pink ones are basically paranormal energy drinks, and the slightly darker ones are used to clear your head or help you focus. Those are the only two I know about because there are given out as prizes. Though I'm sure that there are much more powerful ones."

"Woah," I marveled and then eyed his chips.

"Woat sum?" He asked, his mouth full of food.

I nodded, and he dumped a few into my open palms. "So what are the tasks?" I asked after swallowing.

130

"You'll see." Ethan grinned, "They're pretty fun."

I was about to pester him some more, but Ms. Leaf had just jumped out of her tree and called out, "Good afternoon, class."

Ethan hastily stuffed his chips into his back pocket, motioning for me to do the same. I thrusted the chips down my throat, choking slightly. An unexpected pang of sadness hit me in the face as I remembered doing the same with Amy in math class.

"Today, we will be finishing our jungle unit with a task." Ms. Leaf began, her voice airy and mysterious. "The stimulation will be in a jungle. The challenge is to retrieve the red rose in the heart of the forest. Everyone has two hours to find it and make it out alive."

"Alive!" I repeated quietly, trying to stop my throat from closing in.

"Relax," Ethan replied, "No one actually dies. It's just like a video game. After the task, you come back alive and well."

"But Ms. Leaf-."

"Was probably a Broadway performer in her past life." He finished, "She likes to keep her audience on the edge of her seat."

I gulped but turned my attention back to Ms. Leaf. The situation reminded me all too much of the Hunger Games, but I kept my mouth shut, clinging to every word Ms. Leaf said, hoping that it would somehow protect me in the next two hours.

"How am I supposed to do this?" I murmured to Ethan, hoping he couldn't hear how much my voice was shaking. "I haven't been here all year. I don't know how to do any of this."

"Have some faith, will ya?" He replied, "With me as your partner, we'll find that rose in less than an hour."

131

I rolled my eyes but secretly grinned that he offered to be my partner.

"Without further ado, you have two hours." Ms. Leaf finished, cutting slightly as if we had all just received the best performance in our life. With an elaborate wave of her arm, flickering images settled into one very solid and real-looking jungle.

"On your mark, get set, go!! Good luck." Professor Leaf called out.

Everyone stood up and raced to the sea of green, not even hesitating to think about all of the bugs, animals, and poisonous plants that might dwell there. I was about to hang back and ask Ms. Leaf if she had any extra bug spray, but Ethan grabbed my arm and pulled me toward the jungle. Sighing, I plunged in after him, not sure what else there was for me to do.

"None of the other kids are going to try and kill us, right?" I asked, panting as Ethan continued to pull me over roots, and I swatted mosquitos out of my face. I was still envisioning this as *Hunger Games: The Sequel*.

"No-...let's just try not to run into them," He answered, slightly distracted.

Chapter 18

After a few moments of running, the two of us were hopelessly lost. At least, I thought we were, but Ethan trudged ahead as if google maps had been installed into his brain. I tried to follow while swatting mosquitoes out of my face and wiping sweat off my brow. At some point, I saw a beetle as large as my pinky finger and screamed, scampering out of the way.

"Oh, calm down. It's all an illusion." Ethan reassured me for the hundredth time.

I eyed the bug skeptically. "Sure."

Once Ethan judged that we were far enough from the others, he squatted down on a small rock and placed his chin on his hand. "Ok, let's think about how we find the rose."

I shrugged, still standing, "I don't know, maybe we could follow someone who knows what they're doing."

Ethan snapped his fingers, about to say something, when the air was filled with a sound, one that oddly resembled a growl.

"What was that?" I squeaked.

Ethan revolves on his heel, "Jaguar," He whispers slowly.

My breath hitched in fear.

"Back away slowly, don't look at its eyes." Ethan coached in a bare whisper. "If it doesn't see us as a predator or prey, it will leave us alone."

I stared at the ground, trying not to shake. My eyes seemed to have a mind of their own and glanced up at the beast. In all honesty, the jaguar was gorgeous. With its sleek *Empire Gold Mathew Williams #10213* coat covered in dark rosettes, it was easily the most graceful creature I had ever seen. I felt the familiar nagging in the back of my mind where I wished I had my sketchbook with me at the moment. However, all thoughts of the creature's beauty left my mind with its long muscular limbs tensed, and the jaguar lunged.

I screamed.

And then the jaguar was on top of me, its razor-sharp claws were scratching my neck, and I felt blood ooze down. I stayed frozen in fear, terrified of moving. This is it, I thought, my throat closing up. Out of the corner of my eye, I could see a second jaguar pounce on Ethan. My blood began to buzz, my head hurt, and I was dizzy from the blood loss. There were razor-sharp teeth gnawing at my t-shirt.

Suddenly my mind went blank. I was standing in the golden god kingdom, and a figure was approaching me in the distance. Potia, I recognized. He was once again holding the infamous spear. He held it out to me, and for once, I took it quickly. The minute my hands curled around the sharp metal, I was back in the jungle.

The jaguar had just opened its massive mouth, and I gulped, staring at its many teeth. Before I could doubt myself, I thrusted the spear upwards, right through the jaguar's stomach. It howled, and I scrambled away, not wanting to look at the damage. I ran over to Ethan and frantically began to thrust my spear at the jaguar who had him pinned down. My jabs were clumsy, but I was able to avoid decapitating Ethan. The animal's legs trembled, and after a moment, it fell sideways. Ethan pushed the carcass off of his chest, looking as sick as I felt. He was breathing heavily, and it was a moment before we spoke again.

"Are-." My voice squeaked, and I tried again, "Are you okay?"

"Yeah." He breathed, trembling slightly. "It's just an illusion, right?"

"Right." I shuddered, "Just an illusion."

Even as I said it, my brain was having a hard time believing me, the blood felt warm and wet against my skin, and the cuts on my throat burnt. The air was filled with a coppery smell, and I began to breathe through my mouth, ignoring the nausea building in my stomach. The two of us sat on the ground in silence. After a moment, Ethan took a big breath. "That was really scary, but we have to keep going. No doubt we lost a lot of points for getting caught up with the Jaguars. Thank you, by the way. You were great back there."

"No problem," I whispered, still shaking slightly.

"Now we have to get the rose." He contended.

I laughed, hysteria bubbling out of my throat. God, it felt good to laugh.

"Why are you laughing?" Ethan asked incredulously, "We have to win."

I gasped, still laughing, "You're worried about winning? We were almost mauled to death by some wild cat."

"Well, what happens happens. However, if I lose my winning streak, I promise to do a lot more than maul you to death."

"Dully noted."

***

"So what are we going to do?" I wondered. I'd managed to get rid of all the gore and grossness from the jaguar attack with some water Ethan conjured for us.

He gave me a mischievous smirk, "Well, I have one idea. You might not like it."

"Oh god."

"Follow me."

135

He quickly walked towards a thicket of trees. "Ethan!" I called.

Ethan stopped at the base of one of the tallest trees around. He began inspecting the low-hanging branches, "We climb."

"Forget it." I hissed.

"Aw, come on, don't tell me you're afraid of heights." He replied, shaking his head in mock disapproval.

"More like afraid of falling and breaking my neck," I muttered.

Ethan acted like he hadn't heard me. "Just follow my lead, and you'll be fine."

I shook my head about to ask if his definition of "fine" would land me in the hospital when he grabbed onto the first branch. "Each branch has to be at least six inches in diameter for it to be strong enough to hold us."

I rolled my eyes. He didn't really think I was stupid enough to do this. Ethan began taking off his shoes and wrapping his socks around the inside of his arm. I sighed. Well, here goes nothing.

I copied his motions, wishing that I had spent more time with Ms. Leaf. Without warning, Ethan took off. He ran up and placed his right foot on the trunk and pushed upwards, gracefully grabbing a branch that was at least six feet off the ground. I gaped. He couldn't possibly expect me to do that. I could barely make it up a rock climbing wall.

"Come on, Piper!" Ethan yelled impatiently, already hanging on to a third branch.

Swallowing, I sprinted toward the tree. I threw my hands up and tried to kick off. Fail. My hands grabbed air, and I painfully fell on my right hip. "Ow." I groaned.

Ethan laughed.

"Stop smirking at me." I pouted.

"I'm not smirking!" He responded indignantly.

"You're laughing!" I accused

"Not laughing." Ethan bit his lip to hide a smile.

"Well, quit doing whatever you're doing."

"Whatever you say, little miss sunshine."

I shot him a rude hand gesture and ran up again, and after a few tries, I actually managed to grab the bark, only to let go in surprise. Finally, my hands reached the tree, and I was able to tighten my grip. I hung a few feet off the ground, feeling a sense of accomplishment. I pulled myself up and hugged the branch like a koala. I swung my feet back and forth, finally able to my stomach on the bench. I groaned slightly but was able to get my left foot on a small knot and balance myself. Grabbing a branch near my head, I was able to pull myself up a few more feet. Ethan was resting a few branches above me. I slowly began to climb until I was finally next to Ethan. My limbs shook in exhaustion.

"Don't worry, we're almost up," Ethan reassured me.

"Okay," I replied, keeping my eyes focused on the center of the tree to stop myself from looking down.

Ethan distracted me, "Come on, let's go a bit higher. I can't see very well through all of the trees. Oh, by the way, be careful some of these branches look unstable. Trees rot from the inside, so always test branches even if they look sturdy."

I didn't have enough energy to reply with a sarcastic comment, so I just nodded.

Ethan stood up and began to test the branches he found safe.

"I think we can go about ten more feet until the branches can't support us anymore," Ethan concluded.

Once he has chosen the branches he classified as study, Ethan begins to climb. I gulp down my fears and feverishly wipe my hands on my shorts, trying to stop them from slipping.

I took a deep breath and tentatively reached up, trying to grab the next branch without losing my balance. I was so on edge that the slightest movement could have thrown me off. Trying to calm down, I think of the wonderful view I will be able to see once I make my way to the top. As I began to daydream, the traction on my feet slipped. "Crack," the wood under my feet broke. I screamed, trying to grab a branch.

My none dominant hand clung to a thin branch as my feet dangled. I let out a string of curses, flailing my feet, trying to wrap them around the trunk. After two tries, I managed to hug the thinning trunk. "I'm ok. I'm ok." I panted.

Ethan yelled my name from the canopy, "Piper!!!! Piper, what happened!! Are you okay!"

"Yeah, I just slipped," I replied breathlessly

"You sure you're good?" He inquired.

"Yeah yeah," I noted, trying to sound casual.

"Ok, we're almost at the top," Ethan called.

I swallowed and continued my ascent. Left arm, right arm, left foot, right foot. At last, I made it to the top.

I moved my eyes from the center of the tree to the view. It was breathtaking. I understood the saying "On top of the world" more clearly than ever. Adrenaline coursed through my veins, and I laughed. The entire ground was spread out for me to see. The vast forest with large canopies and beautiful colored birds. My fingers itched to pull out my sketchbook and capture the beauty, but losing track of everything around me and sketching had gotten me in trouble before.

I stopped abruptly, realizing something. "Ethan? How are we planning to find a tiny rose from up here?"

"Well, it's not just some ordinary rose." Ethan replied, lowering his voice, "It's *The Rose*."

I raised an eyebrow. "Is that a TV show?"

He sighed, looking slightly put out. "No, it's a rose that is channeling some of Ms. Leaf's power. As long as you look on the godly side of your mind, it will be easy to spot from here."

My cheeks grew red as I asked yet another question, "And I do that by…"

"Just unfocus your eyes and try to start channeling from Potia, except instead of concentrating on fire, try channelings his vision."

"Uh, okay?" I replied, ignoring how strange that sounded. I let my thoughts drift to Potia while still keeping a very firm grip on the trunk. I tried to imagine his woodsy scent and aura of power. The air seemed to buzz with electricity, and my pupils dilated. Opening my eyes, I could see…power. There was no other way of describing it. It wasn't a color or a substance, more like a feeling. I could feel power pulsating from the ground into the air. There were a lot of areas radiating power. The weaker ones, I would guess were other people trying to find the rose, but the strongest one had to be the flower.

"I've got it." Ethan and I declared at the same time.

"We need to go north to that odd cave in the shape of a tiger mouth," I said, summoning my sketchbook to draw a map.

"Alright." Ethan went on, "Let's go get this rose."

I looked down. The ground was at least twenty-five feet away.

Ethan noticed me eye the tree. "Oh, we're not going down the tree that way. We would lose too much time."

"I swear if you suggest we jump, I will push you into the jaguar den." I threatened.

Ethan laughed, "Relax, I've got us covered." And with that, he summoned a…

***

I took a step back (well, as far back as I could stand without falling into the tree canopy).

"Nuh-uh," I said, my voice trembling with fear.

"Oh yeah." Answered Ethan with a glint in his eyes.

I groaned, "why, just, why?"

"Come on, hold your arms out, and I'll strap you in," Ethan said, coming a bit closer.

Unable to believe that I actually agreed to this, I held out my arms for Ethan to pull a few pieces of fabric around my arms. Once he finished, I looked a bit closer. The parachute looked nothing like the ones I had seen in movies.

"Where did you get this?" I asked, making sure to keep my voice light.

"I made it myself.." answered Ethan proudly.

I gulped, "you're crazy."

He grinned, holding out his hand, "I'm freakin' insane, but I'm also your only hope of winning. So what's it gonna be? Sanity or survival."

Shaking my head, I sighed.

"Grab my hand," Ethan said, looking over the edge.

"What? No!" I replied.

"I'm not asking you for a hand in marriage. I'm trying to make sure you don't turn it into a pancake!" Ethan held my hand and jumped, pulling me along straight off the tree.

I let out a high-pitched scream, my life flashing before my eyes.

There was a tingling feeling rushing through my feet. My hands were reaching the air for nonexistent handles. I was frozen in fear.

"Open the parachute," yelled Ethan flying after me. "Open the parachute."

Unfortunately, falling through the air caused my brain to fog up and forget all of its common sense. Lucky for me, the ground rushing towards me at top speed was enough to knock some logic into me. I grabbed onto the strap and was immediately pulled back up into the air. I let out a breath, and I floated down, landing on all fours, shaking violently. Never again, I swore, never again. Ethan landed on the floor a bit more gracefully than I did, giving me a smug look.

"On a scale of one to ten, how much do you want to murder me right now?" He asked, grinning.

"I'm leaning towards the high thirties," I said hoarsely.

Ethan laughed, "Come on, let's go get that rose." He strode off in the direction we had pointed to on the top of the tree, leaving me behind, trying to scramble to my feet.

"You are too competitive for your own good," I called after him. "Actually, I take that back. You're too competitive for my own good."

"I am perfectly aware of that," He laughed, "That's what Ivy always used to say--." He paused, a strange expression briefly crossing over his face, "Let's go."

"Who's Ivy?" I asked, but Ethan was too far ahead to hear me. "Hey wait up."

He paused, "Do you still have the map we drew on the tree?"

"Umm yeah," I responded, recoiling slightly at his harsh voice. "Here."

He took it and began trudging through the dense jungle in silence. There was a spider on his right pant leg, and he didn't flinch. I sighed, deciding that the trees would probably be easier to talk to than Ethan right now. I was surrounded by long billow trees covered in vines.

"Hey Ethan, hold--."

"Shhh."

I crossed my arms, "Don't shush me."

He slapped a palm over my mouth and pointed at a cave, and then moved his hand to point at two figures.

I cursed. There were two people who had already beat us to the cave. I saw a petite girl with a tight brown ponytail tucked under a baseball cap. She gripped a massive black whip that was twice her size. Her short sky-blue skirt didn't have a speck of dirt on it, and I got the impression that she didn't need to climb a tree to find the cave. Next to her stood another girl wearing a brown beanie that covered hot pink hair. She was leaning against a massive club that was covered in dangerous-looking spikes and was flexing her biceps. The only thing out of place was a large spot of burnt flesh on the top of her exposed shoulder. It was red and throbbing, looking as if it had happened recently.

"That's Abi Golben and Essie Dixon," Ethan whispers. "They are a complete menace and almost always win these challenges. Essie is the daughter of Professor Leaf, and her Dad is a *lisad*. That's a creature that can teleport. Don't let her cuteness stop you. I swear in my life that she is a bloodthirsty killer. Abi is the pink girl, her mother is human, and I think that her father is the god of metalwork. They are the scariest couple in the art realm."

I snorted quietly, "Seriously? Bloodthirsty killers, you're taking this wayyyy too far."

Ethan shushed me again, and I rolled my eyes, "Okay, so what's the plan?"

I shrugged, "I don't really know, but I wonder why they're just standing there? I mean, their cave is less than ten feet away from them. Why don't they just walk in?"

Ethan shook his head, "I honestly don't know. Let's just try and sneak next to them."

I bit my lip but didn't protest. Something about this seemed off. We doubled back and scampered between trees to avoid detection. The grass squelched under my feet, but Essie and Abi didn't turn. "What's going on?" I whispered to Ethan.

He shrugged, "I don't know, but the cave is right there. I'll make a run for it.

He stood, but I grabbed his arm before he could move, "Stop." I hissed, "Look at the writing over there."

"The what?!" He asked, bewildered, crouching down next to me.

I rubbed my eyes, "When I wandered into the cave of Charlid, there was a sort of writing on the side. It was something that claimed that the cave belonged to the realm of Charlid. And look at some sort of engravement on the side of the rock there."

Ethan leaned closer and cursed, "We have a problem."

"Why what does it say?"

Ethan ran a hand through his hair, "Now it makes sense that Essie and Abi are just standing there. There's a barrier of dark fire."

"Dark fire?" I replied, slightly panicked, "Potia told me about that. Even he can't go through it without the proper protection. I bet that's what happened to Abi's hand."

"I don't suppose Potia taught you the proper protection," Ethan asked, his nostrils flailing slightly.

"Would I really be standing here panicking if he did?" I hissed sarcastically. I took a breath, "Okay, look, first, we've got to get rid of Essie and Abi, right?"

"Yeah, maybe we could create some sort of distraction, maybe make some jaguar noises?" He suggested.

"I've got a feeling that they won't be scared by the sounds alone." I responded, tapping my chin pensively, "Maybe we could make some sort of shadow. You can hit them with your knife. It doesn't actually kill them, right?"

"I believe the technical term is stab." Ethan corrected. "And no, they would just be disqualified from the game."

I rolled my eyes and told him to shut up. "I've got an idea. Can you sculpt a wind-up toy? Those things are really loud. Preferably in the shape of a jaguar. I'll take care of the shadow."

As he worked, I focused on channeling Potia, a small flame erupted in my hand, and I focused on increasing the brightness. I shielded the light with my body, hoping not to give us away.

"On the count of three, chuck the ball as far as you possibly can," I told Ethan.

"Umm...okay?" He replied, confused.

"One…..two…..three!!!!!" I whispered.

Ethan wheeled back his arm and threw the contraption so it landed a good 100 feet away. The ball started yelling. Essie and Josh perked up, looking alert.

"Now what?" He asked.

I pushed the ball of fire like a bowling ball, so it sat right before the screaming toy but stayed out of Essie and Abi's view. Moving my hands around, I made the toy's shadow move up and down. It sort of reminded me of shadow puppets, but a lot more flammable.

"Go, go!" I directed Ethan, sweat beating down my forehead as I tried to keep the fire burning.

Ethan crept ahead, and I shut my eyes, feeling squeamish. I knew that it was all an illusion, but I didn't even want to see that. Unable to resist, I peaked and was surprised that the floor wasn't bathed in blood; instead, Emmie and Abi disappeared.

"Ethan!" I cried.

"I'm right here." He replied, standing near the mouth of the cave. "Those girls aren't going to forgive me. They hate losing."

"Where did they go?" I asked.

"Where everyone goes when they die in this class, back to the clearing." He replied, "Now, how do you think we can get into the cave before someone else finds us."

I ran my fingers over the writing, "How are we supposed to get the rose."

"Well, I have an idea," Ethan said tentatively.

"Oh no."

"It's a good one, I swear." He pushed. "Can you take out your *pindres* and turn it into a sharpie?"

"Umm, okay, sure," I answered, waving my hand.

Ethan began drawing weird symbols on the ground. He traced an odd fire shape and a twisted-looking sword.

"What are those for?" I asked curiously.

"I need you to draw these on my forehead with your *pindres*." He answered seriously.

"You must be joking," I said, amused. "You want a tattoo on your forehead? How about your ankle or shoulder."

Ethan rolled his eyes," Just do it. I think that it will protect me from the fire."

"And if it doesn't," I asked nervously.

"Well, then, I hope you like the smell of burning flesh." He replied, grimacing.

Swallowing, I walked over to him and began to draw on his forehead. I snickered slightly, taking a step back.

Ethan frowned, "You better not have written a loser."

"Tempting as it was, I was able to control myself," I replied dryly.

Ethan ignored me and slowly began to walk to the cave. I held my breath. If this didn't work, then I don't know what would. Ethan raised a quivering hand to the field and slowly walked through on edge as if he thought it was about to bite him. Pushing his arm forward, he carefully brought it through the cave's mouth. I closed my eyes for a minute, praying that it would work. I had completely forgotten that everything here was a game.

Ethan let out a whoop, and my eyes flew open, "Piper, it worked!"

I grinned and pumped my fist in the air. "Yesssss, go grab it!"

Ethan curled his hand around the flower, and at that moment, a massive blast filled the stadium. I jumped, thinking that we were being attacked, but Ethan just grinned, "Don't worry, that's just the victory cannon."

Ms. Leaf's airy voice filled the air coming from what I assumed were invisible speakers, "The winners today are Ethan and Piper. Congratulations, please join me back in the classroom."

I was about to ask if we had to make our way back through the jungle when my body began to float upwards. "What's happening?" I cried in panic.

"Relax." Ethan answered calmly, "This is how we are reborn back into the classroom."

"Reborn?" I asked skeptically.

"I don't really know how it works. It's pretty advanced channeling."

I closed my eyes and relaxed my limbs. My entire body was tingling, and I felt like a cloud. I laughed out loud, my inner six-year-old flipping out.

Chapter 19

I opened my eyes and found myself looking up at the sky. I felt lightheaded, as if I had just woken up from a disoriented dream. I sat up, rubbing my eyes, and the first thing I saw was Professor Leaf holding out her hand. "Come, you may pick out your reward."

I stood up, dusting off the back of my pants, and followed her as she walked toward the magical rose tree. I smiled, feeling lucky for the first time in what felt like ages. I couldn't believe we had won. Sure, most of it was thanks to Ethan, but I hadn't been completely helpless. As I walked up to the golden roots, ready to grab one of the sun-kissed petals. Professor Leaf floated towards us.

"The petals I offer are courage, an escape from reality, a reliever of negative emotions, focus, and a bright idea. Which do you wish to possess?"

I wondered. I had no idea what the future held for me. After everything I had gone through today, though, I thought that an escape from reality would be better than anything else that was offered.

"Escape from reality, please," I said. At the same time, Ethan said, "Reliever of negative emotions."

We both looked at each other and then looked away, neither of us asking because neither of us wanted to answer.

"How do we use them?" I asked quickly, trying to break the building tension.

"Ah, you must put the petal upon your tongue and allow it to dissolve. Once used, the effect will last for an hour. Use it wisely." Answered Professor Leaf looking pensively at me and Ethan as if she were trying to read our minds. I wrapped my sweater around my chest, feeling exposed.

"Well, thanks, Ms. Leaf," Ethan said and hurried out the door. I frowned quickly, grabbing my bag and running after him. As I caught up to him, his face was pale, and his hands were balled into a fist.

"Hey, be careful. You'll break the petal," I said softly, trying to loosen his grip. I noticed his stoney expression and became concerned, "Ethan, what's wrong?"

"Nothing." He grunted, quickening his pace, so I had to run to catch up.

"Are you sure because--." I started.

"Yeah, I'm great. Hey, I forgot something. I'll see you at dinner." Ethan told me, his expression still tense.

I stayed standing in the hallway, wondering if I should go after him. I was confused. What had happened? One second we were laughing about the rose, and the next, his face resembled my moms whenever I did something wrong. Well, he had made it clear enough that he wanted to be alone. Sighing, I followed the crowd of students heading back to the cafeteria.

I sat down at the first table I saw, not even noticing the dirty looks some of the other students shot at me. I pulled out my sketchbook to draw up a slice of pizza when Eveda shook me out of my daydreaming (more like a day nightmare, come to think about it). "Hey Eveda, what's up?"

Her features were contorted into anguish, and panic wrapped its long fingers around my throat. "Piper, quick, Ethan's in the nurse's office. Come on." She hurried out of the room, and I grabbed my sketchbook before following her.

"Wait, what happened to him!" I hollered, but Eveda didn't slow down. "EVEDA!"

I raced across the narrow hallway and down a flight of steep wooden steps, hastily yelling apologies to everyone I bumped into. As we ran, my heart pounded, and my entire body felt like it was on pins and needles. Why hadn't I gone after Ethan? Everything I seemed to do was wrong. Before I could get too deep into my pity party, Eveda stopped running, and I skeeted to a halt to avoid crashing into her. She opened the door to a smiling Nurse Alice, and Eveda let out a sigh of relief. "So everything's okay?"

Nurse Alice's smile grew even wider, "No, it's awful. Gods, I haven't had this much fun in ages."

Eveda frowned, and I resisted the urge to slap Nurse Alice across the face. Instead, I ran over to a bed that hadn't been occupied the last time I was here. Bile rose to the back of my throat, and my vision grew blurry as I looked down at him. I tried to fight the nausea while wiping my sweaty hands on the side of my jeans.

My breath hitched as I asked, "What's happened to him?"

The light side of his face was mangled in a way that I could barely recognize him. There was a long bloody gash running from his forehead to his chin. The rest of his face had turned a sickly shade of green. There was a small amount of hair in the wound near his cheekbone, and I resisted the urge to vomit.

"Ethan!" I yelled, struck with horror and feeling dizzy. "What's wrong with him!"

"The same thing that happened to Bella," Eveda replied, her voice shaking. "Luckily, Nurse Alice had already extracted most of the hair of Charlid."

My heart fell as I turned around to look at Bella, who was in the northern part of the room. She hadn't moved from where I had seen her last time. "Is he, is he going to--." I trembled, not being able to finish my sentence.

"No," Eveda replied sternly, "We were lucky enough to find him before the hair dissolved and blocked off an artery. In fact, he should be up and running by tomorrow morning, isn't that right, Nurse Alice."

Nurse Alice pouted, "Well, I suppose...but can't I keep him, just for a little bit longer. Maybe he needs a few more tests done or even--."

"No," Eveda replied firmly.

"Where did you find him?" I asked, desperate to change the subject before either Eveda or I strangled Nurse Alice.

"In a broom cupboard, Arius-yes Arius," She said, sighing at my expression of confusion, "found him." She answered gratefully. "Now Nurse Alice needs to go back to unclogging the hair, and I assure you that's not a pretty sight. I'll bring you to your room."

"But-."

"No," Eveda said sternly, leading me outside.

I turned to Ethan quickly and began to whisper, "Goodnight, Ethan, please get better. I can't-I don't think I could survive this place without you."

Eveda led me to my bed, and I numbly followed the image of Ethan's wound imprinted on my brain. The thought of the hairs of Charlid left me queasy, and I tried to keep my few bites of pizza down. I pushed my temporary dorm room open and sat down on the bed, feeling a sense of defeat. Why I thought I had a chance with Charlid, there was no way I could possibly defeat him. He had been around for ages and had just dispatched the one person who was going to help me. I lay back, trying to stop tears from running down my cheeks.

I quickly found out that sleep was no longer an escape. I found myself playing hide and seek with a woman dressed in green leaves.

152

"Come and find me," She replied in a sing-song voice.

I ran and ran towards the tent, frantically looking. I felt something brush against my arm, and something sharp stabbed into my arm. Teeth.

I gasped, waking up in a cold sweat. Panting slightly, I threw the cover over my head and shut my eyes tightly. My mind still raced, and I decided now would be a good time to put Ms. Leaf's flower petals to good use. I tentatively pulled off the covers, half expecting something to jump out at me. I slipped out of my sweaty jeans and pulled on a nightshirt that I found in the blank white closet. I tiptoed over to the table and reached for the flower. Before I could wrap my hands around it, the petal fell off the nightstand. Groaning, I bent over to pick it up when it lunged under the bed. I let out a series of colorful curses, getting down on my knees and extending under the bed, trying to grab its petal. It floated away into the air, and I banged my hand on the frame. Gritting my teeth, I lunged again, and the petal flew up into the air. Ink began to appear on it as if an invisible hand was writing on it. *Keep This For Later,* it read.

And with that, it floated back onto my nightstand. I sighed, wishing that I had chosen a petal that didn't have an opinion. Too tired to fight, I grabbed my *pindres,* deciding to draw up some chamomile tea.

Taking a sip, I feel myself calm down. Sighing contently, I lay back in my bed when I saw something flash in front of my window. Tip-toeing over, I looked down to see a hooded figure creeping around the grounds.

Biting my lip, I leaned further through the window, the cool night air whipping my hair into my face. I recoiled suddenly when the smell of moldy fish hit me in the face. Holding my nose, I tried to lean over this time, a sight more prepared for what awaited me. Leaning through again, I waited for my eyes to stop watering to look at the figure. It seemed to be carrying something in large buckets. The liquid inside was sloshing around noisily. I glanced down curiously, wondering if this was a normal occurrence.

The figure was running across the lawn quickly, though the bucket was clearly too large for them to carry. The cloaked creature clumsily lifted its leg as the content of the bucket spilled over. Even three stories up, I could see the panic in their stance as they frantically tried to mop it up. My eyes had already started to feel heavy again, and I decided to tell Ethan about it in the morning. He would probably reassure me that creepy figures that smelled like sulfur crossed the lawn holding suspicious substances regularly. And with that reassuring thought, I collapsed back onto my bed.

***

The next morning I opened my eyes to the cheerful sunlight streaming into my room.

I cursed with annoyance remembering I had forgotten to close the blinds when last night's events flooded back into my mind. I remembered the cloaked figure and the sloshing bucket. Quickly getting dressed in a pair of jeans and a blue button-down t-shirt that I had found in the closet, I left my room to go to the dining hall, hoping to see Ethan there. I was not disappointed to find him sitting at a far table, looking tired but very much alive. I gave a very uncharacteristic squeal and ran up to him.

"Oh my gosh, you're alive. Are you okay?" I asked, desperately glancing up at his wound.

"Yeah," he replied, keeping his eyes trained on his cereal.

"Do you remember what happened?" I interrogated. "I didn't hear anything except that Arius found you in a broom cupboard after you had been attacked."

"It's sort of blurry," He answered. "I mean, I wasn't really paying attention to the door because I--er." Ethan trailed off. I pretended not to notice. He cleared his throat and continued.

"Anyway, I heard the door open and felt something slash across my face. The weird thing is that I didn't hear the door close. All I saw was Arius's face until I passed out." He frowned. "I was probably just disoriented from the venom."

"Yeah, probably, "I answered, unsure what to make of that. "Well, anyway, I saw the strangest thing last night," I told him, giving a quick recap.

Once I finished, Ethan ran his hand through his hair and thought. "I've never seen some creepy dude walking through the lawn, but this place is filled with weirdos, so..." He said, trailing off.

Before I could respond, the room exploded in noise and shouted, traveling around the room.

"What's going on?" I yelled, my heart still pounding from the shock.

"Someone stole *deleva* from the golden god kingdom. It's a special mixture of the nectar from their flower and all three brothers' urine." Ethan replied after taking off his *pindre* and putting it up to his ear. "It makes the drinker a deity. It's one of the most guarded possessions there."

"Is that a radio too?" I asked, motioning to his *pindre,* still processing that he was holding his ivy leaf bracelet up to his ear.

"Huh?" He asked, confused, and then looking at it, "Oh yeah. But you don't understand. This is really bad."

I shrugged, licking yogurt off my spoon and scrunching up my nose. "The three brothers must be pretty stupid if someone managed to steal it. But seriously, their pee? That's disgusting. This one kid at

155

my old school was dared to drink their friend's urine last year, and they had to go to the ER."

"No, no, you don't understand." Ethan repeated in a panic, "What do you think Charlid would do if he got his hands on something as powerful as that."

I cursed.

He grimaced, "That pretty much sums it up."

I opened my mouth to say something else when Eveda's voice silenced everyone in the room, "QUIET!" She bellowed, "I understand that there had been something stolen from the Golden God kingdom, but at this point, it is none of your concern. So it would be in your best interest to continue your day as normal." She said tersely before sitting back down. The room was filled up with a soft murmuring.

"Wow," I whispered to Ethan, "She seems tense."

"Who wouldn't be?" He replied, looking down at his cereal.

"I wonder how anyone could have stolen it. I mean, aren't the three brothers supposed to know and see everything? How could anyone slip past them?" I asked, cleaning up my breakfast and sliding out of my chair.

Ethan shrugged, clearly as mystified as I was, looking down at his watch. "Hey, what class do you have next?"

I summoned my sketchbook and flipped to the page where Eveda had drawn my schedule. "Ummmm, I had sculpture. How 'bout you?"

Ethan grinned, "Same here."

I let out a breath I didn't know I was holding. "Where is it?"

"I think we have it in the garden today." He replied, looking out of one of the stained glass windows.

"Oh, that sounds great." I said and then bit my lip, unsure as to how I was planning on asking this next question, "Ethan?"

"Yeah?" He responded with a mouthful of cereal.

"I was thinking about this last night." I began, "And I was wondering, I was wondering if you if you wanted to come with me to find Emensaly. I get it if you don't want to because it's crazy and dangerous, and you probably don't--"

"Of course, I'm coming." Ethan scoffed.

"Are you sure?" I asked, not believing him.

"You think I'm going to let you save the world yourself?" He asked, "What kind of a person do you think I am? I wouldn't do that to the world."

I would have punched him had I not been so grateful.

Chapter 20

The courtyard was gorgeous, and it could put any botanical garden I had ever been to shame. I saw every flower imaginable, Lilys, tulips, Orchids, carnations, Sunflowers, Daisies, Hydrangeas, and more. There were twelve students propping easels up next to a massive stone birdbath and another class that was stacking rocks into elaborate sculptures that didn't seem to obey any laws of gravity.

"It's one of the most beloved areas of the art realm," Ethan explained.

"I can see why," I replied, using all my self-control to stop my jaw from dropping.

About a hundred meters away from where I was standing, the neatly cut grass ended and turned into an unruly forest that had a sweet yet menacing charm to it. It looked like something out of a fairy tale. As my eyes feasted on the wonders of the meadow, Ethan led me over to a tall woman with blue skin and dark cornrow braids that faded into blue. The woman had a wedge-shaped nose and thin pale pink lips. She was wearing a pair of dark blue overalls that were splattered with mud. I didn't register much about her except that she was quite literally floating.

"Is she-."

"Floating? Yeah." Ethan replied unconcerned.

I swallowed, "right, okay, cool."

"Good morning, everyone." The blue lady said.

"Good morning Professor Evergreene." The class replied.

"Now, class, today I have a treat for you. We will be looking for *pofors* in the Art Realm Forest. Can anyone define a *pofors*?"

A girl in the front with flat shoulder-length brown hair answered immediately, "*Profors* are used to create divine objects. It's a type of nutrient found in soil, and if sculpted in a correct mold, it can be used to create an object of power. Unlike our *pindres* it does have a mind of its own. *Pofor* is sometimes used to create tools for deities." She sounded as if she had swallowed the textbook.

I gawked, "Okay, so it's basically just divine dirt?" I murmured.

Ethan grinned, "Yeah, pretty much."

"Correct Sadie." Professor Evergreene praised, "Now *Pofor* is an incredibly rare type of mineral, but we are fortunate enough to have some in our very own forest. Today we will be pairing into partners and go scouting in our forest looking for some *Pofor*. Once you have half of a bucket full, report back, and you can begin to sculpt. Everything is due by Friday." She waved her hand and then began handing out red buckets.

"Yo Ethan wanna be partners." A burly guy in a neon green t-shirt and auburn hair called.

"Nah I'm with Piper." He called back, accepting a red bucket.

"SIMP!" The guy yelled, "Ay Mason, how 'bout you--."

I flustered, "You don't have to. I mean, thanks I-."

"Eh, don't worry about it," Ethan replied, "That guy's a jerk. He'll louse around in a tree scaring the *pofor* away with his shirt."

I laughed, cocking my head sideways, "How do you scare away a mineral."

Ethan laughed, "You're in for a treat. Come on."

We began to walk to the woods when Eveda frantically burst towards Professor Evergreene, "Alessandra, come see this."

159

Professor Evergreen dropped her bucket and hurried over, "Eveda, what's wrong!?"

Everyone in the courtyard rushed over and tried to get a glimpse of what Eveda had been pointing at. As I managed to push myself to the front, I didn't understand what the problem was. There was a small bundle of lilies growing out of the grass, similar to the ones that I had seen in the Golden God kingdom.

"What's the big deal?" I asked Ethan, "They're flowers. We have them all over the courtyard."

Ethan paled, looking down at the shrub. "Yeah, but those are special to the Golden God kingdom; they only grow when Deleva has been sprinkled onto the ground."

"So what?---ohhh." My heart raced as I realized what had happened, "Do you think the thing I saw last night had stolen the Deleva? It seemed concerned when it dropped whatever was in the bucket."

Ethan bit his lip, "I don't know, but you should probably go tell Eveda about it."

I nodded, pushing my way through the crowd.

"Eveda, EVEDA!" I yelled, trying to get her attention along with the twenty other people surrounding her.

"Yes, yes, Piper dear, " she replied, and I was surprised to see that the bags under her eyes had gotten darker.

"I saw this figure outside my bedroom last night," I explained, giving a quick recap.

Eveda pressed two fingers to her temple and took a breath. "LOCK UP THE REALM!" She yelled into a microphone that hadn't been in her hand a moment before. "ALL STUDENTS, RETURN TO YOUR ROOMS IMMEDIATELY."

I took a step back, and my heart raced. I turned around and ran towards Ethan.

"What did you tell her!?" He asked, eyes wide.

"The same thing I told you!" I responded as we ran into the building.

I huffed, trying to keep with him, the winding staircases getting the better of me.

***

I had returned to my room, the stress of the day getting to me as I began to hyperventilate on the bed. At some point, I heard a knock on my door, and it took me a few tries to get up. "Who is it?" I called, hoping my voice wasn't shaking.

"It's Eveda!"

I threw the door open frantically` for any news. "What's up? Any news?"

Eveda stood in the doorway and looked like she had recently been pulling her hair, "We don't have any news yet, but that's not why I came. See, my mother wants to see you."

My eyebrows flew into my hairline, "I have a grandmother?"

Eveda sighed, "Yes, and she always chooses the most inconvenient times to visit. Doesn't care that there are chaos spirits running around as long as everything goes according to her plan."

I gave a small chuckle, "And what does that have to do with me?"

"She wants to meet you," Eveda answered as if it were the most horrible thing that she could wish for.

I smiled despite her mood, "Cool, when?"

"Right now." Eveda said curtly, "Grab a jacket. Let's go."

Running to my closet, I pulled off the nearest hoodie and pulled it over my green tank top.

"So, is she a deity as well?" I asked curiously, hurrying to keep up with Eveda's long strides.

"Yes, I made her one after I became a goddess," Eveda answered, her tone indicating that it wasn't one of her better ideas.

"What is she the goddess of?" I asked, not taking the hint.

"Fashion." Replied Eveda as if it were a curse word.

"How old is she?" I asked, still fascinated about how time works here.

"In human years? 87." Answered Eveda.

"And in your years?" I asked, scared but curious.

"Oh about 312 years." Replied Eveda casually.

"Oookay then," I said, trailing off my voice, extremely confused and disoriented, deciding now was a good time to change the conversation.

"Actually, I have been meaning to ask you something, how old is the art realm? It looks incredibly developed but haven't you only been a goddess for 15 years, so how are there so many other god's here as well?" I pondered.

Eveda thought for a moment. "It's because time goes a lot faster here than in the human world, remember? A day here is an hour there. So for here, I have been a goddess for a few hundred years, give or take."

I panicked all of a sudden, coming to a realization my voice had left me as I placed my hand on the wall to stop myself from falling.

Finding my voice again, I croaked, "Hold on, so if I age a year here, then it's only been fifteen days in the human world."

"It's complicated," Eveda replied, choosing her words carefully, "People will physically age at a similar rate, but mentally it will be a bit different."

I nodded, pretending to understand her, "Oh, riiiiight."

Eveda stopped in front of a door that was painted gold and covered in colorful ribbons. She knocked twice, and the door opened, revealing a very stylish older woman. She was wearing sparkling stilettos that were six inches tall and a pair of white and gold jeans with a diamond-encrusted belt showing off her thin calves. Her black top had frills on the bottom and near the arms, with shiny cobalt blue peeking out from the inside. The long neck line showed off her delicate collar bone and fair skin. Blue and gold hoop earrings hung from her ears, matching the many bracelets along her arms. There was a necklace that spelled out *artists* in diamond letters. Three rings adorned her long bony finger, three rings blue and one gold, and one silver, each an inch long.

My eyes trailed up to her cherry-red lips and high cheekbones. Her long false lashes matched the shiny rose petal pink eye shadow on her eyelids. Long hair poured over her shoulder like a golden river of curls. There was hardly a wrinkle on her face, making her look 20 years younger than I was told.

"Wow." was all I was able to get out.

"She recently discovered botox,"

My jaw hung open.

"Close your mouth before a pixie flies in," I shut my mouth.

"Ahh, Piper, darling nice to finally meet you," My grandma said in a sing-song voice, coming over to embrace me. She smelled like expensive perfume and foundation.

I heard Eveda sign noisily, sounding annoyed while muttering, "The things I put up with to live with my mom."

The louder she said, "You have ten minutes, mom. I need Piper back after that."

My grandma gave her a million-dollar smile, "Well, that's wonderful. Come in, come, Piper. Can I offer you some Buzzlebird Tarts I imported from the Flitter realm?

"Uhh, sure, thanks," I replied, feeling slightly underdressed in the posh room, wearing a grey hoodie and a pair of jeans.

She pulled towards two plushy pink chairs around a roaring fire and set down a plate of the "Buzzlebird Tarts." I grabbed one and popped it into my mouth. I nearly spit it out. It felt as if I had thrown fireworks onto my tongue. Trying to suppress a gag, I reached out and gulped down some of the tea that she had set down next to me.

My grandmother chuckled, "Sorry, I didn't mean to scare you there."

I gulped, trying to blink tears out of my eyes, "it's all good."

She laughed and apologized. "How are you enjoying the art realm, my darling?" She asked, her topaz eyes gazing into mine.

I cocked my head, "I'm enjoying it more than I thought I would." I replied truthfully.

164

She clucked in sympathy.

"So you're related to Eveda?" I asked, trying to be polite.

"By blood, yes, but I sometimes doubt it. Between us, I think she's jealous." My grandma answered.

I nearly spit out my tea, laughing, "What?!"

"I mean, just between the two of us." She continued, looking at the door. "She just can't dress as well as I can."

I pretend to zip my lips, "Not a peep, grandma."

"Ahh." She slapped my knee, still laughing, "Don't call me grandma. Makes me feel old, my name's Carina."

"Okay, Carina." I giggled, looking around.

"You have a very nice room," I said politely, looking around at the golden silk hanging from the windows.

Carina laughed, "Oh, this is nothing you should see in my closet."

I turned to look as she walked towards a massive purple door with baby pink crystal stars jutting out like door knobs. She pulled the closet door open, and my jaw dropped. The closet was bigger than the room itself. It looked as if it had come right out of a Barbie movie. I walked towards it, wondering if it had been angled to look larger, but as I made my way inside, I realized that wasn't the case. In fact, the closet seemed to go on forever in all directions. I grinned, wishing Amy was with me to see this. Grandma-I mean Carina, began explaining each article of clothing to me.

"My third husband gave me this scarf on our second anniversary. Not sure why I still have it. Oh, and this belt is from Sacs. I bought it when I visited the human world back in '89. Wow, I haven't worn this dress in ages, I sewed it for Eveda years ago, but she claimed it was too scandalous."

165

The tour continued and probably would have gone on for twelve years had Eveda hadn't burst in, her face contorted into an expression of anger and panic. "Time to go Piper!"

Carina rolled her eyes, "I love Eveda to death, but she can be so uptight." She whispered to me

I giggled, giving her a quick hug as Eveda tugged me away, "I'll talk to you again soon!"

"Oh wait, dear, I have a present for you!" She called before Eveda could drag her out.

I looked at her in excitement, "Oh no, grand-- I mean Carina, I can't--." I blushed, wishing that I could give her something in return.

"Oh, Piper, don't worry about it. Here come." Carina walked to her closet.

I glanced at Eveda, waiting for her approval. She nodded once, and I grinned at her, "I'll be quick." I promised.

I followed Carina, and she pressed a small box into my hand. "Just a little get-to-know-you present, Piper."

I smiled, pulling the ribbon on the box and opening it. Inside lay a flashy ring. It was an inch thick with gold platings and a massive emerald in the center. A bit too flamboyant for my liking, but I slipped it onto my thumb. "Thanks, Carina," I said with a grin. She gave me another hug, and I skipped out of the room to Eveda. She was checking her watch frantically, looking more annoyed than my real mom, wait, no fake mom...nevermind. I looked at Eveda, trying to figure out if I was irritated or understanding, but when I was about to open my mouth, an alarm began blaring through the halls. 1 pressed my hands against my ears and looked around in a panic.

"What's going on? I yelled as the loud gong began pounding my head, blocking out all other sounds. Eveda yelled something at me, but I couldn't hear her. She shook her head, grabbed my arm, and dragged me to the dining room where all of the adults of the art realms were gathering their students and children. Eveda waved her hand, and the gong stopped just as quickly as it had started. I let my hands drop from my ears and tried to calm my pounding heart.

"Eveda, what's going on?!" I asked loudly, my ear still ringing.

She didn't respond, running over to a group of deities. Someone tapped my shoulder, and I nearly jumped out of my skin.

"Piper, what's going on." Ethan's voice asked, and I spun around to face him.

"I don't know," I replied truthfully, tucking a strand of hair behind my ear. "Has the bell ever rung before?"

He turned white as a sheet, "Well, once, but... never mind. That can't be happening again."

I was about to ask him what had happened when Eveda called for quiet.

"It seems," She began, holding her head up, "That our situation is worse than we had predicted. The three brothers have just notified me that Charlid has produced offspring that are part human. They process the ability to travel between realms."

There was a collective gasp, and the room was filled with panicked whispers.

"How did this happen?!" I asked Ethan desperately.

He furrowed his eyebrows together, "Someone must have entered the Realm of Charlid and brought humans in."

"But then this must be going on longer than we thought." I whispered, my blood turning to ice, "If they are traveling through the realms on their own, they can't be that young."

167

"At least eight years to travel without an adult," Ethan repeated, his voice so low I could barely hear. He cursed.

"Because of this change, there will be new rules in-placed," Continued Eveda, silencing all whispers, "No children are allowed into the forest. We do not know the power of these new in-betweens, so they could be lurking anywhere. The only time you may leave your room is for any sort of training, medical emergency, or other situation that can not be postponed. If anything changes, I will have a deity escort you out either to safety or--Gods forbid, battle. This is for your protection. Please do not disobey."

Eveda stood down from the podium, and the murmuring continued. She made her way toward and began to speak quickly as if she were a recording, "Piper, you will begin searching for Emensaly in the morning. Finding her is more important now than ever. You may choose whoever you wish to accompany you." She turned away to a man who had green and webbed frog-like hands.

Heat crept up my spine, and my eyes went in and out of focus. Ethan was saying something, but my ears felt like they were stuffed with wet cotton. I stumbled, and my legs turned to lead, and bile filled the back of my throat.

"E-Ethan?" I asked, my voice feeling as if it were a million miles away.

Something grabbed my hand, "What did Eveda say?" A voice asked, sounding like it was under water.

"I-I." I tried to respond, but my heart was pounding so loudly that I couldn't hear my own thoughts.

"Piper!" A voice yelled, and I felt a hand slap me across the face.

I shook my head and rubbed my stinging cheek, my vision clearing, "Ow."

"Dude, what happened?" He asked, his voice laced with concern. "What did Eveda tell you."

"I-" I gulped, trying to focus on my breathing and not the words that were coming out of my mouth, "leave tomorrow."

"*We* leave tomorrow," He corrected, his green eyes earnest, "You can't honestly think I'm letting you do that alone."

I felt like collapsing at least that one ray of sunshine, breaking through the cloud, "Bu-but, how, Ethan, how are we going to do this? We're thirteen. I've never even been outside the country, I---."

"Piper, Piper," He said in a calm voice, "Chill out. We'll be fine."

I was about to burst out with more hysteria when Eveda began speaking again. "Everyone will go to their dormitories tonight. Professor Evergreene, and Master Revac will bring you tonight. Do not open the door under any circumstance unless the pledge of the art realm is chanted."

I was barely listening, my breathing still uneven, and my heart racing a million miles a second. The students began moving to the door, and my legs followed even though my mind was on a different planet. I don't remember going up the stairs and down the hallway. I must have unconsciously put my pajamas on and gotten into bed. My mind was a numb shell, and my stomach was a bundle of nerves.

***

I woke the next morning feeling slightly lightheaded as three knocks on my door woke me up and began reciting some pledge I didn't understand and then permitted me to go to breakfast. Sitting at the table, I pushed my scrambled eggs around my plate, my stomach too tied up to eat anything.

"Morning," Ethan said, his smile looking a bit strained.

"Hey," I replied, my mind replaying all of the different ways that I might die today.

We ate in silence, only breaking it to tell each other to eat while consuming nothing ourselves.

Eveda entered the dining room, her hair a bird's nest and the bags under her eyes a profound shade of purple. She made a B-line towards us, and I straight, shoving my hands in my pockets to stop them from shaking. "Hey Eveda." I greeted, my voice a few octaves too high.

"Hello, darling." She replied, her voice rushed, "Come with me, you too, Ethan, since I assume you will be accompanying Piper."

I stood, knocking over my glass of orange juice in the process, cursing. I leaned over to mop it up, but Eveda stopped me, "No time for that, follow me."

I left my uneaten eggs on the table and followed her, stealing a glance at Ethan. Eveda led us back up to our dorms and sighed, "Piper, I apologize for springing everything on you so quickly. This is all happening very fast. It's stressful for all of us, but I need you to stay strong."

I nodded, focusing on how to breathe.

Eveda gave me a strained smile and handed me a weird fluffy *thing* with fangs the same color as *Walnut Nom. 61*. "Here you go, begin packing your things."

I took a step back, eyeing it wearily, "Uhhh, what *is* that?"

"Packmares." Ethan and Eveda both replied.

"And those are....?"

"Creature from the *furi* realm. They're dead useful on long journeys." Ethan replied. "They speak up to two-hundred languages and can hold up to three tons worth of luggage and make it seem as if you aren't carrying anything?" Eveda added.

I gulped, "I'm supposed to put my stuff in that? It has fangs!"

"Fangs to protect your belongings." Ethan explained, giving me the "duh" expression.

"Ah, okay," I said, looking skeptically at the large brown furry bags. Both were incredibly shaggy and resembled under groomed sheep. It also didn't escape my notice that the *packmares* had the last syllable of "nightmares" in it. This journey was starting off just great.

"Well get packing." Eveda said, "And hurry up."

I nodded, tentatively grabbing the *packmare*. Walking down the hallways, I opened my door and randomly began pulling clothing off the closet that had appeared when I first arrived. I dumped all of my things onto my bed, unsure of how I was going to get it into my *packmare*. The only opening was guarded by fangs, and I sorta planned on keeping all ten fingers.

"Oh, come on, I don't bite." said a disembodied, annoyed male voice. I jumped as my heart skipped a beat.

I cursed. "Who's in my room?" I asked, trying to sound braver than I felt.

"Down here, princess," It taunted.

I moved my eyes down to look for where the sound was coming from, but all I could see was my *packmare*.

"Hold on, are you my *packmare*?" I asked now, more curious than frightened.

The voice sounded offended as it replied, "I have a name, you know."

I laughed, "Riiiiight."

"My name is Grassian Machilo Atticus Prescot Sebastian Hubert. Thank you very much." The *packmare* answered in a snotty voice.

I laughed, "You're joking."

The fangs on the backpack seemed to snap, "I most certainly am not. How dare you insult my honor. I should have you beheaded for such treason--."

I snorted, "Dude, chill. How 'bout I call you Grass, it sort of sounds like your first name."

An angry voice filled the room, "The absolute nerve of some in-betweens, my ancestors used to be worshipped by your kind, we were raised onto a pedestal and adorned with flowers, we were--."

"Clearly working with someone else." I interrupted impatiently, "Now open up, Grass. I got to put my stuff away."

The *packmare* growled but unhinged his jaw. I tentatively balled up my shirt and dropped it inside, "Hurry up, I haven't got all day." Grass snapped.

I retracted my hand just in time to avoid getting it a bit off. "Careful." I scolded, "I need my fingers."

If a *packmare* could roll its eyes, I'm sure Grass would have. Luckily I was able to get the rest of my stuff in and keep injuries limited. After packing toiletries, snickers, clothing, the petal I had won in survival 101(that still wouldn't let me eat it), and the ring my grandma gave me, I hung Grass's sloth-like arms around my shoulders. I was surprised at how normal it felt, almost like a backpack minus the claws, of course. I exited my room and made my way back to Eveda. Ethan was already waiting there, and Eveda was looking around distractedly. "Ah, wonderful, there you are, Piper.

Both of you come with me. I'll take you to the flower garden and explain the map before you leave.

She turned on her heel, and we ran to keep up.

"Map?" I whispered.

Ethan only shrugged.

Eveda brought us to the door that led to the flower garden. She handed us a standard map of the color Chanterelle Beige #6185-31 that was worn and crinkled. There were hundreds of different flowers scattered all over the map. Some of them had small prints next to them, while others remained undefined. The oddest part was that it seemed to glow green in a few areas.

"This is an *ivela* map," Eveda proclaimed, handing it to us, "It's the biggest export of the art realm. It is a map of the flower garden. Some of the flowers are labeled by *blanxies*, realm explorers while some haven't been investigated yet. There are different types of maps, but they are especially useful for finding specific items. If you can't remember where you got your buzzleber tarts, the map can tell you which realm to look in. In this particular map, the setting has been switched to finding any type of earth channeling. It displays which realms Emensaly might have visited."

I gulped, looking at the map. There were more than a dozen glowing orbs dancing across the paper, "we have to visit all of them?"

Eveda pursed her lips, "I certainly hope not. I pray that you will find some sort of clue as to where she is in the first few realms. Oh, and remember, the only way back to the flower garden is to go back where it dropped you off."

The part of my mind that hadn't really caught up with the gravity of the situation vaguely wondered how a deity could pray.

"Well, if there are no more questions…" Eveda asked, trailing off.

I had a million, most of them starting with, "What if I die?" but I managed to stay quiet.

"Good luck dears." She replied, giving us both a quick hug, "You'll be fine."

And with that, she led us out to the flower garden and closed the door, clearing in a rush to go back to whatever realm leaders did. I looked back, realizing how quickly that had just happened. We were actually going to go look for Emensaly.

I turned to Ethan taking a big breath, "Right, this is actually happening." I held the map up, "Where to, captain?"

He laughed, trailing his finger over the paper, "How about *Ledolish* land? It doesn't seem all that dangerous. I'm pretty sure they're just these small dwarfs that like to cook."

I had a strange thought of being Snow White. " As long as we don't meet Grumpy, I think we'll be fine." I laughed at my own joke.

He furrowed his eyebrows, "Who?"

I rolled my eyes, "What exactly did you do throughout your childhood?"

He opened his mouth to protest, but I interrupted him, "What does their flower look like?"

Ethan squinted, "It kind of looks like a gingerbread cookie. According to the map, it should be somewhere to our left."

I turned, trying to navigate around the flowers that were as tall as my waist. "Ummmm, I think I see it." I pointed to a flower that was about twenty feet away.

I pulled Grass off my back to stash the map. I pried open up the fangs when they immediately snapped on my finger. I retracted my hand and let out a yelp.

I cursed loudly. "Dude, I'm not stealing anything. It's already my stuff."

I heard a snore, "Oh, oops, sorry." Grass replied, not sounding apologetic at all. "I was sleeping."

"Uh-huh, sure, whatever, just open up," I said, trying to keep my voice leveled. Grass slowly, slowly opened the fangs. I groaned and reached inside, and forcefully pulled the fangs apart to open the bag.

"Oww." Grass moaned, "I think you broke my jaw.."

I ignored him and threw the *packmare* over my back. I ran after Ethan, careful not to bump into the surrounding plants. We approached the flower, and the smell of Christmas filled my nostrils. The *Autumn Bronze Nom. 2162-W3* colored petals were decorated with red, white, green, and yellow frosting. They looked so crispy and soft that I was positive that it was real cake batter. Leaning over, I took another whiff. Ethan had already sculpted two *onres* and handed me the odd straw contraption. Thanking him, I bent over slightly and stuck the straw into the nectar. Taking a long drink, I relished the taste. It was liquid gingerbread. The tingly taste stuck to the roof of my mouth, and I grinned.

Soon the warm sensation began to spread over me, and I received the uncomfortable feeling of having my molecules rearranged. I groaned, knowing what was about to happen. Everything became a blur as I began spinning through space. Getting so dizzy that I thought I would black out, it finally stopped, and I landed flat on my back, trying to get back my balance. Black spots danced in front of my eyes, and I put my hands up to my head, trying to stop the spinning. Next to me, I heard Ethan groan and saw that he looked as green as I felt.

"I hate doing that," mumbled Ethan, still trying to get up.

I stood looking and looked around. It wasn't exactly what I had envisioned. There wasn't a single dwarf singing *Heigh Ho*. There wasn't much of anything here, to be honest. Ethan and I stood in the center of a large piece of land. It was as if we had gone back in time and entered a 1950 black-and-white sitcom show. The sky and the ground were all the same depressing shade of grey. It was as if someone had spilled a can of *Kendall Charcoal #HC-170* paint onto the realm. "What the…"

I turned to Ethan, my feet crunching in dry soil, "Ethan, Ethan, I think we're in the wrong place. We--." My voice was cut out by the sound of a gunshot, and I dropped to the floor in terror and screamed.

Half a second later, a silver bullet landed right next to where I had been standing the previous second. I screamed again. Ethan looked around and panicked.

"What's going on?!" I hissed, "Where are the singing dwarfs?"

Ethan commented and looked around in panic, "We have to get to that city over there. We're too exposed here."

"What if we're in the wrong place?!" I yelled.

"We can't go back. A flower needs an hour to produce nectar and rejuvenate, so we can't get back to the flower garden."

"We should get to that city," I said, pointing at a few run-down buildings, maybe twenty meters in the distance. Well, maybe the word "city" was a stretch.

Ethan nodded, still lying on the ground next to me. I lifted my head upwards slightly to look at the city, hoping it would provide shelter. To be honest, it looked more like a pile of broken rocks. My heart pounded into my chest as we crawled towards it on our stomachs. My eyes were darting back and forth in panic, and I prayed that no one would see us. I inhaled a bit of dust and tried to choke down a cough. The silence was deafening. The wind was whistling faintly, and I could hear the faint sound of explosions richting from the direction of the city. Part of me still couldn't believe it was real.

We hadn't witnessed any more gunshots, so perhaps the one before was a stray, and no one had seen up. At last, we arrived at the "city." I stood tentatively, dusting off my shirt, and winced slightly at my scratched elbows. The shards of glass in the soil had been yet another unpleasant surprise.

One of the slightly more intact houses had a few dwarf-like creatures inside, and I motioned Ethan toward it. "I guess we are in the right spot." I shrugged, gesturing to the Ledos.

We walked through the wooden door, and I was immediately overpowered by the smell of hard liquor and stale bread. I scrunched up my nose and tried to breathe through my mouth. There was one dingy light bulb in the center of the room that was flickering on and off. The windows were covered by mildew, and the floor creaked with every step I took. The wooden walls seemed to be disintegrating and peeling off by the second. There was a slight buzz of chatter and glasses clinking through the room.

"I have a feeling underaged kids shouldn't be in here." Said Ethan rubbing his shoulders uncomfortably.

"Yeah, well, I have a feeling that this isn't the place we saw on the map," I replied, sounding a lot more confident than I felt.

I grabbed Ethan's sleeve and pulled him to the closest Ledo, one which was swaying back and forth. He was wearing patched-up overalls and a tee-shirt that was covered in so much filth that I couldn't tell what the original color was. There was a suspicious liquid running down his chin, and it was caught in his frizzy goatee. His mouth hung open, and his *#N210-7 Havana Coffee Matte*-colored eyes dropped in exhaustion. He seemed to be having a conversation with himself. There were mops of *Green Garden Sage #235-Fd2* hairs on his head, each standing up as if they were about to be struck by

177

lightning. His face was a map of scratches and wrinkles, each uglier than the next. Despite all of that, I could see his ribs protruding out of his overall, and his arms were skinnier than twigs. Everything within five feet of him smelled of rotten gin. Swallowing down the bile that had crawled up my throat, I approached him.

"Hello," I said as pleasantly as I could, with the smell so overpowering I could almost taste it.

"Giii-Giiiraaaaffes aarre iilliteeeraaate." He slurred with a hiccup.

I straighten my spine, wiping my sweaty palms on my jeans.

"Um, right," I replied, trying to keep my voice leveled. "Could you tell us what has happened to Ledolish Land?"

"Ledooo's reevolllt," He putting his finger up as if he were giving a lecture, "Mmmad at Giraffes, hehe, griiiaffes. Stooopid Giraffes. Girrrraffes illiteraaate, ignooore threattt letters." He continued, eyes glossy, drifting around the room. "Goonnaa, uh gonnaaa revolllt."

I rolled my eyes, getting ready to stand up. This was pointless. Maybe we would have better luck with a Ledo who was actually sober. Ethan, on the other hand, leaned forward, interested.

"Are you getting any of this?" I asked him.

"Yeah, I think so." He replied. "The people here are called Ledos, right? We read how this was a dictatorship. I think the Ledos are revolting against the dictators."

"How did you get all of that?" I asked, amazed.

He pointed to a bunch of signs on the wall. Most of them had images of crowns being destroyed and giraffes dead on the floor. One read, "Ledo's rid of the giraffes." "Get the crown." "Steal back our rights." "Submit the threat letters to HB152."

I dropped my head into my hand, "Of course, the one time we need to be in Ledolish land, they are in the middle of a revolution."

"I bet the dictator is hushing it all up, or else all of the realms would have heard about this by now." Replied Ethan.

"Okay...." I said, realizing we were getting off-topic. I turned back to the Ledo. "We were wondering if you have ever heard of someone named Emensaly. You see, we are looking for her."

"Aaaah I-I had a friend named Emms-," He replied, crossing his eyes, "They, I--." The Ledo frowned and changed his train of thought, "Giiraafes are Illlllliterate."

I groaned, "Let's go. I bet the chair would be easier to get answers out of than this buzzed idiot."

Ethan sighed, "Yeah, you're probably right." We turned around to leave when we were stopped by a young Ledo. She had patched-up brown boots. She was wearing a pair of baggy trousers that were covered in rips and a dirty yellow cardigan that was missing three buttons. Her face was tear-stained, but her shoulders were squared. She was shorter than Jack. In fact, she only came up to my ribs, but her face had lost its child-like roundness. She could maybe pass for ten. Her shoulder-length *Webster Green (HC-130)* hair was filled with knots, and the bags under her eyes were the same shade as *Perfectly Purple Matte #PPG1176-7*. Her feet were bare and calloused, which seemed dangerous considering the rubbled that littered the street. Still, there was a gleam of determination in her eyes that unsettled me.

"I couldn't help but overhear that you were looking for Emensaly." She said in a high squeaky voice.

"Bet you could." I murmured while Ethan answered, "Yeah, we are."

"I've seen her before." She replied, going up on her tippy toes, her voice businesslike.

"You have?!" I asked excitedly, forgetting everything my Dad ever taught me about bargaining, "Do you know where she is? Can you tell us?"

The girl pressed her fingers together just like Ernst Blofeld from James Bond.

"Let's talk in a place that's more private." She said, trying to sound superior.

I repressed a sigh, of course. We were probably running a wild goose chase. I looked at Ethan, and he shrugged his shoulders, "We don't have any other choice." He said, quiet enough for only me to hear.

I rolled my shoulders back, trying to release the tension. Well, here goes nothing.

***

The Ledo girl led us out through the door and walked through the mostly deserted streets. There were a few Ledos huddled around a dumpster fire and another one who I convinced myself was sleeping. The girl crawled between two buildings that were on the brink of collapsing and crab-walked under a pile of charred wood. After getting my pants and palms, all cut up, she led us through a small hole that opened up to a tiny shack. The dusty floor was uneven and had pieces of splinters popping up. There was a dirty grey sleeping back in the corner straw on top of a thin moth-eaten blanket. To the left, a dark brown pot over an empty fireplace. Their small window was covered in a thick layer of dirt that made it hard to distinguish where the glass started and the wall ended. I saw a beetle skittering across the flooring, and I flinched, taking a step back. I didn't realize that my jaw had dropped open until Ethan nudged me. I felt a wave of sympathy. This was no way to live. Newfound respect was born for the girl.

"Make yourself comfortable." The girl said sarcastically.

180

I squatted down, not trusting the floor. I had a feeling that I couldn't get a tetanus shot anywhere around here.

"So I hear you are looking for someone named Emensaly." She began, still standing.

"Yes," Ethan said simply, mastering the poker face.

"I know where she is." The Ledo replied firmly, "But I won't give that away for free."

"What do you mean?" I asked, keeping my voice leveled like Ethan's.

"My name is Marlee Swoles. I want you to help me get my sister Riley back." She answered, sounding as if the phrase had been rehearsed hundreds of times. Her voice was stern, but there were tears pooling in her eyes.

"What happened to her?"

"The giraffes took her. She was stealing bread from their storage supply because we were starving. They took her to the prison underneath the castle." Her voice was leveled, still sounding like she was reading off a piece of paper. "Help me get her back, and I'll tell you where Emensaly went.

"Deal." I said immediately, while Ethan replied, "No way." at the same time.

"What is wrong with you?" I hissed. "This is our best shot?"

"How do we know that she actually has information about Emensaly? Besides, do you know how deadly it will be to break her sister out of prison? Be realistic. "

"What other leads do we have?" I asked crossly.

"No, I understand why he wants proof, and I can show it to you." Said Marlee calmly as if she was finally certain of something, a little bit of life returning to her voice. "Come with me."

Marlee led us to the dirty window and showed us a small plant that seemed to be growing out of a slightly cracked flower pot. It was a small lily similar to that had brought me to the golden god kingdom. It had four petals red, blue, white, and a thriving green. It was a sign. As if that wasn't enough, when I unfocused my eyes the way to see the aura, it was pulsing green.

"Wow," said Ethan.

"Where did you get it?" I asked breathlessly, inching closer.

"Emensaly gave it to me," Marlee answered smugly.

"What?" I asked, feeling as if my mind couldn't take it anymore.

"It was a while ago," Said Marlee, "It was when I was with Riley. There was a woman who came to our door and asked to spend the night. She seemed so powerful and kind that we helped her. In the morning, she was gone, the seed left in her place. It blossomed in less than a day, pulsing earth power."

"So where is she now?" I asked eagerly.

"Well, I can't tell you that, or else you won't find my sister." Replied Marlee, pouting her bottom lip.

I groaned slightly, "Fine, but I hope you have a plan. I'm not Frank Morris or anything."

"I've only been in the castle once." Marlee answered truthfully, "But I know someone."

"Who?" asked Ethan, his expression still guarded.

"Officer Jaxon." She answered, walking over to the sleeping bag and began rolling it up. "He's my main source of income. I clean out Ledo houses that have been destroyed by the giraffe bombing. He has an obsession with hoarding treasure and pays me for whatever I find."

"And?" I asked impatiently.

"And, he works at the palace. Maybe we can barter some sort of priceless artifacts in exchange for information and access to the prison."

"Riiight, and you think we are carrying thousands of dollars worth of treasure?" Ethan interjected, his voice dripping in sarcasm.

"Well, I assume since you're from the art realm, you can handle creating a bit of fool's gold," Marlee said cooly, raising an eyebrow.

I stepped between them before Ethan could respond. "How did you know we are from the art realm?" I asked, biting my nails.

"Ledos don't see the way you do. We see auras. Everyone has a different one, and it reveals a lot about you. For instance, your gender, your parentage, your power, your name, and your age etc. It's sort of how snakes see with infrared. We see your character."

I rubbed my bare arms, feeling exposed. "But won't Officer Jaxon know that these treasures are fake? If he knows we come from the art realm, I mean."

Marlee grinned, "I have that covered. There are ways to block off being read by a Ledo. I've got something that will change how they read you."

"How?" Ethan asked, his voice no longer tense.

She rummaged through the sleeping bag and pulled out two small circular cases. "Contacts."

I cocked my head to the side, "You're joking."

Marlee shook her head and turned the case around to read the label, "Land: *Athletic realm,* Channeling power: *speed,* Name: *Anna,* Age *15,* Mother: *Ager, tree spirit*: Father: *Igoris, the deity of sprinting.*"

My jaw fell open, "You got all this from a pair of contacts?"

She grinned, "Yup."

"Where did you get those?" I asked, getting a bit closer.

Marlee laughed, "I could tell you, but then I'd have to kill you."

"I can't tell if she's being sarcastic or not," I murmured to Ethan.

She held up the other pair of contacts, "Here, Ethan, these are for you. Land: *Athletic realm,* Channeling power: *sprinting,* Name: *Maxen,* Age: *16,* Mother: *Magis, Ledo citizen,* Father: *Igoris deity of sprinting.*"

She handed us the light blue cases, and a sly smile crept across her face, "Put them in, and I'll call Officer Jaxon."

I took it tentatively, unscrewing the top. "Has anyone ever used these before?"

Marlee ignored me, and I took it as a sign to be warned.

I looked at the small piece of plastic, cringing away slightly. My mom had once gotten her contact stuck in her eye and needed to go to the emergency room. I wasn't really willing to go through that experience. Ethan looked just as uncomfortable as I felt. Taking one out, I tried to steady my hand and place it right into my eyes. I lifted the eyelid the same way my mom always did. It took a few tries until I was brave enough to actually stick a piece of plastic in my eyes. Blinking a few times, I rolled my eyes around, waiting for the contact to take place. When the world came back into focus, my mind seemed to change slightly. Instead of admiring the architecture as I had been before, I wondered where I could hang a basketball hoop and how quickly it would take me to do twelve laps around the room.

"This is weird." Ethan declared, looking at his hands as if it were the first time seeing them.

"When this is over, I want my sanity back," I mumbled, jumping from foot to foot.

"What do you want us to build?" Ethan asked, turning to Marlee.

She shrugged, already heading out the door, "I think he likes snakes." She called and slammed the door, causing the flower pot to shake.

I stared at Ethan in confusion. "Ummmm, any ideas."

He shook his head, already summoning a slab of clay out of his *pindre*, and glaring at it.

I put my fingers to my temple and tried to brainstorm. After a few minutes, I let out a breath of annoyance. This was the worst possible time to have an artist's block. What was going on?

Ethan snapped his head up, "The contact! I bet that's why we can't think of anything."

I slapped my forehead, "Of course." I reached up and tentatively took them out and put them back into the case. "We'll just have to put them back in when Officer Jaxon's here."

***

I stared at my paper, my brain going back to normal, "So let's do something flashy."

He nodded, placing his hands on his chin, "Some kind of jewelry that makes him feel powerful. Like a scepter."

"Oooh and crown." I said, then frowned, "Or is that pushing it?"

Ethan shook his head. "No, it's perfect. Let's get started. Who knows how long we have 'till Marlee gets back."

Nodding, I began to sketch the layout of my scepter. I lightly began tracing my outline, letting my hand take over. I wanted a golden rod as the base, and then I could work my way up. After a few rough drafts, I found my favorite and began. I planned on having a long golden rod with an elaborate snake climbing its way up. The snake had originally been green, but I decided sliver would look flashier. The scales were tedious, to say the least. Each one had to be drawn precisely in the shape of a diamond. Trying to make everything symmetrical, I ended up having to discard my paper when my eraser ripped a hole into the paper. Groaning in frustration, I began again.

My hand was cramped, but I added the shadows onto the diamond and highlights to the glinting silver. My fingers were covered in light green pastels, and I cursed, wiping them on my jeans, praying that they wouldn't leave an imprint on the gold. I set my blending stump and scrutinized the sketch. The diamonds were somewhat asymmetrical, and the forked tongue looked lopsided.

"Hurry!" Ethan urged, glancing out the window.

Before I could lose my nerve, I waved my hands, and the scepter peeled off the page, falling into my hand. I grinned, looking at it from every angle. It wasn't as bad as I had imagined.

It was bigger than expected but was more or less what I had intended. The golden rod in the center is about two inches in diameter. The silver snake curled its way up, its diamond-shaped scales glittering like silver gems. The massive emerald that sat on the top glinted in the dim light. The snake's head was a bit farther above the emerald and gave off the impression that it was guarding the precious jewel. A silver forked tongue lashed out of the snake's unhinged jaw, ready to attack at any moment. The only issue I realized was that there was no way of holding the rod without gripping the snake's scales, making it somewhat uncomfortable to touch.

Ethan was putting the finishing touches on his sculpture. Once satisfied, he waved his hand, and the crown grew to look like a gorgeous article of jewelry. It looked realistic enough to sit on Queen Elizabeth's head. The base was gold with a silver snake in between each of the longer piercings on the top. The two of us had decided to go with the treasure that belonged together. The snakes slithered along between the pointy headband. Its green eyes were expensive-looking emerald, and its tongue flicked out, revealing a sharp green jewel. If I squinted, it looked like an expensive disco ball.

I glanced out the window nervously, "Let's clean up and put the contacts back in. Marlee will be back soon."

"Okay."

We cleaned everything up into our *pindre* and popped the contacts back into our eyes. It was a little easier, but I still felt squeamish imagining a piece of plastic in front of my pupil.

Leaning against the wall, I pulled Grass the Packmare off my back and began tossing him in the air.

"Ow, what-ooff, mhwa." Grass yelled, letting out a muffled yelp. "Stop that this instant."

I laughed, setting him down. "Chill out."

"I will not chill out." Grass grumbled, "Why are we in Ledoish Land? This place is a death trap. Are you two suicidal? The Ledos are undergoing one of the deadliest revolutions in history."

I froze, "You knew!"

"Well, obviously," Grass replied smugly. "The giraffes are trying to cover it up, but people talk."

"And did you possibly think to tell us about it before we drank the nectar!?" I growled, my voice rising.

Grass began to say something but was interrupted by Marlee barging through the door, breathing hard. She began speaking in a rushed whisper. "He's coming, " I told him to wait outside and give me time to make the room decent. Here's your story. I told him that the two of you were exploring a cave in the fizzing mountains and came across the treasure. You were coming to visit Max's (Ethan's code name) Mom. Then you ran across me. Don't tell him what you are getting out of the deal. That'll just raise suspicion. Don't tell him we're saving my sister either."

"Okay," Ethan said as I repeated the information under my breath.

A deep voice that resembled a foghorn bellowed, "Miss Swoles, are you there?"

Marlee straightened her overalls and ran to get the door. "Remember the plan." She mouthed to us before opening up.

A large man who was nearly as wide as he was tall walked in and towered over Marlee. His beady eyes bulged out under his hooded eyelids, revealing black eyes with white pupils. They were too far away from each other to make up for his tiny nose. He smelled like hair gel and quesadillas, a scent that triggered my gag reflex. There were three *dark Evergreen #164-Fd3 hairs* on the top of his bald hair that was combed back as if that somehow made him more attractive. His massive neck rolls were big enough to hide at least three cans of soup. Tiny eyebrows looked like they had been sewn into his forehead and looked out of place in the sea of the *Orange Sherbet #98YR 65/33* skin.

"Ah, Marlee," He huffed, wiping sweat off his brow, "I'm getting old. This walk becomes longer every time."

188

Marlee muttered something under her breath that sounded a lot like, "Well, maybe if you weren't fatter than an adult elephant-."

Officer Jaxon pulled off his white coat and turned around to find a place to put it. "My, my, Marlee, didn't you tell me that you were cleaning up? Everything's covered in at least three layers of dust."

Marlee bit back a response, her eyes throwing daggers at an unaware Officer Jaxon. I glared at him as he draped his blingy coat over one arm. I was amazed that he could even hold it. The article of clothing was covered in so many gold and silver buttons it must have weighed over a ton. It looked like an over-decorated chandelier you don't trust yourself to walk under in fear of it falling on your head.

"Ah, here are your visitors." Officer Jaxon said, his voice becoming nearly as oily as his head. "Very nice to meet you, Anna and Max."

Ethan and I both bowed the way Marlee had instructed. I hoped that the dim light of the shack masked the disgust on my face. "We come from the athletic realm," Ethan said, his voice displaying no emotion. "We were visiting the Fizzing mountains and found many incredible objects. Marlee said that you were interested in bargaining."

I pulled the scepter and crown from my packmare, unwrapping them. Ethan and I decided that it would be smart to wrap the treasure in cloth to make it look as if we had been traveling. Officer Jaxon's eyes widened, and he took a step towards the "priceless" objects, "My oh my, these are exquisite. You found them in the Fizzing Mountains."

Ethan nodded once.

He reached for the scepter, but I pulled my hand back. "Not yet," I said firmly as if trying to get a child to obey me. Realizing that might not be the best way to approach him, I cleared my throat and tried again. "We need information on how to access the prison."

He clapped his meaty hands together, displaying the fat golden rings adorning his fingers. "Well, that's a large request, isn't it?" he asked, laughing. "I'll tell you what. Give me the scepter and the crown, and then I will give you the information you want."

I snorted, "Fat chance."

Officer Jaxon frowned, "Secrets are not to be taken lightly. Unlike objects, you can not give back information."

I crossed my arms. As easy as it would be for us to catch up with Officer Jaxon if he tried to run away, I had a feeling he had a lot more leverage in this realm than we did. Who knows what type of creatures and people he had at his disposal?

Marlee took a step forward, "We'll give you the crown once you get us into the castle unharmed, then the scepter once we escape *with* our prisoner."

Officer Jaxon rubbed the back of his neck, "Are you sure you want to go to prison? Who do you plan on breaking out? I assure you there is nothing more than psychotic Ledos in there."

Ethan grabbed Marlee's arms and stopped her from lunging at Officer Jaxon.

"We're sure," I affirmed, watching Ethan wrestle with Marlee from the corner of my eye.

Officer Jaxon pulled at his shirt collar, eyes darting between the treasure and the door. "Children, I-I don't know what to tell you. I haven't been down to the prison in years. Can't I offer you something else?" He asked helplessly, "Gold? Power? Food? I, for one, can never say no to a good fritada."

I resisted the urge to roll my eyes, "No. Give us access to the prison. If you refuse, there are many other people willing to bargain for these treasures. We met a few people in the Flitter Realm willing to pay a hefty price." I said, making that last part up. The Flitter realm was the only one I could remember, thanks to my grandma's tarts.

"Children look at it from my perspective." He begged.

"Don't think I can get my head that far up my butt," I muttered, and Ethan suppressed a laugh.

"It's illegal," Officer Jaxon continued, "I could lose my job. In fact I should report you to the authorities right now. Yes I will do that. Of course if you gave me your treasure I could turn a blind eye in your direction." He said, changing tactics.

"Well then that might be a problem. My friend and I might just leave. I'm sure we could find other people who will value the treasure more than you do. Come on Pi-Anna." Ethan said, pretending to open his packmare.

"No, no, no, don't do that." Jaxon interrupted, stepping closer to Ethan.

Ethan continued to pack his stuff, acting as if he didn't notice.

"Fine, fine you win, don't give the treasure away." He caved, in a desperate voice.

I reminded myself to praise Ethan's acting skills later.

Chapter 21

"Getting you to the prison will be the simplest part. I thought that we could give you some sort of costume, to make it look like you are giraffe staff. Perhaps a chef, we could get you into the building by saying that you're delivering food to my suite. Yes, yes that's a good idea. Very believable, I have chefs coming in 24/7." Officer Jaxon planned, licking his lips.

I refrained from commenting.

"How will we get from your room to the prison?" Ethan asked, absentmindedly playing with his finger.

Officer Jaxon looked around, as if trying to think of an idea.

"How about we deliver food for the prisoner?" Marlee asked, sitting up.

"Yes, yes good." He replied, "I'll have someone escort you three to the dungeon."

"How do we break, Ri- I mean the prisoner out?" I asked, praying Officer Jaxon didn't notice my slip.

He frowned, "I'm not sure how the prisons operate. I'm sure that the guards down there have specific keys for each cell but I'm not certain what other barriers stand between you and this illegend prisoner."

I suppressed a groan, "Well that seems reliable. What are we going to do about the guards? I highly doubt that they will peacefully stand next to us as we remove the er..prisoner."

Ethan spoke up, "What about that thing you did in survival 101 with the wind up toy. Maybe we can cause some sort of distraction or noise, make them leave the prison for some time."

"I can arrange that." Officer Jaxon said, "I'll raise the alarm for the west hall."

"Perfect." Marlee grinned, "Then we'll sneak out of the prison and find our way to an exit."

"Wait wait." Officer Jaxon interjected, "What about my treasure, you have to give me the scepter before you leave."

Marlee rubbed the back of her neck uncomfortably, "Can't Pi-Anna and Max bring it to you?"

"No!" Ethan and I both yelled.

"You'll just slip right out through our fingers," Ethan said, raising his voice.

"What if we give it to you before we go into the prison?" She asked, her voice having gone up a few octaves.

"Forget it." I said frustrated, "How do we know he won't throw us in prison the moment he gets what he wants."

Officer Jaxon held a hand up to his heart in feign shock, "I would never-I am a man of honor."

"Spare me." I interrupted, holding my hand up.

"Why can't you just come back to my room and I'll escort you out?" Officer Jaxon asked, his voice confused. "You'll be safest when you're with me."

Marlee was quiet but after a few beats she sighed, "Okay sure."

Officer Jaxon stood dusting off the back of his pants, "Well if that settles it I'll send someone to bring you your costumes. Try to be quick, I have a dinner party at six that I can't afford to skip."

Bet you could, I thought bitterly.

193

He turned and pulled open the door. After it swung shut I let out a breath. This was it, we were actually breaking someone out of prison. I still didn't totally understand how we had gotten into this situation. Somehow I had gone from complaining about the song Baby Shark to intruding in on a Ledo rebellion and breaking some kid out of a Giraffe prison. I rolled my shoulders back, well, at least I wasn't camping.

***

The next half hour was a special type of torture. Ethan, Marlee and I paced around the room creating a dent in the bare floor. I hated waiting, the entire mission was terrifying enough without me having time to mull over all the different ways this could end badly. After ten minutes Ethan suggested that we began to pack up the treasure into our packmares.

I picked up my packmare, "Open up Grass."

"Stop calling me that." he muttered indignantly, "Are we still with that Ledo chick?"

I frowned at him, "I need to put the scepter away."

"What's my real name?" He asked, jaw still clamped shut.

"I don't have time for this!"

"What. Is. My. Real. Name?"

"Ummm Sir Gracius Sebastian, something, something." I tried massaging my temple.

If a packmare could roll his eyes, Grass probably would have, "Close enough." He murmured, opening his mouth.

I cursed and dropped the scepter a bit more forcefully than necessary. There was a knock at the door and I dropped Grass in fright. A muffled, "What the-." Came from him.

"Who is it?" Ethan asked Marlee in a hushed whisper as she peaked through a hole in the door.

"A Legif." She replied. "Probably the one Officer Jaxon sent."

"A what?" I asked, trying to keep my voice low.

"A Legif." She replied, still turned away from me, "In Ledolish land there are different classes of power, kinda like castes. Ledos are on the bottom and Giraffes are on the top. Legifs are sort of in the middle. They aren't as short as Ledos, but haven't been promoted to full giraffes. The highest possible position is royal giraffe, but you only get that title if you're related to the dictator himself, or part of his private cabinet."

"Wait but we were almost as tall as Officer Jaxon. Won't people notice that we don't look like Ledos once we put on our costumes?"

Marlee shook her head, "The contacts will take care of that," She explained while opening the door.

The Legif walk in a I was suddenly overpowered by the scent of cologne. I'm not talking spritz spritz, this was full blow middle school boy cologne, as in dumping the whole bottle on their head.

Breathing through my mouth I took a step back. He was smiling entusaitically, his green eyebrows hiding beneath his thinning sage hair. He was breathing heavily and holding three large packages in his wrinkled hands. "Officer Jaxon asked me to give you this." The Legif said, bouncing on the balls of his feet nervously.

He handed us a bulky parcel that must have been our costumes.

"Ah, thanks," Marlee said, taking it from him and trying to close the door. The Legif stuck his foot inside, and leaned . "Do you need any help changing or..."

Marlee gave him a look of disgust and shot up a rude hand gesture, "Get out of my house."

"Aw come on, baby." He said pushing into the room.

I looked at the Ledig in horror, "Get out."

I swung the door shut, hitting the freakish Legif as he let out a satisfying yelp.

I cursed softly, "Geez, that guy's-."

"Crazy." Ethan finished. While Marlee said, "Disgusting."

"Anyway, put on your costume quickly." She interjected, looking giddy.

"Right, right," I replied, ripping the packages open. There were three white aprons, cream-colored slacks, and the same-colored shirt. In the next one, there were three pairs of contacts with random Ledo names and a pair of instructions on how to use them. In the third box, there was an assortment of pastries that made my mouth water. At first, I thought they were for us, but a note explained that they were our props and we were supposed to bring them to Officer Jaxon. I pulled the white clothing over my jeans and t-shirt and tied one of the aprons around my waist.

"Good thing Officer Jaxon didn't deliver these," Ethan said, holding up a pair of contacts.

"Oh yeah, that would have been a nightmare." I replied, "He'd know that the treasure's fake if he saw us replace our contacts with these."

"We should probably bring the contacts you're wearing right now." Marlee added, pulling a pair of contacts out of her eyes and replacing them with the ones officer Jaxon gave her, "Just in case he wants his back."

"Wait, you've been wearing contacts the whole time?" I asked, hiding my sneakers under a pair of white cloth.

"I don't need people recognizing me." She said, with a tone of finality that stopped me from prodding.

Once we had adjusted all of our aprons and blinked our contacts into place, we began the walk to the castle. Marlee led us out of the door and towards the giraffes' castle. It wasn't incredibly far from her shack, a ten to fifteen-minute walk. As the three of us maneuvered between the dilapidated buildings and destroyed streets, I was surprised by the number of dirty looks shot my way. There were Ledos squeezing out of the rubble to glare at us, their hungry stares following our every move. I kept my head down, wishing that I could throw the box of pastries down at their feet. They deserved it so much more than Officer Jaxon. I tried to avert my gaze from them and tried to focus on the palace that was looming in front of me.

It looked as if I were gazing at a portal. The building shined with power and light. The white walls had a tint of *Opalescent Pearl #173d-2DA* making it shimmer in the light. I wondered how they made it look like the sun was shining onto the building. There seemed to be an invisible barrier that extended 100 meters in every direction of the palace bathing the area in artificial happiness. The landscape looked like a half finished drawing, as if someone started coloring but gave up halfway through. There were four massive towers that grew out of the center making it look like a sand castle.

"Sheesh, no wonder the Ledos are revolting," Ethan whispered.

"Yeah." I agreed, "Imagine living in a tiny little shack and seeing that every morning."

We continued walking in silence, maneuvering between broken street lands and shattered glass that littered the street. I looked down at Marlee's bare feet, wondering how she was planning on walking over it, but she marched over, unflinching. I followed her lead (grateful for my converse sneakers) until a sign taped to a somewhat intact building distracted me. There was a black a white picture of a ledo no older than fifteen. There were 12 freckles splattered across her nose and her hair in two braids. She was holding a prison plaque, and underneath the picture were the words written:

"VEGA FLINT HAS FINALLY BEEN CAPTURED. THE MURDERER OF THE ROYAL GIRAFFES HENRY HUSRON, MASON GEONE, KENDALL GREENE, AND ADENTA MORGAN. INSTIGATOR OF THE FIRE THAT BURNT DOWN THE MAURA TOWER, DESTROYING HUNDREDS OF IRREPLACEABLE DOCUMENTS. IF ANYONE HAS THE ADDRESS OF ANY OF HER RELATIVES, PLEASE DO NOT HESITATE TO COME FORWARD FOR A REWARD.

Ethan pulled my arm, "Come on, Piper, we have to get to the castle."

I followed him back to Marlee, still distracted by the paper. I felt as if I had seen her before somewhere. She brought us to a small door on the left of the massive entry and hesitated before knocking twice. My stomach flipped, and I held my breath. Here goes nothing…

The door was opened by a massive Ledo. She was as tall as Officer Jaxon but seemed to be made of pure muscle. The moment she saw us, she rolled her eyes. "SOMEONE GET OFFICER JAXON DOWN HER RIGHT NOW!" She yelled, fingering the ax on her belt.

I gulped.

Officer Jaxon appeared a few moments later with a cupcake in hand, his eyes widening slightly when he saw us. "Hey Macy what's up?" He asked the woman, eyes darting back and forth.

"You ordered more food!" She asked incredulously, motioning at the three of us. "Listen Jaxon," She growled, "We talked about this, you can't keep ordering Ledos from the city to bring food. Those rats are dangerous, the next thing you know they're planting bombs in our bedrooms and burning down buildings."

Marlee stared at her feet, suddenly looking very uncomfortable.

The guard continued, her voice rising in anger, "If I see one more slimy little ledo within ten feet of me, I will break every bone in their body and burn them alive. In fact, maybe I should start with these three."

Ethan let out a small noise that sounded like a balloon deflating. I hid my hands under the box, hoping that no one noticed how they were shaking.

"I need my food supply coming in 24/7. I'm not going to inform the guard patrol/or order the Ledos in the kitchen around every time I have a craving for sushi. The cities of Ledos have perfected the art of food, and I refuse to eat anything less than the best."

"Listen Jaxon. I couldn't care less about your sushi cravings or the fact that you've achieved the goal of becoming the size of a small killer whale. If I see one more group of ratty Ledos standing in front of my door, I will not hesitate to put their severed head on a pedestal right next to yours."

I took a step back and prayed that this guard's bark was worse than her bite.

Officer Jaxon nodded, "I one-hundred percent agree. In fact, let's begin by showing these Ledos who are their boss."

I gulped, not liking the sound of that. Ethan took a step back, "What the--Ahhhh!"

Office Jaxon had lifted a massive wip. No, why on earth would he brandish a whip in our direction? We were allies, right? I looked around at Ethan and Marlee, both who seemed to be confused and panicked. The whip cracked, coming down hard. My eyes widened as

199

the leather twisted and came down towards me. Ethan and Marlee scattered left and right, but my legs stood frozen in place. My right arm protected my face. The whip wrapped around my arm, and pain exploded throughout my body. I gripped my wrist tightly, realizing in horror that my entire arm was covered in blood. It felt as if someone had lit my arm on fire. Stars danced in front of my eyes as I whimpered, stumbling backward. My stomach felt heavy, and I resisted the urge to throw up. Tears welled in my eyes, and sweat pooled around my hairline.

It seemed as if sharp needles were stabbing every part of the skin.

Ethan yelled out a curse, completely losing the character, and ran over to me. His face was red, and his eyes shot daggers and Officer Jaxon.

"Now now hush down." Said Officer Jaxon in his disgusting oily voice. "None of that, or you'll be next."

Ethan seemed to be shaking, but I weakly pulled his apron and managed to shake my head slowly without passing out, hoping he got my message.

"Come with me." Said Officer Jaxon, turning around as if nothing had happened.

The other guard smirked in my direction. I weakly tried to stand up and tried to ignore the flash of lightning in my arm. A whimper escaped my mouth, and I stumbled forwards, following officer Jaxon.

Ethan scowled, clenching his fist into his arms. He turned his gaze to me, "Can you walk?"

I swallowed and nodded, not trusting myself to speak. Ethan grabbed my cookies, and I cradled my injured arm, following Officer Jaxon into the castle. After we had walked a good distance away from the other guards, Ethan began to shout, "WHAT IS WRONG WITH

YOU! YOU COULD HAVE KILLED HER! YOU COULD HAVE---."

Officer Jaxon held up his hand, "You, sir are at a seventeen, and I need you at like a three. Don't go yelling and blowing out the cover. As for whipping Piper, that was all part of the act." He continued unapologetically.

Ethan looked as if he were about to commit murder, and I quickly spoke up. "Where." I winced, "Where are we g-going now?" I asked, holding back tears.

"Hmm, well, I suppose I ought to get a bandaid before you bleed out." Office Jaxon said lightly, his oily smile never leaving his face.

I balled my good hand onto a fist and glared at Officer Jaxon, "You've got to--."

I stopped mid-sentence. The guard from earlier had just rounded the corner, "Everything okay here?" She asked, her suspicious eyes trailing from my balled-up fist to Ethan's glare, "Do we have a problem here?"

"No." Marlee spoke up, her face pale and eyes wide, "No, we don't."

The guard let out a cool laugh, "Well then, carry on."

She walked away, and once out of sight Officer Jaxon raised a hand to his lip, signaling for us to be quiet. For once, I didn't argue and tried to keep my whimpering to a minimum.

***

We arrived at Officer Jaxon's room a few moments later. I stood in the doorway, cradling my arm, not sure what to do.

"Bandages are in the second cupboard to the left," Officer Jaxon explained while sitting down on a massive plump arm chair. "Try not to get blood on the floor. I just had the place vacuumed."

Clenching my teeth, I walked over to the cabinet, and Ethan helped me pull out a pair of bandages.

I sat down on the floor and held my arm out in front of me. "Hold still," Ethan instructed.

I complied, trying not to wince as he poured a clear liquid down my arm. I bit the inside of my cheeks, trying to ignore the stinging pain. I wrapped a bandage around the cut, hoping to make the bleeding stop. My head felt woozy as I gulped down a glass of water I found on the nightstand.

"Want me to sign it?" Ethan asked, eyes dancing with amusement.

I rolled my eyes and laughed, "I'll pass."

He grinned, "Your loss. Some people would kill for my autograph."

Officer Jaxon walked up to the three of us, "All right, you have entered this castle, hand over the crown."

I looked at him, my astonishment quickly turning to fury, "You're kidding, right? The deal was, to get us into the castle *unharmed*."

Officer Jaxon's eyes flashed, "You are in no position to bargain. Give me the crown."

Ethan stood up to protest, but Marlee interjected, "Just give it to him, Piper. Officer Jaxon is right. We're in no position to argue."

"Thank *you*, Marlee." Officer Jaxon said, giving us a smug smile.

I gulped down an insult, "Right, yes, of course."

I nudged Ethan, and he mumbled in agreement, reaching into his packmare to grab the crown. Officer Jaxon wrapped his greedy finger around the treasure, pupils widening. "Ahh yes, yes." He lifted the crown and placed it on top of his head, a massive smile atop his face.

"Geez, you'd think he's holding the latest I-phone or something," I muttered.

Ethan rubbed his hands together, "Oooh, I want to tell him so badly. Just to see the look on his face."

"Don't." I advised, "He's our only ticket to Emensaly."

"I know but….." Ethan trailed off.

"All right." Said Marlee, bringing us back, "How are we going to do this?"

Officer Jaxon rubbed his hands together and rolled a metal cart covered in a white silk tablecloth toward us. On top of it, there were three woven baskets, each filled with about a dozen plastic-wrapped meat. The content was soggy, and the color resembled a lemon that was exposed to radiation. I wrinkled my nose at *the Dark Avocado #6007-6A Valspar* meat. "You're not expecting us to eat that, right?" I asked, bile building up in the back of my throat.

"No, no, this is part of your costume," He explained, "You'll be delivering food to the prisoners. Then you may break your friend out."

My stomach rolled. There were people who actually ate this stuff?!

"You can't feed the prisoners that!" Marlee exclaimed, her voice rising, "That goes against everything in the Nourishment Proclamation."

I furrowed my eyebrows, wondering if that was anything like the Food and Drug Act in America.

"What Nourishment Proclamation?" Officer Jaxon asked with a smile creeping across his lips. "The one that hasn't existed since the giraffe took over?"

Marlee bit her lip, trembling with anger, but she said nothing. Ethan shot Officer Jaxon a reproachful look.

"So you'll grab your baskets, and I'll have someone walk you down to the prisons. Keep your head down, and don't look anyone in the eye. We don't need you raising suspicion. Try to avoid talking to people or telling them where you are going. They might notice that you aren't the usual Ledos that bring down the prison food." he explained.

"What if we run into the real Ledos that bring the food?" Ethan asked.

"I will summon them to my room." Officer Jaxon answered, "Yes, they will not ignore a summon from me."

"He's just like a diaper." I muttered to Ethan, "Self-absorbed and full of it."

He laughed, giving me a fist bump.

"Now, before you leave, I'll sound an alarm." Officer Jaxon continued, "The alarm will only be directed to the workers in prison. I'll try to get them all as far away from you three as possible. Once you're down there, try to make a bit of noise. Throw something across the room or set off an explosion. Whatever you can do to distract them."

"I don't suppose you have any spare dynamite," Ethan asked, only half-joking.

Officer Jaxon frowned, "I might. Hold on--."

He pressed a button on the side of his chair, and a few moments later, a Ledo ran through the door, panting loudly.

"Wha-what wrong, your highness?" The Ledos rushed, running a hand through her hair and fixing her tie.

"Go fetch me the dynamite." Officer Jaxon said lightly, waving her away.

She blinks, "But sir, that alarm is only for emerg-."

"GET ME THE DYNAMITE!" Officer Jaxon roared, and I jumped slightly.

The Ledo quivered and stumbled over her boots to run out of the door.

Officer Jaxon clapped his hands together, "Just can't get good help nowadays, can you? Anyway, once you've gotten into the prison, you'll have to find your inmate. I won't be able to assist you, considering that you refuse to tell me who you are breaking out. After that, you need to open the look. There are different locks for different prisons. The first part is accessed by a key, and the second is going to be some sort of pattern or number system. It depends on who you are breaking out."

"How do we get the key?" Marlee asked.

Officer Jaxon pursed his lips, "Well, that's a bit problematic. See, I don't have a key but, but---." He held up a finger as Ethan began to protest. "I do know where they are. The prison guards are each designed to protect a specific key. Every guard has a different key that opens only one cell."

I groaned, "You're kidding. How are we going to get the right key?"

Officer Jaxon grinned and pulled a second bowl off the white cart, unweaving three *Benjamin Moore Dove White #4fd--E2* gloves.

"Well." Ethan declared, "At least we'll look like medieval princesses while marching to our death."

Marlee took a deep breath.

Officer Jaxon gave him a strained smile, "No, these are snatcher gloves. They give your finger bones the ability to stretch and pop out. It's going to help you steal the keys."

I shuddered, "But won't they realize that we stole the keys?"

Officer Jaxon bit his lip, "You'll just have to figure it out along the way."

I gulped, "Right--."

There was a knock on the door that made me just get out of my seat, and a loud voice bellowed, "OFFICER JAXON OPEN UP!"

My spine went rigid with fear. The voice sounded extremely similar to the guard that had stopped us right in front of the castle. Officer Jaxon's eyes grew wide, "Uhhhh, one moment I'm, er, I'm naked."

The knocking stopped, followed by retching. I winced, trying to push that image out of my mind.

"Quickly go through the door behind the red tapestry. It'll lead you straight to the prison." He hustled us away and then quickly fixed his tie. Officer Jaxon stood up and, in a louder voice, said, "Coming!" He made a shoeing motion towards us.

I gulped, looking across the room. Marlee ran across the room towards the tapestry, and Ethan and I quickly followed. Cursing, I turned around and grabbed the gloved and mystery meat off the cart. Ethan and Marlee had already pulled the heavy carpet aside and climbed through a small hole. I rolled my eyes, leaving it to Officer Jaxon to have a secret tunnel hidden behind a fancy tapestry.

***

The three of us trudged through the dark tunnel, which was barely illuminated by light seeping through the tapestry. Marlee stopped us once we were a good distance away from Officer Jaxon's room but still able to receive a bit of light. "Okay, everyone, put a glove on. I found a flashlight in my apron that we can use. This wasn't how we planned for this to go, but it's fine. We'll still manage to break Riley out." She paused, "You guys ready."

"Yup," Ethan replied, and I nodded even though my heart was pounding in my ears.

She gave us a thumbs up and flickered her flashlight on. "Let's go."

We continued walking as our eyes slowly adjusted to the dimness. I scanned the rocky ceiling and cobwebs, hoping to avoid bumping into anything unpleasant. We had been trudging through for so long that I began to think that Officer Jaxon had\ tricked us down the wrong passage when Marlee stopped.

"What's wrong?" Ethan asked in a stage whisper.

"I think we're here," Marlee replied quickly.

I shimmied my way to the front, hoping to catch a glimpse of what they were staring at. There was a small door at the end of that hallway. Well, I assume it was a door. There was a weird fuzz growing on the frame, giving the impression that it wouldn't be easy to open.

"Soooooo, what's the plan?" Ethan asked, turning to Marlee.

She swallowed, "Well, if this door does lead to the prison and Officer Jaxon hasn't sent us down the wrong passage, we should try to find Riley's cell first."

"We can pass out the food until Marlee recognizes her," Ethan exclaimed.

"What about the keys?" I interrupted, "How are we going to know which belongs to Riley's cell."

They shrugged.

"And the alarm Officer Jaxon said he was going to raise. How will he know when we are breaking Riley out?" I questioned, crossing my fingers hopefully.

"We have to wing it," Ethan replied, glancing at Marlee.

She nodded and then turned to the door, "Let's try to open it."

The three of us squeezed around the mouldy door and tried to pry it open. Ethan grabbed the doorknob and pulled, only to have the metal rip off, causing him to stumble back. He looked down at the doorknob, "Well, that could be problematic."

I groaned, slapping my forehead. "Try the cracks along the side." Marlee dug her long fingernails into the small crevice. She cursed, retracting her hand. The fingernail was still in the door frame, no longer in contact with her finger.

"Ethan, can you create a screwdriver?" I asked, now pushing my body weight against the rough door.

"Yeah sure." He waved a hand over his Ivy leaf anklet, but nothing happened. Frowning, he tried again, "Something's wrong with my *pindres*. I can't summon anything."

I turned to face him, "That's bizarre, here, let me try." I imagined my sketchbook falling into my hands, but there was no reaction. I bit my lip, trying to stop panic from forming in the pit of my stomach. "Mines, mines not working either," I said, voice quivering.

Ethan paled, "What!? Why don't--."

"It's your contact!" Marlee exclaimed suddenly, "They block any ability you have to make you more like a Ledo!"

"Well, do we at least get whatever power's Ledo's have?"

"No."

"Right, because that would be too easy."

"Should we take our contact out?" Ethan asked, pushing against the door.

I bit my lip, "I don't think that would be a great idea......maybe as a last resort. It can be our plan C"

"What's plan B?"

"Don't mess up plan A."

Marlee sighed, "Well, this is great. Do you have anything in your *packmares*?"

I pulled Grass off my back and was about to reach in when an idea stuck, "Wait, what about our *packmare's* claws?" I pointed to Grasse's long sloth-like fingernails, "Do you think those could unwedge the door."

Ethan was about to respond when a loud "FORGET IT!" echoed through the chamber.

"Aw, come on, pleeeeease, Grass. We need to get into the prison." I begged.

"Are you kidding me! No way!" He replied, deep voice growling.

"Don't tell me you're afraid of breaking a nail." I grinned.

"Of course not, I just, well I--. ugh fine." Grass gave in, reluctantly

I laughed and carried Grass over to the door. Ethan did the same with his *packmare*. Grass lifted his long arm and dragged his fingernails through the crevice. There was a low screech, and Grass retracted his finger, "Ugh, that was exhausting. Please, put me back on your back."

I rolled my eyes, turning then to Ethan, who had now pulled the door open. With a low squeak, he popped his head out and then closed it just a quick. "There are three guards in my line of sight. One of them could spot us if we climbed out, but the other two were turned away from us."

"What if I throw something across the room?" Marlee asked hesitantly, "They would look away long enough for us to sneak out."

"And then we look for Riley's cell?" I asked, hoping that she couldn't hear the doubt in my voice.

"And then we look for Riley's cell."

***

Marlee gripped her flashlight tightly in one hand and held a glass orb in the other (She wouldn't answer where she got it from though I do remember one sitting on Officer Jaxon's nightstand). Creaking the door open, she wound her arm and then let go. A few moments later, I heard the sound of glass crashing onto the ground. She beckoned us forward, and we squeezed past the door. I hid Grass under my apron and grabbed the basket of "quote-unquote" food. I followed them through the hole into the prison. We quickly walked past the guards who were bent over inspecting the broken glass. I swallowed, hoping that we remained invisible. Marlee was leading us forwards, making her way through the twists and turns.

Whenever we passed a guard stationed at their post, we made sure to pass out food to the weary prisoners. I shivered as the three of us began walking down a flight of stairs. We were getting deeper and deeper underground. I don't consider myself a claustrophobic person, but even I began to break out in cold sweat looking at the dark rock walls.

"Marlee, where are you taking us?" I whispered fiercely.

"I know where Riley is. Just hurry up." She responded, never slowing her pace.

I gulped, about to respond, when a sign stopped me. We passed under a low arch with a sign that said, "Danger, Prisoners here have committed the highest offense. Enter with Caution."

"Marlee, what's Riley doing in an extreme security prison? I thought that she was imprisoned for stealing bread." Ethan asked, voicing my thoughts.

Marlee bit her lip and averted his gaze, "Steal bread is a uhhh, a major offense here. Doesn't matter! We're almost--." She shut her mouth when a guard passed the three of us. His eyebrows were raised, and he stopped right in front of us.

"Since when are ledo chefs sent down here to supply the prisoners here?" His lip curled into a savage expression.

None of us responded.

"Well?" He asked.

"It's a new form of torture called Maggot Meat." I blurted out, hoping he wouldn't see through my lies, "The prisoners here think that this is the normal food, but there are poisons hidden within, not enough to kill but enough for them to wish it did."

The prison guard raised an eyebrow, "And they send mere Ledo's to do this?"

"We're not Ledos." Ethan proclaimed, "We are Legif. The contacts really do their job, though, if they can fool you." He gave a nervous laugh.

The guard began quivering. At first, I thought with anger or fear, but then he did the unimaginable. He burst out laughing. "Oh, oh, that great stuff." He wheezed. "I can't wait to see that. Come on in."

I gave him a smile that probably came across as a grimace. We walked under the arc, and I was immediately hit in the face with the pungent smell of vomit, human waste and perspiration. I covered my nose with my apron, hoping to filter some of it away. My eyes strayed toward the sallow figures sitting inside of the dark cells. There was a small one-way window showing the creatures that were inside. Some were Ledos, some looked like people, and others looked like nothing I had ever seen before. The prison guard walked with us, bouncing on his heels with excitement. "So who are you going to prant first, Gabriel Newton, Mason Gody, Abigail Murphy, Madel, that *drener* whose name I forgot, Oh the dreaded Vega Flint? I'm most excited to see that foul giraffe killing Ledo being tortured. There's also Marlia Germanico, sheesh there's a piece of work--."

The list went on, but something in Marlee's posture changed halfway through. I might have been imagining it, but there was a sort of menacing glint in her eyes. We continued to deliver the food through a small hole in the ground in front of each cell that the inmates would have to pull a rope to get it. The guard was still rambling on and on about how priceless the prank would be when Marlee tapped me on the shoulder, excitement visible in her eyes. "I found her."

"What! Where?" I whispered, still sliding food into the slots.

"Two cells down from this one." She replied and stood to relay the message to Ethan.

I let my gaze flitter down the hall, but I couldn't see into the cell from this angle. Ethan began talking to the prison guard. "So, are you the only one down here?"

"I'm the only living guard down here. There are, of course, shadows in the cell with each prisoner. The shadows keep them stuck in the room. See inside each cell. There is a light that's positioned in a way that their shadows are always in the same spot. Eventually, the person gets stuck to their shadow, therefore, stuck in the cell. I've been working here for a while. Most of the prisoners keep to themself. We've only had a few incidents where Vega Flint tried to escape. She made it all the way to the kitchens by the time we caught her. Good thing she didn't manage to get her hands on any of the knives. Who knows what the ruthless murdering little rat would do if she had access to weapons."

I took a deep breath. This was getting more and more difficult by the minute. Now we had to get rid of some sort of shadow charm on top of everything else. Great, just great. On the other hand, we seemed to have found the perfect prison guard to reveal information. He seemed to be dying to talk to someone. I wondered why he had chosen to come here. I had a feeling that it hadn't been a popularity contest.

"I'll distract him. Check out Riley's cell." Marlee whispered, "Inspect the keyhole with Ethan. It might help you find out which key we need."

I nodded. Marlee pulled Ethan away from the guard and began talking, "So, gone to the gym lately, have you?"

The two of us tiptoed to Riley's cell, and I glanced over my shoulder a few times, trying to stop myself from psyching out. I had to trust Marlee. Ethan and I crouched down in front of Riley's cell. I had gotten a glimpse of her. Her dark green hair was plastered against her face. Her shallow cheeks gave off an undead aura. Her skin looked like saran wrap that had been stretched too thin. The only thing alive about her were the few freckles scattered across her cheekbones and

213

nose. There was something about Riley's face, though. It looked familiar. It might have just been because she was related to Marlee but had the feeling that there was something more. I shook that thought aside and focused on the lights shining down. Looking down at her shadow, I noticed that there was something unusual about it. The *Dovetail SW# 3543* colored silhouette that was displayed across the asphalt concrete floor looked alive. It flickered like a broken light bulb.

"Does she look familiar?" I asked, bending over to join Ethan.

"Huh, I don't know, maybe." He traced his finger over a smooth circular ridge with a small dent in the shape of a heart underneath it, "Is this the keyhole?"

"Umm, I don't know, maybe," I replied distractedly, "Do you think Marlee might be lying--."

"I've seen this before!" Ethan grimaced, still looking at the keyhole, "I've--I don't." he groaned in frustration.

"Ethan, take your contacts out," I instructed, suddenly realizing what was wrong.

"What?"

"Take them out. You might be able to recognize the pattern and where you've seen it before." I said, no longer thinking about Riley.

Ethan reached up to his eye, wincing slightly, "Good idea." He pulled the contacts out, holding them on the top of his finger pad. "I got--." Ethan cursed suddenly. He leaned forward too far and grabbed the door with his hands.

"No!" I whispered in despair, "No, no, no, your contacts!"

Ethan took a deep breath, and I tried to swallow, nausea and panic creeping up my throat. "What are we going to do?" I asked, biting my lower lip.

"I don't know!" His voice was harsh. He took a deep breath, "Look, it's fine. There's nothing we can do about it--." Ethan cursed, changing the subject, "I know where I've seen this before. It's exactly the same as a bracelet, the one worn by Officer Macy."

Chapter 22

"Macy." I repeated, "You mean the guard that threatened to break every bone in our body and burn us alive if she ran into us again?"

"The very one."

"Great, just great." I tried to swallow the bile rising in my throat. Macy would probably skewer us into shish kabob if the three of us came within ten feet of her. I tried to clear my head and focus on the big picture. We were wasting so much time! According to my (not so accurate mental calendar), we only had three to four days until Charlid would be released into the world. What were we doing in Ledolish land helping some girl rescue her (maybe psychotic) sister? Didn't Marlee care about saving the world? I felt a wave of anger toward her. Marlee had to realize that even if we managed to break Riley out of this impenetrable prison, she would still be in hot water if Ethan and I didn't find Emensaly. What was Marlee thinking would happen if the two of us were murdered during this suicidal mission? No one else was jumping up and down, volunteering to find Emensaly. I took a deep breath and tried to focus on everything from Marlee's perspective. Maybe she wasn't willing to live in a world without Marlee. I wondered if I was willing to live in a world without Jack. Tears pricked the back of my eyes, threatening to flow over, and I blinked them away, concentrating on Ethan's words.

"What are we going to do?

"Do you think that we could go back up to Officer Jaxon's room? Officer Macy may still be up there. We could use the gloves to get her bracelet." I asked. I tried to pretend I wasn't actually going to do this. I was just summarizing my new favorite movie or something.

He massaged his temple, "And then we have to manage to sneak back down here, open Riley's cell, get past some other obstacle behind her door, get rid of Riley's shadow, and then manage to sneak out without Officer Jaxon seeing my eyes. Oh, and Marlee has to tell us everything she knows about Emensaly."

"Seems doable."

***

Ethan and I had decided that it would be best if he hid near the exit while I fetched Marlee. She was trapped by a prison guard who seemed to be talking a million miles a minute. As I approached, Marlee shot me a look that clearly said, "SAVE ME!" I had the feeling he would take until the end of time unless someone tied a gag around his mouth. I approached and grabbed Marlee's arm.

"We need to go back to Officer Jaxon's room," I said quietly, hoping no one else could hear me.

Unfortunately, it seemed that I hadn't mastered the art of whispering because the prison guard whipped his head up and narrowed his eyes suspiciously, "What is your business with Officer Jaxon?"

My heart jumped into my throat, "busted," I thought, clenching my leg muscles and preparing to run.

"He organized this prank on the prisoners," Marlee interjected, thinking quickly.

I shot her a look of gratitude and wiped my sweaty palms on my apron.

The prison guard laughed. "Ha! I never thought that old geyser had it in him. Good to know he isn't holed up in his room surrounded by gold and eating chocolate.

"Wow, the rumors of his reputation have made it all the way down here." I marveled under my breath.

"Why do you have to leave already? There are still so many prisoners you can poison." He whined, suddenly sounding like a bratty ten-year-old. I resisted the urge to roll my eyes.

"Could you deliver the rest of the meal packets for us?" Marlee asked sweetly, all evidence of the harsh woman gone from her voice.

"O-of course." He replied hastily, stumbled over his feet.

Marlee smiles, "Thanks." She leaned up and kissed him on the cheek.

I stared at her in amazement and astonishment, but she ignored me. All the kindness vanished from her gaze to be replaced with steely determination. "Where's Ethan?!"

I bit my lip, hesitantly looking at the prison guard, who was practically sashaying through the dark hallway. "His contact fell out."

"What!" Marlee whispered. She stopped running and turned to face me. She cursed, "That's bad, that's really bad."

"Yeah, I figured that much out for myself, thanks," I replied.

She scowled, "Well, where is he? Please tell me you at least managed to figure out which key will break Riley out."

A wave of panic crashed over me as I thought about Officer Macy. I quickly shoved that emotion away and focused on one that I was somewhat more familiar with, rage. "Listen, Marlee. This is getting out of hand. Don't you realize that we'll all be in danger, Riley included, if you don't give us information on Emensaly? I mean, Riley will be just as comfortable in her cell as in your little house if Charlid manages to escape. Ethan and I just asked you for a small bit of information while you're asking us to risk our necks!!!! It's getting out of hand, Marlee." I tried to sound sophisticated, but my voice had begun to rise. I opened my mouth to continue, but Marlee had heard enough. Her eyes seemed to glow, and I took a step back. It was ridiculous to be afraid of her, though. We were allies, right?

"How 'bout you listen to me, *Piper*," Marlee snarled, her character changing so suddenly I felt as if I had just met her. I began to wonder if the tear-stained little girl who had just missed her sister was another act. "We are getting Riley back. If not, I will turn you and Ethan in, and I'll get Riley back myself. I've gone too far and suffered too much to lose Riley again. And once I've got her, there will be some changes in this realm."

I looked up at her in confusion and fear. I had a feeling that she wasn't just talking about saving Riley. "Marlee, is there something you're hiding from us?" I hated the way my voice squeaked at the end.

She ignored me and walked away. I was hit with the impression that she should look taller.

I walked after Marlee, my mind running a million miles a minute as I trudged behind in silence. What was she talking about? Has Marlee been lying to us? What were her real plans? I contemplated all of these questions, desperately wishing that I could read her mind. There was another question that had been gnawing away at me. What had Riley really done? I was becoming more and more uncertain that petty theft was the only crime that she had committed. I risked a glance at Marlee, but her face betrayed no emotion.

The two of us quickly made our way back to Ethan. As we approached the arch that had the massive sign hanging from the top, a spark of panic erupted in the pit of my stomach. Ethan wasn't there. "Ethan!" I hissed, praying that nothing had happened to him, "Ethan, where are y--."

A hand clamped over my mouth. I jumped, the adrenaline pumping through my veins as I prepared to fight, "Piper, it's me, chill." Ethan's voice whispered.

I settled down, my heart racing. I took a deep breath and turned around to scowl at him.

"Sorry for the scare. I was hiding. I didn't want anyone to see my eyes." He turned to Marlee.

She winced, "Oh, that's bad."

Ethan grimaced, "Yeah, I thought as much. I don't suppose you have any more that you could spare."

Marlee shook her head, "No, I left them all in the house. Did you bring the ones that I gave you earlier from the Athletic Realm? Maybe we could convince Officer Jaxon of the other ones and beg for another pair."

Ethan grimaced, "I left them at your house. I didn't think that it would be a good idea if Officer Jaxon saw me carrying them."

"Why didn't you put it in your packmare?" I asked, scratching my chin, "I thought that no one but you could access your packmare."

Ethan groaned, "I'm not going to lie. I completely forgot about that."

I straightened, suddenly having an idea. "Ethan, what if you use your *pindres*? Could you make yourself contacts?"

Ethan looked doubtful, staring down at his Ivy leaf anklet. "I'm not sure that's how it works."

"It isn't," Marlee replied, her voice rushed. "Contacts are created in the image of a Ledo, or Legif, or Giraffe. You need two Ledos, Legifs, or Giraffes for the process. When you put the contacts in, you basically look like the child of the two Ledos, Legifs, or Giraffes. So unless Ethan gets an eyelash from two Ledo, he can't do anything."

I cursed.

Marlee ignored me, "And how exactly are we supposed to get through the prison with Ethan looking like that."

"I feel offended."

"You know what I meant." She replied as she began walking through the passageways. "Officer Jaxon's no Einstein, but I'm pretty sure he'll be able to put two and two together if he sees Ethan's from the art realm."

"Why don't I just hide inside the passageway?" He asked in a hushed whisper as the three hid behind an open door as a female guard with a sharp knife passed us.

I swallowed my panic before answering, "How will you help us get Officer Macy's bracelet?"

Ethan frowned, "I can use my *pindre*. That's got to help somehow."

"Hold on," Marlee muttered. She pushed us into an empty cell and shut the door. I felt a wave of trepidation hit me. I tensed my legs, getting ready to run, thinking that Marlee was about to lock us in here for the rest of eternity. Thankfully she made no move to grab the deadbolt or door handle. Ever since her little speech, I didn't trust her.

Marlee looked over her shoulder before talking, "Ethan can you pull some sort of arty stuff and get yourself a disguise? Or maybe something to hide yourself."

"Arty?"

"FOCUS!"

"Fine fine jeez." Ethan waved a hand over his *pindres,* and a slab of clay fell onto his hand. He scratched his chin, thinking for a moment and then turned to be. "Do you think that I could create a curtain, I could hide behind it, and it would change to fit the walls behind me? I just have to make sure that no one ever stands behind me."

I shrugged, "I suppose you could, but I thought you could only create stuff that didn't have a mind of its own or magical powers. Like a flower or a cup."

He frowned, "Can you paint it? Marlee describes the walls to her."

"What about *Profors*?" I asked, thinking about the magical clay that I learned about in the art realm. "Doesn't that have a mind of its own?"

"Hmmm." Ethan said, "I think I have some…" He closed his eyes and gripped the Ivy leaf around his anklet. A few moments later, a few ounces of a clay-like substance that was the color of *#2d45 Satin Gold* appeared in his hand. Ethan opened his eyes and frowned, "I could have sworn I had more."

"Just spread it over the surface of the curtain," I recommend checking my watch frantically. It was 9 pm in the art realm. We have wasted an entire day here. Ethan shot me a quick look of panic, clearly thinking the same thing as me. He has already begun molding his clay into a small slate with round ridges that look like a curtain on wheels.

"Okay, Piper, the walls all looked pretty much the same," Marlee explained, in a low voice, checking the small window by the door to make sure we were still hidden. I could barely make her face out in the dim light as she began to talk. "I assume you saw the walls when we walked to Officer Jaxon's room."

I frowned, "In case you don't remember, I was a bit preoccupied, but the blood pooling around my arm."

"A simple "NO" would have been sufficient, but okay. All the walls are white with grey marble. In some other places, there are either massive floor-to-ceiling windows and red curtains. If we stick to the main hallways, then that should suffice. Oh, and of course, the prison walls."

I nodded, vaguely remembering now that she had described it. "Ethan, how should I paint it?"

Ethan bit his lip. "I'm going to create a curtain the size of my palm. I'll grow it once I transform the piece. I think I'll be able to make it big enough to hide myself. I've made four curtains and coated each with the *Profors*. If you paint all four and I layer them, the *Profors* should be able to camouflage me with the wall. Granted, this is all a very big *if*."

I swallowed, not fully understanding everything that he just said, "Soooo, I just paint the four pieces of clay."

"Yes."

"Got it," I replied, reaching out to take them from him. An idea struck me. "Ethan, can you make me a case to hold my contacts while I paint?"

"Sure."

***

We worked quickly, frantically glancing at our watches. Once I had taken my contacts out, I was back in my element. My hands were itching to get a hold of a paintbrush, and I managed to paint the four tiles in under twenty minutes. My stomach rumbled again, and I tried to ignore the gnawing hunger. When was the last time I had eaten? This morning? Has it really only been half a day since I left the art realm? It felt like more than a century.

Once I had put the finishing touches onto the marble paint, Ethan smeared the *Profors* onto the surface. Once everything sparkled with the golden clay, he waved his right hand, and the clay curtains tripled in size. I grinned as the wet clay transformed into a massive silky tarp.

The wheels on the bottom and the metal rail on top were flickering in and out of sight. Ethan stood behind the curtain, and I had to squint my eyes to make out the difference between the delicate ruffles.

"Ethan, move the curtain around. Let's see if it makes any noise." Marlee instructed.

I stood next to Marlee, awkwardly waiting for Ethan. Something tapped me on the shoulder, and I jumped in a panic, nearly hitting my head on the low ceiling. I turned around and heard Ethan say, "Well, I guess the curtain works."

I glared, my heart still beating a million miles a minute. "As long as you don't bump into people, you should be fine." I said, "Oh wait, I can see your hair, just a bit at the top. Crouch down."

"The one day I regret not brushing my hair," Ethan mumbled.

I reached out the touch the curtain and felt the silky martial glide through my hands like water. Walking around the side, I saw Ethan crouched down in an awkward position leaning against the wall. I giggled while taking in the scene. The curtain was barely tall enough for Ethan, and he had wrapped the extra material around his sides, leaving only his back exposed, which was plastered against the wall. Clearly, the curtain was a little smaller than we had anticipated. The veil was somewhat see-through, so Ethan could make out the outlines of people and figures. Not the most convenient solution, but hey, it worked.

"Piper, I get that we want to help Riley, but I think we should get go--." Ethan began but quickly stopped when he saw me pressing a finger to my lips and shaking my head frantically.

"Talk later." I mouthed, cocking my head towards Marlee.

He looked confused but nodded. I glanced at Marlee, who was opening the door and looking left and right to make sure the path was clear. "Piper follows me out, and Ethan trails behind her."

"If something happens, just whistle, Ethan," I told him quickly, putting my contacts back in. "We won't be able to see you."

"Got it." He muttered from somewhere on my left.

Marlee trudged through the door, holding her high. I followed her, turning around to face Ethan. "You good?"

"Yup," he whispered from my right, and I reeled around to where I heard his voice. I squinted, trying to make out the pattern of the curtain fabric, but my eyes didn't see anything out of the ordinary.

I took a deep breath of the musty prison air and began to walk. The population of guards became denser and denser the closer we got to the exit. I got the eerie feeling that it would be more difficult to exit this place than to enter it. As soon as that thought entered my mind, a prison guard took a step in front of Marlee and raised his hand. A menacing expression adorned his face, and his hand was a little too close to the revolver in his right pocket for my liking.

"What business do the two of you have here?" He said, raising his voice.

"We were delivering food," Marlee explained, voice even, but I could see her hands shaking slightly.

"And you left your basket in the cell." He asked, eyebrows raised.

Marlee opened her mouth to respond but closed it, lost for words. An idea flickered through my brain, and I took a step forward before I could lose my nerve. I spoke up, "One of the prisoners," I said with a fake sob. "They--oh, they grabbed me! I don't know how, but they were trying to escape!" I buried my head in my hands, realizing that I sounded more like a rhinoceros with a cold than a crying Ledo.

The guard ignored my tears but gripped his revolver tightly, "Which prisoner?"

"They came from that direction!" Marlee proclaimed, pointing to the far side of the hallway, opposite to the one that we just came from.

The guard lifted his revolver out of its sheath, and I took a step back, fear gripping my throat. I prepared to run, thinking that he was going to shoot us for lying, but the guard turned and ran down the hall, yelling into a walkie-talkie. I took a deep breath and felt Ethan's curtain brush against my back. "Oop, sorry, Ethan," I muttered, still panting with fear.

"No problemo."

"Hurry up!" Marlee commanded.

I rolled my eyes. "What's her deal?" Ethan asked from behind me.

"Not sure," I admitted. "But earlier, when I told her that I wanted to back out of the mission, she started yelling at me. Starting saying that she was going to change things around here and needed Riley for that. Then she said that she would turn us in and lock us in prison down here."

"Yikes." He replied, "I had a feeling that the innocent little girl was just a facade."

I gulped as he confirmed my suspicion.

Chapter 23

The rest of the walk was uneventful. The only guards that we saw were hedging in the direction Marlee had pointed out to one of them before. I almost felt bad for the prisoners that they were going after. I turned to Marlee, "How much farther to the passageway! I'm a little scared as to what will happen if the guards realize that no one stole our baskets and come after us."

"Relax," Marlee instructed her in no way resembling a look of relaxation. "We're almost there."

"Everything good back there, Ethan?" I asked once we passed through another empty hallway.

"Yup." He replied. I tried to place where his voice was coming from.

"How do you know the way around all of these passages?" I asked Marlee a moment later.

She didn't respond (not that I expected her to anymore, she gave a new definition to selective hearing") and kept walking. I rolled my eyes in her direction. I trudged behind her for another good five minutes. Right before I was about to ask if she had gotten lost, Marlee stopped in front of a space in the wall. I leaned in closer, trying to make out what she was looking at in the dim light. I stopped the outline of the wooden door that we had entered from. I grinned, even though we were a far way from success. At least we were getting somewhere. I looked left and right, tugging Marlee's sleeve, when I saw a pair of shiny black boots turning the corridor. "A guard is coming. Hurry!"

Marlee didn't have time to respond when Legif turned the corner and saw us staring at her, our guilty eyes wide in fear.

"What are you looking at?" She snapped. "Move along!"

I glanced at Marlee in a panic, who was lost for words. Slowly she turned and began walking down another hallway, this one with three guards standing in a row in front of the cells.

"What do we do?!" I hissed.

"I don't know.' Marlee admitted out of the corner of her mouth. "We need to get to that door!"

I shook my hands nervously and continued to follow Marlee in silence. She turned another corner, this one completely deserted. "Ethan, can we hide back there with you?" I asked feverously.

"Umm, that might get a little tight--." He began, but Marlee cut him off.

"Good idea Piper. Get behind him." Marlee instructed, sounding bossy.

I gulped, trying to find where Ethan was.

"I'm right here!' He called, sticking out a hand, having sensed my thought.

I walked towards his hand and then flattened myself against the wall. Ethan stood crouched over awkwardly with his back flattened against the wall. I deflated. There was no way that I would fit back there. One of my limbs would hang out, or I would trip and sprawl over the dirty floor and destroy the curtain.

"Hurry up Piper!" Marlee commanded her voice impatiently.

I took a deep breath and tried to flatten my stomach. Leaning against the wall, I inched my way behind Ethan. The curtain moved a few inches forwards, but Ethan grabbed it. I gripped my elbows to my sides as Ethan pulled the fabric around us. I was painfully aware of the fact that my hair was pressed against his neck, and his back was glued to my chest. I took a slow breath, "Are we hidden, Marlee?" I

228

asked, my voice squeaking a bit at the end when Ethan accidentally stepped on my toe.

"Well....," She hesitated, "It's not so back. Let's just hope that the guards are farsighted."

I groaned, sweat trickling down my neck.

"Let's just get to the door. Marlee, how are you going to hide? I have a feeling we won't have enough space for you back here." I said, my voice muffled by Ethan's left knee that had just collided with my stomach. I winced, catching myself using my forearm. I winced, the skin still tender from the whip.

"I'm going to leave through the main entrance." Marlee said simply, "I know my way around the castle."

"How?" Ethan and I asked at the same time.

"Don't worry about it." She called, already walking back through the passage.

"Wait!" I whisper-yelled and shuffled against the wall with Ethan.

"Ouch, stop, Ethan, my chin."

"Your elbows lodged in my rib cage!"

Our banter continued as we followed Marlee. She walked past the previous guards with confidence, and Ethan and I tried to keep up. Marlee turned the corner, and I could vaguely make out two female voices conversing across the corner. I guessed that it was Marlee talking up the guard that had stopped the three of us earlier. Ethan turned the corner, and I could hear Marlee's hysterical voice a bit more clearly.

"Ma'am, I'm lost. Please help find the exit." She sniffled loudly.

"What business do you have down here anyway?!" The guard yelled, her voice echoing off the chamber.

Marlee quivered, and I couldn't tell if she was acting or for real. I guessed a bit of both. I wondered how she was planning to get the guards' attention away from the door. I looked closer and noticed that Marlee's were rotating ever so slightly to the left, and the guards were unconsciously following. I marveled at how easily she deceived people. My mouth tasted sour, and I began to question how much she was deceiving us.

After another painfully slow two minutes of Marlee distracting the guard, she had turned 180 degrees. Ethan and I crept towards the moldy door. Grunting, we managed to lean against it and push it open. Thankfully it swung silently. I lifted the base of the curtain off the floor and stepped onto the ledge, making my way through the door. Ethan pushed it shut behind us and pulled the curtain off his head. I noticed that his forehead was matted with sweat. I fanned myself with one hand, trying to fend off the warmth.

"Well, that was something," I said, leaning against the wall. Now the rush was over, my heart was pounding in my ears, and my breath hitched.

"Yeah." He replied, wiping his forehead.

We sat down in the hallway to catch our breath. I took a half-melted snickers out of my *packmare* and broke part of it off for Ethan.

"Do you think that Marlee will actually be able to get back to Officer Jaxon's room?" I asked, breaking the silence.

Ethan shrugged, "I don't know, but something about her unsettles me."

I nodded, munching the chewy bar, "Did you see how easily she changed her personality based on each guard that she encountered? What if that's what she's been doing with us."

230

"Exactly." Ethan agreed. "I'm also finding it hard to believe that Riley only stole bread. I mean, what's she doing locked up in the super dangerous prisoners' cell."

"Maybe Riley isn't her real name!" I gasped, "Remember when the prison guard down there was listing the names of the prisoners? Marlee perked up halfway through, but he never said, Riley."

"Creepy." Ethan decided, "Not to mention the fact that she was wearing contacts when we saw her at the bar. She took a pair out before she put the ones Officer Jaxon gave her in. When you asked her why she was wearing contacts, she just told you not to worry about it."

"That tends to be her answer whenever I ask her anything," I muttered, annoyed.

"Are we sure that this information is worth it?" Ethan asked tentatively. "This has gotten out of hand."

I bit my lip, thinking. Marlee had been lying to us. She had threatened me and put our lives at risk. She knew this castle from head to toe and never told us anything about herself. I vaguely wondered if she was a runaway princess but dismissed the idea immediately. It didn't make any sense. On top of that, the "proof" that she really had information on Emensaly was a tiny little shrub and a good story. We already knew how well she could lie.

"Let's go back to Officer Jaxon's room." I decided, "Maybe we could give him the scepter, and he'll let us go free. We can go back to the flower garden and look at the map Eveda gave us. Marlee isn't worth it."

"You're right." Ethan agreed, fiddling with his anklet. "She isn't worth it. We don't have time to run through Ledolish land when Charlid is planning his escape in a few days."

I nodded and finished up my granola bar. I stood and dusted the crumbs off my lap. "Let's go."

***

Ethan and I walked through the tiny hallway lodging the curtain behind us. It wasn't all that heavy, but the wheels kept getting stuck on the ridges in the uneven floorboards. I maneuvered around patches of mold the color of a lemon that had been exposed to radiation. Having slipped in it twice already, I was careful to avoid doing so a third time. The dim light in the hallway came from small cracks in the wall. Most of the time, I could only see a few feet in front of me. Unfortunately, since I had put my Ledo contacts back in, I couldn't summon fire. Both of us were panting from the exertion. For the first time, I wished that I had participated in the school track instead of walking behind everyone gossiping with Amy. Though, if I'm being honest, this is probably the best workout I have ever done. Forget the Chloe Ting workout. Just break a Ledo out of jail, and boom, you'll drop five pounds immediately.

"Wait, I think I see the tapestry!" I called Ethan. "Just one more flight of stairs.

"Okay," Ethan replied. He lifted the metal rod on the bottom of the curtain, and I grabbed the top, lugging it up.

Once we made it to the landing in front of the red and gold tapestry, I quieted my breathing and peaked through a tiny hold. I gasped, "She's here!"

"Who, Marlee?" Ethan exclaimed, astonished. "No way. I can't believe it."

My mouth hung open, and I swallowed my disappointment, "I guess we can't ditch her anymore, can we?"

Ethan shook his head, "I don't think so."

I groaned, "Great, just great!"

"Should we go back and find another exit?" Ethan asked doubtfully.

I shook my head, "Think about it. Marlee clearly knows the castle better than we do, and she needs Officer Jaxon to help her get in and out. If she doesn't know any of the secret exits, there sure isn't a chance of us finding any.

Ethan sighed, "So what? We just keep helping Marlee."

I shrugged my shoulders, "Something tells me we don't have much of a choice."

Chapter 24

"So, how do you want to do this?" I asked, looking from Ethan to the curtain. "Should I hold the tapestry up and let you push the curtain out? You still have to hide your eyes from Officer Jaxons."

"Yeah yeah," Ethan nodded, "Just pretend you're stretching or something. I'll wheel myself to the door."

"Okay." I agreed, "Can you whisper something to me when I leave to go with Marlee so I know that you're coming with us."

"Sure. I'll whisper 'Pineapple,'" Ethan grinned.

I sighed. "Whatever makes you happy. Oh, and if Marlee and I get kicked out, can you try to get Riley out? The chances are slim, but maybe you can break her out, and Marlee will still help us."

"Gotcha."

I turned to the tapestry and pushed it to the side. Once underneath it, I lifted my arms to make it look like I was stretching. Feeling ridiculous, I held it up high and felt Ethan brush past me. "Pineapple." He whispered in my ear.

I rolled my eyes.

"Anna?" Officer Jaxon said in surprise.

I looked around. Was there another person in this room?

"Anna, what are you doing!" Marlee asked, glaring at me.

I blushed, remembering what my contact's name was (the ones Marlee had given me). "Ju-just stretching." I stuttered, walking forwards to Officer Jaxon and Marlee. They were sitting across from each other in plushy red arm chairs. Officer Jaxon leaned against his chair in a relaxed fashion while Marlee sat on the edge, looking so uptight that I could have sworn it looked like someone had tied a wooden rod to her back.

Officer Jaxon was frowning at me, "Where's the other one? The-the boy, what was his name? Max?"

I nodded, swallowing a lump in my throat, "Uh huh."

"Well?" Officer Jaxon asked impatiently. Marlee squirmed next to him.

"Oh, he, uh, he died," I exclaimed. I saw Ethan make a quick appearance standing right behind Officer Jaxon. He shot me a WTF look.

Realizing that I didn't sound sincere, I tried again, scrunching my face together to make it look like I had been crying, "Yes, he died." I get a dramatic sniffle. Marlee looked like she was about to strangle me.

"And how did he die?" Officer Jaxon asked, amusement fluttering across his features.

"He slipped on the, uh, stairs," I replied. My face turned beet red. I began praying that the floor would swallow me whole.

"Hmm." Officer Jaxon responded, looking unconcerned, "My condolences."

I nodded vigorously, "Yes, thank you, I'm sure that Eth--Max would appreciate that. It is very sad that he, uh, fell down the stairs."

I made a mental reminder to slap myself when I got the chance. I had a feeling Marlee was planning to do the same.

Officer Jaxon changed the subject, clearly unconcerned about Ethan, "Now your friend Marlee here has told me that she needs to find Officer Macy. Do you know what she needs from there?"

I opened my mouth to respond, but Marlee shook her head slowly. "I, um, I don't know what we need, sir."

Officer Jaxon rested a hand on his chin and stared at Marlee intently. "What exactly does Officer Macy have to do with breaking someone out of the dungeon."

"That is none of your concern," Marlee answered.

"And what is your prisoner's name again?" Officer Jaxon asked, frowning.

"I never told you." She replied coolly.

He scratched his neck, "Well, I don't know much about the dungeon, but I sure know what key Officer Macy guards, and if that's what you want, then you can march right out of my room."

"We don't need her key!" Marlee exclaimed, her voice raised. She took a deep breath and calmed herself. "It is none of your concern what we need from Officer Macy. All we ask is for you to tell us where she is."

I swallowed my fear as the gears in my brain began turning. Why was Marlee lying about the key?

Officer Jaxon stood, his face slowly turning a shade of *ARTEZA Magenta Acrylic Paint #22*. "Listen to me, Marlee. I can't have you running around this castle, doing Giraffe knows what. The exchange was to help you get into the dungeon and break your prisoner out. I don't know what you're trying to do or trying to free, but I'm sick of it. This has gotten out of hand! You better give me the stuff that was promised and then GET OUT!"

I froze, fear pounding through my veins. If we were thrown out, would Marlee still give us the information? Probably not. I risked a glance at her, and by the expression on her face, I knew that she wouldn't yield any information until she got what she wanted. My instincts told me that her information was valuable. I tried to deny it, but even with my limited experience with this world, I could tell that the little shrub she had shown us was powerful. We needed her information about Emensaly.

"But Officer Jaxon, there must be another way--." Marlee began, but Officer Jaxon cut her off.

"Another way to what, bribe me? He scoffed. "Forget it."

Marlee shot me a desperate look. I bit my lip, unsure what to do.

"What are you waiting for?!" Officer Jaxon, his face still purple. Come to think of it. This was probably the most stress that he had ever been under in years. He was probably ready to go back to lying on his bed eating sushi and pie.

"Wait, look. We really need to break this prisoner free!" I exclaimed suddenly.

"Why is that?" He asked suspiciously.

"Well…" I trailed off, looking at Marlee. Her expression was unreadable. "We need to find Emensaly. Charlid is going to break out in a few days. Without Emensaly, the entire world will go to hell. You-everyone will be in so much danger if Charlid breaks free!"

Officer Jaxon kept his expression neutral, "And you think Emensaly is being kept in our prison? Oh please. I'm done with these lies you're feeding me. GET OUT RIGHT NO--."

"No, stop. Isn't there anything else we can bargain for?" Marlee asked desperately.

"NO!" Officer Jaxon roared, "NOW GIVE ME THE SCEPTER AND GET OUT."

I gulped, turning around to open my *packmare*. For once, Grass didn't argue with me. I pulled his jaw open slowly, praying that a brilliant would strike me. I dug my hand inside to look for the scepter when my fingers curled around the ring my grandmother had given me. I rubbed my finger against the gold band and green emerald. I bit my lip, wondering if it would work. There was a small chance, but that was better than none at all.

"Officer Jaxon?" I asked, my voice squeaking a bit at the end. I cleared my throat, "I have something you might like.

***

He scowled at me, "If you think I want anything more to do with the three of you little rascals, you can--." He stopped his mouth from falling open when he saw the ring.

I held it in front of him, a bit startled by his reaction. Marlee was looking at it in astonishment. "Where did you get that?" She asked breathlessly.

I slipped the ring on and off of my finger. "My grandma gave it to me."

"That's a *Grizet* ring." She exclaimed.

"A what ring?" I asked, confused.

"It's the most high-end company in all the realms. It's like the Gucci of our world." Ethan explained. "But even more rare and expensive."

"I heard that you have to wait 56 months to get one of those rings!" Officer Jaxon murmured, practically drooling.

I resisted the urge to roll my eyes at them. Seriously get a grip. I looked down at the ring again. Well, now that I knew that it was all expensive and rare, I didn't really want to give it away. I scoffed at my grandma. I guess as the deity of fashion. It was her duty to own all of the high-end brands. Still, I couldn't believe that she had given me this piece of jewelry. It must be worth a fortune.

"Say, who is your grandma?" Officer Jaxon asked gently, all menace gone from his voice.

"Her name--." I paused, remembering that I was supposed to be from the Athletic realm. "Umm, she owns a small Jewelry store. Her name is Amanda." I fibbed. Jeez, these lies were getting hard to keep track of.

"Ah, ok," Officer Jaxon said politely, clearly to focused on the ring to call me out on my lies, "How about you give me the ring now, and I'll tell you where Officer Macy is? Then you give me the scepter right before you leave."

I bit my lip and looked at Marlee. She nodded. "Sure," I replied, turning back to Officer Jaxon.

His face lit up like a Christmas tree, and Officer Jaxon jumped out of his seat with more agility than I had ever seen from him and ran across the room to grab a piece of paper. "Here's a blueprint of the castle. This is my room right here. If you turn left and go up the first big staircase, you'll find a hallway. The silver door belongs to Officer Macy. Now I'm not sure how you are planning on getting inside. Officer Macy only has one door that you can get to."

"Do you know where she is right now?" Marlee asked, leaning over the paper to get a better look.

Officer Jaxon frowned pensively and then checked his watch, "She spends most of her time in the training hall, sparring with other guards. It's getting late, but she's probably still down there. She takes her duty very seriously. You'll probably find her there."

"Where is the training hall on the map?" I inquired.

He scratched his chin, "Dear me. I can't quite remember. I haven't been there in ages. I think that it'll be down in the basement. Go down this staircase and turn left. Wait, no, turn right. There should be a sign that shows you which was. Worst case scenario, just ask someone and tell them you have to clean the towel mats. Those things are always disgusting." Officer Jaxon traced the roots with a pen. "All right, good luck. You still have the Thief Gloves right?"

"Yes, sir," I replied.

"Good now, hand over the ring and get on with your little plot." He instructed.

I hesitantly dropped the ring into his awaiting palm. I knew that it had to be done but I wasn't completely comfortable with giving Officer Jaxon a present my grandma had given me. He licked his lips and slid the massive ring onto his pungy pinky finger. His eyes were glowing with excitement, "Ah yes, gorgeous..."

Marlee made a revolted noise in the back of her throat. We stood and made our way to the door. I turned around, hoping to spot Ethan. "Watermelon." He whispered in my ear, "Uh, no, wait, I mean pineapple."

I chuckled softly and walked out the door. Officer Jaxon was still cooing over his ring and didn't give us a second glance. I walked through the door, hot on Marlee's heels. "Hey Ethan." I muttered, "Can you make us some cleaning supplies? It'll help us sell our story."

"Sure one sec." He replied as we began walking through the castle.

Marlee found the gym easily, which made me even more curious as to how she knew the castle so well. Maybe I shouldn't have dismissed the runaway princess theory so quickly. The space looked relatively normal, and I could tell it was a Legif and giraffes-only gym. Marlee would be way too small to use any of this equipment. It had a musty sorta smell, like body odor and Febreze. Thanks to Ethan,

I was holding a mop and bucket while Marlee carried Clorox wipes. The stairs on the way to the gym were a bit tricky with Ethan's curtain, but there weren't many people for us to run into at 10 p.m. I yawned, feeling exhausted and famished. All I wanted to do was lay down and eat a big helping of mac and cheese. Promising myself to do that the moment all of this craziness was over, I began walking deeper into the gym. It was quieter than I had expected. There was no music or low babble humming through the air. All of a sudden, a loud groan pierced through the air. It was followed by another and another.

"Umm, maybe we should come back later....?" I whisper, feeling uncomfortable.

"Don't wimp out now," Marlee exclaimed and trudged straight towards the sound.

"Should we er..."

"Let's let her go first," Ethan replied, still hidden by his curtain.

Marlee raced back towards us, her smile unsettling, "I found her, come on, guys!"

I exchanged looks with invisible Ethan before running after her. Marlee stopped right behind a massive exercise bike and motioned for us to follow her. I crouched down next to her and looked at Officer Macy. She was standing a few hundred feet away and looked like she was having a party. There were earphones plugged into her ears and she was dancing around like a maniac. There were two dumbbells lying forgotten on the side of the mat. Ethan pulled the curtain off his head to get a better view.

"Oh this is priceless." He laughed, pulling his phone out of his pocket.

I wanted to slap him for recording but after the nightmare Officer Macy put us through, I'd be glad for her to get a taste of her own medicine.

241

"Focus, Focus," Marlee commanded, clearly not understanding what an incredible opportunity this was for Officer Macy to go viral. "Look, I see her bracelet! It's sitting there, right next to the dumbbells."

"Okay, how should we do this?" Ethan asked.

"Ethan, I'll take your curtain and a glove. If all goes well, I'll be able to grab the bracelet and get out of here," Marlee instructed. "You guys are my backup."

"Back up?" I mouthed to Ethan, and he shrugged.

"Okay," Marlee whispered, hiding behind the curtain. "Here goes nothing."

I held my breath and waited to see what would happen. My heart was beating a million times a minute as I watched with trepidation. Time seemed to slow down, and I was starting to think that Marlee was walking backward. I was about to begin hatching a new plan with Ethan when the sound of metal hitting the floor rang through my ears. Ethan cursed. I turned to see what had happened and saw Marlee sprawled across the floor two feet away from the dumbbells.

"Oh no no no no, no!" I whispered, holding my breath. If Officer Macy killed Marlee, we wouldn't find anything out about Emensaly, and the information would end with her, oh, and I suppose it would be sort of sad.

I grabbed Ethan's hand, squeezing it so hard that his knuckles cracked. Officer Macy turned around slowly, pulling her earphones out as she did. Her face turned magenta. "WHAT ARE YOU DOING HERE, YOU LITTLE RAT!"

Marlee was still on the floor, her entire body quaking in fear. She didn't respond.

"WELL?! ANSWER ME!" Officer Macy ran to Marlee and grabbed her apron. "I'M GONNA KILL YOU!"

Marlee turned pale, but held Officer Macy's gaze (a bold move considering how much spit was flying out of Macy's mouth). Officer Macy loomed over tiny little Marlee, and I noticed for the first time how much of a height difference there really was. Officer Macy lifted her fist, about to strike, when Ethan suddenly yelled, "WAIT!"

Officer Macy stopped in her tracks, looking at Ethan. "Well, well, what do we have here? Looks like a little scum from the art realm. Ethan miraculously stayed calm, "I'm going to need you to unhand my friend over there." He motioned towards Marlee.

Officer Macy laughed, "Or what?! Are you going to paint me?"

I cursed under my breath, still hiding behind the treadmill. What was he planning on doing?

"Careful with that tone," Ethan advised, and I wanted to scream at him to stop being a smart mouth.

"Or what?" Officer Macy growled.

"Or I'll expose you," Ethan replied simply. His smile grew wicked, and he pulled his phone out of his pocket. "You're a great dancer."

Officer Macy's mouth dropped open. "You. Wouldn't. Dare."

"Oh yes, I would."

She growled like a lion and lunged at Ethan, "GIVE ME THE PHONE! GIVE ME THE PHONE!"

"I downloaded it to the cloud!" Ethan yelled, jumping out of the way. "It doesn't matter if you break my phone or my neck, for that matter. Anyone could still access it in my drive."

Officer Macy's paused, narrowing her eyes, "You piece of--."

"Calling me names won't help your cause." He said simply as if explaining something to a dramatic 4-year-old. "No, if you do want to have this video deleted, I recommend that you let me and my friends go. Don't mention our presence to anyone."

A vein in her forehead throbbed, and her hands were curled into a fist. "Very well," Officer Macy said, swallowing her anger. "Go."

Ethan pocketed his phone, and Marlee stood up in amazement. I saw her tuck something into the pocket of her apron before she lifted the curtain off of the ground. I dusted myself off, and the three of us walked to the exit following, leaving a steaming Officer Macy behind us.

As soon as we entered the stairwell, I let out a breath of relief and squealed with excitement. "Good idea Ethan." I grinned, feeling breathless, and he high-fived me.

"I've got the bracelet!" Marlee said, her face shining with happiness.

Ethan pumped his fist in the air and drew the curtain back up.

"Oh hey, can I see the video?" I asked, turning towards him as we began walking up the stairs.

He winced, "No can do. My phone died halfway through. I'm not even sure the video was saved."

I froze, staring at him. "You're telling me that you built your entire plan around a dead phone?!

"Yup," Ethan remarked.

"I'm going to kill you." I glared, holding a hand to my chest in an attempt to calm my pounding heart.

"You and Officer Macy can take turns," Ethan replied cheerfully.

Chapter 25

Ethan, Marlee and I ran as fast as we could trying to get back to Officer Jaxon's room. The hallways were mainly deserted except for a few disoriented strangers and guards who were too tired to say anything to us. We probably looked like a few custodians who had a job to get done, thanks to our handy cleaning supplies. Officer Jaxon hadn't said a word when we came bustling into his room. He was still sitting in the same position we had left him in, coddling his new ring as if it were a puppy.

We dove through the tapestry and ran down the slippery stairs. I managed not to fall the entire way down, only stopping once or twice to catch my breath. "Come on!" Marlee yelled, her voice filled with panic and excitement. I groaned, starting to understand what my mom meant whenever she said, "Don't get mixed up with the wrong crowd."

At last, we arrived in front of the familiar wooden door. Ethan situated himself behind the curtain while Marlee pushed it open. Ethan had created some new baskets and filled them with more mystery meat. I wasn't sure how much longer we would be able to keep milking the whole, feeding the prisoner's story. We creeped out of the wooden door, looking left and right. Marlee led us down a passageway and kept her head high when we passed the first guard. His green hair was matter against his face, and he seemed to be playing on his phone. Each corridor had the same iron door with one-way glass. I tried to avoid looking inside of the cells. Prisoners inside didn't seem quite human. Some had cuts and infections across their face, while others seemed to be lying in their own waste. All of them bore the same expression. One of hopelessness and despair. Each and every one of them looked broken. My mind was filled with images of how they might have been treated.

"Stop!" A gruff voice said, bringing me back to the present.

Marlee halted in front of an important-looking man with a uniform. "We need to deliver food to the prisoners."

"No one is allowed into these cells," the officer said, gesturing to his left. "There has been a rumor of a prisoner grabbing a basket from the foot patrol. We are investigating the premise."

My heart leaped into my throat the same way it always did when we were stopped in these hallways. I waited for Marlee to brush off his words and get us out of here.

"Don't worry, sir, we're going this way." She replied, pointing to her right. In the dim light, I noticed a sign that said, "WARNING: High-Security Prison."

The officer frowned about arguing when a different voice rang through the room. "Officer Agel, we've got a new lead."

He turned away, forgetting us, and ran down the other hallway. Skipping merrily, Marlee hopped down the stairs and ran down under the sign.

"Well, here goes nothing," Ethan muttered, and I heard the faint tap of his feet go down the stairs.

I followed, running down to Marlee. Walking through the door, I noticed that the guard we had previously met down here was snoring, fast asleep. "Does anyone know when his shift ends?" I asked, not really expecting an answer.

"In fifteen minutes," Marlee replied, running down to Riley's cell. "He told me earlier."

I shook my head in amusement. Ethan stepped out from behind his curtain and joined Marlee at Riley's cell. Marlee had already pulled the silver bracelet out of her apron and pushed it into the ridge in the cell wall. There was a faint click, and the door swung open. Only instead of revealing Riley, we found ourselves standing in front of a second door. I slapped my forehead. The only out-of-the-ordinary aspect of the door was a golden doorknob in the center and the one-way window. Marlee reached forwards and touched the knob only to quickly retract her hand. She cursed, "It burned me."

I looked at her hand in astonishment, the flesh had turned a nasty shade of red, and her skin was peeling. I turned to the doorknob and took a closer look. I blinked in astonishment, realizing that the doorknob wasn't completely solid. There was a glass case around it, and a substance that looked like liquid gold was sloshing around inside of it.

"What the--?" Ethan asked, leaning over next to me. "That's bizarre."

I bit my lip, squinting at the doorknob. I felt as if there was a sort of tugging sensation in my gut. It was pulling me towards the doorknob, practically begging me to touch it. I reached up, feeling hesitant. There was something blocking me.

"Fire," I muttered, the words tumbling from my lips without passing through my brain before.

"Piper, what are you talking about?" Ethan asked, but it sounded faint as if he said it from a great difference.

I wrapped my hand around the glass, ignoring the searing pain in my left palm. My body felt warm. It buzzed as if alive. Red dots danced in front of my eyes, and I suddenly realized that they were on fire. I thrashed around, covering my eyes with my hands, trying to extinguish the flame. My brain felt as if it had been replaced with smoke, and I opened my mouth, preparing to scream. Suddenly a voice rang clearly through my head like a lighthouse clearing the fog. "Piper, you need to calm down. Control the flame before they consume you. Stop fighting it, join it, and reign it in."

Tears would have been flowing down my face if my eyes weren't so dry, "I-I can't." I sobbed, my chest heaving.

"Control it." The voice instructed before fading away.

I took a deep breath, and the flames receded slowly at first. My body cooled, and I managed to get my bearings. I focused on the feeling of my feet touching the concrete, trying to find my center of gravity. I opened my eyes slowly, expecting the worst, but was amazed to see that they were still functioning. I began to wonder what on earth had happened when I realized that there was still a dark haze that filled the room. Smoke. I squeezed my eyes shut, fighting the panic swelling within me. I took a deep breath, my lungs filling themselves with clean oxygen. Perhaps it was my connection with Potia that rendered me safe against smoke. I opened my eyes again and squinted, trying to find Marlee and Ethan. The smoke wasn't that thick. I could see a good 5 feet in front of me. Where were they? What had happened? That last thing I did was grab the golden doorknob. Then everything was on fire. I took a step forward, calling out their names, when I felt my feet come in contact with something. I straightened my arms to stop from falling.

My heart leaped into my mouth once I looked down at what had caused me to stumble. A sob built in my chest, "E-Ethan!" I yelled, looking down in horror. Tears cascaded down my cheeks as I looked down at his body. He lay sprawled across the floor, his mouth hanging open slightly. I fell to my knees, taking in the sight of his grey skin and thin frame. Has the smoke done this to him? Why had I been spared? Did the voodoo doorknob have something to do with Potia? I crawled closer to Ethan, tentatively resting my injured arm on his palm.

Ethan gasped, a loud sound that echoed through the silent room. His chest began rising and falling, and his eyelids fluttered open, revealing his green eyes. "Ethan!" I whispered in relief, lifting my hand off of his palm. The moment the contact ceased, his head felt bad, and his pulse was still. My heart began beating again faster and faster as I made the motion to grab his hand. The moment our skin touched, color returned to his face, and he managed to sit up.

"Don't let go of my hand," I instructed, my voice still shaking.

"Why was I on the ground?" Ethan asked, sitting up and leaning against the wall.

I shrugged before responding, "I think that it had something to do with that doorknob. The moment I touched it, everything went to hell. I felt like I was on fire. Then I heard a voice. I think it was Potia, he extinguished the fire, but now there's this weird smoke. If I'm not touching your hand, you'll pass out."

Ethan gave me a strange look, still holding my clammy hand. "Do you think the doorknob is somehow related to Potia?"

I bit my lip, "It might. That would explain how I managed to survive touching it and stay awake with the smoke."

"I wonder how far the smoke has spread," Ethan questioned, "If it's gotten all the way through the dungeon, it might work to our advantage to get out of here."

"We need to find Marlee," I instructed, my heart finally returning to its original pace. "Then we get Riley, break out of this place, get our information, and then finally leave this hellish place."

"Good plan," Ethan replied, standing up. "Only problem is that our plans never seem to go the way we hope they do."

I ignored him, hoping for our sake that he was wrong. My eyes scanned the room, trying to find Marlee. At last, they focused on a small, crumpled-up figure curled up on the ground a few feet to my left. "There she is." I breathed, pointing at the lumpy blob in the corner.

"Where?" Ethan asked, squinting his eyes.

"Right there, to my left," I replied, pointing again.

"Oh, I see her."

We walked towards Marlee and were surprised that she was so far away. Hadn't she been standing right next to us? Was she planning on running away, leaving us to the mercy of the smoke? I felt a small stab of betrayal but wasn't surprised in the slightest.

"She was going to leave us here, wasn't she?" Ethan asked venomously.

"Looks like it," I said, fighting the urge to leave Marlee's pathetic little body on the ground. We had been through too much to stop now. She needed to tell us about Emensaly.

"Wait, Piper, stop," Ethan said, pulling me away from Marlee. His face was a mixture of awe and anger.

I took a step closer, trying to see what he was looking at. My eyes trailed away from Marlee, and I saw a second figure curled up next. Riley was out of her cell.

Chapter 26

"She got Riley," I whispered, looking down at the two girls that lay in front of us. "She broke Riley out and was going to leave us there to die. After everything we did to help her."

"That little rat!" Ethan fumed, having picked up a few cusses thanks to Officer Macy.

"She was going to leave us there to die," I repeated, the words having sunk into my skin. I finally realized the type of world this was. People were willing to steal, kill, betray, and lie for anything. Family first had a different meaning down here. My hands balling into fists, and I narrowed my eyes. I took a closer look at Riley. Even through my anger, I still had the nagging sensation that I had seen her somewhere.

Ethan cursed and moved closer to the two sisters. "Wake them up." He said, his voice angry. He straightened, "Let's see what they have to say from themselves."

I obliged, still holding Ethan in one hand. I bent over to rest my thumb on Marlee's forearm. Her eyelids fluttered, and she woke up with a start. She lifted her head, eyes widening when she saw Ethan's expression.

"So," I asked, "You thought you would go on a little detour and show Riley around?"

Marlee took a deep breath, "It wasn't like that. I swear I, I wasn't trying to--."

"You betrayed us." Ethan snared, "That's all there is to it. After everything that we did for you, you betrayed us. Left us here to die."

Marlee held his gaze for half a second before responding, "Piper was on fire, and you were choking on smoke. There was nothing I *could* do. The smoke confused Riley's shadow after the door burned down. I managed to grab her."

"Don't lie to us," I hissed, "Now, I couldn't care less about your sister or about, but what I do care about is Emensaly. Tell us where she is. After that, you can go back to living your pathetic little lives."

Marlee was unfazed, "Get us out of here, then I'll tell you."

Ethan laughed though it sounded more like a roar, "You are in no position to bargain, you psychopath!? There is no way that we are helping another hair on your head."

"Actually, I am in a position to bargain," Marlee said with a slow smile creeping across her face, "Piper, the fire burnt your contacts. How exactly are you planning on getting out?"

"I'll find a way." I bluffed.

"But you promised to help us escape!" Marlee pouted as if this was all a game to her. In the back of my mind, I vaguely hoped that Riley was slightly saner than Marlee.

I chuckled without humor, "Are you trying to give us a lesson on integrity? Ha, funny. Now tell us where Emensaly is."

Marlee opened her mouth to protest when beside her, Riley began to stir. Her eyelids were fluttering, and she tried to lift her arm.

"We need to run before the guards wake up!" Marlee said urgently.

"What is this ``we``?" Ethan asked, scowling, "There is no more ``we``!"

I tugged his arm, and I heard a loud groan coming from the entrance. "Hurry, the guards are walking up."

I stood, but Marlee grabbed my arm. She lifted Riley's hand and placed it on my shoulder. Riley let out a gasp, fully walking up. "Agh ge-off me." I struggled, but Marlee held on firmly. For someone so tiny, she had a firm grip.

"Let go of her!" Ethan yelled, pulling on Marlee's waist.

I tried to pry Riley off, but her fingernails dug into my shoulder blade. "Ah stop it. That hurts."

Riley grinned, showing her *Banana Yellow #53d4 shade 6* teeth, "Good."

I shuttered, trying to inch away. Something about her smile was even more terrifying than her scowl.

"Who's there!" A weak and unfamiliar voice yelled. I could barely make out his silhouette, but he seemed to be struggling to stand.

"We're wasting time." Malree hissed, "Piper, just get us out of the dungeon."

"La la la la wasting time all the time." Riley croaked and swung her head back and forth. I leaned away from her, trying to escape her awful breath. Gagging slightly, I sighed and began running out of the dungeon, with Marlee holding one hand, Ehan the other, and Riley still giving my shoulder a death grip. We got past the first guard, who didn't seem to have managed to regain the feeling in his legs. "Stop!" He yelled, helplessly trying to crawl after us.

"Which way, Marlee!" I yelled, no longer caring about being discreet.

"Left left!" She called, her voice panicked.

I turned about to continue running when Riley suddenly pulled me back. I cursed, stumbling backward. "Riley, what the-." I gasped, stopping midspeech. Riley still had her fingers wrapped around my forearm, but she was turned to face a prison guard. Marlee was looking at Riley. Her expression laced with a mixture of confusion and amusement.

"What is she doin---AHHH." I let out a scream. My eyes focused on Riley. She had grabbed the hand of a male prison guard and bit down on his finger.

The guard screamed but was unable to move his hand away due to the smoke. I looked down at Riley in horror, wincing at the sound of bones cracking. I forced down nausea and tried to pull Riley away. She was licking her lips, eyes wide with amusement. She threw her head back and cackled. Yeah, she definitely did more than steal bread.

***

I swallowed another scream, "Marlee, what's wrong with your sister?"

Marlee looked at me, "Oh, don't worry, she's just having fun."

"Well get her!" Ethan yelled, running an agitated hand through his hair. "Piper and I need to leave!"

Marlee sighed, "Time to go, V."

I raised an eyebrow. Since when was V an abbreviation for Riley? Riley rolled her eyes and stood. I inched away from her as far as I could, with her still keeping a death grip on my shoulder. "RILEY, MOVE!" I hissed.

She ignored me. Ethan grabbed my other arm and began pulling me away while Marlee pushed Riley. An expression of adorning was displayed on her features as she looked at Riley. I gulped down my fear.

"They're both psychopaths!" I whispered to Ethan, and we continued running down the hall.

"I've come to that conclusion myself, thanks," Ethan replied, pumping his legs.

I struggled to keep up with him, panting with the exertion. Marlee was keeping up just fine, but Riley seemed to be pulling me back. It appeared that she had created a game out of pulling my hair whenever we saw another guard sprawled on the floor.

"Will you quit that!" I hissed, trying to slap her hand away.

Riley grinned and answered with another tug. I resisted the urge to strangle her. Instead, I focused on navigating. Ethan finally stopped pulling me and pushed the moldy wooden door open with one hand. I made the motion to step through the door when Marlee held me back. "We can't go through Officer Jaxon's room." Her eyes glazed over to Marlees, who was pulling strands of hair out and flossing her teeth with it. I suppressed a shudder.

"What is your problem!?" I asked, clenching my fists together. Marlee was getting on my last nerve. I had half a mind to lunge at her and tackle her to the floor.

She bit her lip, probably concocting more lies in her head. I rolled my eyes, turning to follow Ethan to the door. He shot Marlee a rude hand gesture and opened his mouth to argue when the sound of footsteps filled the hallway. Marlee turned around, distracted, and in my panic, I ran through the door. Looking frantic, Marlee glanced back and forth between the hallway, Riley and the door. In a split second, Marlee grabbed Riley's arm and tugged her through the doorframe. Ethan slammed the door shut, and we all took a deep breath. Marlee took her hand off my shoulder and turned to me, fuming. Riley was leaning against the wall, humming a song that sounded a lot like a funeral dirge.

"We can't go back to Officer Jaxon's room," Marlee said, pacing back and forth.

"And why not?" Ethan asked, exasperated.

Marlee paused and then something in her expression changed. "Well, you two don't have your contacts in. Officer Jaxon will know that the treasures are fake."

I shook Ethan a look of hesitation. Marlee actually had a good point. Ethan looked back at Marlee, ignoring her previous statement, "What are you hiding from us."

She tucked a strand of hair behind her ear and looked up at us through her green lashes, "I'm not hiding anything, Ethan."

I clapped loudly, interrupting their banter, "Helloooo! We need to move! Who knows when the guards will find the door."

"But the contacts--."

"We'll figure that out when we're walking!" I said, my voice becoming hysteric. "Move!"

For once, they actually listened to me, Marlee grabbed Riley, who had begun a cheerful conversation with the wall, and Ethan followed me up the stairs. Marlee and Riley began talking in hushed whispers.

"Any brilliant ideas?" Ethan asked helplessly.

I frowned, "Honestly, I'm just hoping to run through Officer Jaxon's room and then find a different exit from there. If we're lucky, he'll still be distracted by the ring and ignore us."

"Luck tends to disappear when you lean on it," Ethan muttered.

"What do you think Riley did?" I asked, glancing over my shoulder.

Ethan shrugged and rubbed his neck furiously. "Not sure, but it might not have been our smartest move to unleash someone in that mental state and who spends time in the part of the dungeon with high-security measures designated for highly dangerous prisoners."

I felt a shiver run down my spine. What if Riley attacked us down here? Would we be able to defend ourselves? What if we couldn't? Marlee had already stabbed us in the back. Did they really need us anymore? They could leave our bodies down here. No one would notice. I wondered if they had realized that as well. We needed our information. We really needed it. I stopped walking, realizing that I was standing right in front of the tapestry that led to Officer Jaxon's room.

"Ethan!" I whispered. "Psst Ethan."

"Yeah?"

"Let's corner them, get the information out now!"

Ethan swallowed, "Got it."

I turned around to them and contorted my face into what I hoped was a menacing expression. "Marlee, we got you out. Tell us where Emensaly is."

I stood before her, gritting my teeth and not moving. Riley's lip quivered, and she burst out laughing, "Oh, you don't--," She gasped for breath, "Go there want." She pointed at Ethan, "Not with him!" Riley doubled over, clutching her stomach as if it were the funniest joke that she had ever heard.

I shot Ethan a confused look, but his expression was stony. I took a step back, "Marlee, tell us, you'll regret it if you don't."

I bit my lip, not sure if he was bluffing. Marlee glared at us, but then her gaze shifted to the tapestry behind us, "Uhh, guys, we have a problem."

"Yeah, we do," Ethan began, "You won't tell us where Emensaly is."

I turned around, realizing that I was standing in the folds of the tapestry.

"Anna, Max, Marlee?!" Officer Jaxon's voice called, "Is that you? Did you get your prisoner?"

I froze, staring at the others, petrified.

"Hello?!" Officer Jaxon said again, "Children are you there?"

"Run!" Ethan whispered.

I prepared to bolt, already down two flights of stairs, when light flooded into the stairwell.

"Oh, there you are!" Officer Jaxon stated. "Are you ready to give me the scepter?"

I stood with my back facing him, petrified. My feet were stuck to the ground, and I vaguely noticed Marlee and Ethan looking down the staircase as well. Even Riley had the right mind to stay still.

"Children?" Officer Jaxon said, "Why won't you turn around? Have you gone mad?"

His hand gripped my shoulder, and I felt a wave of fear as Officer Jaxon turned me around.

I stumbled slightly and accidentally met his gaze. His eyes flashed menacingly, and his face turned magenta. "YOU LITTLE ART LIARS!" He screamed, spit flying in my face. YOU'RE NOT FROM THE ATHLETIC LAND? YOU'RE FROM THE ART REALM!!! THE PAYMENT YOU OFFERED ME WAS FORGERY?"

Officer Jaxon lifted a fist about to pummel me when Riley tapped him on the shoulder. Marlee lunged to grab Riley, but she was too late. Officer Jaxon turned to face her, and his expression turned from anger to pure terror. He let out an uncharacteristically high-pitched scream. Marlee pulled Riley away from Officer Jaxon, who was lifting a shaking finger, pointing towards Riley. "V-Vega Flint, y-you u-unleashed Ve-Vega Flint."

Officer Jaxon leaned against the wall looking faint, and I blinked in confusion. Vega Flint? Marlee said that her name was Riley. Understanding rushed through my brain as all the puzzle pieces clicked together. That was why Riley had looked so familiar when I first saw her. I had seen her face on a poster when we were walking from Marlee's house to the castle. Terror washed through me, and I understood why Officer Jaxon was quaking. The poster said that Ri-Vega had murdered a handful of important Giraffes and Legifs. It also made sense as to why Marlee was wearing contacts. She didn't want everyone to recognize her as Vega's sister. I felt a shiver of fear and a bit of guilt, realizing what we had done. Ledolush land was already in such a bad place, had Ethan and I made it worse by releasing Vega? Marlee (if that was even her real name) had said that she was going to change Ledolish land, whether it was for better or for worse. I didn't want to be here when it happened.

"Run!" Marlee screamed, pushing past Officer Jaxon who was still quaking in his boots. I looked at Ethan for a second before tensing my legs and chasing after her.

The four of us ran through Officer Jaoxn's room straight through to the door. "It's locked!" Ethan yelled, shoving against the will all of his might. My vision grew hazy with adrenaline and terror.

"The window!" Marlee yelled frantically, grabbing Vega's hand and tugging her towards the massive, floor-to-ceiling windows. Grabbing the burgundy curtains, she tugged them away from the glass, moonlight flooding into the bedroom.

Officer Jaxon took that moment to regain his senses and ran into the room. "Stop it right now!" He yelled, running to the other side of the room. His hand slammed over a gold button, and I took it as our cue to leave. He looked around in a panic and picked up a glass orb that was sitting on a coffee table, and threw it at us. It missed by several feet.

Marlee began frantically working on the switch next to the window with no luck. Impulsively I grabbed the black desk chair next to Officer Jaxon's bed. Before common sense got the better of me, I threw it out the window. The glass shattered on impact, spider web-like cracks forming across it. Without a second glance, Marlee grabbed Vega's hand and jumped through the opening. I looked at Ethan in panic, and he bent over cautiously, looking down. There was a clatter of footsteps, and Officer Jaxon was yelling in the background.

"JUMP!" I yelled, pushing Ethan out. I shot one more glance over my shoulder and saw the door being thrown open by a very angry Officer Macy.

Chapter 27

I hit the ground faster than I could say ouch. My hip bone throbbed painfully and my bandaged arm stung as I rolled onto my other side. Grateful for the wet grass that we landed in, I pushed hair out of my face and looked up at the broken window. It stood at least twelve feet above us. Groaning, I pushed myself up and turned to Ethan. "You good?" I asked, getting to my feet.

He cursed, "Guess that's what I get for pushing you out of the tree in survival 101 class."

I managed a small smile. Groaning, Ethan sat up and then took a sharp breath. "Gah, my wrist."

I frowned walking over to him. As soon as I saw his hand in the dim light my stomach gave a lurch. The skin was already turning a nasty shade of purple, and the wrist, which was bent at an odd angle, had begun swelling. Ethan poked it tentatively, wincing.

I cursed, "Ethan that looks really bad but we need to get going. The guards will see us not to mention the fact that Marlee and Vega are getting away. Can you, can you walk?"

He took a deep breath, "Yeah yeah I-I'm fine. Let's." Ethan let out a gasp of pain and I felt like the worst friend in the world. "Let's go."

He held up his good hand, and I pulled him upwards. I looked around trying to find Marlee. We had wasted a little over two minutes here, who knows how far away those two could get. I closed my hand into a fist and then opened it again producing a small flame. Holding my hand high I squinted trying to see Marlee and Vega. I looked off to my left seeing two figures running away from the castle.

"Ethan, I found them," I said, running down the grassy hill.

"Great." He winced, trying to keep up with me. "Also, can you turn the flame off? You're setting off a beacon for everyone and there are like ten people trying to kill us right now."

"Actually, I think it's more like twenty-five." I corrected, panting. I closed my fist to extinguish the flame.

I pumped my legs as fast as I could trying to keep up with Marlee and Vega. They had already run down the stone path straight into the Ledo village. Losing sight of them I slowed, not sure in which direction they had gone.

"There!" Ethan declared, pointing down one of the many dirt roads.

We followed it, turning left past a halfway demolished building and I nearly crashed into a Ledo wearing a parched up clock. They bared their teeth at me and grabbed something inside of their clock. Ethan grabbed my hand and pulled me away quickly. I could barely see anything in the dim light but I didn't risk a fire. Glancing over my shoulder nervously I could make out the silhouettes of guards running down the grassy hill from the castle. Breathing deeply I continued to follow Marlee and Vega. Running past another door and around a flickering streetlight, I caught a glimpse of the two sisters. They seemed to have stopped running and were looking at an engraving in the wall.

"Quick, trap them!" Ethan said.

"Cover me if guards come!" I replied, rubbing my palms together.

I opened my hands, and a roaring fire appeared in my hand. Marlee and Vega turned around staring at me in terror. Even Ethan took a tiny step back. I took a deep breath and tried to remember how to link myself to Potia. I felt heat build up in my stomach and I raised my hands farther apart. Adrenaline coursed through my veins, and my arms began shaking with the exertion. Channel it from your core, I

263

remembered from Potia's lesson, Don't fight it, join it. Breathing in through my nose, I imagined the flame building with every breath. The wall of *Angelus Red #45fd2* colored flame grew until it was big enough to surround the two sisters.

Marlee's jaw dropped and Vega grinned in amusement. She hobbled over to the wall of the flame and stuck her hand inside. My insides squirmed and I looked away, trying to stop the smell of burning flesh from reaching my nostrils. The wall of fire shrunk with my concentration and I made an effort to put it back up. Vega shrieked and stepped away. A second later she made another grab for the flame. Marlee was ready and quickly pulled Vega away. Ethan raised his eyebrows in their direction but said nothing.

"Let us go!" Marlee yelled, trying to hold back a squirming Vega.

"Where is Emensaly!" I barked, sweat dripping down my brow from the exertion and heat.

Marlee took a deep breath, "Vega and I are both part of a revolution. We've been trying to overthrow the Giraffes for our entire life."

I gritted my teeth trying to stop my arms from shaking. Ethan asked the question that was running through my head. "And what exactly does that have to do with Emensaly?"

"I'm getting there," Marlee grunted, trying to control Vega from running into the flame. "Emensaly came to visit us, she wanted to help us. Told us about a time when her brothers took away her will, she said that she was trying to make sure that would stop happening in all the rest of the realms. She gave us maps through the castle and helped us kill a few giraffes. Vega got caught and when I came home, Emensaly was all panicky, she said she couldn't be captured, she said that she would never go back to her brothers. Emensaly told me that she was going to take some time off in Teyar Skies. Whatever that means."

I heard something stumble behind me. I turned around, quickly losing control of the fire. It dissolved into embers that flew away in the wind. Ethan was leaning against the wall, his face having turned *Chalk White, Benjamin Moore #45S2*. His eyes were wide and every inch of his body was shaking. Marlee and Vega had already fled the premises and there wasn't a soul in sight. The clack of soldiers had already superseded, they must not have been too willing to enter the Ledo town at night. What was Ethan scared of?

"Ethan?" I whispered, tentatively, "Ethan, what's wrong?"

He opened his mouth and closed it again. Two words tumbled out of his mouth in the form of a whisper, "Mud dragons."

Chapter 28

I stared down at Ethan, fear blossoming in my chest, "What's--what's so bad about mud dragons?"

Ethan didn't respond but the terror in his eyes said enough. I was about to ask again when I heard a gruff shout come from somewhere on my left. "Spread out! Those kids have got to be here somewhere. Dead or alive! If you find Vega Flint do not attempt to hurt her, call for backup. That girl is unpredictable and deadly."

I immediately recognized officer Macy's voice. Cursing I grabbed Ethan's good arm and pulled him away from the guards.

"Do you remember where we landed?" I asked Ethan desperately, as we ran through the dark streets. The only way back to the flower garden was to go back to the spot where it dropped us off.

"Huh?" Ethan asked, looking up, his eyes darting around nervously.

I sighed, "Nevermind."

I looked at the castle, the clearing that we had landed was outside of the Ledo town opposite to the castle. I bit my lip, wondering if google maps worked in this realm. "Let's go this way." I decided, grabbing Ethan and pulling him forwards. He stumbled for a second and then began to run next to me.

What was wrong with him? The words Teyar Skies had triggered something inside of him. Had he been to that realm before. Had something happened to him. My mind was reeling with ideas when I suddenly hit my right toe against an uneven stone and went sprawling. Grunting I pushed myself off the dirt and tentatively touched my lip. I winced, realizing that it had been split open. My bandaged arm stung due to the fact that it had caught me on my way down. Ethan stopped for a moment and offered me his good hand. Grabbing it, I pulled myself up and dusted off my dirty chef costume that I was still wearing.

"Ethan?" I asked quickly, as if I were talking to a spooked animal, "Ethan are you okay?"

Stupid question, I know. Obviously he wasn't okay.

"I can't go back there." Ethan said hoarsely, "I-I can't."

"Oh, well, you don't have to come with me," I replied, my spirit falling quickly. I tried to hide the disappointment and fear in my expression. Ethan wasn't going to Teyar Skies with me. I knew that I shouldn't be surprised. After his reaction to Marlee's statement, there was no way that he wanted to go. Heck, I didn't even want to go. I knew that I had to find Emensaly. This was my mission. Ethan wasn't obliged to come. I was lucky enough that he came to Ledolish Land with me. Still, a small selfish part of me wanted to get down on my knees and beg for him to come with me. I shook that thought out of my head and turned away from the castle.

"Let's go, we don't want the guards to catch up with us." I smiled, trying to keep my voice light.

I began running, with Ethan right next to me. I looked over my shoulder trying to make sure no one was following us. I heard Ethan say something and I quickly became hopeful. "What was that?" I called.

"There's the bar that we started in. I think if we follow this road we'll be back in the clearing." He replied, voice unreadable.

"Oh." I proclaimed, mentally slapping myself, "Oh right, yeah, let's go that way."

Ethan began jogging down the dirt road avoiding piles of rock and debri. Sighing, I ran after him. Soon enough we were standing at the edge of the Ledo village a few steps away from the clearing.

"Do you remember where we landed?" I asked, hating the tension between us.

"No." He replied, rubbing his hands up and down his arms.

I exhaled, squinting my eyes, trying to focus. Having an idea, I unfocused my eyes the way Ethn taught me back in survival 101 class. Maybe the spot would appear if I focused on the godly side of my mind. I tried to imagine channeling from Potia's sight. Abruptly a flash of green light appeared in the middle of the clearing a few hundred feet away from us. I grinned with relief. Thank goodness I could find it. Concentrating on that spot I managed to make the light reappear three more times. My legs shook with exhaustion, channeling his sight wasn't nearly as easy as channeling a flame.

"I've got it." I declared, pointing to a small patch of land where I had seen the green light flicker.

Ethan opened his mouth to say something when a massive boom echoed through the town. Without thinking twice we ran out of the town straight into the dead clearing. "Get down on your knees!" I yelled, when an odd bullet that looked like a feather flew a few feet past my face.

Ethan obliged and we began crawling toward the place where I saw the flash of light. It was around twenty feet away, but I wasn't sure if we would make it. I could tell that Ethan was distracted. His eyes seemed somewhat unfocused, and I tried not to panic. "Ethan, hurry up!" I begged, already a few yards ahead of him.

Ethan made no motion to show that he had heard but began moving a bit faster. "LOOK OUT!" I yelled as another feather bullet landed in the spot he had been in before. Just a few more feet, I repeated in my head. Just a few more--, AHHHHHHHH. I screeched as one of the feathers lodged itself into my right hand. Shaking my fingers in pain, I whimpered, pulling the odd contraption out. I wiped my hand on my apron, trying to ignore nausea threatening to take control.

"It was supposed to be right here!" I yelled to Ethan, my heart still pounding in my ears.

He looked around wildly and then suddenly grabbed my hand. I felt touched at first thinking it was an action out of kindness, but then wind began to whip around my hair. Light blared in my face and my body began to spin wild. I grasped Ethan's hand desperately. When I felt like I had lost all sense of direction and gravity, I landed on my behind upon a patch of wet grass. Am I dead? I wondered, squinting up at the clear sky. I gripped my head trying to keep it from spinning. I saw a long green stem to my left and realized that we were in the flower garden. We were alive! I felt like rejoicing but my happiness was short-lived. I would be going to Teyar Skies now, and Ethan wouldn't be coming. I swallowed a lump in my throat, feeling the familiar sense of panic, settling in the pit of my stomach. Maybe I could just lay here for the rest of my life. I could become used to the calming feeling of grass beneath me.

I let out a small groan. Everything hurt. My hip bone was throbbing painfully, and the stinging in my hand and forearm hadn't subsided. If anything, the travel from Ledolish land to the flower garden had made it worse. Oh, and I was tired, so tired, I felt like I could win a sleeping competition with Sleeping Beauty. Feeling sorry for myself, I rolled onto one side and looked for Ethan. He lay somewhere to my right, looking downright miserable. A very small, cruel side of my mind suddenly thought, serves him right for abandoning me. I quickly vanquished that speculation. Ethan had done more than I could hope. He deserved to have some peace of mind, especially if I was about to screw up the world by failing. Don't think like that. My subconscious scolded me. You can find Emensaly. The inaccuracy of that statement made me laugh. The only way that I would find Emensaly would be if she bit me on the nose. Groaning, I sat up, massaging my shoulder that (surprise, surprise) was also in pain.

"Ethan?!" I called, my voice weak. Clearing my throat, I tried again, "Ethan!?"

"Yeah, what's wrong!?" He replied, sitting up, his eyes darting around in a panic.

A wave of guilt hit me, "No, nothing, don't worry." I paused, trying to figure out the best way to phrase this. "Ethan--what happened back there. One minute you were fine, and the next you, well, you kinda--." I stopped, unsure how to continue.

"I'm fine." He replied, gruffled. Then he winced, "Gah, my wrist."

I jumped up, fearing the worst. Walking over, I bent down to examine Ethan's wrist. I cursed, looking closer. The skin had turned a dark magenta, and the hand was swelling awkwardly. Ethan gritted his teeth and took a few shaky breaths.

"I can make you a bandage and some ice." I offered lamely.

Ethan gave a quick nod. Fingering my *pindre* I summoned my sketchbook and quickly began to draw. Waving my hand, a black and white bandage appeared on my hand. If the situation wasn't so dire, I might have giggled. I guess using a pencil wasn't a great idea when you were trying to summon objects out of your *pindres*.

I tentatively lay the ice onto his swollen wrist and began wrapping the bandage around. Once I finished, he stood staring out into the horizon which had turned a pretty shade of *Farrow and Ball Middleton Pink No.247* paint. I cleared my throat trying to talk to him again, "Ethan, maybe we don't need to go to the Teryar Skies, there's always the possibility that Marlee was lying to us."

Half of me hoped that it was true. Ethan might be willing to go somewhere else with me. Of course, there was always the possibility that he didn't want to keep looking for Emensaly after our little adventure in Ledolish land. Another part of me was desperately praying that our time spent trying to free Vega wasn't in vain. "I'll look at the map Eveda gave us," I said when Ethan didn't reply.

I shrugged Grass the packmare off of my back, sighing, knowing what was about to happen. "Well, well, well, look who survived Ledolish land. Good for you, princess."

I gritted my teeth, "Shut up, Grass, I need the map."

"Do you need it, or do you want it?" He asked in a sing-song voice.

I took a deep breath, "I will rip you in half."

Grass chuckled, "You're so passive-aggressive. No lady should behave like that."

"GRASS!" I screeched.

"Fiiiiiine." He surrendered, stretching open his wide jaw.

Once I was sure that he wouldn't clamp his jaw shut the moment I stuck my hand inside, I snatched the map and shouldered Grass. Looking down at the worn paper covered in green markings, I searched for a realm named Teyar Skies but couldn't find it.

"Hey, do you know where," I paused, not sure if Ethan could handle hearing the words again, "That realm Marlee told us about is?"

Ethan opened his mouth as if the words pained him to speak. "It's-hehem-it's also known as the mud dragon realm."

I bit my lip, wondering if I should go over and comfort him or if he would want to be left alone. I decided to look back at the map and search for the Mud dragon realm.

Placing my finger on the spot, I felt a mixture of dread and anticipation when I saw that there was a large green orb positioned right next to a doodle of what I assumed was a mud dragon.

271

"Um, okay, so maybe we, I mean, I need to go to the mud dragon realm," I said, my spirits falling.

"Don't go." Ethan said hoarsely, "If you value your life, don't go."

I blanched, my fingers feeling numb. "Well, that's just perfect. I was running out of nightmare fuel for a moment there."

Ethan didn't respond. Before I could say something else, I heard a loud screech that sounded a lot like tires skidding across asphalt. I jumped up in a panic, thinking that we were being attacked. I whipped my head around to see what had made the noise. There was a fancy dark blue car standing between a massive sunflower and a neon blue orchid. It was covered in constellations and had gold strips on the side, running from door to door. Even though I wasn't a fan of cars, I could tell this was expensive, maybe a Bentley or a Porsche

"What the--?" I wondered, and Ethan even looked up at the automobile.

I scrambled to my feet, hoping that I would be able to defend myself or run away. A moment later, the car door opened, and a posh woman stepped out of it. My heart beat calmed as I took in her shiny pantsuit that matched the design on the car. I squealed, "Grandma!!"

I ran towards her and wrapped my arms around her.

"Now, now, you'll wrinkle my clothes." She complained but grinned and didn't pull away. "So, did someone call for a ride?!"

Chapter 29

"What are you doing here!?" I asked, confused but thrilled.

"Well, I thought that you might want somewhere to stay the night. Eveda told me that you guys might need a safe place to spend the night. Almost every realm has been attacked by chaos in-betweens, and so many people have gone missing after venturing out into the flower realm. This place is crawling with Charlid babies."

I shuddered at the thought, "How...pleasant."

"Mhm. Oh, and I almost forgot, Eveda wanted to talk to you."

My face split into a grin as I looked around, "No way, really!? Where is she?"

"Oh, still in the art realm, but she asked me to give you a light bloom. The two of you can talk to each other." My grandma said as she passed me an odd contraption that looked like a flashlight with flower petals attached to the top.

I took it, vaguely remembering Eveda explaining that light blooms could be used as communication devices. I flicked the little switch on the bottom, and the petals began to glow. I immediately heard a crackling noise that sounded like static, "P-Piper! Piper, are you there?" I heard Eveda say.

"Yeah, I'm here!" I replied, feeling a sense of homesickness and excitement.

"Are you alright? Have you been making progress?!" She asked, sounding stressed.

"Oh yeah, we're doing great." I lied, feeling guilty. "Everything's just fine." I looked over at Ethan, who was still sitting on the grass, depressingly looking at the sky. "And how are you?"

"Oh, Piper, I wish I could deliver some good news, but the art realm isn't doing well. We've had five attacks in the past two days, and they just keep coming. I neve expected there to be so many in-betweens. Humans must have been smuggled into the realm of Charlid for longer than we suspected. And the art realm isn't the only place suffering. The pixie realm is nearly abolished, and kayider land is running out of resources." Eveda sounded exhausted and close to tears.

Wishing that I could offer some comfort, I said, "Well, don't worry, we're really close to finding Emensaly. She's practically already back in the golden god kingdom." Once I said it, I wished that I could bite the words back. It was stupid to give Eveda false hope. I was about to tell her that I was exaggerating slightly when she began to speak again, "Oh, that's wonderful, Piper. Thank you for that. I hope you're staying safe. I've got to run. Love you!"

The petals stopped glowing and closed in on themselves. I looked down at the flower in my hand, feeling as if my chest was filling up with water. Love you, two simple words that held more weight than the sky. She had said it like a promise, but for some reason, I saw it as a threat. Was the 'love you' only a result of what I had said, the false statements I had concocted to make her happy, or was there more to it? A motherly side, a side that loved you even if you did screw up the world. Would she still be saying love you if I didn't find Emensaly. 'Love you' was thrown around so vaguely nowadays that I had seen it wear a thousand different meanings. It could be used as a lie or a mask. Some saw it as a vow, while others read between the lines and acknowledged the emptiness behind it. What had Eveda meant? Was this a 'love you' with no strings attached? Did a 'love you' like that even exist? I rubbed my eyes. The exhaustion of the day had taken its toll on me. Maybe Eveda was the type of person who used love you as a goodbye, someone who threw the phrase into every sentence without a second thought.

I sighed, turning my attention back to my grandma. "Do you think she's going to be okay?"

My grandma didn't reply. She was squinting off into the distance, looking alarmed.

"Grandma?" I asked, my concern growing, "What's wron--."

I was cut off by the sound of a massive explosion. I was thrown off my feet, and my senses seemed to turn off for a moment. I landed with a loud thump, the grass not nearly as forgiving as I had hoped it would be. I looked around wildly, trying to figure out what had caused the havoc. My eyes rested on four teenagers who were standing a few feet away from us, weapons at the ready. I gulped, my heart quickening. They wore nothing but an unfashionable dark cloth that stretched from their neck to their knees. I could already imagine my grandma shuddering at the unflattering fabric. Their skin was covered in marking the same color as *Metallic Dark Gold No. 321* paint. Straining my eyes, trying to take a closer look, I realized that the symbols looked identical to the ones that were carved into that cave that I ventured into that fateful night I went camping. These are chaos in-betweens.

My throat closed in fear, and I tensed my legs, ready to bolt. Before I could think of a plan, one of the chaos in-betweens let out a low whistle. I barely had enough time to think, 'what the-' when they lunged. I let out a scream, and my grandma jumped into a fighting stance. She raised her hand, and strips of fabric shot out of her palms. The metallic fabric straightened and began loping its way around the in-betweens. They struggled against the bonds before hacking their way out with sharp-looking knives. My grandma shot another pair of ribbons their way, but they were prepared this time. Two of them slashed the material out of the air and lodged forwards. The other two advanced in my direction. I scrambled to my feet, looking around like a caged animal. Ethan still sat on the ground, looking pale. He seemed to be living in his own head, completely oblivious to the danger around him. I glanced over at my grandma, hoping that she could help me, but she seemed busy enough sparring with the other in-betweens.

The two grew closer, and my mind reeled a hundred miles a minute as I tried to figure out what to do. 'Use the spear,' a voice said in my head. Of course! The spear that Potia had given me. I took a deep breath and tried to focus. I pictured a fiery spear appearing in my hand. I tried to imagine the scene that Master Reverac had created for me during defense class. I pictured the chaos in-between cowering under my foot, and I held my spear high. My hand suddenly felt very heavy. I looked down and saw the massive spear sitting in my palm. My entire arm shook, trying to hold the heavy metal up, but I hoisted the four-foot-long weapon and prepared myself for the chaos in-betweens.

The chaos in-betweens charged towards me and I automatically took a step back. The girl held a chainsaw, and the boy sported a mace. I began to wish that Potia had used a more modern weapon, a nice machine gun that I could fire from far away. Unsure of what to do, I held the spear in front of me, hoping that it would be useful for defense. I swung it back and forth, trying to copy what I had seen in movies. I managed to hit the boy's mace and completely humiliate myself in the process, nearly stumbling into a five-foot-tall daisy.

The two came closer, taking their sweet time clearly; they didn't see me as a threat. Though if I was being honest, I was about as menacing as a puppy on a skateboard. Taking a deep breath, I tried to summon fire. Gritting my teeth, I opened my hands expecting to see a miraculous flame appear, but only a few sputtered into view, I felt a wave of exhaustion hit me, and I stumbled back. I took a step back, my panic turning to full-fledged terror. I shot a look at my grandma, hoping that she could come to rescue me, but she was in the middle of a deadly-looking dance with two other chaos in-betweens. Ethan still lay behind me, about as useful as a sack of potatoes.

The boy let out a bark that may have been that version of a laugh. He exchanged a few words with the girl in their language. I realized that the only reason that I was still alive was that they were laughing too hard. I couldn't tell if I was supposed to be embarrassed or offended. The boy rubbed his hands together, and I lifted my spear in front of my face, hoping that it would protect me from whatever was about to happen. Instead of hitting my face as I thought he would, the boy opened his hands, and darkness pooled in his palms. I had enough time to gape in confusion before he blasted the darkness toward my body. I had the good sense to try to avoid it, but my feet weren't nearly as graceful as I had hoped. I ended up sprawled on the floor, the darkness missing my torso but wrapping itself around my ankles.

I squealed like a wounded animal jumping up and down as the top of my sneakers burnt off. Tentacles crawled out of my sneakers. It took me a few moments for me to realize in horror that those were my toes. I let out a scream scrambling backward, desperately trying to escape the slimy black limbs protruding out of my shoes. Tears of frustration and anxiety pooled in my eyes when the two chaos in-betweens chuckled loudly.

The girl stepped forwards and said something that sounded suspiciously like, "My turn."

I gulped, turning around, ready to bolt, when something heavy hit my back. I hit the ground with an oomph. I struggled to get up, trying to turn around, but there seemed to be an invisible force holding me down. I struggled against the bonds, but they seemed to get tighter the more I moved. My breath quickened, and my heart felt like it was about to explode out of my chest. My spear had flown out of my hand and now sat directly next to Ethan. I tried to stretch my hand out and reach it, but my attempts were fruitless.

The chaos in-betweens walked around and stood in front of me. The girl motioned towards Ethan, and I let out a scream, thrashing against my bindings. The boy said something in return and then bent down to get my spear. I felt a tugging sensation in my guts, and I roared in anger. They. Could. Not. Touch. Potia's. Spear. I kicked my legs up and down, my voice growing hoarse from the screaming. They ignored me, and the boy grinned, wrapping his hands around the metal base of the spear.

There was a sudden flash of white light, and I was temporarily blinded. The tugging in my gut subsided, and my muscles seemed to collapse in exhaustion. I opened my eyes, scared of what I might see. My eyes first found Ethan, who was still sitting in the grass, now undisturbed, still holding his wrist. The next thing I saw was the spear. It was glowing dimly, radiating power. What my eyes didn't see was the chaos in betweens. In their places were piles of ash. I gulped, starting to understand what had happened.

My grandma was standing a few feet to my left, panting, but she looked unharmed. I tentatively tried to stand, letting out a breath of relief when I realized that I could stand. My toes had also returned back to normal. The only evidence that tentacles had once been there was the tear at the front of my shoes. Dusting my pants off, I looked back down at my spear.

"Did you do that?" My grandma asked hesitantly, a mixture of admiration and fear in her voice.

I opened my mouth to respond, "I-I don't know." I replied weakly. My head spun, and the world seemed to tilt. My legs were shaking with fear and exhaustion. I had been awake for almost twenty-four hours in this crazy world, nearly dying more times than I could count. The stress was over, leaving exhaustion in its place. Still, as I looked around, fear began stirring inside of me, waking my senses. Had I murdered all of those in betweens? Had Potia's weird spear had something to do with it?

The in-betweens would have killed us without a doubt. Still, their death wasn't something I wanted in my hands. Would people mourn them? Families, lovers, friends? How much pain I had caused with my actions. Had our lives been worth it? I shook the thought out of my head, ignoring the guilt pushing down my feeble barriers. Everything would make sense in the morning. Maybe I would wake up and realize that all this was a bad dream. Granted, I had already said that twice in the past two nights, and most of my hope had diminished. Even my weird brain couldn't think of something this lunatic.

I was dimly aware of my grandma walking over to Ethan and waving a hand over his wrist with her eyes closed. Numbly I stood, following the two of them, but my grandma stopped me, "Piper, your spear." She said gently, "We don't want anyone touching it."

I nodded, turning around to grab it and put it back into my *pindre*. So she had seen the chaos in-betweens pick up the spear. Maybe it had some sort of defense mechanism that kills off enemies. A small part of me hoped that I could just blame everything on Potia, his spear, his problem. With that in mind, I ran back to my grandmother, hoping that there would be enough space for me to lie down in her tiny car.

My grandma opened her purse and began rummaging around for car keys. I looked at Ethan, whose eyes seemed to have glazed over. I stared at him for a moment, my panic returning at full speed. What had happened in the mud dragon realm that left him this shaken? Would I come back with these kinds of emotional scars? I took a step closer to Ethan and wrapped my arms around him. I wasn't sure if a hug was exactly what he needed. In fact, he didn't seem to acknowledge my presence. I sighed, wishing that he would return the jester, but his arms hung loosely by his side.

Tears pricked in my eyes, but I blinked them away. I hadn't quite realized how much Ethan meant to me. Was this going to be our last day together? Was I brave enough to go to the mud dragon realm alone? If Ethan went back to the art realm, would I ever see him again? If, by some miracle, I did manage to find Emensaly and convince her to come back with us, was I going back to the human realm? Could I go back to normal life after everything I experienced here? I shook my head, trying to clear my thoughts. I was too tired to think about this. It's tomorrow's problem.

I heard my grandma clear her throat behind me, and I quickly let go of Ethan, my cheeks burning. "Come inside, dear." She said kindly, "You must be exhausted."

I nodded, not fully trusting myself to speak. Turning around, I stepped up into the car. My jaw dropped the moment my eyes settled on the interior. I rubbed my eyelids together and then looked again. "What the?" I said, trailing off.

"Do you like it?" My grandma asked, helping Ethan inside. "Eveda helped me design it."

I gulped, "Wow, this is crazy."

It truly was. The inside was slightly larger than an average hotel room and far more luxurious than any I had seen before. There were three mattresses on the left, each continuing the constellation pattern that the exterior of the car had. The *Midnight Blue 1 qt. #N480-7 Behr Marquee* bed sheets were covered in gold stars and beautifully drawn patterns. There were silky blue tarps hanging from the ceiling that trailed to the wall giving off a sort of fancy circus tent vibe. Hanging from the very top was a crystal chandelier that bathed the room in blue light.

I suddenly felt very underdressed in my dirty jeans and ripped apron. There were three large doors that led out of the room, labeled as *closet, bathroom,* and *driver seat.* I was only slightly surprised by the fact that the closet door took up half the wall. There was a small white coffee table next to a gold couch laden with fruits and snacks.

My grandma smiled kindly and walked over to us, "I laid your pajamas on your beds. Go get dressed and get something to eat. I'll let you rest. Oh, Piper, could I borrow you for two seconds?" She beckoned me over to one corner of the room, and I followed, somewhat confused.

"Piper, about your friend, why is he so…" She waved her hand vaguely in the air, her expression troubled.

I sighed, shooting a glance at Ethan, who was lying on the bed, "I'm not sure." I admitted, "I think that Ethan's gone into shock. It first happened when one of the Ledo we met told us that Emensaly might be in Teyar sk--I mean, the mud dragon realm. I think he's been there before."

My grandma tapped her chin pensively, "My, my, you were in Ledolish land? You've been busy. Don't worry about your friend. Everything will be better in the morning."

I nodded and watched as she slid open the door that led to the driver's seat. I stayed there for a moment, looking down at my bed in longing. As much as I wanted to collapse on the mattress and sleep for the end of time, I knew that I would regret it if I didn't get something to eat and take a shower. I was covered in soot, dirty, some mysterious green sludge, and crumbs.

"Do you want to use the bathroom, or can I go shower?" I asked, lifting my pajamas up.

Ethan shook his head in reply.

"Thanks," I said, trying to hide my sigh as I walked to the extravagant bathroom door. Inside there were beauty products covering every surface available. There were enough shampoo bottles, conditioners, moisturizers, and other random products, to fill at least three Sephora's. I grabbed the nearest bottle of soap and hopped into to shower. As I wiped the grime off of my skin, my thoughts drifted to today's events. I had hardly thought that we would have survived Ledolish land, and with the small amount of hope that I had allowed myself, I thought that Ethan and I would be celebrating. Instead, he became a terrified shell of his former self, and I was plagued by fear and exhaustion. Would the Ethan I knew return in the morning? At this point, all I could do was hope.

I sighed, trying to push those thoughts out of my head. Resting my head against the cool marble of the shower and taking a deep breath, calming my racing heart. Everything would be better in the morning. Everything would be better in the morning. I repeated it in my head like a mantra over and over. I tugged my pajamas on and headed back outside.

Ethan was lying on his bed, now wearing pajamas, still unresponsive. I took a step closer, trying to see if he was breathing. An idea struck me, and I quickly ran to Grass, my *packmare*. I prepared myself for an argument, but he ignored me as I tugged open his mouth to reach inside. I could hear him snoring softly. I snorted. Some protector he was. I dug around, trying to find the petal that I had won in survival 101 class. When I tried to use it, the petal slipped away from me and said, *Keep This For Later*. Maybe now it was later. Was the petal saving itself for Ethan?

I straighten, heading over to the mini bar on the left side of the car. "Ethan, do you want some tea?" I called as I began boiling hot water. "Ethan!" I yelled again, and he sat up instantly, his eyes wide.

"Yes?" He asked, his voice unreadable as he slumped back down into the mattress.

"Would you like some tea?" I tried again and attempted to be patient.

He shook his head.

I gritted my teeth in frustration. "I'm going to make you some tea. Okay!?"

Ethan shrugged, and I opened my hand, dropping the rose petal Ms. Leaf had given me. I walked over to Ethan and handed him the cup. "Drink," I commanded.

Ethan lifted the cup to his lip, taking a small sip. I gazed intently at him, waiting for some kind of result. Ethan ignored me and set the nearly full cup on his nightstand.

"Drink all of it!" I commanded. My voice was harsher than I intended it to be.

Ethan gave me a confused look and took another big gulp. I observed him intently as if he were a science project that I didn't quite understand. All of a sudden, his posture slackened, and an odd smile spread across his face. Ethan turned to face me. His gaze was so full of love that I took a step back. What was going on?

"Don't run from me, Ivy." He proclaimed, with his goofy smile, "Ivy, Ivy, where are you? Don't worry. The mud dragons aren't here."

My blood ran cold, and I fell onto my mattress in fear. Ivy. Ethan had mentioned her a few times before, his expression always clouding when he did. Did she have something to do with mud dragons? Was that why Ethan went mad when the mud dragon realm was mentioned? I looked back at Ethan, who lay on the mattress, whispering to himself. My eyes were dropping with exhaustion. I would figure everything out in the morning. I thought as I turned off the light switch. I would figure everything out in the….

Chapter 30

I was running through the dark streets of Ledolish land, my heart pounding in my ears. A shadow was chasing me, its face constantly changing shape. First, it was Officer Jaxon with his massive whip, "YOU LYING ART THIEF." He yelled, chasing me through the alleyways.

Mid scream, his face morphed into Officer Macy's. "COME BACK HERE, YOU LITTLE PUNK. I'M GOING TO MAKE YOU PAY."

The shadow then turned into a man's face with blue ram's horns. "Your search is useless. Give up now, Charlid has won."

I screamed, ducking below a low awning, hoping to find cover. My foot got caught on a rock, and I went sprawling to the floor. I let out a hoarse scream as my body hit the chipped cobblestone. The shadow loomed over the head, its face flickering in and out of view. I squirmed in terror, trying to get to my feet. A sharp gust of wind rustled the air bringing along an earthy scent. It seemed to carry a voice. "You'll never find me, Piper. Better give up now." The shadow cackled menacingly and lunged, its mouth wide open. I screeched with terror, shielding my face with my arm. The world went dark.

***

I awoke to a throbbing pain on the left side of my head. I groaned, massaging my temple, trying to remember where I was. I was lying on something hard, though I specifically remember falling asleep on a very comfortable bed. Groaning, I pushed myself up, trying to get my bearings. Had I been taken out of my grandma's car?! I squinted, looking around in the dim light, I could see the vague outline of beds and sofa that I had seen before I went to bed, but the question still stood, what was I doing on the--oomph. The floor moved underneath me, and I crashed headfirst into the mini-bar. I whimpered, rubbing my scalp.

284

A thought entered my brain, was someone...driving the car? I wobbled slightly, trying to get to my feet, as stars danced in front of my eyes. The car lurched again, and I grabbed onto my bed, trying to balance myself out. I vaguely wondered if the car was driving on its own. Was it even possible for a human to drive this badly? Cursing and sputtering, I stumbled to the front of the car where the door that was labeled *Driver's Seat* was. I heard a sort of maniacal laugh coming from the other side, and I began to wonder if I should have brought some sort of weapon. Against my better judgment, I slid the door open, about to jump into a fight stance, when I saw the silhouette of my grandma.

I rubbed my eyes, "Gra-grandma?" I asked, through a yawn, "What are you doing?"

She gave me a wild grin, "I'm driving, trying to keep the chaos in-betweens off our tail."

I gulped as she took a sharp left to avoid a three feet tall tulip that was nearly smashed against the windshield of the car. "Are you sure that's such a good idea?" I asked hesitantly, gripping on the doorframe to avoid falling on my rear end. I didn't know what would happen if we ran over one of the flowers, but I didn't think that it would have a positive result.

"Of course, it's a good idea." My grandma scoffed, "Besides, I don't drive much anymore, not since my third husband and I got a divorce. You know, I'm not sure what I saw in him besides the fact that he was good in--."

"Woah, okay, that's enough information, thanks," I said, holding my hand up, cheeks turning red in embarrassment.

My grandma laughed, "Right, right. Anyway, you should get back to bed, it's late, and you've got a big day ahead of you."

My shoulders sagged as memories of yesterday began flooding into my brain. "Are you picking us up tomorrow night," I asked in a hopeful voice.

My grandma sighed, tapping her fingers against the wheel and looking at me through the rear-view mirror, "I don't know. It depends, they might need me in the art realm, and you two might not be back yet. I promise I'll try."

I nodded, trying to hide my disappointment. "Oh, ok. Well, good night Grandma." I stepped through the door frame and slid the door closed.

"Good night Piper." She called back.

I stumbled back to my mattress, not bothering to lift the blanket off the floor, before I collapsed with exhaustion and fell asleep.

***

I awoke, the light streaming onto my face, bleeding through my eyelids. I groaned, throwing a pillow over my head. "Ten more minutes," I muttered, feeling like I was back home in my bed, my mom shaking me awake for school.

"Wake up, sleepy heads." my grandma called in a sing-song voice.

I rolled over and groaned, looking at the alarm clock next to my bed. "What the--it's six a.m."

"Exactly." She said as if it were perfectly sane for someone to be awake at this hour.

"That's not normal." I heard Ethan call from across the room, and my heart suddenly spiked up. All exhaustion was forgotten. Was Ethan talking again? A grin split my face in two. See, I knew everything would get better in the morning. Did this mean that he would come to the mud dragon realm with me? I banished the thought from my head. I wouldn't make him do that. Even if he was better today, yesterday was still proof that he couldn't handle talking about mud dragons, much less confronting them. I put my poker face on and took a deep breath.

I sat up, "Ethan! Oh god, how are you feeling?"

"I'm fine. Why?" He replied casually, though I saw his ears turn red. I could see my grandma frantically shaking her head in my direction, holding a finger up to her lips.

"Oh, never mind," I answered quickly.

The room became an awkward sort of silence. Ethan began making his bed, and I quickly followed his lead. Once I finished, I walked towards the bathroom to brush my teeth when my grandma stopped me. "Where do you think you're going?"

I paused, "To the bathroom...?"

She pouted, "Without me?"

I heard Ethan snicker in the background, and my cheeks grew hot, "Are you out of your mind?"

My grandma frowned, "I want to help you get ready."

I cocked my head to the side, "I know how to get ready."

"Please darling. I haven't gotten to give anyone a makeover since this dreadful fight with Charlid began." She begged.

"So for three days." I calculated, not budging.

"Piper..."

I sighed, rolling my eyes, "Fine."

My grandma clapped her hands together, grabbing my arm and dragging me to the bathroom.

"Help me!" I mouthed to Ethan, but all he did was give me a thumbs up and laugh.

I rolled my eyes, trying to be annoyed with him, but I was still drunk on the thrill of him being back to normal.

My grandma closed the bathroom door and rubbed her hands together, and pulled a curling iron out of her draw. "All right, sit down."

Sighing, I obliged, lowering myself onto a light blue chair, "Can we do this quickly, I sort of need to get ready to go to the mud dragon realm. Who knows how much time I have to look for Emensaly."

My grandma grinned, "Oh don't worry darling, you'll have plenty of time. Relax your face muscles, you're two young for crow's feet around your eyes."

I resisted the urge to roll my eyes yet again. Instead I rested my eyelids, as my grandma began applying creams, powders, and steam to my face. After an eternity of plucking, dusting, and curling, there was a knock on the door.

"I need to use the bathroom!" Ethan called. "Are you two almost done there?"

"Yes!" I yelled back, before my grandma could answer.

She sighed, and finally let me stand. My eyes drifted to my reflection in the mirror and I took a step back feeling startled at the foreign face that stared back at me. It looked like me using some sort of snapchat filter. My cheekbones certainly weren't that high nor was my hair that shiny. I touched it self consciously, attempting to act indifferent.

"You can come in Ethan!" My grandma called, practicing fluttering out of the room like a happy fairy.

I followed, her shaking my head trying to focus. I grabbed Grass off of my night stand and got ready to head out the door.

"Wait, Piper. You can't leave yet." My grandma called, her head burrowed in her closet.

"Why not?" I asked, already knowing what she was planning to say.

"Well you can't leave looking like that!" She proclaimed.

I self consciously looked down at my sweat pants, and hoodie, "Why not."

"Oh darling, please, I'm the *goddess* of fashion, I can't have my granddaughter running around in sweats. Oh please, Piper, let me dress you just this once."

I sighed, "Okay fine, make it quick."

She squealed, and began running to a sewing machine that suddenly appeared on the coffee table. I cocked my head to the side wondering why I couldn't just take something out of the ridiculously big closet. A sudden thought popped into my head and I quickly yelled, "Make sure I'm wearing pants, no skirts, I'm trying to fight mud dragons not seduce them."

I bit my lip looking frantically at the bathroom door. I didn't need Ethan freaking out at the word mud dragon again. Thankfully, he didn't seem to hear me.

My grandma pouted, "Ok darling whatever you say."

I smiled at her and shook my head. Normally I would have been thrilled to play dress up with my grandma. In fact that would probably be the first thing I would do if the world didn't fall to pieces, but I was a little too concerned with looking for Emensaly to pretend to be my grandma's doll.

With that in mind I quickly began raiding her minibar and snacks. I wasn't sure if I would have the time or energy to summon something while in the Mud Dragon realm. As I had learnt from my time in Ledolish land it might be a good idea to bring more than half a snicker bar. Grass didn't protest, and I had the feeling that he was still sleeping. I probably should have woken him up but the quiet was a nice change of pace compared to his running complaints. Ethan had begun packing his *packmare* as well and I wasn't sure what to say to him. Was there some sort of protocol to confront someone after they freeze up due to the mention of mud dragons and then begin canoodling some person named Ivy?

Right before I let my eyes drift back to the floor Ethan met my gaze. I bit my lip, not sure what to do. Ethan took a breath, "You ready for the mud dragons?"

I started not sure how to respond. After a beat I nodded my head.

He gave me a half smile, "Good me too."

I grinned, unable to hide my relief, those three words turned my entire perspective around. I could already imagine escaping the mud dragon realm with Emensaly on one side and Ethan on the other. Attempting to appear nonchalant I nodded, "Cool, cool."

Ethan laughed, "Very."

My grandma walked in, with twelve outfits, six on each arm. Ethan gaped at her, "You sewed all of those in twenty minutes!?"

She laughed, "Don't be ridiculous, I also sewed myself a new denim dress and created a resin necklace, they're all the range now-a-days."

I shook my head but felt a small spark of excitement run through me, this reminded me of when Ami and I would go into designer stores and try all the fancy clothing on. I felt a pang of homesickness wash over me as I thought of her. Was she worried about me? How many hours had passed. I had been gone for three days so that made it three hours in the human world. Did my parents know that I was missing? Were they still sleeping?

"Okay Piper, here are your options." My grandma began and held up the first outfit. "So I was first thinking about this pants suit. It comes with this oversized blazer, and silky grey trousers. I thought it might bring out your eyes."

"Grandma, I don't need to look good while trying to slice a dragon in half," I replied checking the clock that read 7:30 a.m.

"Doesn't mean you can't look good while doing it." She pouted. "Besides I was going to have you and Ethan be matching."

I slapped my forehead and Ethan let out a laugh, "We can't have that." He said, grinning goofily, "Besides Piper doesn't want me showing her up in the outfit."

My palms twitched with the urge to slap him, and I turned back to my grandma, "Do you have any jeans, maybe a simple t-shirt…?"

My grandma sighed, "I'll let this fashion offense slide because you're stressed about the mud dragon but the moment you come back---."

I laughed, "You got it grandma. Now, jeans."

She smiled, "Give me five seconds."

Ethan and I watched curiously as she waltzed to her sewing machine and waved her hand quickly. Fabric appeared beneath it and the machine began humming quickly.

"Why doesn't she just take stuff out of her closet?" Ethan asked me.

I shrugged, "I don't think that's how she does stuff. I've got the feeling my grandma is the type of person who only ever wears an outfit once."

Ethan chuckled, "Yup, you got that right."

***

After my grandma finally decided on the perfect outfit for Ethan and me, the two of us were allowed to leave. I was jumping from foot to foot in trepidation in my new high waisted jeans and flowery top that my grandma told me would make me feel like a million dollars. After thanking her for her kind gifts, we made our way out of the car in search of the flower of the mud dragon realm.

I shoulder my *packmare* and squinted into the morning sun, "Should I look at the map Eveda gave us to see what the flower that transports us to the….mud dragon realm looks like?" I gulp, still afraid that Ethan would go into shock again whenever I mentioned that realm. I knew that I should have confronted him about last night, the tension was so thick that you could cut it with a knife. I turned to him, building up the nerve to ask, but kept my mouth closed like the coward I was.

"No need, I know where the flower is," Ethan said, turning north.

Another puzzled piece clicked together in my brain. So Ethan had been to the mud dragon realm before, and something had definitely happened to him, but what was it?

I ran after Ethan for a few minutes before he stopped in front of a large daffodil that was up to my chest. It was shaped like a daffodil but its texture and color were strange. It looked like it had been carved out of a muddy type of wet clay. The edges were choppy and frayed as if an inexperienced carver had done it. The petals were *Behr Toasty Gray (N320-2)* color, instead of the traditional yellow.

"Do you have an *onre?*" Ethan asked, rummaging through his *packmare.*

"Yeah, I'll get it," I replied, pulling Grass off my shoulder.

"Hey princess. Your boyfriend back to normal yet?" Grass asked, in his boisterous, unfiltered way.

I saw Ethan's cheeks turn pink and I gripped Grass tightly. "I liked it better when you were asleep. Now, open up, I need my *onre.*"

Clearly, Grass thought that he had tormented me enough and stretched his mouth wide open to allow me to grab the straw-like contraction, also known as an *onre*. Ethan stuck his *onre* into the center of the flower and drank the nectar. I quickly followed his lead. Taking a long sip, I immediately recoiled. The nectar was thicker than I had expected and had a sort of acidic taste, like shoe polish. As I tried to wipe my mouth on my shirt, I realized that there was also a small hint of fresh fruit, as if someone had poured gasoline on top of an apple. Before I could ponder the taste any longer, my body jolted backward, and I had the sensation of being jolted through a vacuum. My skin prickled uncomfortably, and I could feel my eyes rolling to the back of my head.

At last the spinning stopped, and I landed on my back like a pile of bones, Groaning I tried to turn. "It really doesn't get easier does it."

"Ughhh nope," Ethan murmured, clutching his lower back.

I stumbled, to my feet, ignoring the protest from my screaming muscles. I held a hand up to shield my eyes and looked around. The first thing that caught my eye was the sky. It was an electric shade of purple. It was somewhere between *Neon Apple Barrel 21062E Acrylic Paint* and *Fluorescent Paradise Purple #25533d.* "Well this is a strange place," I noted thoughtfully, my eyes straying down the *Magnolia Home by Joanna Gaines Matte Tint* grey-green ground.

"Strange is one way to describe it," Ethan said nonchalantly. Something flashed in his eyes but disappeared so quickly that I thought I might have imagined it.

"You good," I asked, offering him my hand and pulling him up.

"Yeah I'm fine." He replied, his eyes darting around the landscape.

The two of us seemed to have landed on some sort of hill, it had bumpy ridges, and stange circular shapes that were nearly three foot wide each. The hill had a steep downward edge that led to flat ground. Oddly enough the hill was a slightly more green shade than the rest of the land.

"Does this hill look, I don't know, unusual?" I asked, feeling apprehensive.

Ethan turned to me and then looked down, what every he was about to say was drowned out by a massive rumbling that sounded like thunder. I whipped my head around "What was---ahhhh."

The ground had suddenly begun moving underneath my feet. I stumbled backward, breathing heavily, when a hand clapped over my mouth. "Don't scream," Ethan instructed, his voice shaking slightly. "We're on one."

"We're on what?" I asked, my voice muffled by his palm.

His eyes grew wide, and his voice trembled, "We're on a mud dragon.

***

I stared at him in horror, my heart falling to the pit of my stomach, "We--we, how are we going, to get off. Doesn't it make us feel?"

Ethan glanced over his shoulder in fear. "I think it's asleep."

The ground er, I mean mud dragon, shook again and my palms began to sweat. "Ethan, we need to get off here."

I grabbed his hand and the two of us began wildly running down the body of the dragon. I stumbled downwards desperately trying to find my footing. The mud dragon's body began turning downwards, leading to his underbelly. I tried to get down when the ground let out another lurch and I saw my life flash before my eyes. I had to get out of here. My legs were wrapped around the mud dragons torso and I squeezed them praying to stay latched on. I reached down to grab a hold of the grass in the attempt to study myself and crawl off.. I held onto the blades of grass and was surprised at how sturdy it was. Normally grass would rip out. I let a bit of my weight move down to the grass and unfastened myself from the great.

A hundred things happened at once. I lost my grip, and the ground began to shake even more ferociously than before. Then I heard a noise. It was the loudest sound I had ever heard. I thought that the world was breaking in half. I instinctively clapped my hands over my ears to make them stop. Big mistake. I lost the only balance that I had left and fell backward, hitting my head. My vision ebbed, and stars danced in front of my eyes.

"Piper!" Ethan yelled frantically.

I whipped my head around looking for his voice. My head spun madly right before I landed in a large puddle of something wet and smelly. I thrashed around and got a mouth full of mud.

My head throbbed painfully, and felt like it weighed a million pounds. Bits and pieces of memories flooded into my brain and I sat out quickly trying to scamper away from the beast. Ethan grabbed my hand and pulled me downwards. He held a finger up to his lips, trembling slightly. "Wait." He mouthed.

The two of us lay in the mud for an eternity. I tried to slow my breathing, and prayed that the creature wouldn't notice us. At last Ethan stood, backing away slowly. I matched his pace, trying to soften my steps. It was difficult to concentrate with the pounding in my temple, but I managed to keep a clear head. I followed Ethan as he began running towards a massive swamp forest maybe half a mile away. The air was so thick with humidity that I had trouble breathing. My sneakers couldn't get any traction on the muddy ground and I spent more time trying to get up than actually running. By the time Ethan stopped I was out of breath and covered from head to toe in slug.

"What's wrong--oh," I said, looking at the terrain that began curving upwards into a steep hill.

"Yeah." Ethan replied, "Any idea on how we are going to get up there?"

I shook my head, bouncing from foot to foot. "Have you tried running up?" I asked.

He nodded, "No use."

"Lemme try." I went up my tip toes and pumped my legs upwards. My foot slipped and I fell forwards, my front being splattered with mud.

Ethan grimaced, "Yeah we need a different solution."

"Can we go around?" I asked, turning my head left and right.

Ethna frowned, "It's about a day's walk to get around this hill. Plus we would be a lot more exposed before entering the mud dragon city."

"Could we use our *pindres*?" I asked skeptically.

Ethan frowned, "What would we summon? A grappling hook?"

I shrugged, "My grappling skills are a bit rusty."

"Ummm what else could we do?" He muttered pacing.

"Wait, what about our *packmares*?" I asked, an idea forming in the back of my brain. "I bet they are good at climbing with those talons."

"And Eveda said that they are able to hold up to ten tons." Ethan finished high-fiving me.

I took Grass my packmare off of my back and tapped him loudly. " Grass? You there?"

Grass let out a pompous sniff, "Of course I'm here where else would I be. For further refer--hold on a minute, why am I covered in filth? WHY AM I DIRTY!? I HAVE ONE TWELFTH ROYAL BLOOD, NO PRINCE SHOULD BE TREATED THIS WAY. I DEMAND TO BE BATHED AT ONCE."

I bit the inside of my cheek to stop myself from responding rudely. I needed to stay on Grass's good side, that is, if he had a good side.

"I have a proposal for you," I said sweetly.

"I already refuse-." Grass started but I cut him off.

"I was wondering if you were any good at climbing."

Grass paused his yelling, "Of course, I can climb. I was champion of the Mountain Games back in '07 and--,"

I cut him off quickly before he started talking our ears off with his victories. "That's perfect, you can climb us up the hill, if you could hold on to the mud with your long sloth talons then we'll be up in no time. You see, I need to get to the swamp forest up there. I'll use you and Ethan will be his packmare." I responded by trying to sound convincing and kind.

297

"First of all," Grass began, "Never compare me to sloth. I am far more evolved than that clumsy, dreadful creature, and second of all, no. I am made to carry heavy loads and stay on your back. I will not be used as a harness or rope to pull two heavy ungrateful in-betweens up a muddy hill. And before you start telling me how worthy your cause is and how selfless that two of you are risking your life, spare me. No amount of charity can get me to ruin my nails."

"Please Grass, I'll do anything," I begged, glancing over at the mud dragon. Was it my imagination or did it sound like the snores were getting fainter.

"I will not be swayed." Grass said with finality.

I changed tactics, "Fine, maybe I'll go back to Eveda and ask her for a new packmare. And then you'll have to go back to your realm unannounced and tell them that you lost your job. Didn't you tell me that honor was important to a packmare the first time we met."

Grass was silent, "I-well, that's completely besides the point."

"No, I don't think that it is."

Grass waited a few beats and let out a discontent sigh, "Alright I'll do it."

I let out a breath of relief. "Awesome. Thanks Grass you're the best."

"Yes, yes, I know I know. Now place me against the hill and hold on. I'll climb up and you can just walk normally using me as a grip." Grass explained.

"Got it," I replied, curious to see how the *packmare* moved. I had only ever seen Grass open his mouth before.

I helped Grass up against the hill, leaning forwards to make sure that he had a tight grip. Grass lifted one arm and slowly began climbing up the hill. I was once again reminded of the way a sloth moved. I walked a few feet up along with Grass and kept a firm grip on his back. It was a slow process but I had to admire the *packmare's* stamina. Though I would never admit it out loud, Grass was incredibly strong. He managed to pull me up the entire way. On the other hand, the climb felt longer than it should with Grass constantly complaining how heavy I was.

"I'm going to need a massage after this." He grumbled once we were up. "I'm so sore."

Ethan took a deep breath and plopped down on the floor. He held a hand up to his heart, and I doubled over, trying to catch my breath. I was filled with adrenaline and wanted nothing more than to run as fast as I possibly could in the opposite direction. I took a breath and turned to Ethan. "That-that was terrifying," I admitted sitting down next to him. He was breathing heavily.

"I certainly wasn't expecting to meet a mud dragon that early." He replied.

"Where to now?" I asked. Ethan hadn't really confirmed if he had been to the mud dragon realm before but I had sort of turned him into my tour guide. Maybe he would know the safest way around. Though by the way his eyes flashed everytime the mud dragon realm was mentioned, he may not have had a very safe experience here.

"We should go through that swamp forest. It leads us straight to the mud dragon city. At least that's what everyone calls it. Each mud dragon ruler names the city after themselves. Unfortunately rulers only tend to last a few months before a bigger and tougher mud dragon kills them and takes the crown." Ethan proclaimed, pointing to a massive cluster of trees to our left. "Our best bet to find Emensaly would be to go there."

"Well, that's reassuring," I muttered. "Say, Ethan, do you know how to navigate the city?"

Ethan didn't respond for a moment. After a while he shrugged, "I honestly don't know how much it has changed."

The statement didn't do much to reassure the butterflies in my stomach. I was beginning to doubt Ethan's ability to face this realm. Would he crack and become imprisoned in his mind all over again? I sighed and looked to my right, wishing that we could stay where we were. Sure, we were standing in a muddy swamp filled with mosquitos and exposed to any mud dragon that looked in our direction, but at least it wasn't surrounded by trees. The memories of our camping trip were too raw in my mind. I wondered what my family was doing right now and how much time had passed with the time difference. Were they still sleeping? Had they woken up to find me gone? Did they cry or not care? I dug my nails into my palms. Of course, they cared, right? My heart ached, and I felt another pang of sadness. I missed them.

Ethan began trudging towards the marsh forest. I followed him inside. It was downright miserable. My shoes were soaked through in seconds and as stylish as my jeans were, they were unfortunately not waterproof. The muddy water rose up to my shins, and bugs the size of my thumb swarmed around my head. They clung to me like burrs, no matter how much I tried to swat them off. The air was so thick with humidity that my shirt was doused with sweat. Reeds clung to my legs and brushed against my skin uncomfortably. I could hear the crickets of frogs and other marsh creatures in the air causing me to shudder in fear and discomfort every few minutes. I ran my hands up and down my bare arms trying to protect them.

"Are we almost there?" I asked, trying to keep my voice light.

Ethan pursed his lips, "Almost. But there's something about this marsh that is odd. Mud dragons normally inhabit this area, I'm not sure where they all are. We've gotten lucky."

I wanted to point out that I felt nowhere near lucky but I had other pressing questions, "Say, Ethan." I began tentatively, "How do you know so much about--" I waved my hand in the air. "This place. Have you been to the mud dragon realms before?"

He paused, "I was here before it was the mud dragon realm."

I sighed, wonderful, another straight answer. I waited for him to say more but he seemed to be lost in a memory. He continued to walk forwards, and I quickened my pace trying to keep up with him. We walked for another good ten minute until Ethan finally stopped a few feet from the edge of the forest. He took a deep breath and then stopped shuddering slightly, "Well here we are." He proclaimed, making his way through the last thicket of trees. I emerged the swamp gratefully, while scratching the many bug bites that were forming on my legs. My eyes fell on the Stone city and my jaw dropped. "Oh my God it's massive."

"Yep," Ethan said unenthusiastically.

I gulped, and began walking down towards the stone city. There was a humongous grey wall that had to be over twenty feet tall surrounding the city. "I don't suppose you know how to get us through that?" I asked, fearfully.

Ethan pursed his lips. "Let's get closer, maybe we'll find a way in."

I nodded, shuddering slightly. We approached the wall cautiously and the closer we became the more apprehensive I felt. The two of us soon realized that the wall was created to keep larger creatures out of the mud dragon city, not tiny little humans like us. There were massive cracks along the bottom of the stone making it easy enough for the two of us to slip through. I squeezed between the two stones and just like that, I was in the mud dragon city. I lifted my head up to look at the massive structures around us. I had known that mud dragons were big but looking at their structures sent a shiver down my spine.

"I wonder what Emensaly's doing here?" I told Ethan, confused, "Does she like spending time with these horrible creatures?"

Ethan gulped, "I have no clue. But if she's here then we're here. We can't leave 'till we find her."

Chapter 31

Ethan and I encountered the first mud dragons, we watched them enter a stone plaza as we squeezed ourselves inside a crack between two buildings. The one advantage to being so tiny was that we could hide easily. Ethan told me that our best chance of survival was to stay hidden. The two mud dragons walked in front of us conversing in their language that sounded like an assortment of clucking and wheezing.

"I wish that we could understand them." I muttered, "It may help us get a better understanding of what's going on right now and where we can find Emensaly."

Ethan bit his lip, "Let me try something." He waved a hand over his *pindres* and a small stack of gold clay appeared before him.

"*Pofor*?" I asked, referring to the mineral in the clay that had a mind for itself.

"Yep." Ethan replied, molding the clay with concentration, "I stocked up in your grandma's car right before we left. I thought it might come in handy."

I grinned as he began to sculpt the clay into something that looked like an ear trumpet from the 18th century. "Errr, what exactly are you making?"

"I'm hoping that the *pofor* will be able to translate the mud dragon language for me. I'm not sure if it will work but I can't think of anything else to do."

I crossed my fingers, as Ethan lifted the golden trumpet up to his ear. After a few minutes he lowered it with a groan. "Nope. Nothing."

My shoulders fell in disappointment. "What now?"

"Should we just walk around?" He asks, squaring his shoulders as if preparing for a fight.

303

"I guess…" I decided, feeling hesitant. "Should we try to get a closer look at the stone plaza? That's where all the mud dragons were headed. Maybe we can take a look around? It may even be easier to navigate if all the mud dragons are in one spot."

"Sure. Let's do that." Ethan replied, swallowing hard.

"Why are you so afraid of mud dragons?" I blurted out. "I mean my grandma told me that they aren't any worse than Ledos."

"Well then, your grandma's probably never been here before," Ethan said harshly.

I took a step back, surprised.

"Piper I'm sorr--What was that?!" He asked, fear leaking into his voice.

"What was what?" I asked, looking over my shoulder in fear.

"Nothing I thought I heard--nevermind."

I let out a breath of relief when I heard a gruff voice behind us, "I wouldn't be so quick to dismiss that thought."

I turned around and let out a scream. Ethan stood paralyzed pressing himself against the wall. A massive mud dragon stood in front of us. It's massive head poked into our small hiding place. It's head peeking into through the crack between the two buildings showing off the bright *Aqua Horizon MAG109* colored scales. There were two horns on the top of its head each as long as my forearm. The mud dragon's icy eyes reminded me of cracked marbles jammed into an eye socket. Fear froze my brain and the only thing I could think to say was, "You speak English?"

The mud dragon roared and laughed, its warm breath filling the cavern with the smell of fish, "I do, thanks for noticing--ahh Ethan, I thought I recognized you. Good for you, coming back home. You

304

didn't have enough of this place did ya? Wanted to visit your old home. Maybe look for Ivy?"

I turned to Ethan who was shaking from head to toe. "I-it's you. You, you."

"Yes?" The mud dragon said pleasantly, "Come on, Ethan, finish the sentence."

"You killed her." He yelled, tears pooling in his eyes, "You killed her without a second glance. I'm gonna kill you--."

Ethan ran straight toward the mud dragon with his fists raised. The mud dragon watched with a bemused expression, lazily flicking his tail back and forth. Luckily enough, my body chose to regain its sense at that second, and I grabbed hold of Ethan. "Stop, you can't fight a mud dragon," I yelled in panic.

"I don't care," Ethan gasped, struggling against my hold, "I'm going to kill him. For her, she didn't deserve to die."

The mud dragon laughed, "Oh yes please, yell at me. All that blood pooling into your head is good for circulation. You're going to make such a great meal."

I gulped, "Ethan run!"

I bolted off running from the mud dragon hoping there was another exit on the other side of this crack. The sound of my feet hitting the ground echoed through the small hallways and I heard the mud dragon chuckle. "Oh this is just too easy."

A scaly claw wrapped itself around my waist and began to pull me out of our little hiding space. I screamed, "LET ME GO LET ME GOOOOO!"

I tried to push myself against the mud dragons hold. I saw Ethan trying to grab onto the walls, and pull himself away. "Let me go!" I yelled between breaths, scratching and biting the thick scales holding me back. Tears were flowing freely down my face, mixing with sweat and mud. The horrible creature was gripping me so hard that I couldn't feel my legs. I thrashed around like a fish out of water trying desperately to escape the mud dragon's clutch. The claw squeezed tighter around my mid second squeezing my ribs tightly. I gasped, trying to breathe. "Too tight." I panted.

The mud dragon chuckled. "Trust me. I could make you hurt a lot more. Now quite squirming before I 'accidentally' crack a rib. You too, Ethan."

I froze, wanting to keep my ribs intact. My mind raced, trying to find a way out of this situation. I could feel the cool metal of my *pindres* pressed against my collarbone. Could I summon Potia's spear? Could I light the mud dragon on fire? Causing a flame to erupt would probably hurt Ethan more than it would affect the mud dragon. I closed my eyes and tried to summon the spear to my hand. I grinned, feeling the long metal base of Potia's spear. I turned around to see that the mud dragon was pulling us out of our hiding spot. 3, 2, 1. I lunged and tried to drive the spear straight into the mud dragon's eyes.

I prayed for victory, but luck wasn't on my side. I miscalculated, and my spear ended up a few feet away from the mud dragon's face. If I hadn't been terrified, I would have died of embarrassment. If that wasn't bad enough, the mud dragon took my spear between its teeth and pulled it out of my hand. "Hey!" I yelled, making a grab for it, my hands coming a bit to close the creature's teeth for my liking.

The mud dragon threw its head back and made a sound that sounded like a squirrel having an allergic reaction. It took me a moment to figure out that the mud dragon was laughing at me. Tears appeared in his icy blue eyes, "Oh wow that was amazing, you're rid- -." It gasped, "Ridiculous."

I frowned. Well, at least the mud dragon wasn't eating us. I wasn't sure if I preferred this, though.

The mud dragon continued laughing, Ethan and I exchanged confused looks. The mud dragon finished its chortling and returned its gaze to the two of us. "You guys are lucky I'm full. You know what, since you made me laugh girly, I'll let you live another night."

I cocked my head out the side, "So you're letting us go?" I asked.

The mud dragon began chuckling again and didn't respond. It took Potia's spear out of its teeth and threw it over his shoulder. I felt a pang of misery listening to the clang of metal against rock. That was going to be hard to explain to Potia.

***

A horrible grin spread through the mud dragon's face as he began walking through the streets.

"So tell me more about Ivy. Do you miss her? Aww you do cry?" The mud dragon asked, baring his fangs.

Tears trickled down Ethan's face, and he clenched his fist, his face turning red with rage.

"Hmm," said the mud dragon, its voice dripping with malice, "Is she, is she dead?" It asked with fake concern. "Oh, I wonder who killed her?"

My eyes grew hot with tears, and I swallowed hard.

"It was you!" Ethan screamed, "You murdered her, you disgusting, filthy awful-"

He let out a string of curses, and the mud dragon threw him onto the ground. Ethan hit it with a thud and groaned. He rolled around and tried to stand. I could vaguely see blood trickling down his nose.

"No! Ethan!" I yelled, sobbing. My mind went white with rang, and I let out a scream. I channeled Potia and let a jet of firefly into the mud dragon's eyes. The mud dragon's claws unraveled from my

307

waist, and I dropped to the floor. Pain shot through my right leg, but I ignored it. The mud dragon yelled in anguish, covering its eyes with its hands. A crossbow appeared in Ethan's hands, and he began shooting toward the dragons. "Get its eyes," I screamed. Channeling more of Potia's fire.

The blue mud dragon took a step back, its claw covering its face. "SOMEONE GET THOSE CHILDREN!"

Ethan and I gulped as two mud dragons began circling us. Ethan let arrow after arrow fly, but they bounced off the creature's thick hands. I tried to channel Potia, but the red mud dragon grabbed my hands and tied them behind my back. The other picked Ethan up by his leg and began to sniff him. The yellow one gargled something in the mud dragon language. The blue mud dragon that first found us blinked a few times and then held his claws out. Ethan and I were both dropped into his awaiting hands.

It growled and squeezed us together tightly. "Don't try anything else, you little squirts."

I gulped and shot Ethan a look. He shrugged helplessly (As best as he could with the mud dragon's claws squeezing him). "Wait." He mouthed. "Inside."

I nodded, praying that he had a plan. My legs had begun cramping up, and Ethan's bloody nose was dripping onto the hem of his shirt. I shivered with fear and exhaustion. This wasn't how our trip to the mud dragon realm was supposed to go. Ethan and I weren't supposed to run into any mud dragons. Our plan had been to sneak around alleyways and avoid the stare of any creatures. Now we were being squashed by some delusional mud dragon who has a connection to Ethan's mysterious path, and we were probably being brought to his kitchen to be boiled alive. I was starting to think that our time in Ledolish land wasn't even this unlucky.

"Where are you taking us?" I gasped, struggling against the claw jamming into my torso.

"Where are you taking us?" The mud dragon imitated in a high-pitched voice and then laughed. "Don't you like surprises, girly."

"Not when they end with me stuck on a shish kabob," I replied, trying to push myself upwards.

"What about you, Ethan? You've been awfully quiet."

"I tend to shy away from murderers and sociopaths," Ethan told the mud dragon, holding his sleeve up to his nose.

The mud dragon chucked and motioned to me, "Then what are you doing hanging out with this one?"

I rolled my eyes, "Very funny."

The mud dragon began walking towards a massive stone structure. It had a brown flag and blue flag hanging over the side, with a massive reptile drawn on the front. (Clearly, mud dragons weren't artistic talents, as they were at being cruel people eaters).

The stone structure would have been unimpressive if it weren't for its size. It seemed to stretch on for acres. The mud dragon lifted us up and carried us through a dent between two stones that I assumed was the door. If this creature hadn't been planning on eating us, I would have definitely recommended some interior designers. Every single room was the same *Aged Stucco Grey #70YY 46/053* color. Not to mention the fact that the walls were so rough I could have rock climbed my way to the ceiling and back. Ethan and I were carried to a room all the way to the back until the mud dragon finally unleashed his dreadful hold on us.

I took a few breaths and touched my tender ribs which were already beginning to bruise. I looked around the room as we were inside and took a few steps backward when I saw warm air gushing out of ventilators in each of the four corners of the room.

"Where are we?" Ethan asked with a trace of fear in his voice.

"The sauna." The mud dragon replied with a cruel grin curling across his face, "I like my meals steamed."

Chapter 32

The stone door slammed shut behind us, leaving the two of us in the sauna. I paced back and forth pulling my hoodie off my head and rolling my jeans up. "What are we going to do, what are we going to do?" I moaned, wiping sweat off of my forehead.

"Calm down." Ethan huffed, wiping his hands on his shorts, and pulling his sweater off. "We'll find a way out."

I slid down the wall and sat down next, I bit my lip hesitantly, "Ethan, I'm really sorry about Ivy. You don't have to explain anything but I just want to let you know that you can talk to me." I finished, lamely, my facing turning red.

Ethan shuttered despite the heat, "Thanks. Ivy was, she was my sister. We used to live in Teyar Skies."

"That's what Marlee called this place right?"

"Yeah well Teyar Skies doesn't exist anymore," Ethan replied plainly. "The mud dragons took it over."

"What? How?"

Ethan sighed, "When we first met I told you I had lived in the art realm my entire life, but that isn't entirely true I moved here when I was seven. I was telling the truth when I told you my dad was Loget, but he isn't the god of air dry clay he is the god of *revis*. That's the holy mud of Teyar Skies. That's what this place was called before the mud dragons took it over. The mud that you see on the ground used to be *revis* but it's been polluted by the mud dragons. Ivy and I were both born in Teyar Skies." He took a shaky breath.

"You don't have to--," I started but Ethan cut me off. It was as if everything was coming up like a waterfall of words and he didn't know how to stop.

"Ivy and I were raised here, and it was the greatest place ever, this was the only place i had ever known and i never really planned on leaving it. But, then the mud dragons invaded the days after Ivy's tenth birthday. It was all so chaotic I--." He stopped, lost in thought. "No one knew what to do. The mud dragons were picking people up left and right. Someone had the idea to run to the flower garden to escape. The mud dragons weren't really focused on killing people, they just wanted the *revis*, our sacred mud that we used for sculpting. My dad was helping get all of the families out and I was too scared to do anything. We were taking these carts in groups of seven to get to the flower garden. I had been hiding under my bed, scared to move. My mom was loading everything in the cart and she couldn't convince me to leave. She gave up and loaded Ivy in the cart without me. As they rolled out the cart Ivy jumped out realizing that I wasn't with them. She came back for me, she convinced me to go with her. We ran to the flower garden on our own. I wasn't very fast and she had to slow down to help me. There was a mud dragon chasing us, Ivy's hand slipped out of my grasp when I was transported to the flower garden, and she never followed." Ethan bit his nail not looking me in the eye.

I leaned over and wrapped my arms around his stiff shoulders. I slouched feeling as if I were about to collapse underneath the story Ethan had just told. There were so many horrors in the world, I couldn't even see the point in coping with it anymore. Even if we did find Emensaly and stop Charlid from escaping into the human world, there would still be Ledos being tortured by the giraffes. The mud dragons would still be in control of Teyar Skies, and Ivy would still be dead. The three brother deities would still be horrible leaders, ordering everyone around while sitting on their stupid flying cushions without any sense of justice. Was there a point in even trying? It would be so easy to just let the mud dragon's eat us. Maybe wherever I end up in my next life I wouldn't be chasing after some crazy deity that probably didn't want to be found in the first place.

But what about Jack? A little voice asked in my head. I won't ever eat another peanut butter and jelly sandwich with him. I wouldn't ever be able to laugh with Mom or listen to Dad's corny jokes. I wiped my face on the back of my sleeve and turned to Ethan.

"Ivy came back for me" Ethan repeated, grief returned to his features, "She was the bravest person in the entire world, she jumped out of the cart to save me. I didn't want to go with her at first. I couldn't imagine any place being safer than underneath my bed," Ethan's hand shook and his eyes misted, "If only, if only I had gone with them in the first place, if only, Ivy had left me there. She would be alive."

"Oh no Ethan don't say that, it wasn't your fault, you were just a little kid and--."

Ethan let out a humorless chuckle, "You haven't even heard the worst of it. My mom, when she saw that I had made it to the flower garden without Ivy, she threw a fit. I don't think I ever saw her so angry. Everyone was yelling and the entire flower garden was chaotic. My mom told me that I would never be half the person Ivy was. According to her, Ivy didn't deserve to die but...buy I did, and sometimes, sometimes I believe her--." Ethan's voice was empty as if every emotion had been drained from him making his words seem as if they were carved from ice.

I stood, "No Ethan. Stop it, you didn't deserve to die then and you don't deserve to die now. We're going to find a way out of here."

"My mom went back, she went back to Teyar Skies to find Ivy and I didn't even try to stop her." Ethan continued like a broken record box. He didn't seem to have heard me. "For the first half hour that she was gone I let myself imagine what our life would be like if they returned. My mom would forgive me and Ivy would tell me everything would be okay.

"After two hours I had begun to wonder if they would come out at all. After five hours most people had left the flower garden and taken refuge in the art realm. I sat in front of the mud dragon flower for two days before my dad came looking for me. I didn't want to leave, I wanted to sit in front of the hazelnut colored flower."

I held a hand in front of my mouth, unable to speak.

"I didn't want to go with him but I had learned my lesson about not listening to people when they told me to come with them." Ethan finished bitterly.

My eyes filled with tears, and slid back down next to Ethan resting my head on his shoulders, the horrors that he experienced were ones that no seven year old should ever be forced to go through. "Oh Ethan…" I trailed off, not sure what to say. How do you comfort someone who was currently standing in the place where all their scars were formed? How do you help someone without having gone through their situation, or been part of their life during that time? I sighed wrapping my arms around Ethan hoping that it was enough comfort, it was certainly all that I was able to give.

***

I took a deep breath and stood, "We need to get out of here. I can't--we can't stay here. I refuse to sit here like a lamb to the slaughter, while the mud dragon prepares us for his dinner."

"You're right we're going to escape. What's our exit strategy?" Ethan asked, shaking his head as if to clear it.

"Our what?"

"Oh my God, we're going to die."

"Calm down, calm down," I said, biting my pinky nail. "Maybe we can move the stone that the mud dragon set in the door."

"Want me to summon an ox from my pindre. Or perhaps a lever."

I scowled, "Hey at least I'm trying."

Ethan scratched his head, "What about the vents. The ones that are pumping the hot air into the room?"

The two of us walked to the other side of the room, and I stuck my head over one of the vents and Ethan did the same. My eyes watered, and my hair matted itself against my forehead as I leaned over the small holes. I shot a glance over at Ethan and wondered how he was so calm. It was as if our conversation never even happened. How could he act as if nothing had ever happened to him? He's acting, I realized after a moment, he's been acting his whole life.

"These vents have burning flames beneath them, and it appears to be boiling water." Ethan realized, "That's what's causing the water vapor."

"Could we crawl through the vents," I asked, already knowing the answer.

"Not unless we want to be boiled to death," Ethan replied.

"Wait, I have a solution!" I said.

"Great."

"It involves fire."

"Absolutely not," Ethan responded, shaking his head and wiping sweat from his forearm

"You may have some creepy fire retardant skin but I unfortunately don't."

"Just hear me out," I answered, a plan already forming in my head. "We need something to lift the grate, like maybe a long hook or something. One it's open I might be able to squeeze through and you

315

can lower me down on a rope or something. Then I'll extinguish the fire and you can follow me."

"You're insane." Ethan marveled.

"I know right, isn't it great?"

***

Ethan began molding a hook out of clay for us to pull the grate and I sketched out a long rope to lower myself down. This will work, I thought to myself. This has to. I couldn't stay here and be eaten by the mud dragons, especially not after Ethan confided his story in me. These mud dragons wouldn't get a bite out of me, not without a fight. As I finished the ropes outline, I grabbed my colored pencils and began shading. Waving my hand and brown metal rope coiled into my palm. "All right have you got the hook?" I asked, staring over the grate apprehensively. The drop didn't look that deep, maybe ten feet or so. My hands shook slightly as I began examining the boiling water. I wasn't sure if I would be able to survive the heat. Potia wasn't really the deity of boiling water. "Hey Ethan," I said, "I'm not exactly sure if I can survive the water."

Ethan stopped sculpting and stared up at me, "Umm….okay, then how are we going to do this."

I bit my lip leaning over the side and looking down the grates. Ethan bent over and joined me. "Can you touch fire?" He asked, after a moment.

I nodded, "I'm pretty sure that I can, but I have a bad feeling about the water."

Ethan tapped his chin twice, "Could you swing around the water. The pots are a few feet wide, I'll hold the rope for you. If you let go at the right moment then you'll land right between two pots."

"And then I'll extinguish the flame and move the pots so you can come down too." I finished my heart already racing a mile a minute, "That seems fool proof."

Ethan rubbed a hand down his face, "You're right. There's too much that could go wrong, I don't want you to be boiled to death."

I gulped knowing that I would regret saying this, "No, we need to get out of here, if I have to jump over a pot of steaming water so be it."

"You sure?"

"...Yes, I'm sure."

Ethan rubbed his hands together nervously, "Well then, help me pull up the grate."

Ethan hooked the long piece of metal to one of the grates and the two of us began to tug. My hands began to blister as we pulled but the metal came out easily. I threw it aside and handed Ethan one side of my rope, "Don't you dare let go." I warned, trying to contain my terror.

Ethan nodded grimly and I shook my limbs out. I let my feet drop through the hole ignoring the slight sting of my exposed ankle pressed against the scalding rock. Ethan tightened his grip on the rope and lowered me down slowly. My knees passed through the hole and then my hips squeezed through. Part of my shirt lifted when my stomach passed through, and the hot rocks pressed uncomfortably against my skin. I was so close to the water that my leg tingles with pain and had turned a nasty shade, of *Fire Engine Red #34F31*.

I swallowed the nausea that came with stinging in my calves and took a deep breath trying to calm myself. I pulled my knees up to my chest hoping to alleviate the pain. I was maybe four or five feet over the water, and the heat was unbearable. My entire body was doused in sweat and my head pounded relentlessly. My muscles were screaming in protest, and I strained them in the hope to keep myself from falling in. I kept my grip tightly on the rope climbing a bit higher every few moments, due to the fact that my hands kept sliding back down.

"Ready to start swinging?!" Ethan called his voice tight with exertion.

"Y-yeh," I choked back, weakening, hoping he heard me.

"Hold on tight." He yelled.

"Really? I hadn't thought of that." I wanted to call back, but all that escaped my mouth was a soft whimper.

I reached my hand up and pushed it against the warm rock. The rock began swinging back and forth slowly. I blinked sweat out of my eyes and gritted my teeth trying to find the perfect moment in the land. There were two other pots on either side of me but the one on the right was slightly farther away. I pushed harder and let myself swing again. I counted to three in my head and tightened my biceps, I let my fingers uncurl from around the rope and my legs extended.

I let myself fall forwards and realized in a split second that I had jumped too late. My left foot landed on the cool stone floor but my right foot wasn't as lucky. It landed straight in the fire of the pot that I had jumped towards. I let out a scream, fear washing over me like a wave. I pulled my foot outwards and hopped like a madman howling in fright.

"Piper Piper!" Ethan yelled, sticking his head through the hole in the grate. "What happened, are you okay? Calm down!"

I took a deep breath and tried to steady myself. An odd smell had filled the room and I immediately recognized it as burning plastic. I looked down at my right foot and realized in horror that my sneaker had melted off of my foot. The panic returned, and I squeezed my nails into my palms, attempting to control it. My sneaker was completely ruined, but my foot looked completely normal. The skin was intact and shone with a rosy glow. Relief flooded through me and I let out a breath. "I'm okay," I said softly and then raised my voice. "I'm okay!"

"Phew," Ethan replied, "So...I don't really want to rush you after everything but could you please extinguish the flame, my face feels like it's about to melt."

"Yeh, one sec," I answered, still giddy. I curled my hand into a fist and squeezed it together tightly. It felt as if the fire were alight beneath my palm and I pressed harder trying to rid the oxygen around it. At last the flame sputtered and went out dropping the room's temperature as it went. I drew up a few ice cubes and plopped them inside of the pot, hoping to cool it down. As I waited, I also pressed a few ice cubes against my forehead and arms trying to battle the warmth. Once the metal pot was safe enough to touch I pushed it out of the way to give Ethan a safe place to drop. Feeling pleased with myself I dusted off my hands and looked up. "You can come down now!" I called.

Ethan began sliding down the rope far more graceful than I did and jumped down to the floor beneath him. "How did you fasten the rope?" I asked, looking up.

"I stuck the metal hook into a small gap in the floor and tied the rope around it. The mud dragon may see it and know which direction we went but hopefully we'll be long gone by them."

I froze, the gravity of the situation finally hitting me. "Ethan, we just escaped from a mud dragon prison, if anyone catches us...." I tried off in fear.

Ethan looked like he had just swallowed a frog, "We just can't get caught."

I nodded, hoping I didn't display my fear, "Right, don't get caught."

Chapter 33

Ethan and I began to walk around the room. It was still steamy, but the temperature had gone down a considerable amount. The room wasn't very large by a mud dragon standard but the door that led out was still around fifteen feet tall.

"Any ideas?" Ethan asked helplessly.

"Uh uh, don't look at me." I replied, holding my hands up, "I just figured out how to break out of the sauna."

Ethan rolled his eyes, "Just try to push it with me."

The two of us learned our backs against the wall and pushed with all of our might. I tensed my biceps and groaned after a few moments, "This wall must weigh a thousand pounds."

He held a hand up to his forehead and looked up. "Is that a door knob?"

I looked up and followed his gaze. There was a large piece of stone that jutted out of the door, maybe eight feet up. I bent my legs and jumped, attempting to grab it.

Ethan laughed, "What are you like, 4'6?"

My cheeks grew warm, "I'm 4'11." I shot back. "Or 5'1 on a good day."

He grinned, "I'm practically twice your height."

"You are not!" I replied indignantly, getting up on my tippy toes, the top of my head reaching a little past his nose.

"Move aside shorty," Ethan said, rubbing his hands together and bending his knees.

I raised my eyebrow, keeping my feet on the ground.

He sighed, "Move aside, please."

I grinned and got out of his way.

Ethan rolled back and forth on the balls of his feet and launched himself upwards. His hand skimmed the bottom of the doorknob, and he fell back down, stumbling slightly.

I laughed, "Not so manly now, are ya?"

He rolled his eyes, "That was just a practice round. I can totally reach that."

I stuck my tongue out at him, "Uh huh."

He didn't reply, only bent down again to try and reach the door knob again. I sat down and watched him jump up and down like his feet were on fire.

"Should I draw you up a rope?" I asked after he failed to grab the door knob for the fifth time.

Ethan rubbed his neck, "Yeah... not gonna lie, that might be a smart idea."

I laughed and summed my sketch book out of my *pindres*. I sketched out a quick rope and tossed it to him. Ethan caught it with one hand and jumped again. He wrapped a rope around the stone and held on tight. The stone began turning slightly, and the door swung open. I jumped out of the way to avoid being squished against the wall.

Ethan whopped and pumped his fist in the air.

"Nice job!" I called back as quietly as I could.

Ethan jumped down and put the ropes in his backpack. We walked through the doorway and I shut it behind us, "Best to cover our tracks." I decided, and Ethan nodded in agreement.

We walked through and began making our way through the hallways. "Everything looks the same!" I complained as we passed through the third stone archway.

"Let's try and find a window," Ethan suggested.

I sighed, scratching a piece of dried mud off my forehead, "Good idea."

We tentatively tiptoed through the passageway jumping at every sound, thinking that it was a mud dragon hot on our trail. The halls were completely silent; the only sound came from Ethan's rapid breathing and by beating heart. We turned left, then right, and then left again. My head spun, trying to figure out where we were. The entire house was a labyrinth, and the two of us were getting more and more lost by the second.

"Haven't we already passed this?" I said, motioning to an uneven stone pillar with rough edges.

Ethan scratched his chin, "We need a better way of getting around. Let's stop traveling the main hallways. I don't think that there are any windows or doors here."

"Good idea," I replied and turned left at the nearest intersection. After a few more twists and turns, a door appeared in front of us. I bit my lip, trying to contain my excitement. For all we knew, this door could lead to a kitchen or something.

"Should we go in?" Ethan asked, rubbing his hands together apprehensively.

I gulped, looking up at the menacing door, "We sure aren't getting anywhere wandering through these halls waiting for a mud dragon to come scoop us up."

Ethan sighed, "I was afraid you'd say that. Ok, help me push it."

***

The door led to an empty bedroom. Everything was twice as big as what I considered normal. The room was a lot more advanced than I had expected it to be. The bed was adorned with silky red sheets, and there was a lamp near the side of a mahogany desk. The walls were grey, rough stones, but they matched the rugged aesthetic of the room. The top of the bed was a few inches taller than me, but I could see eclectic purple light from the strange sky streaming in from what I hoped was a window.

"Look, Ethan! I proclaimed, pointing up at the light, "I think there's a window. Maybe we can climb out of it."

"Let's climb up onto the bed," Ethan suggested, "We can get a better view of the window and maybe find a way out of it."

"Ok." I agreed, jumping upwards, trying to reach the top of the bed. My nail skimmed the top, but I fell back down.

Ethan laughed, "Next time we travel somewhere, we should visit a place that isn't bigger than the Planet Jupiter."

"And a place that doesn't have blood thirsty animals that eat people." I continued and immediately wished I could take back my words.

Ethan looked down at his feet and didn't respond.

"Hey, no-wait, I didn't mean that." I blabbed.

"No, don't worry about it," Ethan said, meeting my gaze. "She's dead. I get it. I know."

323

I gulped, trying to figure out what to say.

"Do you want a boost?" He asked.

"A what?"

"A boost." Ethan repeated, "To get up on the bed."

"Oh right, yeah, sure, thanks."

He got down on one knee and held his palm out in a cup shape. I lifted my right leg and jumped, trying to grab the mattress. My legs swung wildly as I tried to hold onto the comforter. My foot collided with something soft, and I heard Ethan let out a noise that sounded like a squirrel getting decapitated.

I winced, "Ooooh, my bad."

"Don't worry about it." He said, his voice muffled.

I bent, slid my arms forwards, and sat down on the mattress. Ethan jumped up next, pulling himself up next to me.

"There's the window." I declared, turning around and pointing at the open space.

The two of us ran across the mattress, which was about as big as my bedroom, and made our way to the open window. I stuck my foot into the ridge of the bedpost and climbed up the couched size pillow to reach the ledge. I stretched my arms up, trying to reach the ridge above the bed. My fingers curled around the stone, and I kicked my feet against the wall to pull myself up. Ethan came up shortly after, and we peered down the open window.

"Sooo……." I began, holding onto the side of the window, and the cold air stung my face. "This is a little higher than I had anticipated."

324

I felt the ground sway beneath me, and I dug my fingers into the stone, breathing through my nose. Ethan ran a hand through his hair in frustration, "Sheesh, it's like fifty feet."

"How many stories high are we?" I asked, looking down.

"It doesn't matter?" Ethan replied, "The mud dragons are so big. This could be one story high.

I gulped, "That's comforting."

"Should we summon ropes?" He asked, rubbing his hands together.

"There's no time." I said, glancing at the door, "Let's tie the blankets together. We can climb down on those."

Ethan nodded and hopped back down to the pillow. We made our way across the mattress and tried pulling the comforter off the corners of the bed. Unfortunately, we soon learned that a blanket that was nearly four times the size of a normal one was also four times heavier.

"What about the sheet?" I asked, wiping my forehead with my arm.

"Good idea."

We tugged the thin fabric off of the bottom of the mattress and hauled it up to the window sill. It wasn't the prettiest, and if any mud dragon walked in after, they would definitely know that we had been here, but I hoped that we would be out of there by the time any of the mud dragons woke up. Ethan held the bed sheet tightly with one hand and dangled it out of the window.

"It's not long enough!" He called, looking over.

"Let's cut it in half!" I replied, "Then we can tie the ends together."

Ethan nodded and summoned a blunt knife from his *pindres*. I held each edge of the sheet and pulled them apart as Ethan sliced the sheet in half. I ran over to the two edges and began tying them together.

"Double knot it!" Ethan called, glancing at the door nervously.

I complied and got the sheet a quick tug to make sure it was secure. I threw one side of our makeshift rope to Ethan, who grabbed the top and began climbing back to the window sill. A thumping sound echoed through my skull. At first, I thought that it was my heart beat, but Ethan quickly corrected me.

"Do you hear that?" He asked, his voice filled with fear. "It sounds like...footsteps."

I glanced at the door and gulped, "Quick, tie the bed sheet to the window. We may not get another chance to escape."

Ethan wrapped the thin cloth around a small ridge that stuck up near the center of the window sill. I grabbed the bottom of the sheet and threw it out of the room. It dangled for a few moments, and my heart fell when I realized that it was nowhere near as close to the ground as I had hoped. "We're still going to fall around ten feet."

Ethan rubbed the back of his neck, "We really need to stop escaping from windows. What's wrong with a nice door? Or maybe even a crack in a wall."

I sighed, "Clearly, fate has it out for us."

I heard the low squabble of mud dragon voices, and my blood went cold. "Quick, quick climb out," I whispered, shooting terrified glances at the door.

I swung my leg over the side of the window sill and began to slide my way down as quickly as possible. The fabric stung my bare legs, but I just slid faster. I was below the window sill when I heard the unmistakable noise of a stone door swinging open. Ethan, who was a few feet above me, let out a yelp as a massive sound exploded through the halls. With the mud dragon's roar, my eardrums popped, and a ringing sound filled my skull. Stars danced in front of my eyes, and I scrunched my shoulder to my ears, unable to cover them with my occupied hands. My entire body was frozen in place as I gazed up at the window. Ethan's hand was still on the stone ledge, and he made no indication that he was going to move it. As I looked up at him, something in my brain clicked. I would not let him die the way Ivy did. I will not die the way Ivy did.

"ETHAN, MOVE!" I immediately began scuttling up the sheet to him, moving at breakneck speed.

I tugged his foot twice, and he shook his head as if trying to shake off water. He took a breath and immediately began sliding down. I kept my gaze on the window as the entire stone house began shaking as if the mud dragon was running across the room. My heart leaped into my throat as a familiar shape poked its head out of the open window, silhouetted against the run.

A scream escaped my mouth, and the mud dragon cackled, "You didn't really think that you would escape. Did you?"

It's *Fresh Artichoke Behr Logo M340-5* colored talons, swiped across our makeshift rope cutting it clean in half. The bed sheet fell almost comically, and my hair flew into my face. I grabbed onto the rope pulling it towards myself in the hope of keeping myself afloat. My eyes were squeezed shut with terror, and my vocal cords were growing hoarse. The wind rushed past me, and my heart jumped into my throat in fear. The ground was growing closer and closer.

I suddenly let out a yelp of pain as my arm felt as if it were being ripped from its socket. My head was spinning as I couldn't disorient myself. I was positive that I was flying upwards, but that was impossible. I opened one eye, realizing that I wasn't dead. I turned to Ethan, who was clutching onto the sheet with dear life. I looked down, noticing that we were a little more than five feet off the ground. I spin my head around to look upwards. Our rope wasn't attached to the window we had fallen from, and the mud dragon was no longer looking out the window. It probably presumed we were dead.

I huffed, slightly trying to find my voice, "How-." I cleared my throat, "How are we alive."

Ethan turned his head as well and responded breathlessly, "The sheet got stuck, right there, on this hook. That's the only reason we're alive."

I looked down, trying to slow my beating heart. A small hook in the wall, was all that it took to keep Ethan and me from crossing to the other side. My head spun, realizing it how one tiny little bump in the wall saved my life. Might even save the world if the two of us managed to find Emensaly. Did the creator of the house know that the little ridge would keep our hearts beating? Let us continue to live our lives? Surely not. I wondered if I had ever created something that saved someone's life. Would I ever have this big of an impact on someone else? I shook my head to clear my thoughts. Now wasn't a time to be philosophical. We need to get out of here. I touched my shoulder tenderly to make sure that I hadn't dislocated it.

"Did you get hurt?" Ethan asked, noticing my motion.

I rolled my arm backward, "I don't think so. How 'bout you?"

Ethan shook his head, "No, we got lucky."

"We sure did," I said, glancing back up at the ridge in the wall.

I slide down the sheet, wincing slightly, my palms and calves raw with rope burn. I dropped the last few feet rolling to the ground, being covered with yet another layer of mud.

"Do you think the mud dragon is going to follow us?" I asked, apprehensively looking up at the window.

Ethan rubbed his hands together, his gaze darting around. "Not sure. Let's get out of here before we find out."

I grabbed my packmare, off the ground, ignoring Grass's indigent shrieks, and followed. I gripped my shoulder tightly as the two of us walked in silence. Ethan pointed, towards a small ridge between two rocks, near the edge of the city and recommended we go there. It was smaller than our previous hiding spot, but I wasn't keen on staying anywhere close to the mud dragon that had found us. Still, I followed him. He lowered himself between the two rocks and tugged his knees up to his chest. I slid down the wall and sat next to him.

"What are we going to do?" I asked, peering out of the hole to make sure no one had spotted us. The purple sky was dimming, and there were only a few mud dragons left in the city.

Ethan shrugged, "Does it make me a bad person if I just was to stay right here for the rest of my life and never face the world again?"

I sighted, resting my head in my hands. "No, it doesn't. I want to do the same thing."

"It's crazy, isn't it?" He asked, "What we're expected to do?"

I sighed, "We're only 13. We're kids! I'm not even allowed to boil pasta on my own."

"I can't believe I signed up for this," Ethan replied, laying down against the cool stone and resting his head on his packmare.

"You and me both," I responded, looking down at the floor longingly. We sat in silence for a moment, gazing up at the *Eggplant Cream #42d3* colored sky. We sat there, not completely comfortable, knowing that we would have to get up in any second. I was looking back at the mud dragon's house, wondering if Potia's spear was still in front of it. Was the spear lost forever? I turned my focus away from the thought. I wouldn't worry about that right now.

"We can't stay here, though." I continued after a beat, ripping off the bandaid. "You know that."

Ethan sighed, "I do. It's just--." He waved his hand in the air helplessly. "You know."

"Yeah," I responded, still looking up at the sky.

Ethan was the first to stand, and I followed soon after. We didn't want to go back out there. The mud dragon had spooked us. It was different from the Ledos, and we hardly stood a chance with these creatures. We couldn't talk our way out or fight them. The mud dragons were bigger and faster. Our only advantage was being small enough to escape notice.

"Back to the city?" Ethan asked, tentatively

"Back to the city."

Chapter 34

The night was normally a time that was considered scary. It was when monsters came out, and people were hurt. The stone city wasn't like that. Ironically, it was the opposite. The plum-colored sky cast a warm glow on the stone houses that made them look like glow sticks. The air was cool, and a soft breeze blew my hair out of my face, carrying the soft chirps of birds. This is what Teyar Skies must have been like, I realized. One look at Ethan's pained expression proved that I was right.

Ethan trudged around the edge of the stone city, and I followed his footsteps. He was barely looking at where he was going. It was as if he had memorized the route by heart. I wanted to ask where he was going, but I was afraid of interrupting him as if it would break some kind of spell. He stopped a few feet in front of a small hut. His mouth hung open slightly as his eyes were swimming in memories. I looked at the hut in surprise, and realized two things. First, it was human-sized, scaled to fit a person, not a mud dragon. Second, it wasn't made of stone. The walls were wooden, with bright green paint peeling off the side. Was it a remnant of Teyar Skies? Why were we here?

"Ethan?" I asked softly, "What is this place?"

He shuddered slightly before responding. "This is my old home."

***

My jaw dropped, "What!?"

Ethan nodded, still looking at the wooden house as if it were made of gold.

"But, I thought the mud dragons destroyed everything." I continued.

Ethan walked around the hut, "The other half is caved in. I guess they thought it wasn't worth destroying completely."

I watched him walk towards the rickety wooden door. He reached out to grab the doorknob but hesitated before touching it. It was as if he feared the house would disappear if he held it.

"Go ahead." I was encouraged.

Ethan wrapped his fingers around the metal handle and took a long breath. "Here goes nothing." He muttered and pushed it open.

I walked in behind him, my eyes widening as I looked around. The other side of the building had caved in, showing the stone city. The interior of the house was slightly ruined. The stuffing was coming out of the sofa, and a soft bed of mold was growing in the kitchen. Ethan pressed his hands against the damp wooden walls as if they could come to life. I walked through to the next room and saw a small white cot leaning unstably to one side. I ran my hands over the peeling paint and retracted them immediately when my eyes made out the writing on the headboards. *ETHAN.* The handwriting was so similar to my brother Jack's. My heart felt as if it were about to split in two.

I squatted down to look under his bed. I could clearly see where Ethan had been hiding and was amazed that Ivy had managed to pull him out. Though by the scratched marks on the floor board, it seemed as if it hadn't been easy. My eyes began to prickle, and I blinked quickly, trying to make them go away. I kept my gaze on the floor, it was awful how destroyed the house was. The bed was barely able to stand and there was a puddle of rain water gathering beneath it. There was also something growing through the floor board where Ethan's scratches were.

I bent over to take a closer look at the small scrub that was growing. It was somehow familiar…. "Hey Ethan!" I called, getting up and taking a step back, "Ethan get in here!"

I heard a scuffle of footsteps, and Ethan appeared in the doorway. He took a sharp breath at the sight of his room. "Look down here," I instructed, bending down to reveal the small plant.

I motioned towards the shrub, hoping to distract Ethan from the scars on the floor. His eyes trailed over the small weed, only straying down to the floor for a moment. "It's the same as--." He stopped, looking down in surprise.

"It's the same as the one Marlee had." I continued, "The one Emensaly gave her."

Ethan's eyes glazed over as he looked at the plant's area, "It radiates Emensaly's energy."

"What was Emensaly doing here?" I asked.

Ethan didn't seem to hear me, he was suddenly staring at the puddle. "Piper, this water, can you see the bottom?"

I squinted, looking down closer at the puddle. At first glance, I had assumed that it was simply too dark for me to see the bottom. I tentatively reached my hand into the water, not sure what to expect. It was cold, colder than I would expect rain water to be. I retracted my hand quickly, feeling uncomfortable. "Why is it so cold?"

"I'm not sure." He replied, still looking at the puddle. He reached towards the puddle and stuck his hand inside. Ethan leaned forwards, and the water was so deep that it went up to his sleeve. He let out a small yelp and pulled his arm out. He cursed, looking down, at his finger.

"What, what is it?" I asked, looking down at the puddle suspiciously, wondering how it could be so deep.

"I touched something, and it moved," Ethan replied, shuddering.

My jaw dropped, "Do you think something lives there?"

"I think it's a *Fortant*."

"A what?" I asked, once again being reminded of how little I know about this world.

"It's something that transports you to another realm, without having to go to the flower garden, they were made illegal back in 1980 because they could unbalance an ecosystem, so the only people able to create it..." Ethan began, his words rushed in excitement, "Are deities."

I let out an uncharacteristic squeal and looked down at the puddle, or *Fortant*, as Ethan called it. "Are you saying that Emensaly created this?" I asked, my face flushed.

Ethan grinned and nodded, "I bet it leads to whatever realm Emensaly went to next!"

My heart raced, and a jolt of excitement flared through me. Was this it? Was this all that we had left of the mission? I felt an odd feeling course through my veins. It was strange, I had only been gone from my home for a few days, but it felt like a millennial. It was almost as if I had gotten used to the prospect of running for my life. That was ridiculous, though of course, I was ready to go back home. But what was home now? My place in Seattle with my family? Or the Art Realm. Would I really be able to go back to my normal life after everything that had happened in the past few days? I gripped my head, trying to clear my head, I didn't have time to focus on that right now. Ethan and I needed to figure this *Fortant* out.

"So, do we just jump in or.....?" Ethan trailed off, looking down at the dark puddle.

I wasn't totally keen on swimming through a dark puddle, unsure of what was beneath me, but unfortunately, we didn't have another choice. "We should probably draw up some gear." I decided, summoning my sketchbook from my *pindres*.

334

"Do you know how to scuba dive?" Ethan asked skeptically.

I froze mid-sketch, "Oh yeah, that could potentially pose a problem."

Ethan laughed, "Yeah..."

"Can't we just youtube it or something?"

He rolled his eyes, "You think you can learn how to scuba dive in five minutes off youtube?"

I shrugged, looking down at my sketchbook, "I mean......maybe."

Ethan grinned, "As much as I'd love to see you try, maybe we save that for another day and try to find another way through the *Fortant.*

I sighed as we sat in silence, trying to brainstorm. Ethan scratched his head, and I looked at the *Fortant* in dismay. "What if we don't overcomplicate it?" He asked, summoning a slab of clay. "Let's just try to see what realm this goes to."

"Okay...." I said, the gears in my brain turning. "Let's just create a pair of goggles."

Ethan nodded and worked quickly, fashioning a pair. He waved his hand, and they fell into his hand as I stared down at the puddle in fear. "Do you want to go into the puddle, or should I?" He asked.

I bit my lip, "I'll do it." I blurted out. It was my mission, all of this was my fault. I wasn't going to let Ethan risk his neck because I was a coward.

"You sure?" He asked, still holding onto the goggles.

"Yup," I answered before I could regret it.

He handed me the plastic toy and I strapped them over my face. Ethan began to chuckle and I held up a finger. "Not. A. Word," I said, knowing full well how ridiculous I looked.

Ethan pressed his lips together, and let out a laugh, poorly disguised as a cough. I rolled my eyes and turned to face the puddle. I gulped, and crawled towards it, after pulling my socks, shoes and sweater off. I dipped my foot into the water and let out a small gasp. "It's freezing." I hissed, cursing.

Ethan grins, "That's tough."

I shot a rude hand gesture at him and took a shuddering breath, dropping my foot back into the puddle. Gritting my teeth, I lowered my legs into the icy water, shivering vigorously.

"You good?" Ethan asked, all humor gone from his voice.

"O-oh y-yeh, I-I've n-never b-been warmer." I chattered.

"I see that dropping into a basin of freezing water hasn't affected your sarcasm."

I ignored him and gripped onto the side of his bed. I had lowered far enough that the water was up to my chest, my legs grew numb, and shivers ran up my spine. I curled my toes, losing feeling in them. My bare feet burned as the icy water sloshed against them, and my hands began shivering.

"You've got this!" Ethan encouraged.

"E-easy f-for y-you t-to s-say," I said, quivering as I looked down at that water. It was all the way up to my chin. Taking a big breath, I lowered my head completely underwater. Icy waters filled my ears as I submerged completely. Swimming downwards I squinted, trying to make out the different shapes in the dark water. There didn't seem to be anything around me, only a rocky outline a few feet below me. My lungs felt tight as if my hands were squeezing around them. Still shivering, I swam upwards again, returning to Ethan. I broke the surface, gasping for air.

"Did you see anything?" Ethan asked, leaning over to look at me.

I took a big breath before responding, "I think I saw a rock. It might have been nothing, but it's the only thing I saw for miles. The rest is just empty dark blue water."

"Is it saltwater or freshwater?" Ethan asked.

I scratched unsure. "L-LTemme check." I stuck my face back into the freezing water, trying to figure it out. As I came up, I licked my lips, pensively. "This is strange, but it tastes, sweet."

Ethan frowned, bending over, to sniff the water. "That's....weird." He replied finally. "I've never heard of, *sweet water.*"

I shuddered, "A-as l-long as it isn't a-acid I t-think we're f-fine."

Ethan nodded, "Do you think you can get a better look at that cave?"

I shivered at the thought of swimming deeper into the strange realm. "Ok."

Taking a gulp of air, I turned and dived deeper into the water. I propelled myself forwards as quickly as possible, my lungs already tickling slightly. I looked around trying to find any sort of live in the *FolkArt Acrylic Paint Azure #213d* waters. What could Emensaly possibly be doing here? My ears popped as I descended further and I was painfully aware of my lungs screaming in protest. I swam to the bottom of the rock that was floating in the center of the empty realm. I blinked a few times, my head becoming heavy. I swam towards a small hole near the center and caught a glimpse of something. Something that was impossible. There was a burning fire inside of the rock.

***

I propelled myself upwards as quickly as I could. Sticking my head through the whole I appeared next to Ethan, sputtering and coughing.

"Woah are you okay?" He asked, reaching over to pull me back onto the ledge. "You were down there for a long time."

I let out another series of coughs, before responding. "I-I saw f-f-fire. Down, i-in the r-rock. I-its the c-c-cave."

"Fire!?" Ethan asked incredulously, "But fire needs oxygen to survive?"

"T-there may b-be o-oxygen in the c-cave?" I proclaimed, my lips turning blue.

"Can you go down there again?" Ethan asked, "Maybe you could get into the cave. Look if Emensaly's there."

I took a big breath, smiling thinly at the irony. My adventure started when I entered a cave, now it's ending in another cave. Crossing my fingers, I turned around and dropped back into the freezing water. I let myself float for a few moments before kicking my feet to descend. My ears popped and my lungs shuddered. The sweetwater brushed against my lips, leaving a strange after taste in my mouth.

My heart was beating madly, as I approached the floating rock. My chest was on fire. I needed to breathe. I kicked around trying to find the entrance to the rock, panic choking me as much as the water. My eyelids felt heavy, by the time my pupils finally focused on the small fire within the rock. I propelled myself forwards with my numb limbs attempting to get closer to the cave. My chest aches, and as I swim to the opening. Almost there, I push, almost there--. Cold water fills my nose, causing a massive headache to explode in my head. I

338

wrap my hand around the opening, on the rough surface of the rock. Gasping, I lift myself through the opening, taking greedy gulps of air.

I pulled myself into the warm room and collapsed upon a dark green carpet. I stood on all fours, coughing water out of my lungs. My limbs shivered, and I began crawling towards the water, towards the warmth. My sore lungs felt as if someone had filled them with needles, and the back of my throat burned. My breathing was heavy, and my only goal was to make it to the fire. I stuck my hand inside, ignoring the way my sleeves fringed and burnt. Warmth spread through my body as a rosy glow returned to my skin. As I thawed my frozen hands, I began to look around the room. It had green leather upholstery and *New Shamrock Acrylic Set Hue 2452* colored walls. Plants hung from the ceiling in messy tangles, looking like my hair when I forget to brush it. There were two *Benjamin Moore Dark Olive* set chairs, stationed on either side of the hearth. The chairs were made out of clear green stones that were beautiful but probably really uncomfortable to sit in. I paid no attention to the one on the left as the woman sitting to my right was the one that interested me. There was a pot in her lap but her eyes were closed and I could just make out green lashes, connected to her earthy colored eyelids. Her lips were cracked, resembling soil that had been exposed to the sun for too long. Her hair had a green tint to it, and there was something timeless about her, she could pass for fourteen, or forty.

My heartbeat in my chest in anticipation and excitement. Was this Emensaly? Was this the goddess I had risked my life to look for? The pulsed with a sort of heat, one that didn't come from the fire, it was radiating off of her. I let my eyes unfocus for a moment trying to look through my deity eyes. The power shone from her so strongly that my eyes began to burn. So this was her. I realized, my heart leaping into the air. I had found Emensaly.

I felt like whooping but there was no time for that. I stood quickly, nearly stumbling into the hearth, the sole of my already melted shoe coming off completely. I ran up to her and patted her arm gently, "Emensaly? Emensaly?"

She awoke with a start, her eyes brows narrowing in anger and fear. I felt an invisible force hit me in the gut, knocking the wind out of me. I landed in the fireplace with a start, coughing and sputtering. Emensaly raised an eyebrow, her eyes following my, "A daughter of Potia are you? I'm assume you bring nothing but trouble to my doorstep."

"Please, Emensaly, you have to listen to me." I pleaded, my words blurring together as I rushed to get them out, "The wall to the realm of Charlid is breaking down. We need you back in the golden god kingdom. The creatures of Charlid will escape and destroy the world."

She scoffed, sitting up in her chair and crossing her arms, "Who are you and what are you doing in my house!?"

"My name is Piper Hart." I said quickly, hoping to get back on track, "I've been searching for you for the last three days. The world needs you. Your brothers---."

"Don't speak of my brothers." She hissed, and I took a step back wishing I could eat my words. I had forgotten that Emensaly despised her brothers after they murdered a human she had fallen in love with.

"But ma'am with all due respect we need you!" I tried backpedaling hoping to get her on my side.

"That's nice to know." She replied, sounding sincere, "Should give my brothers a nice amount of trouble. As I'm sure you know they have taken pleasure in my misery. I might as well return the favor."

"Emensaly, I get it, you're mad at them for stopping you from seeing your soulmate Charles, or whatever, but that was centuries ago. We need your help! If Charlid escapes, you're in just as much trouble as the rest---." I began, but she cut me off

"You don't understand, do you?" She asked, her eyes blazing, "A deity is given one soulmate. They don't get countless re-dos and second chances. They find that one person, that one creature, and they fall in love forever. Without them, there's a part of the deity missing. It will be missing for the rest of time itself. Forever and ever. My brothers took that from me."

I bit my lip, trying to figure out a way to get the tension levels down in this room. As bad as I felt for Emensaly, I couldn't give into my sympathy just yet. I needed her, and frankly I couldn't believe that this was the actual goddess I had been looking for. I had imagined that she would be kind and willing. Supportive of our cause. Instead she turned out to be a nature deity nursing a two-thousand year old heart break, and seeking revenge on her brothers that caused it. And here I was thinking that I wasn't in middle school anymore.

"You wouldn't just be saving them!" I replied, raising my voice, using my last resort. "You would be saving everyone. My friends, my family, myself, every creature alive right now, that deserves to live!"

"SILENCE YOURSELF!" Emensaly snapped, her eyes glowing with fury. "All I hear in my my my my my, I've been hiding for over a dozen centuries and every intelligent form of life hadn't changed in the slightest. You're all still selfish little creatures that die at some point, why not speed up the process."

I took a step back becoming fearful. Wow what a pessimist I thought vaguely. I had the mind to tell her that maybe sitting on an uncomfortable chair made out of emeralds was causing her mood, but I decided that it may not be the greatest approach. I was about to say something else but Emensaly was on a roll.

"Did you know that my brother's still benefit from my misery? The flower garden that you used to transport yourself to this realm, you see that as a happy place don't you? Well let me tell you this, my tears nurtured the soil and my sobs sprouted seeds. Now people come and go upon the ground I wept on, all of them, simply using me."

"Yeah I can see how that has made you bitter…" I trailed off.

341

"I couldn't care less about their little dispute with Charlid. In fact I relish the thought of someone challenging their throne it's about time they learn what pain is."

I resisted the urge to gasp, I mean I had a brother so I totally understood sibling rivalry. But saying that your sibling deserves to be thrown off the throne by the father of evil, Charlid himself, was a bit far.

"Listen, I know the three brothers have their faults." I began hoping that my next argument would sway her, "Trust me I've met them, but imagine Charlid on the throne right now. Everything would be a hundred times worse. Besides, things aren't all that bad with the three brothers ruling now are they?"

Emensaly turned to me, so we stood eye to eye and let out a dry laugh, "Do you really believe that Piper Hart? Tell me Piper, was the Ledo situation, *not so bad*? How about your little friend Ethan hmm. The mud dragons invaded his home killing his mother and many others. Was that *not so bad*. Charlid is practically already ruling. Evil takes many forms, my brother's just so happen to be one of them.

I opened my mouth to respond, trying to find a counter argument, something to prove that the leaders of the realms weren't as corrupted as Emensaly was making them out to be. "She's right isn't she?" a little voice in my head asked. I squeezed my fists trying to ignore it. Well parts of it at least, no matter what she said I knew that Charlid was worse than the three brothers. The amount of pain and torture that he had put some people through was unacceptable. However, before I could continue trying to convince Emensaly, I heard a wet slosh from the entrance of the room.

I turned my head to look at the entrance and was surprised to see a hand grab onto the side of the mouth of the cave. I went to the center and saw Ethan attempting to enter. "Ethan!" I yelled, rushing over to him. I grabbed his hand and pulled him through the hole in the rock, helping him slosh into the room. Ethan landed in the center of

Emensaly's living room with a wet squish. I cursed, "Ethan are you okay?"

"You were down there so long." He replied with a gasp, shivering slightly. "I...thought...something had...happened." Ethan puffed between every few words, trying to get his breath back.

"Ethan, Ethan, Ethan she's right here! Emensaly, we found here." I squealed, "We did it!"

"What!? Where--." He paused suddenly, his features contorting into one of recognition and then disbelief. "I-Ivy?" Was all he managed to get out.

I frowned, wondering if his brain had been damaged from being underwater too long, "Ethan, no that's Emensaly."

"That's Ivy." He insisted, firmly, he turned to Emensaly, doubt creeping into his voice, "Right?"

Emensaly held a hand over her mouth, and stared at Ethan, her eyes filled with pain.

"RIGHT?" Ethan yelled, his voice, shaking but not from the cold.

My eyes almost popped out of their sockets when I saw Emensaly nod her head one. Her thin lashes were coated in tears, and she blinked them away one by one.

"But, but, Ivy's dead." I managed, hoping I didn't sound too blunt.

"Are you dead?" Ethan asked, his voice so small, that I could barely make out the small spark of hope within it.

Emensaly, or Ivy swallowed once before responding. "No, no I'm not dead. I am Ivy. Well I supposed you could say I was her."

Ethan didn't respond, his eyes wide and overwhelmed. He didn't ask and I had the feeling that he didn't want to lose the small shred of hope by asking questions. I stared at her, waiting for more.

She took a shaky breath, "I've been many different people. I've found that it's the best way to hide my true identity. Many people had been searching for me. My brothers have been searching for me, it hasn't become an open investigation but they know that they are more powerful with me. They do it in secret, not wanting to confirm the rumors."

I stared at Ethan as he heard Emensaly's tale. He was still as stone, his face emotionless. The only indication that the story had any effect on him was how his nails were digging little crescent shapes into his palms.

"I can't ever stay in one place forever. When the mud dragons attacked, I thought that it would be the perfect opportunity to leave. You have to understand that you were safer off thinking that I was dead." The last sentence Emensaly spoke was more of a plea than anything.

Ethan looked as if he were trying to swallow a particularly large fly, he blinked a few times before responding, "I've thought you were dead for the past 13 years. Every single day I've woken up and blamed myself for your death. You were the most important person in my entire life...was that person even real?"

Tears threatened to overflow in Emensaly's eyes as she listened to Ethan's words. "I promise, oh Ethan I swear it was all real. I loved you but I had to leave you."

"You're a coward," Ethan said slowly, his face betraying only the barest hint of pain, "I've suffered since the day you left, thinking that you were dead. I've been mourning you the entire time you've been in hiding. All because you can't bear facing a feud you had with your brothers ages ago. You called people selfish, and you know what, you're probably right about that. But let me tell you this, you're just as bad if not worse than everyone else."

"No, no Ethan I swear, I never wanted this for you I thought, I thought...."

"Well we don't always get what we want do we?" Ethan asked bitterly.

"Please Ethan."

He didn't respond, staring anywhere but Emensaly's face. I bit my lip unsure what to do. Emensaly was certainly not going to help us, and I didn't want to put Ethan through another minute with her. She didn't deserve his company anymore than he deserved her guilt. I wasn't sure what I was supposed to do. Were we going to leave Emensaly here? Ethan looked ready to bolt out of the room and Emesaly, stood a few feet away from him silent tears running down her face. As I stood deep in thought I heard another slosh. It was similar to the one Ethan made when he entered the rock. The three of us turned to see the unawaited visiter.

"Arius?" I asked, looking at the ¾ deity that worked for Eveda, as he pulled himself through the hole in the rock. I ran over to help him up, "Arius, what are you doing here?"

I bent over to help him up and I immediately noticed a difference in the way he looked. The last time we had met his skin shone like gold and his muscles bulged more than the Rock's. Now they sagged limply, as if dumbbells had been permanently attached. The bags under his eyes proved that he hadn't been sleeping well as did his bloodshot eyes. They were darting back in a nervous fashion as he regarded Emensaly. I shot a glance at Ethan who had calmed down enough to look confused.

"Who are you?" Emensaly demanded, straightening herself. "Get out."

345

Arius didn't respond, but simply scuttled towards the mouth of a cage like a scared rat.

"Arius, what are you doing here?" I asked, trying to figure out why he was acting so strangely.

Arius didn't respond to me either, he stood at the entrance of the cave bouncing from foot to the other nervously. Emensaly walked up to him, "If you don't answer me I will personally throw u out of this house and--oh." Emensaly paused watching a woman appear through the hole in the rock. Unlike Ethan or Arius, she entered, gracefully, water dripping from her long dark hair turning into ice before it hit the floor. The temperature in the room seemed to drop a few degrees causing me to shudder.

"I'm afraid that won't be necessary." She said, her voice cool. "Arius is with me."

"And who might you be?" Emensaly asked, sneering.

I was starting to get the feeling that Emensaly wasn't the type of person that would invest in a welcome mat.

"Introductions can come later." The strange woman said her voice firm. "For now." She lifted her hand, causing Emensaly to float in the air. A mixture of panic and confusion shot across her face as her feet dangled a few inches off the ground. Ethan and I glanced at each other in panic, neither of us aware of what was going on. Emensaly balled her hands into fists, causing plants to begin growing around the woman's ankles. The woman's concentration broke for a moment allowing Emensaly to fall back to her feet. She rolled to the ground and put her hands up in a fighting stance, shrubs erupting all around the room, encompassing the deadly woman.

"ARIUS, HELP HER!" I yelled as Ethan and I backed away from the two women in their deadly dance. We knew better than to get involved. If there was one thing that I had learned from our adventure was that when deities were mad, you got out of their way. Arius didn't

346

respond, simply turned to face the tall women with black hair. Emensaly had her pinned against the wall by a cactus when Arius lunged. I crossed my fingers, hoping he would be able to get rid of the women, but instead of reaching for the intruder, he jumped on top on Emensaly. I screamed and he drove her to the floor, allowing the dark-haired women to escape the deadly plants. Emensaly attempted to rise, only to have a massive rock smacked into her head by Arius. The intruder waved her hands, and a cocoon of air began forming around the Emensaly, keeping her trapped within.

"WE HAVE TO HELP HER!" I screamed, shooting a glance at Ethan. He hesitated for a moment before responding. He waved his hand, and a crossbow appeared in one hand and a knife in the other.

I rubbed my *pindres* like a genie lamp praying that Potia's spear would appear in my hand even though I had lost it somewhere in the mud dragon realm. I was delighted to find the warm metal in my hand, as the tip of the spear erupted in flames. I ran towards the inturter ready to turn her (and maybe Arius) into a roasted shish-kabob. I lunged towards the fight where the dark haired woman had Emensaly trapped inside of a tornado and Arius battled against a patch of thorny roses. Ethan fired his crossbow at the women but they only seemed to agitate her as they bounced off her thick skin.

I ran towards her with Potia's spear in hand hoping to do some real damage. I lunged forward awkwardly, (still not totally sure how to use a spear) and the tip of the metal scratched along the woman leaving behind a trail of black liquid which I assumed was her blood. She hissed slightly, her concentration wavering, dropping Emensaly from within the tornado. The nature deity dropped to the floor, with an ungraceful *phump* and steadied her.

The dark haired woman sneered, lunging towards Emensaly, darkness pooling in her hands, "My my you're getting old aren't you Emensaly."

"Who are you?" Emensaly gasped, as massive rose thorns began growing from her hands, like weapons.

"I'm Linge." The woman replied, a grin curling across her features as they noticed Emensaly's horror.

Emensaly attempted to hide her horror and pushed towards Linge with her thorns. I could tell who would win. I didn't know where Linge came from or who trained her, but she had the upper hand. Emensaly was already weakening, as dark spirals began shooting towards her, making little nicks and cuts on her face.

Ethan as I watched in fear as the two continued their deadly dance. I wanted to help Emensaly but I had the feeling that I wouldn't survived being hit in the face with one of those dark spirals. As I watched intently I felt as if a snake were curling around my waist. I turned to see Arius behind me and Ethan his hands up in a fighting stance. There were ropes coiling around our feet holding us in place. I tried to jump away from them as they continued to wrap around my ankles.

Ethan hacked him away with his knife and launched at Arius a murderous glare in his eyes. I did the same with my spear and lunged towards the three-quarters deity. I stabbed left and right trying to get past Arius's defenses, yet everytime I managed to nick or scrap him, another pair of ropes held me back. I rubbed my hands together channeling the fire of Potia. A flame erupted between my hands as I threw it towards Arius with all the force and might that I had. It singed the left side of his body, causing him to howl in pain. I ran closer to Arius ready to impel him with my spear when my entire body was thrown backwards against the wall as if it were attached to a bungee cord. My head in the wall with a loud bang causing stars to erupt in front of my eyes. I saw that Ethan and Emensaly had been given the same treatment and were also pressed up against the wall.

"What the--." I struggled against the wall with all my might. I felt as if I had been stuck to a wall the way a bug might be caught in a spider's net. My feet dangled a few inches off the ground and I pointed my toes trying to touch the floor.

"Linge." Emensaly snarled, attempting to fight against her bonds.

"That's right," Linge said with a sneer.

"Come to do your father's dirty work for him?" Emensaly asked, eyebrows raised.

I glanced at Ethan in confusion, who was Linge's fathers?

"My father is dead." Linge said, a satisfied glint, "I've made sure of that?"

The two of us exchanged horrified glances.

"Charlid is dead?" Emensaly asked, astonishment leaking into her voice.

I felt fear crash over me as I looked at Linge again. She had killed Charlid, the one person that scared the three brothers. If Linge had managed to kill him, who knows what she could do to us?

"What?" Arius asked, looking at Charlid's daughter as if he were seeing her for the first time. "You, why--I mean, yes my queen."

I looked at Arius in confusion, and felt a small stab of betrayal. Since when was this, witch, his queen? I had thought he served Eveda. Nothing made sense, why was Arius taking orders from Linge. Was he no longer loyal to the art realm? I swore under my breath.

"And who are these two lovely children?" Linge asked, her gaze flickering upon the two of us. I felt the urge to squirm away, but I forced myself to look her in the eyes.

"They're the ones that found Emensaly, ma'am," Arius replied, his voice weakening with exhaustion and fear.

349

"Ahhhh yes, Piper and Ethan, how could I forget. You know, none of my plans could have been possible if it weren't for the two of you?"

Ethan and I looked at each other, not daring to speak, but his words were written clearly upon his face. What was Linge's plans?

"Yes yes," She continued, "You know for all your strict moral obligations the two of you make excellent pawns. All Arius had to do was follow you, and you brought me straight to Emensaly."

I felt my face grow hot with terror and anger. What did the daughter of Charlid want with Emensaly? Did they simply want to stop her from uniting with her brothers, or did Linge have other plans for the earth deity? I didn't want to find out.

"What's going on?" Ethan asked.

Melige checked her watch, "I suppose we have some time until the walls break down."

"What walls?" Emensaly asked, her head held high. I could hear a slight tremble in her voice.

"The walls of the realm of Charlid. Though I suppose it is high time to rename that realm, don't you?"

"Arius--," I said, desperately hoping he would help us out of this.

The three-fourths deity didn't meet my gaze, and Linge laughed. "Ahhh yes Arius has been incredibly helpful. He launched the attack on Bella, and Ethan as well."

I could practically hear Ethan gritting his teeth as I clenched my hands into fist.

"Arius doesn't work for you." Ethan said and I felt close to tears "He works for Eveda" He said desperately. I looked around hoping that someone was about to jump out of a pijata and yell "SIKE!"

350

"Ahh yes another wonderful story," Menlige said, with a grin that reminded me of the Cheshire cat. Arius looked at the floor, and shuffled his back and forth. "Arius was one of the first people to discover the realm of Charlid but unlike the others he was one of the few to survive. Arius struck a deal with my father, in exchange for his life, he would bring humans to my father's realms. This gave my father the chance to create his own in-between. No one can leave the chaos realm unless they are an in-between, or part deity, that was how the realm was closed in the first place. With Arius able to leave whenever he wanted, we had an endless supply of humans."

"You're lying!" I screamed, and Ethan let out a roar next to me. "That can't be true." I faltered, "...Right?"

Linge's cackle sounded like a bleating sheep. She walked towards me and pressed her long graceful finger across my cheek, tracing my shallow cheekbones. I tried to turn my head away but it stayed firmly pressed against the wall. I considered the urge to spit in her face but decided that pissing off the most powerful person in the room might not be the best idea. "Arius has been incredibly useful." She continued. "He was more resourceful than I thought was possible for a ¾ deity."

Arius flitched at the words, still looking down at his feet.

"He even managed to steal *deleva*, the food of the deities, to strengthen myself and my father." Linge boasted.

My eyes widened, it had been Arius who had lugged *deleva* acrossed the art realm the night I had looked out of my window. Ethan let out a small gasp letting me know that he realized it as well.

"Yes yes," Linge said, and then turned to Emensaly who had been watching the entire exchange in horror. "Your brother's have gotten cocky. I doubt they ever thought that anyone would attempt to rob them. A three year old could sneak it's way past them."

Emensaly's gaze narrowed. "Let us go right now. You'll regret it if you don't." Linge actually had the nerve to laugh, "Oh really Em. You think someone is going to come rescue you?" She laughed, and Emensaly's lip curled, "Well you really shot yourself in the foot with that one. If I remember correctly, it's impossible for a deity to find this comfy little hideout. Only an in-between can lead a deity to it."

Emensaly, turned to me and Ethan. Her glare could have cut through bone. For once I was happy that she was stuck to the wall.

Linge continued to chuckle, "Oh you didn't think that one through did you? Yes well Arius managed to bring some *deleva* to me and my father. It strengthened us, and built up our army of in-betweens. It's quite masterful, if I do say so myself. Not that you two are going to live to see it." Linge pointed towards me and Ethan. "As for you Em, trust me you'll have a part in this."

My blood turned to ice and I shot a glance towards Ethan. His face was stoic but I could see the real fear in his eyes. This was it, Linge was going to kill us. My eyes became hot with tears and I didn't bother to blink them away. Shame and terror built up in the pit of my stomach. If only I had convinced Emensaly to leave sooner. If only Arius wasn't so weak minded that he was so easily swayed to Charlid's side.

"But Arius you saved Ethan's life!" I yelled desperately trying to get Arius to help us.

Linge laughed, "Of course he didn't. Arius attacked Bella thinking it was you, attempting to stop your mission. That was of course before we figured out how useful Emensaly would be on our side."

"I am on nobody's side--." Emensaly hissed.

Linge continued as if she hadn't heard a thing, "As for saving Ethan's life--."

"Eveda was losing her trust in me," Arius spoke up for the first time since he arrived. His voice was more hollow than I remembered. "I had to save Ethan to stop her suspicious." It might have been my hopeful imagination but there seemed to be a twinge of regret in Arius's voice.

I bit my lip to stop myself from screaming at Arius. I felt no sadness that we lost Arius, all my pity was directed towards Eveda, she had placed her trust and her secrets into him. His betrayal was a conscious decision, one for cold indifference. He took personal gain instead of a loss that could have saved so many. I felt a fresh wave of fury at the two of them and pushed against the invisible barrier with a new vigor. My chest ached and my muscles burned as I attempted to free myself.

I sighed, deciding to conserve my strength. Even if I did manage to push through the binding I would hardly have time to collect myself before Linge stuck me back onto the wall or worse.

"My family's next stroke of luck is all thanks to you Piper," Menlige said, bringing me back to the present.

I froze, "Wha-what do you mean, thanks to me." I sputtered.

"The cave you stumbled upon during your camping trip was one that is sacred to Charlid. By sacrificing your drawings in the fire you gave the entire realm of Charlid access to the art realm."

I stared at her in horror, wishing that I could cover my ears to stop myself from hearing the rest of her sentence.

Linge grinned, enjoying my pain.

"ENOUGH!" Emensaly roared, and a massive explosion of green light filled the room. I slammed my eyes shut to protect them from the blow and the next thing I knew I hit the floor with an uncomfortable *slump*. Ethan was free of his bonds as well and Emensaly stood on the floor in a battle stance.

"What the…" I wondered, as she lunged at Linge. Linge jumped to the side and drew a heavy-looking club.

"Piper, look out!" Ethan yelled and I looked up to see Arius coming at me with a lethal looking knife. I rolled away, scrambling to my feet. Ethan summoned his crossbow and wide, pointy staff. I tried to concentrate on summoning a firestorm from Potia but for some reason it was a little hard to focus when there were four ppl locked in a deadly battle to my left and right. A flame curled in the center of my palm and I opened my hand to make them grow. Emensaly seemed to be holding against Linge just fine but Ethan was straining against Arius. I directed the wall of fire toward him. Arius jumped aside, causing a nearby bookshelf to go up in flames. I put it out as quickly as I could with a wave of my hand. Ethan managed to regroup himself and pulled his crossbow out firing shot after shot at Arius. Unfortunately the arrows were barely able to draw blood, much less distract him.

Darkness pooled in Arius's hands, clearly Linge had been teaching him a few tricks. Ethan danced out of the way from the coils and I held up my hands to block them. I let out a jet of fire toward the coils. They wrapped around the flame extinguishing them with a poof. The coils continued toward me.

"PIPER, MOVE!" Ethan yelled, pushing me out of the way.

I stumbled to the left as the darkness let out a little explosion right where I had been standing the moment before. I picked up Potia's spear from where I had dropped it earlier, advancing toward Arius from the left.

Ethan shook his left foot where his *pindres* resided, and a strange group of clay worms advanced towards Arius. They wiggled towards Arius with shocking speed, climbing up and around him. I quickly noticed that wherever they touched Arius, his skin turned to clay. Ethan squinted in concentration, attempting to keep Arius encased. It worked for a few moments allowing me time to advance toward Arius with my spear. I was a few inches away when Ethan suddenly stumbled against the door, wheezing, with exhaustion. Arius unfroze, but I still whammed the spear right through his gut.

Arius clenched his midsection, his eyes shut in agony. I approached him, making the mistake of letting my guard down. The ¾ deity raised a hand and slammed the darkness toward me. I skidded to my left, unable to fully avoid the dark coils shooting out of his hand. They reached my right arm, and pain like no other erupted from my shoulder to my hand. I watched in horror as the skin turned black and shriveled up like a raisin. Tears sprung to my eyes as I dropped Portia's spear. It hit the ground with the sounds of clanging metal. It fizzled slightly with fire before turning as dark as my arm.

Fear shot through my veins, and my head spun with terror. I had never felt so vulnerable. One of Arius's hands was still clenched to his gut. Clearly, whatever self-healing skills deities had didn't fully work against something as powerful as Potias spear. He lunged towards Ethan, who was still leaning against the door for support. Ethan managed to dodge but fell between Emensaly and Linge. A thorn lodged itself in his side, and his leg got caught with the same dark magic that Arius was using against me.

"ETHAN!" I screamed, watching him collapse onto the floor.

Arius used the moment of my distraction to hit me with another one of his dark coils. It hit my head, and my ears began to ring. My skull felt as if it had been split open. Stars danced in front of my eyes and I stumbled forward a few steps. My head spun, but I lunged at Arius, tackling him to the group. His head hit the floor with a mighty thump, but he managed to throw me off him. I gripped my head, tears spilling down my eyes as I attempted to stand again. Arius let out a thin smile as he stumbled towards me, blood pooling out of his gut. "You should have stayed in the human realm, little girl. This world has no place for a weakling." He managed to gasp out.

He crawled towards me with his hands outstretched when a massive boom echoed through the room. Arius was thrown across Emensaly's now demolished living room, and I heard a familiar voice snarl through the room. "My daughter isn't weak."

Chapter 35

I awoke upon a hard mattress lying between two sterile white beds. I blinked up at the bright white lights, vaguely thinking I was back in my mom's kitchen. The brightness made my eyes hurt, and I pressed a hand against my throbbing forehead. I noticed that my right hand was bandaged in a soft white cloth when the memories flooded back into my mind. Arius had attacked us, Linge and Emensaly were fighting, and had Eveda come in? Was my mind going insane?

I tried to sit up, groaning as every muscle in my body ached. "Careful." A nurse said, easing me upward. "You took quite the fall."

"Where's Ethan," I asked, suddenly alert. "And Eveda, and Emensaly---."

"Shhhhhh." The nurse hushed, fixing my bandage. "Everyone's alive."

I bit my lip, looking around the infirmary. I didn't miss the fact that she said that everyone was alive, not okay. The office was much more crowded than the last time I had visited it. There were over 50 people within the room, and maybe a dozen doctors and nurses hustling around helping patients. I noticed a familiar figure and began waving my hand to beckon her over. "Eveda!" I called, hoping she would hear me.

The art goddess turned towards me and was at my side in three long strides. "Oh, Piper dear, thank goodness you're okay!"

"Eveda what happened?" I asked desperately, "Where's Emensaly, Ethan, Linge--."

"Everything's alright." She began calmly, but I interrupted.

"I heard you when I was fighting Arius, right when I passed out."

"Piper, I need you to calm down for me to explain it." Eveda began.

I nodded sheepishly, and she began to talk. "Potia was the first to notice that you were in trouble. See, when you channel from him, you are essentially taking strength from him. Now since you're an in-between, you can't really leech him of all of his strength. But when you start summoning more fire than you normally do, Potia begins to feel it. He alerted me at once that you may be in trouble. He was able to see where you were using the fire. The two of us got there, and you had already taken care of Arius." Her eyes hardened, and she looked at me in concern. "He..he died a few moments after we arrived. The spear is potent to even the most powerful deities, Arius didn't stand a chance against it. Potia and I were able Emensaly against Linge. She's been badly injured and has lost all of her ability to channel, for now."

"What do you mean, for now?" I asked, the familiar feeling of panic settling in my heart.

"Well, we were both concerned with protecting you and Ethan, she managed to escape."

"WHAT!?" I yelled, causing a few nearby nurses to shoot me angry looks.

'I don't want you to worry." Eveda said sternly, "The realm of Charlid, or whatever it's being called right now, has been sealed off better than ever, and Linge's power has been leached away. She can't cause any more damage."

I sagged against still not fully convinced, but I decided to let it go. Everyone was ok, for now at least. Linge didn't manage to capture Emensaly and Ethan and I were alive. My feelings towards Arius were much more jumbled up. My stomach churned at the thought of me killing someone. I could still picture the exact moment when I drove the spear into his gut. I thought that deities couldn't die. Would I have still tried to hurt him had I known the damage I could have inflicted?

Of course, a logical part of my brain said he was going to kill me. Still, I felt a bit of remorse toward the ¾ deity. Ending up in the realm of Charlid could screw with anyone's head. Would I have ended up at Linge's side if I had accidentally transported myself into that realm? I shook my head, not wanting to think about it.

"Where are Emensaly and Ethan right now?" I asked, badly disguising the fear in my voice.

"Ethan is in a stable condition, in the other infirmary." Eveda confirmed, "He had a concussion and some internal bleeding, but he's going to be just fine."

I swallowed my horror and nodded.

"As for Emensaly," Eveda tensed. Clearly, this was a slightly more difficult matter, "She is with her brother for now...."

"Gotcha," I replied, not wanting to think about what was going on there.

"Sleep now." Eveda commanded, "You need to rest." She placed a cool hand on my forehead, and despite my protests, I fell into a dreamless sleep.

***

I stayed in the hospital for a few more days until I was finally released. My right arm was still in a sling, but I was able to walk on my own. Ethan was freed the same day, and the two of us wandered through the art realm asserting damages. The chaos in-betweens annihilated the entire place. I blinked tears out of my eyes, and I saw paintings, sculptures, and other gruesome sights, all wrecked because of Charlid, Arius, and Linge. As the two of us navigated around the rubble, I worked up the courage to ask Ethan about Emensaly.

"So, have you seen Emensaly yet?" I asked, hoping Ethan wouldn't storm off.

He sighed, sitting down on a bit of chipped-off marble, "She came to see me, twice, actually. This first time I pretended to be asleep, but the next one--." He broke off, lost in thought, "She wanted to apologize again. I'm not really sure what to do. I-I can't forgive her, not yet, at least."

I nodded, unsure what to say. Something told me that there wasn't a protocol for what to say when your dead sister turned out to be a missing goddess in disguise. The two of us walked in silence for a while, each lost in thought. "What do you think Linge is doing right now?" I asked.

Ethan shrugged, examining an oil painting with a dent in the center, "I'm not sure. She probably went back to the Realm of Charlid. Without Arius, she doesn't have anyone passing information to her from the other realms."

"I'm sure she'll stay put there." I replied, mostly to reassure myself, "Maybe for a little bit, at least. She needs to regroup."

"Yeah." He agreed, "Especially with Emensaly back in the picture. With any luck, she'll work with her brothers to keep her trapped in her realm."

I nodded and crossed my fingers.

"Are you going back to the human world?" Ethan asked casually.

I bit my lip, still unsure. "I honestly have no idea."

Ethan was about to say something when I heard Eveda's voice ring out in the hallway. "Piper Hart, please come to my office."

Ethan and I looked at each other in confusion. I had the strange sensation that I was being called to the principal's office. I shrugged it off and began walking down the hallway on the left. I hadn't been here long, but I was still able to remember the way to Eveda's office. I waved to Ethan and told him I would find him later. I weaved through the uneven hallways until I found the one that went straight to Eveda's office. I knocked twice, taking a big breath. Eveda opened the door with a smile. I walked inside, about to ask why I had been called inside when I spotted three people. My jaw dropped, and tears formed in my eyes. Standing inside her office was my family.

***

After a tear-filled greeting and a lot of explaining on my part, Eveda asked the question that had been burning in the back of my mind since this morning. Was I going to stay in the art realm? My mom looked at me expectantly, but I didn't meet her gaze. After a few beats, I let out the decision I had come to the night before. "Mom, I'm really sorry," I muttered softly.

She held her hand up to her mouth, and tears filled her eyes. I blinked a few times. No, I was not backing out, "I want to stay."

To my surprise, it wasn't my mom who responded but my dad. His voice was a lot deeper than I remembered. "Honey, are you happy here?"

I nodded, afraid that if I opened my mouth, I would only begin to cry.

"Come visit us," Jack said, poking his head out from behind my mom's legs.

"All the time." I said, with a thin smile, and I ruffled up his hair, "All the time."

Chapter 36

Ethan and I ate breakfast in the hall the next day with my family. They had decided to stay the night, though my mom nearly passed out after finding out about the time difference. "So...so no one would realize if we were gone for a day? They would think it had only been an hour." She stuttered.

I nodded uncensored, licking yogurt off my spoon. "Pretty much yeah."

Ethan laughed and bumped my brother's fist. I turned to look at them. Ethan had created three race cars out of *pofor,* and they were zooming in between cups and plates as Jack laughed hysterically. My dad had just joined us, still confused about how to order. "How's it going?" He asked.

"Well, no one's tried to kill me yet," I said with a smirk.

"Really? Those are your standards?" Dad asked, his eyebrows shooting into his hair.

"Well, I've begun to lower my expectations," I responded with a laugh.

He was about to say something else, but Ethan interrupted him. He was holding his *pindres* up to his ear and grinned, guess what. "Emensaly started working with her brothers. They've begun exterminating the realm of Charlid."

I smiled down at my plate and piled bacon onto my fork. Maybe there was hope for this world after all.

CPSIA information can be obtained
at www.ICGtesting.com
Printed in the USA
LVHW050825130623
749536LV00032B/425